Christian's Quest Through the Modern World

PILGRIM'S PROGRESS

TODAY

LAEL ARRINGTON

Bringing Truth to Life
P.O. Box 35001, Colorado Springs, Colorado 80935

OUR GUARANTEE TO YOU

We believe so strongly in the message of our books that we are making this quality guarantee to you. If for any reason you are disappointed with the content of this book, return the title page to us with your name and address and we will refund to you the list price of the book. To help us serve you better, please briefly describe why you were disappointed. Mail your refund request to: NavPress, P.O. Box 35002, Colorado Springs, CO 80935.

The Navigators is an international Christian organization. Our mission is to reach, disciple, and equip people to know Christ and to make Him known through successive generations. We envision multitudes of diverse people in the United States and every other nation who have a passionate love for Christ, live a lifestyle of sharing Christ's love, and multiply spiritual laborers among those without Christ.

NavPress is the publishing ministry of The Navigators. NavPress publications help believers learn biblical truth and apply what they learn to their lives and ministries. Our mission is to stimulate spiritual formation among our readers.

www.navpress.com

ISBN 1-57683-261-9

Cover design and illustration by Kelly Noffsinger
Creative Team: Don Simpson, Greg Clouse, Harold Fickett, Amy Spencer, Pat Miller

Arrington, Lael F., 1951-
Pilgrim's progress today : Christian's quest through the modern world / Lael Arrington.
p. cm.
ISBN 1-57683-261-9
1. Spiritual life--Christianity. I. Title.
BV4501.3 .A78 2002
248.4--dc21

2002004814

Printed in the United States of America

1 2 3 4 5 6 7 8 9 10 / 06 05 04 03 02

FOR A FREE CATALOG OF
NAVPRESS BOOKS & BIBLE STUDIES,
CALL 1-800-366-7788 (USA)
OR 1-416-499-4615 (CANADA)

To my friend
Lindsey O'Connor
without whom this book would never have begun

And to my life partner,
Jack,
without whom it would have never ended as it did

WELCOME, FRIEND

I've been sitting around (for a couple of years, actually) having the greatest conversation with John Bunyan. Listening mostly. He's the only author friend I have whose book is still in print 324 years later. (Most of us are lucky to get past four.) I've discovered we have a lot of things in common: we're worried about the violence and destruction in our cities; we've learned to take the Enemy seriously; Vanity Fair is as huge a temptation as ever; and Giant Despair's castle is still almost always booked solid.

But of course things *have* changed. Worldly Wiseman no longer points us to the Mountain of Morality so much as to the Hills of Inner Light. We don't just doze off for a short nap in Pleasant Arbor. We camp out there for tens of thousands of leisure hours. We are a HeartLand full of compassion, yet we have a strange way of showing it to the very old, young, and weak. We are Nomads of the Heart, restlessly seeking something to satisfy this ravenous appetite we have for the kind of depth and meaning, intimacy and adventure that is *still* only found at the foot of the cross and the gate of Celestial City.

It's been a conversation as much about our turbulent times as about the longings of our hearts. And on that point I am deeply grateful to John Eldredge, Brent Curtis, and Leighton Ogg for joining in. The idea for chronicling Pilgrim's adventures through our new millennium was conceived as part of a talk I gave to John's students at Focus on the Family Institute. With his books *The Sacred Romance* and *Journey of Desire* and his words, John has challenged me to think deeply about God's Kingdom Story and the chapters yet to come.

The conversation really livened up when Eugene Peterson, author of *The Message,* joined us. After NavPress and I decided to partner together on this book, I said, "Please send me every bit of *The Message* that's complete." To read my original draft of the first three chapters BTM (before *The Message)* and everything that was written ATM is to see how Peterson set me free to create my own story with energy and risk. I clipped an advertisement where Peterson is holding the Bible, saying, "Who did I think I was to rewrite the Bible?" It gave me hope. I had often said the same about rewriting Bunyan.

My husband, Jack, sat in on a lot of the conversation. It's wonderful to be married to a resident theologian of the first order. Every creative type needs a theological check when she tries to write about the Trinity. "I see dead people," I told him, when I was writing the chapters on heaven and hell. He tried his best to keep me in scriptural bounds. Any wild pitches are mine. Occasionally my son, Zach, and his college buddies would rumble through. Many of the creative and humorous touches in these pages were "borrowed" from my son, especially chapter 5.

A host of others wandered in and out of the conversation—Chuck Colson, Bill Hybels, Ravi Zacharias, Os Guinness, John Piper, Larry Crabb, Gene Veith, C. S. Lewis, Anne Lamott, Kerby Anderson, Francis Schaeffer, Douglas Coupland. A shot of Truth from their books and messages, and Christian's story would take a completely unexpected turn. Paul Barker gave me an invaluable glimpse through the keyhole at corporate Vanity Fair.

But this book was such a risk. I needed cheerleaders, and Lindsey O'Connor and Carol Kent were the first to pick up their pompoms. So many of my fellow AWSA authors in the cheering section prayed me on. On the front porch swing, waiting at the tanning salon, reading aloud on family trips, my own Community Mom friend, Vivian McMullen, faithfully read the rough drafts and let me know if it galloped along fast enough to keep a busy mom burning the pages. (I had to fix several places.) I sent my editor, Harold Fickett, reams of chapters. He sent me back tight, incisive, every-word-counts critiques. "I'm quite pleased; you just need to cut it by seventy pages." I will never write like Harold. But I'm deeply grateful he tried to teach me what he knows.

To my King, this is my gift of worship to you. Take the gold and silver and precious stones, the Truth and Life and seeing what is *real,* and let it rise above the dross and scatter it abroad in hearts. *I can't wait to see you at the finish!*

Now, if you'd like to grab a cup of coffee, join us. I guarantee you will *love* these people, especially John Bunyan. You'll probably want to take him out personally and have your own conversation with his original pilgrims. If you get a little toasty by the fire and nod off, well, that's okay. Because now that I've finished writing the story, it may be less of a conversation,

more of a dream,
sometimes glorious,
sometimes a nightmare . . .

As I slept, I dreamed a dream.
In my dream the man began to run . . .

Chapter 1

On a perfect blue-sky day, Chris Adams sipped his Dr Pepper while his best friend, Sam, interrupted their conversation to check his pager. The light breeze ruffled the scalloped edge of the umbrella over their table. Further out on the sidewalk, Friday afternoon traffic was picking up as people slipped out of the surrounding office buildings to welcome the first truly flower-blooming, bird-singing weekend of the season. Over the rim of his glass, Chris watched Sam's face tense and his gaze harden as he scrolled down the message on his pager. In any visit with Sam, who directed a local security agency, Chris could count on waiting through at least three or four beeps. Sam passed his pager over to Chris.

"N.E.S.T. deployed one hour ago," Chris read. "What's N.E.S.T.?" he asked.

Sam opened his wallet and started counting out his money. "It stands for Nuclear Emergency Search Team. Punch the green button to scroll on down."

Chris scanned Sam's face for any hint of black humor, but found none. He punched the button and read, "Dirty material smuggled across border." He punched it again. "Highest alert next seventy-two hours." With each punch his pulse and breathing quickened. Chris returned the pager to his friend, who was pocketing his wallet.

"Don't worry." Sam's tone was not reassuring. "You know we get a steady stream of this stuff all the time."

"You get a steady stream of watch-out-for-nuclear-warheads-lying-around?"

Sam's face relaxed slightly. "Don't worry," he repeated as he stood to go. "There's really nothing we can do about it anyway," he squeezed Chris's shoulder in parting, "unless we were the praying kind."

Chris stared after his friend, wishing he didn't have to leave, until Sam disappeared in the pedestrian flow. He longed for someone with whom to mourn the death of his false sense of security—what was left of it. Turning, he gazed in the direction of the Foothills Nuclear Plant, twenty miles away, and for the first time in his life wondered what he would do if he saw a mushroom cloud fill the sky. Maybe he *would* run to St. Mark's around the corner and try a prayer.

He sighed a long, weary sigh, laid his money on top of Sam's, and pushed his chair in. *Shake it off.* Time to kill a few last rats and enjoy the weekend. Live the dream. Poke the enemies in the eye with his rock-climbing, four-wheeling, freedom-filled weekend. He picked up his Dr Pepper and took one last swig.

A blast rattled the windows and made him splutter Dr Pepper down his shirt. His stomach fell away. Terror and adrenaline radiated out over every inch of his body. When it had happened before, he had paused to get his bearings and look for smoke, then walked briskly in the other direction. But today his mind reeled, his glass clattered to the table, and he clung to his chair for a few seconds, eyes sweeping up and over the buildings. St. Mark's steeple glinted in the sun.

When his mind had finally refocused, he managed to turn around. From the middle of the next block, where his marketing firm was located, a much-less-threatening cloud of smoke billowed up. Instead of relief, he felt a second, more specific surge of fear, and he took off running toward the smoke. At the corner he met a frantic counter-wave of people fleeing the explosion. *How could we get hit twice in one week?* On Monday, a Northside High School student had gunned down seven classmates. Now this.

When he reached the middle of the block he could see that the smoke was not coming from his office, but the bank next door. Terrified bank workers and pedestrians choking from the dust and smoke were strewn over the sidewalk. Peering past them he saw a huge crater. From the looks of a burning chassis, it appeared that another car bomber had given his life as an exclamation point on some incomprehensible political or religious statement. The façade of the bank building had collapsed into the crater, and passersby were already at work pulling people out of the rubble. Chris dove into the debris near a small patch of fire where he could see a young woman trying to push out. He leveraged his weight and moved aside a metal beam, freeing her. Chris carried her clear of the crater, where emergency medical aid was already being given to others.

He could hear sirens and the whirring of helicopter blades overhead. He didn't have time—or the ability—to think about events around him. He sprinted back over to the rubble. A man was trying to drag a teenager out from under a tangle of sheet rock and metal. The kid screamed as his leg caught. Chris ran to them and, with everything he could muster, managed to pry open a space wide enough so the man could pull the kid's leg free.

As he was being carried out, the youth cried, "Where's Jason! He was walking right beside me . . . "

Chris looked into the eye-smarting, smoky tangle and saw an arm and a leg. Yanking from every direction, he finally found an angle from which the debris began to give. He threw some hot steel bracing aside, partially uncovering the bleeding body. He looked around for help, but everyone else had more than they could manage.

This kid, he saw, had red hair. Somewhere deep inside a switch was thrown. He attacked the rubble like a man possessed, ripping out buckled metal, ceiling tiles, and insulation until the kid was free enough that Chris could drag him clear. His ashen face ripped Chris's gut. He shouldered the youth in a fireman's carry and headed for the other wounded laid out on the sidewalk.

"Hang on! You're going to make it!"

A paramedic, who had just arrived on the scene, ran over to him. Together they lowered the boy down. As soon as Chris got a good look at the boy's ashen face, his hopes sank. While the medic probed and listened for a pulse, Chris looked around at the other injured. Some lay quietly; others cried and writhed from burns, but the worst had some color in their cheeks.

The medic looked up and shook his head and then moved over

to another victim. Chris looked down at the freckled redhead and tried desperately not to make the connection with his brother and that other tragic day. Deep inside his heart, smoke escaped from the cracks around the door he had shut on fiery, painful memories that threatened to explode. All he could think to do was run.

Chris skirted the crater and ran down the sidewalk into the lobby of his own building. He pulled up in front of the elevators, jabbing the button repeatedly. His thoughts caught up with him in the ride to his sixth-floor office, where he worked as senior account manager. *The suicide bomber, the kid at Northside, how could anyone, especially a kid so young, be so filled with hate and destroy so much?* He longed to sort through this with Meg. Whenever there was a crisis he couldn't help thinking how much he still loved her. But Meg was out of his life. She had returned his ring; broken off the engagement. The black hole she had left gathered in the tragedy of today's events and opened up a yawning pit in his stomach. Hadn't his own rage destroyed their dreams?

Passing the conference room he glimpsed a handful of staff in front of the television, watching a live aerial shot of the street outside. Others peered directly out the shattered window. At his approach, the account managers gathered around the water cooler broke off their hushed conversation and stared silently after him.

Chris walked straight past his administrative assistant, Sherry, and into his office. He grabbed his workout bag from under the credenza, checking for his running shoes. He took a moment to look around at his office—the job his one remaining prize. Slick mountings of his award-winning advertisements hung interspersed with photographs of grateful clients who ruled this corner of the world. His desk's balky drawer, top one on the right, rested askew, not quite closed. He had never succeeded in persuading maintenance to fix it.

He stepped out of his office and told Sherry: "Please cancel my appointments. All of them."

He found his car in the garage and turned left out of the parking lot. On the radio the mayor was making a bid for everyone to stay calm and off the streets so the emergency vehicles could do their work. Talk stations were besieged by callers venting their frustrations with car bombers, teenage terrorists, the mayor, border security, gun legislation, the school board, Northside High School campus security—you name it.

Once inside his front door, Chris made straight for the bedroom, shedding clothes along the way. He threw on his running suit, grabbed his tennis shoes out of his workout bag, and pulled his backpack down out of his closet. Collecting gear and supplies from his dresser, the bathroom, and the pantry, he stuffed his pack and headed for the door. Then he stopped. He looked down at the car keys in his hand, and after thinking a moment, threw the keys back toward the kitchen table.

He slammed the door behind him and began to run. He hadn't run far when his cell phone in his backpack played "Take Me Out to the Ballgame." His pager went off as well, even as the phone rang. While both complained, he flung them as far as possible into a weedy field. "Life!" he cried. "Life!"

A few hours later Chris lay stretched out on a motel bed, fully clothed, arms up, elbows crooked, fingers locked under his head, staring out the window at a neon vacancy sign blinking against an inky sky. He could sense the evils out there celebrating an extraordinary week, dancing in the darkness to the pulsing rhythm of the signs. The bottom letter shone through his window. Y . . . Y . . . *Why? Why was he running? To escape the violence?* What scared him the most, he knew, was his suspicion that the violence had taken hold of him and there might not be any means of escape. A video of intense regret rolled in his head, the worst scenes featuring him yelling fiercely at Meg, shoving her aside as he stormed out of her apartment. In one he had even left fingerprint-shaped bruises on her throat. Why was *he* so angry?

Chris reloaded his mental VCR with happier episodes—romantic highs with a series of bright, funny brunettes (and one blonde); roasting marshmallows on the beach; riding horses in the mountains; candlelight and romantic dinners on the floor. He also scanned his personnel file—a series of jobs that looked fun and challenging. But the women and the jobs, though intensely exciting at the start, gradually became dull, boring, in fact intolerable. *Why do the bursts of fun and happiness in my life always give way to disappointment and loneliness?*

He didn't feel the old highs and lows anymore. Life seemed flatter, shallower, like he was always bouncing along the surface. In recent years, the empty feeling of boredom had come to be one of the causes of floating. Which he found himself doing at that moment—floating, that is—a good ten inches off the bed's mattress.

People never used to float. The initial reports had been a surprise—entire audiences of daytime talk shows, crowds of cheering fans at ball games, even a conference of academic types studying the artistic merit of pornographic films. Eventually, it had become commonplace at everything from political conventions to church. People just floating a foot or two above their chairs. Sort of a "natural high" enjoyed by large groups engaged in amusement, shopping, parties, or any activity where there were likely to be balloons and banners.

The more Chris pondered the whys of his life, the higher he floated. He hated the Big Questions because he had no answers. *Why are we here? I don't know. Let's just go to the mall and buy something.* He knew the unanswered whys were also connected to the floating. Unlike the group experience, private floating was usually associated with melancholy and depression. He had heard of people who committed suicide after extended periods of air-time.

Irritated, he reached down for the remote control on the bedside table and switched on the television, looking for something to change his focus—something with serious *substance* and *weight* to get him back down on the bed. He despised floating, both in groups and alone.

As he surfed the channels, most of the shows only made him float higher. He was about to flick past a stadium full of people when he realized they were not watching a game. This crowd was, with few exceptions, planted firmly *in* their seats. The camera switched to the podium where Evangelist's piercing blue eyes, square jaw, and strong Southern cadence drew Chris in.

"We tend to live as if the small story of our lives is all there is. We like to feel we're in control and can plan the future."

The camera slowly pulled back from Evangelist's face, panning the stage loaded with flowers and city officials. Pulling back further, it panned the seven white caskets lined up across the football field right below the makeshift stage.

"And then a day like Monday comes along. Where were you when you heard the news of the shootings at your school? And today's bombing? I've spoken to parents who were at work, mothers at the mall who got calls on their cell phones. One mother told how she walked in after a morning at her health club and picked up a message on her answering machine: 'Mrs. Smith, I just wanted you to know that Heather is here in the emergency room. In case something happens . . . she wants you to know that she loves you and her dad very much.'

"Now let me ask you, how many of you felt in control at that point? We can work hard and play hard and make our plans for the next chapter of our lives, and then one day 'the evil enchantment of worldliness' is broken. We see things as they really are.

"We realize that life as we know it is held together by shared ideas and commitments and values that are losing their hold on us. And we wonder why. Relationships that we counted on enjoying forever are gone, as is the illusion of control. We have been touched—smashed even—without giving permission. And the small story of our lives we were writing? Some anonymous director has called in a new scriptwriter who has loaded the script with action and violence, but the real thing is not exciting or entertaining. It leaves the survivors raw and bleeding on the *inside*."

Chris stared at the screen, shocked that Evangelist might have something to say to him.

"Which brings us to God, because only God can comfort us when we are hurting this badly. Only God is a Rock when we are so out of control. All of us long for depth, for substance to our lives, for intimacy that never fails or disappoints, for connection to some meaning beyond our own small stories. Only God can give it. Pursuing Life in any other direction leaves us floating like an empty soda can in a watery ditch."

As Chris listened, he began a gradual descent; he was still floating but not at so great a height.

"We need God. If you're out there tonight floating and wondering, 'Where do I find true Life?' or 'How do I find God?' let me tell you: Do you see the Narrow Gate? Even if you can't, if you see the shining light on the horizon, go directly for it. Eventually you *will* see the gate, and when you knock, it will open for you. And take along God's Story and read it."

Once again firmly on the bed, Chris replaced the remote control on the nightstand. He sat up and noticed the Bible there. His hand hesitated, but he picked it up and began to read. He closed it and doubts assailed him. He felt his feet leave the floor, and he hovered, inches above the bed. He opened the Bible again and began to read. Again he sat solidly on the bed. *Oh, God . . .*

Suddenly a sense of urgency overtook him. He jammed the Bible in his backpack and took off toward the light.

In a mini-mart the next day, Chris found a CD version of the Bible, as well as his favorite, Dr Pepper. He planned on listening to the entire Bible through the earphones of his portable CD player as he made his way over the plain toward the Narrow Gate.

He stood in the checkout line next to a guy with gelled hair, flowing shirt, and sunglasses, who radiated charisma and charm. The man pointed to the bank bombing headlines by the register. "What a tragedy, huh?"

"Things have been pretty crazy around here," Chris said. "I heard Evangelist speaking last night on TV at the memorial service for the school shooting . . . "

"The shooting, yeah, we heard about it too," his face clouded with concern as he offered his hand. "Name's Worldly Wiseman."

"I'm Chris." The guy had a good PR shake.

"Yeah, I was just on my way to talk to the families about sharing their stories. I'm a movie producer. What did Evangelist say?"

"He said some things that really hit me." They walked outside and pulled up by Wiseman's shiny black convertible. "He said if I wanted to find real Life, that this . . . " Chris pointed down the road, "this leads to the Narrow Gate, which is *the Way* to find God in my life."

"Oh, I see." Wiseman's show of concern seemed to shift gears a little. "I hesitate to say this, but . . . " he paused, obviously torn about sharing sensitive information. "There's not a more dangerous way in the world than the one to which he directed you. I can't even *begin* to tell you all the stories I've heard of the sorrows and pain of what you call 'the Way.' It's extremely narrow and exclusive. And the company . . . " he shook his head and lowered his voice, "so many extremists—which in a way is nice; at least it keeps them off the better roads."

"There are *better* roads to the light than through the Narrow Gate?"

"Chris, *all* roads lead to the light. Jesus isn't *the Way;* he's one *option*. He's not *the Truth*—merely a viewpoint, and certainly not *the Life,* just a lifestyle.

"How else can we respond to all the different truth claims, all the unique cultures and religions out there? Do you want to join the intolerant bigots that claim their narrow view of truth is true for everyone?"

Intolerant. Bigot. The labels Chris had always tossed around so carelessly had a surprising sting. He squirmed slightly and pretended to adjust the shoulder strap on his pack.

"I mean, how can it be fair for one small group to cram their understanding of morality and 'sin' down the throats of all God's children?" Wiseman's voice had taken on an edge. "When we define truth differently, we're just looking at different facets of the same diamond. As long as we pursue the light in sincerity, we'll reach the same end."

Chris scratched the stubble on his chin and took in the guy's tanned face and "together" look. *Maybe I'm overreacting. It's been a terrible week.* "So you're saying there's another road?"

"Absolutely. Check out these nice wide roads into the Hills of Inner Light. This week's events—they've got everyone in a twist. But what you need is tolerance. Tolerance and openness to all the ways to God. Not the dangers of 'the Way.'"

Looking over a couple of roads that headed up into the hills, Chris hesitated. "How will I know which one is best?"

Worldly Wiseman leaned over and lowered his voice. "Here's the secret: *Follow your heart*. Honest!" He held up his hand as if swearing an oath.

The road Chris chose sloped gently and soon curved along a chattering stream. Butterflies fluttered in search of late-afternoon refreshment, a welcome contrast to the hot, boring plain. Large expanses of neatly trimmed grass dotted with occasional beds of shrubs and flowers made this route a true walk in the park, with the addition of one curious feature: every mile or so large billboards afforded travelers the wisdom of famous quotes. The first was from Confucius: "He who is greatly virtuous will be sure to receive the appointment of heaven."

Soon another road crossed his. Chris hesitated a moment and closed his eyes. He found himself drawn to the new road—a new adventure, one that might be even more inviting!

Gradually his walk in the park turned into a jaunt through fragrant hay meadows broken by stands of rustling oaks. A billboard came up on his right: "It would be the height of intolerance to believe that you would be justified in wanting others to change over to your faith.—Gandhi."

The sky was bluer and the breeze seemed fresher. He was even running faster. Before long he came to another point where the road divided. He stalled at the junction for a full three minutes, trying to get a feeling for which might be the better road. *Maybe this new one looks a little less worn . . . or maybe it's just maintained a little better.* His heart didn't seem to have too much to say about the matter.

He took off down the new lane. The breeze was picking up and blowing the little puffball clouds into ranks of marshmallow men marching south. At least he thought it was south. It was hard to tell with so many clouds.

Another fork in the road. The left one headed toward some pretty steep hills. The right fork seemed gentler, but after he had jogged about a mile down the new road it too headed for steeper terrain. He stopped and finally decided to jog back to his original road. *If I'm going up, I feel like sticking with the other road. Maybe I shouldn't take every new one that comes along.*

His pace slowed as he paused at each intersection, trying to sense which way to go. So many roads. So many choices. It helped if the clouds parted a little and one lane seemed sunnier than the other; and once, as he was thinking at a crossroads, a bluebird sailed by and flew down the new lane. That made it easy.

Traveling deeper into the hills, breathing became harder and his calves began to ache from the incline. In spite of all the exercise, he had to zip his jacket against the wind that was tossing the birches and flattening the marshmallow men into a thick overcast blanket.

Whichever road he chose, wisdom continued to beam down on him from the benevolent billboards: "The heart wants what it wants. —Woody Allen."

Cheered on, Chris kept jogging. Gradually, the hills grew craggier. The trees crowded closer together into a darksome forest. Sunlight gave way to a cloudy twilight as he crossed road after road. Some he took, some he passed by, his apprehension growing. Without some friendly voice, some landmark by which to judge his progress, he felt completely overwhelmed by all the choices he had to make. As he looked around, it dawned on him—he could no longer see the light, only gray twilight in every direction. Being so distracted, he stumbled badly, but instead of falling, he launched upward into the air, floating up over the road a good fifteen feet.

Suddenly, the forest opened up, the hillside fell away, and the road underneath him ran across the top of a huge dam. His momentum carried him out over the dam, and his mood of frustration quickly mushroomed to full-blown terror as he realized that a little pitch to the right or the left would mean drifting down into a large sludgy pit on one side or a deep craggy ravine on the other. The problem was the wind. About twenty feet below him, the road across the dam slid to his left. The wind that had been pushing the clouds around all day was blowing him out over the pit.

Oh, God! he thought, and he meant it, even more than he had meant it in the motel room.

Chapter 2

Gradually his momentum slowed, and Chris began to float down. With frantic swimming motions he turned his floating body around, stretching his full six-foot-two inches back down toward the road. But he was blowing wide of the dam. The pounding in his head grew so loud it drowned out the wind. Refinery-like fumes stabbed his lungs as he descended toward the reservoir of slime. Small islands of rusted barrels and toxic junk rose from the sludge rimmed with faded skull-and-crossbones signs. "Warning: Dump of Despond," the largest one read. His momentum continued to slow until he touched down lightly, sinking ankle deep into the slime, but no further. He clapped his hands over his nose and mouth, but the reeking chemicals invaded his body. A strong metallic tang filled his mouth.

Eyes riveted on the junk and oily goo surrounding him, Chris stood there in a cold sweat. Gradually his head stopped pounding enough to begin thinking "escape." To his right the concrete dam rose twenty feet straight up to the road. All around the pit, forty-foot slopes presented an incline slightly more gradual, but wet with the slow-spilling sludge that continually oozed over the edge and down into the Dump. A low rumble of thunder rolled through the hills.

Aiming for the slippery slope where it looked the least vertical, Chris slogged through the sucking ooze. The warm, toxic, peanut buttery sludge was laced with loops of film and videotape. Every few yards he had to free his feet from the unwound footage. Plowing through truckloads of parental-warning-stickered CDs and bodice-ripper novels, he finally reached the pit wall. But handholds proved as elusive as footholds, and he wound up soaked by the nauseating mess. As he scanned the walls of the pit from one side of the dam all the way around to the other, he saw that the entire surface of the pit was saturated with slime. A couple more attempts to find traction and he gave up, turning his attention to finding something in the sludge that could help him dig into the walls.

He stumbled through reams of legal documents: Jones vs. Jones, Hyatt vs. Hyatt, Escobar vs. Escobar, one open, rusted barrel after another, full of divorce filings. The surrounding sludge was littered with wedding pictures in cracked glass and broken frames. Airline tickets with special instructions for kids traveling alone. Milk cartons bearing pictures of missing children with gap-toothed smiles. Brochures for a battered women's shelter. The fearful eyes stared up at him from the bruised face on the cover. He sank a little deeper into the slop.

Chris headed toward the far end of the pit, where the walls appeared to be lower. Drug paraphernalia was everywhere, and he feared getting stuck by one of the filthy needles. So many of the raunchy CDs and videos he wallowed through were titles in his own collection back home. The more he recognized, the deeper he sank.

Knee-deep in ouija boards, incense cones, and sacred stones, he stumbled through mountains of merchandise plastered with Leos and Virgos, best sellers about the "goddess within" and "being your own master," chakras, and past lives.

Beyond them a charred cross jutted out of a sea of rusted gas cans and hooded white sheets with eye-holes. Overhead a jagged fork of lightning blazed; thunder cracked.

At the far end of the pit he almost walked into a shower of XXX adult videos and satiny pink bunny ears. Looking up, he spied the mouth of a wide tube extending over the edge of the pit. He squished over to where he could see the side of the tube and read the big block letters: "Thou Shalt Not Judge." Underneath was scrawled, "Tolerance Now!" The mouth of the tube began to shake. Hundreds of course catalogs rumbled into the pit followed by a confetti of pennants from prestigious universities that fluttered down and stuck in the waste. Chris picked up a catalog and thumbed the class offerings: "Department of Gay and Lesbian Studies—Special Issues in Coming Out," "Sorcery and Magic," and in another, "Revolting Behavior: The Challenges of Sexual Freedom (with slide-illustrated lectures)."

Whether from the stench or the guilt, Chris's stomach was heaving. Turning back toward the dam, he could see more of the hillside beside it and a billboard mounted there. A familiar face rallied him. Pushing through his exhaustion and a slew of supermarket tabloids, Chris waded close enough to read the sign. It was Evangelist! Fire in his heart, hope in his eyes! The grand old man's billboard featured a quotation very different from the others: "You will know the Truth and the Truth will set you free."

"Oh, Evangelist," he whispered, "I was so foolish to turn away from the Truth."

"Yes, you were, Chris." As if on a live movie screen, the figure of Evangelist dropped his arms, nodded soberly, and actually looked at him. "Why did you to turn off the road to the light?"

Chris's exhaustion and sheer misery pretty well cancelled out his shock to be talking with a billboard. He dropped his head. "I met this fellow named Worldly Wiseman. He assured me this road would be easier. That if I just listened, my heart would tell me where to go."

Evangelist said nothing at first. Finally, he spoke softly, "Your heart, as you have seen, isn't trustworthy. It may seem that as you follow your heart you're somehow being more true to yourself. But Chris, God is more protective of your eternal best interests than even your own heart."

Chris swallowed hard at Evangelist's rebuke.

"Look around," Evangelist said. "Our hearts ooze scum and filth. The overflow runs together and settles in this place. That is why it's called the Dump of Despond."

"It's . . . "—Chris cast about for the words—"it's unspeakably awful."

Again Evangelist paused while Chris shifted his weight from one squishy running shoe to the other. "Chris, Worldly Wiseman wanted to make the cross seem hateful and bigoted to you. But the cross is the truest sign of God's love for us. The greatest love of all is not learning to love yourself, but loving others so much you would lay down your own agenda, your rights, your needs, even your life to serve others, to save them from destruction, like Jesus did. Your heart will deceive you. Better to be guided by your conscience, and your conscience held captive to God's Truth."

"He told me I needed tolerance." Chris glanced back at the dump behind him.

"You must show him a better way," Evangelist said. "Consider this:

Tolerance says, "You must approve of what I do."
Love responds, "I must do something harder;
I will love you even when your behavior offends me."

Tolerance says, "You must allow me to have my way."
Love responds, "I must do something harder;
I will plead with you to follow God's Way,
because I believe you are worth the risk."

Tolerance says, "You must agree with me."
Love responds, "I must do something harder;
I will tell you the Truth, because I am convinced
that the Truth will set you free."

Chris stared at the original quote again on Evangelist's billboard. Wiseman's objections to this one Way to Truth would not go down quietly. "Evangelist, I want 'the Truth that sets me free.' But . . . what is Truth?"

"Can you handle the Truth?" Evangelist's voice echoed down the canyon.

"Please, tell me!"

"Better yet," Evangelist said, "I'll show you. Let the Story begin!"

Trumpets sounded a magnificent fanfare. Evangelist's figure faded and a three-dimensional ocean of undulating images washed out toward Chris, images far beyond the conceptual reach of even the greatest special-effects wizards. "What you're about to see is the

Truth—a glimpse of the heart and glory of God. It's God's grand story—the Kingdom Story."

Ribbons of rainbows pulsed and danced through ancient mists propelled by cosmic winds, synchronized with the most beautiful music Chris had ever heard, performed by hundreds of voices and a vast orchestra with organs, timpani, and cymbals. The ribbons converged, arching into a temple. Through the rainbow radiance, Chris caught glimpses of gigantic pillars, intricate cornices. Behind an altar of fire rose a huge throne on which a figure seemed to be seated, but it was so brilliant he couldn't tell. Maybe just fire from the waist down; from the waist up, a golden sash around a chest and a flash of blazing eyes. He could definitely hear voices, or was it thunder or rushing waters? No, definitely voices, because he also heard laughter.

"This is the fellowship of the Trinity in eternity past—a love and camaraderie so deep that it overflows in its joy and grandeur," Evangelist's voice boomed out. "In fact, the love and joy did overflow to the creation of angelic beings."

Suddenly the air teemed with swirling eyes and precious jewels. God spoke and the eyes gradually sorted out from the jewels, circulating into four pillars. The pillars condensed into exotic six-winged creatures covered with eyes, even under their wings. With faces of a man, an ox, a lion, and an eagle, they stood on straight, powerful legs tapering into calf hooves of burnished bronze. The diamonds, rubies, sapphires, and emeralds coalesced into creatures like men, only vastly more powerful, sparkling in the rainbow light, covered head to toe and wing tip to wing tip with precious stones mounted in sheaths of gold. Yet they flew easily, gracefully.

The finger of God traced out ranks upon ranks of Shining Ones, legions, vast multitudes—gathered in company formation receding into the heavenly mists.

"These are angels?"

"Yes, actually, the ones with all the eyes are the four living creatures who watch before God's throne. The ranks and companies are organized into messengers, guardians, destroyers . . . "

"And the ones covered with jewels?"

"Those are God's guardian cherubs. Magnificent, aren't they?"

"Awesome! Especially the one on the end."

"Yes," Evangelist said, "his name . . . is Lucifer."

At the mention of the name the music went *basso profundo* and ominous. The angelic hosts thundered, "AND THERE WAS WAR IN HEAVEN!" The legions that had appeared in formation now divided and assaulted each other. Chris cringed as beautiful beings, with eyes turned cold and cruel, launched lightning and fiery missiles against their former comrades. God's loyal angel armies hurled back showers of nuclear force.

Directing his troops, Lucifer circled above, a fierce glint of pride glowing in his eyes.

"God had given him so much—beauty, power, intelligence—but he wanted the throne," Evangelist said. "Finally, God threw the traitor out."

Streaking downward toward the pit, ejected from his heavenly home, the glorious jeweled creature slowly morphed into a hideous red dragon. A third of the heavenly host plunged with him. The swirling images, thunderous timpani, and clashing voices subsided to a slower, minor, grieving theme.

"It broke God's heart, you know," Evangelist said. "Satan destroyed so much."

A new wave of images began washing across the screen. A new beginning! There was light! Quasars! Supernovas! Icy green galaxies! Towering pink clouds of nebulae! Celestial events of indescribable beauty—the Universe in all its glory exploded into the air. The morning stars sang together and all the angels shouted for joy.

The beautiful Pleiades, the cords of Orion, the Bear leading out its cubs, then the shimmering blue-green beauty of Earth. Our planet with its rosy dawns, purple twilights; its majestic mountains and restless seas; and, watered by a great blue river in a setting of spectacular trees and flowers, Eden! In the garden, God, with outstretched hand

and the wind of his breath, infused the spark of life into Adam's lifeless form.

Chris stared up from the bottom of the toxic pit. What would it be like to be surrounded by that much beauty? To take a walk with the King of the Universe every day?

"One day," Evangelist's narration seemed to shift gears, "as the King's beloved walked in their garden-kingdom, his arch-Enemy made a play for their hearts."

On the billboard, a snapshot frozen in silence: Satan talking to Eve. And another: Eve eyeing the forbidden fruit. And another: Adam standing silently by, consenting by default.

Chris shut his eyes tight and caught his breath: "Don't do it. Don't do it." But they did it—they doubted God's heart. They wanted control, and the glint of pride flashed in their eyes.

"The Enemy seduced the King's beloved," Evangelist said, "and took them prisoners. The consequences were grim—curses on Adam, Eve, and all creation. And yet, God gave them a promise—a descendant who would finally smash the Enemy." Trumpets, pipe organs, and timpani introduced the Deliverer's theme.

"God called out a nation of people on whom he set his love." On the summit of a mountain clouded with thunder and smoke, God's own hand inscribed his Truth on stone tablets he gave to Moses. "He pursued his beloved people like a husband pursues his bride, but she returned to the Enemy's camp, prostituting herself to other gods, other lovers."

The music tugged at Chris's heart. The chorus seemed to be pleading and pleading for Israel's love, the voices echoing the entreaties of a succession of great, strong-faced men with pain in their eyes, now prostrate before God, now crying out at city gates.

"That's Isaiah," Evangelist's voice whispered, "and Jeremiah, Hosea, and Habakkuk. But God's beloved rejected and abused his messengers, clinging to her adulterous lovers."

On the billboard the Sovereign God of the Universe summoned the Pharaohs and kings of Assyria and Babylon, lining them up to wreak havoc and bring utter destruction on his adulterous beloved. The pit echoed with military cadences, trumpet calls to battle. Voices rose in lament.

He saw Jerusalem breached and burning; soldiers smashing infants on the rubble; the holiest furnishings of the temple melted down and carried away to Babylon.

As the wind died down, Evangelist reappeared on the billboard. "The great King longed to get his beloved back. So he devised the most daring rescue operation. Under the cover of night his only Son disguised himself, left his army behind, and alone, raided the Enemy camp."

The gorgeous strains of Chris's favorite Christmas recording streamed through the gathering darkness: "O come, O come Immanuel." As the sopranos joined harpsichord, recorder, keyboard, and violins, a beautiful series of living Christmas cards filled the billboard.

"Rejoice! Rejoice! Immanuel will ransom captive Israel."

Chris thought back on Christmases full of shopping and partying. He thought perhaps his finest, truest Christmas moments had been those times driving through the snowy countryside with this music playing. *Maybe that ache I felt was God trying to . . . put his arm around me.* He had shaken it off—changed the station.

Soaring phrases of the Deliverer's theme melded into the carols. The Christmas cards gave way to a mosaic of images: Jesus straight-talking with the Pharisees; with his arm around Mary; wiping away his tears as he draws near to Lazarus's tomb; and, on a hilltop overlooking Jerusalem, arms stretched wide in an empty embrace. The mosaic of images took the shape of a cross.

Watching the Son's story, it wasn't Jesus' looks that drew Chris in. Not his image or his style. It was the Truth, strong and transparent. Chris could see it in his eyes.

The cross mosaic blazed and morphed into a rough-hewn wooden cross that toppled forward toward a man. His bloody body was so covered with lacerations and bruises, his face so pulverized and contorted with pain, that Chris didn't recognize him until the picture zoomed in on his eyes . . . it was Jesus! Struggling with the weight, Jesus barely managed to shoulder the cross and hook it over his shoulder.

The symphony and chorus raged as Jesus staggered, dragging the cross through Jerusalem's mobs that screamed for his blood. At the bottom right of the 3D images, the Enemy shrieked in grotesque laughter, his sneering mouth dripping saliva that mingled with Christ's blood in the dirt. Three crosses caught in flashes of lightning. Above the toxic pit, thunder cracked and roared. Finally the shaking and thunder faded to black. Inside the moldy tomb, weeping angels' voices intertwined with cellos, oboes, and tolling gongs over Christ's shrouded body.

"The beloved was still captive and the Deliverer was dead," Evangelist said. "It was a night of ravenous feasting in the Enemy camp."

Then, in an instant, everything changed. The power of God exploded into the tomb, the music exploding along with it. The once-lifeless form began to stir, linen strips unspooled from the body, wounds instantly healed, and the resurrected Christ stood up strong.

Chris let out a "YES!" and punched his fist in the air.

Pipe organs, trumpets, and timpani shook the hillside and the pit. Jesus removed the burial cloth from his head, folded it, and laid it aside. Eyes shining with joy, he raised his hands toward heaven and melded into the light and power that filled the tomb. Drowning out Satan's curses and raging, the loudest chorus of the Deliverer's theme yet celebrated the ransom paid and the prison doors thrown wide.

Evangelist reappeared on the billboard. "It was such an amazing solution. How could people whose hearts are so corrupt . . . " he gestured toward the pit, "be reconciled to a Holy God? If he simply loves us and waves us on in, he's not just. But if he really gives us what we deserve, he denies his passionate love and mercy for us."

"I think I'm getting it," Chris said. It was like looking at the optical illusion of the Old Hag and suddenly seeing the Beauty hidden in plain sight.

A smile spread slowly across Chris's face. "Satan got rolled at the cross!"

"Oh, Chris," Evangelist's tone surprised him, "never underestimate the Enemy."

A slow death-march drum cadence pounded the air. The billboard blazed with thousands of spectators jammed in the Roman Coliseum, whooping their pleasure at the lions and bears tearing the limbs off the Christians and eating them alive. A deacon screamed and stiffened as red-hot brass plates were pressed into the most tender parts of his body. Nero's palace gardens burned with the brightness of believers dipped in hot wax and set aflame. Chris looked away, but he could still hear the roaring flames and screams, the cheers and the drums.

"It didn't take Satan long to come up with a new plan to take control and write his own grand story," Evangelist said. While he hacked away at the moral authority of the church with splits and divisions, he deceived and elevated other great leaders who would create new lies—anything to shake people's confidence in God and the Truth of his Kingdom Story."

On the face of the dam below the billboard, a curious thing began to happen. Chris watched as a picture about three-fourths the size of the billboard flickered on and a new story began. It was Creation recreated—only this time with randomness and terrible violence, without design or purpose. And there was no music. An inhospitable Earth finally calmed down enough for a lucky amoeba to crawl out of a warm pond and gradually transform into a series of bigger, more complex creatures, finally ending with man.

In this version of the story, man and his accomplishments were always the focus. Man's great civilizations and the buildings he built; man's growing knowledge and the technology he produced; man's lively imagination and the art he created; man's ability to reason and the ideas he conceived. Man could build his own Utopia. God was irrelevant. Completely out of the picture.

As the smaller picture on the dam glowed more and more brightly, the big billboard grew dimmer. The music faded as well—no longer full volume.

"What's happening with the images?" Chris asked.

"The brightness of the two different stories reflects how much confidence people have in them." The decades rolled by. Chris realized that the growing brightness of the Progress Story was approaching that of the Kingdom Story. Temporarily set back by two World Wars, the smaller picture surged with power as tumult filled both screens—race riots, demonstrations, assassinations. Love-beaded, tie-dyed hippies celebrated the Age of Aquarius, the triumph of peace and love.

"Then the children of the Progress Story began to grow up." Both pictures filled with images of children crying in court, torn between divorcing parents; sexually active teens crying in doctors' offices; school children weeping over dead classmates. "They realized that the hope of Progress and Utopia was a false hope. All they were left with was their own truths, their own small stories in which to live."

On the face of the dam dozens of smaller pictures appeared, showing nothing more than the small stories of individual lives. "So now one lives in the sports story, another lives in the high school cheerleader story. You see lots of men and women in their own versions of the career ladder story, lots of women living in the find-a-man-and-have-his-baby story. Look closely up on the right and you'll even see a lady living in the church story. Days of activity. Evenings of emptiness. No Big Story to answer the questions: How do I know what's true? Where have I come from? Why am I here? Where am I going? As people lost confidence in the truth and meaning of the larger stories, the floating began."

In the smaller pictures the people were living true to Chris's own motto: "It's all about me, right?" He shuddered. Compared to all those small pictures, both bigger pictures grew faint. And the music faded to background Musak.

"What happens next?" Chris asked.

"This has a while to play out, but eventually it will come to this: God will say, 'You want to reject the Truth? You want to believe lies? I'll send you the best; I give you . . . the Antichrist!'"

All the smaller pictures went dead. The main billboard shone brilliantly with a large, strong, handsome face. The Antichrist's lies of peace exploded into war that annihilated millions. Millions more were slain because of their faithfulness to God.

With a trumpet call to arms, heaven opened and a white horse came charging down. Chris recognized Jesus sweeping past, body bent forward in resolve, eyes locked on the murdering liars below. The armies of heaven thundered after him.

Behind the descending army, an angel standing in the sun cried with a loud voice, summoning all the birds of prey. After thousands of years of grace and second chances, Christ trampled God's enemies. The vultures feasted on heads of state and common people alike.

When Chris could no longer bear to watch the horrendous carnage, he bowed his head, listening, but there was no music to accompany this mourning—only the sound of the wind and the cries of the birds.

Finally, he looked up. The picture followed one large bird. Spattered with blood, it flapped up and away over the millions of glassy eyes of Armageddon.

Satan could be seen below, raging over the battlefield, cursing God. A flash of brightness descended, seized the Enemy, binding him with a great chain before throwing him into the Abyss. His curses and the bloody battlefield fell away as once more the great bird winged its way higher and higher, beyond the highest peaks, circling even the clouds. Finally, at what seemed an impossible altitude, it leveled off and wheeled toward a bright light in the almost inky sky.

As the bird flew on, Chris realized it was flying over the shadowy forms of a great mass of people moving along together, as if in a dark tunnel, toward a bright light at the far end. The bird flew on as the focus shifted to figures somehow familiar to Chris. Oh yes, a couple of scientists from the Progress Story, the cheerleader, and one of the career-ladder men from the small story pictures and right there behind—Chris caught his breath—he saw his own face! He too was walking quietly with the others, moving toward the light.

He could never explain it, but suddenly, Chris was no longer in the pit—he was in the tunnel. He looked around desperately for the billboard but found only the other tunnel travelers moving slowly but steadily forward.

Noticing the surprise and fear on his face, the two scientists moved over to his left.

"You too, huh?" one asked.

"Me too, what?" Chris responded.

"Well, you look just as surprised to be here as we are. We counted on one life and then, lights out—the end."

"You died already?" His mind flitted back to the reservoir of toxic chemicals.

"Oh yes, but here we are. We still *are!* It was supposed to be over!" fumed the other scientist.

One of the husband-baby-Small-Story women turned to them.

"Don't worry. Don't worry. This is turning out just like that best seller I read. We all travel down this tunnel till we reach our angel-spirit guides, who will usher us into the very presence of God. It's going to be beautiful."

The cheerleader looked over, her face drawn in worry and concern. "Oh, I'm not ready for this," she said, tears gathering in her eyes. "I've slept with my boyfriends, even had an abortion. I'll probably have to 'earn my wings' or something. There's no way I'll make it in."

"But what did you think of Jesus?" Chris asked.

"Jesus? I don't know. I never thought much about him at all."

"Oh yeah, that's it," one of the career-ladder men said. "Give us one last round of Come-to-Jesus and we'll all walk the aisle."

A funeral drum cadence and threatening bass chorus rose as they approached the brightly lit mouth of the tunnel. The chorus was singing, "*Media vita in morte sumus.*"

Chris could only think frantically, "Jesus. I'm not sure I said what's in my heart."

"*Media vita in morte sumus.*"

"But I know you're the answer. Please have mercy. . . . "

The tempo picked up as the tenors joined in. "*Media vita in morte sumus.*"

They burst into a huge amphitheater brilliantly lit by a great white throne with a light so clear, it chased every doubt away. The lettering on the fiery gold sash of the One on the throne spelled it out: "KING of KINGS and LORD of LORDS." They could even see the nail prints in his hands. "*Media vita in morte sumus.*"

The cheerleader began to weep; the scientists stared defiantly with clenched jaws, hands, everything; the husband-baby woman frantically tried to reassure herself and the others. "It's all right; it's all right!" she shouted over the chorus. "He loves everyone, you know."

"*MEDIA VITA IN MORTE SUMUS.*"

Chris stood there with the great and small, staring straight at the glory of God surrounded by rank upon rank of massive angelic armies.

"*MEDIA VITA IN MORTE SUMUS*. IN THE MIDST OF LIFE WE ARE IN DEATH."

Chapter 3

The chorus ended abruptly. The books were opened; the air was electric.

To the angels attending him, the King commanded, "Gather my wheat into the barn." Many of the travelers were carried away into the clouds, but Chris and the others he had spoken with were left behind. He kept waiting, but began to realize he was not headed for "the barn." The King looked straight at Chris and his fellow travelers.

"I gave my life to ransom you from the Enemy camp. But you loved his ways so much you would never leave. I kept a quiet patience while you ignored me. You thought I went along with your game, but today I'm calling you to account. There'll be no more playing fast and loose with me. I'm ready to pass sentence. There is no escape and no one to come to your rescue."

"Lord, Lord!" the small story woman cried out, "I read in my book where you welcomed *everyone!*"

"Melissa," the Judge turned his fiery yet tender eyes on the distraught woman, "how many times did I prompt you to read *my* Book? But you never would. 'Why are you talking like we're good friends? You never answered the door when I called; you treated my words like so much garbage.' 'Everyone on the side of truth listens to me.'"

Without warning, a pit that belched sulfuric smoke, from which screams of excruciating pain could be heard, opened right near where Chris stood. The travelers shrank from the blasting heat of fiery fountains and bubbling, molten lava. Hazy tendrils of nauseating organic stench stung Chris's eyes and choked him, clogging his lungs. Closing ranks, a legion of angels advanced toward his group. Sobbing uncontrollably, the cheerleader fell to her knees. Chris shut his eyes and grabbed his head with both hands.

But no angelic grasp caught hold of him. The smoke began to fade, as did the sobs and screams. Only the stench was real, and Chris found himself still standing in it, trembling. "Chris," Evangelist's fading voice whispered, "'your very life is in danger! His anger is about to explode, but if you make a run for God—you won't regret it.'"

Chris glanced around, actually relieved to see the Dump, and tried to get himself under control. Like an electric sign with a short, the low clouds blinked erratically and thunder echoed down the ravine. On the hillside above, Evangelist's picture was fixed on his billboard. But it was only a picture. The Story was over. Feeling as never before the crushing weight of all the toxic crud and guilt in his own heart, Chris began to sink deeper into the ooze.

"Help!" he cried. "Evangelist . . . God . . . please help me! . . . I'm ready to run!"

The more he struggled, the more he sank. Fighting panic, he quieted and in the silence heard a curious noise toward the top of the dam. For the first time he noticed the words chiseled into the entablature there: "You will know the truth—that there is no truth. And the truth will set you free—free to create your own small stories and private realities." Again he heard the noise. Like rats scurrying across the face of the dam. With a loud rip, a crack opened along the length of the entablature, splitting the words in half. Rapidly it widened, spawning other cracks that spread out in a web across the dam. Terrified that the dam was about to burst, and with no idea how to save himself, Chris could only listen while the groaning and popping grew louder.

A huge concrete chunk snapped off the dam and bounced down the ravine on the other side. Other chunks followed until the dam gave one last groan and crashed into the canyon. The entire Dump of toxic waste and debris oozed out of the pit.

As if riding a sinking escalator, Chris flailed around, continually maneuvering back and away from the leading edge of the slow-flowing slop, trying to stay clear of rocks and shifting debris. Already sunk up to his chest, he was more fearful of getting sucked under than getting smashed or crushed into the canyon walls. For hours he rode the toxic tide down the canyon, managing to maintain position, but unable to escape. Finally the canyon walls leveled off enough for vegetation to take hold, and he lined himself up to grab an overhanging tree. Hand over hand he made it to the bank, where he clambered up and collapsed, nauseated from the stench of his clothes and his own skin. There was no way he could even move.

Warmed by the sunrise, Chris roused himself and squinted with bleary eyes at the rosy cloud fingers holding out the bright opportunity of another day. *Amazing. The sun came up again.* He slowly unfolded his creaking body by stages and looked around. He had no pack, no food, and no idea where he was. His one consolation: the light that was again visible on the near horizon. As he stumbled down a hill, he found a path that headed in that direction. Jogging was unthinkable. He was out of the muck, but the tremendous burden of guilt and fear he had felt standing before the throne weighed him down as if he were dragging the entire Dump with him.

Still nauseated, Chris shuffled down a path through land as parched as he was. He observed, though, that the light was getting noticeably brighter. He stripped off his running jacket and then his T-shirt, but the stench came almost as strongly from his own body. Late in the morning he arrived at an impregnable black wall only accessed by the tall Narrow Gate. He trudged up to the gate and knocked, looking down at his greasy skin and pants saturated with putrid slime. *Why would anyone let you in anywhere?* he had to wonder. But he couldn't imagine what he would do if he were turned away. Slowly the gate opened onto a path that headed up a fairly steep hill.

Trudging up the hill, Chris tried to think of the glorious music and God's amazing Story, but it was a losing struggle. He had to concentrate. *Just one foot and then the other* . . . The only music he could hear was the rising choir of crickets. The only picture he could see when he occasionally looked up was the path ascending the unremarkable hill. Toxic sweat dripped off his forehead and collected in the small of his back. His nausea grew worse, sharpened by an empty stomach. Another look up and he could see the top of the hill.

And at the crest stood a cross.

After the grandeur of the heavenly temple and the majesty of the throne of judgment, the stark, barren scene surprised him. Only a windswept hill ascended by a well-worn path. Not even a grassy hill. Patches of dried stubble and weeds covered the sacred ground.

The power of the ancient rough-hewn crossbeams drew him forward. Chris reached out and touched the wood worn smooth by millions of hands before him. Slowly his fingers slid down the blackened polished knobs and cracks as he sank to his knees. He had never felt so dirty and lonely and empty.

"Oh, God. I don't know why, but you have loved me and pursued me all these years," he said, face turned up to the cross, "and for so long . . . I've ignored and resisted you. I'm so sorry. Thank you for making me weary of my life—tired of being a selfish screw-up. Thank you for showing me the Truth. For dying such an awful death on this cross to ransom me from the Enemy's pit. I want you. I want Life. Please fill my empty heart."

Kneeling there, clutching the cross, his nausea slowly drained away, along with his self-loathing. After a long while, Chris stood up. Jogging in place, he swung his arms across his chest and over his head. His burden was gone! The boredom and insecurity and depression and guilt were gone too and he felt a hundred pounds lighter, although his feet were still planted on solid ground.

Partway down the far side of the hill he found a spring gushing with crystal-clear water. Chris waded in and sank back, submerging for as long as he had breath. The bubbling water washed him better than soap, cleaner than he had ever felt in his life. Scrubbed, bleached, detoxed, inside-outside clean. Along with the dirt, his weariness ebbed away. After a good splash and a short soak in the delicious water, he stood up in the chest-deep pool and gazed at the narrow path descending the hill—a new person surveying a new landscape of grace. A new life in a new land opened out before him.

Even as he wished for a razor and clean clothes, two Shining Ones appeared by the pool, dusting what looked like rose petals off their white-robed shoulders. They were breathless and beaming, as if they had been celebrating a World Series–winning grand-slam homer, and it was time to sober up for the official trophy presentation. "Peace to you, Christian!"

"Christian?" He gave them an astonished smile.

"Yes, you're a newly reborn child of the King and you have a new name." One of them laid out a stack of new clothes and gear. "When you are ready you can come to the bottom of the hill and we will tell you about your quest."

Christian donned a fresh-pressed khaki shirt and pants, with the King's crest monogrammed on the shirt, and a camouflage vest. Although it was extremely light and comfortable like a running suit, he wondered at the military style. *What, am I going into battle or something?* He swung his new backpack with padded shoulder straps up on his shoulders and found it much easier to carry than his old one. Energized, he approached the Shining Ones.

The first handed him a small device. "This is your Scroll, where you'll find the Words of Life. You will need it to finish well. Everything else you possess will pass away. But *this* will go with you into the gates of Celestial City." Christian took it, eager to turn it on and explore, but it was obvious there was more, so he tucked it into his pack.

"Look. See this path extending down the valley?" The Shining Ones stood back and Christian gazed at the narrow path fenced on both sides with walls called Salvation, razor-straight as far as the eye could see.

"This is the Way," they said. "It was constructed by the patriarchs, the prophets, Christ, and his apostles, and it is as straight as a rule can make it and the terrain allows. Many paths intersect it, but this is the path that will take you to Celestial City."

Christian looked at the Shining Ones. "I'm usually pretty good with words. But at this moment, nothing comes close to saying what's in my heart."

"We see it in your eyes." Their faces reflected his joy as they saluted him. "For the Kingdom!" they shouted, then melded into the sunshine.

"For the Kingdom!" Christian squinted after them. He looked down at his fresh khakis and fingered the monogram. The crest bore a circle with rays of glory, the cross, and a dove. Like an Olympic athlete ready to march in the opening ceremonies, he imagined himself setting forth, carrying the flag of the Kingdom through an imaginary stadium. The real race was about to begin and he was going for the gold.

Christian hadn't gone far before voices and loud noises behind him interrupted his parade. He looked back to see the strangest sight: two men tumbling over the left-hand wall onto the Way.

A tall, robust fellow, after dusting himself off, greeted him. "Hello there! I'm Jimbo Health and this is my friend, Guy Wealth."

"Hi," Wealth said, adding his greeting. He checked out the crest on Christian's running suit and scanned his backpack and footwear.

"Nice to meet you. My name's Christian. Where are you guys from?"

"Actually, we're from County Prosperity, heading to Celestial City to enjoy *all those blessings* promised there," Health said, fairly bouncing with adrenaline and ready to run.

"All those blessings?" Christian asked.

"Yeah, when you've got your health you've got everything," he said.

"Well, not quite everything," Wealth demurred. Together with Christian they jogged down the stone-walled path.

"Anyway, there's no doubt that Jesus was the greatest healer of all time," Health said. "So if we really want to experience wellness, we just need to slip along this Way and seek healing."

Wealth said, "Don't you think your neighbor will pay more attention while you tell him about God if you wear a Rolex and drive a Mercedes than if you shop the Salvation Army store and ride the bus? God blesses the bank accounts of everyone who walks this Way."

Their smug tone annoyed Christian. "Excuse me, but why didn't you guys come in at the Narrow Gate?"

"The Narrow Gate?" Health shook his head. "To approach the gate from County Prosperity is too far around. Usually our countrymen take this shortcut and climb over the wall like we did."

Christian felt like he was talking with two guys who'd just cut in line at a movie. "I'm a little surprised that if you want to go to Celestial City, you didn't come in through the gate. I mean, isn't that what the Lord of the City asks?"

"Well, the important thing is that you find healing," responded Health. "And prosperity," added Wealth. "And besides, it doesn't matter how we get on the Way. You came in at the gate and we came in over the wall. What's the difference? If we're on it, we're on it. The bottom line is, we'll all arrive at Celestial City and enjoy health and prosperity forever."

"That, my friends, is where you may be disappointed." Christian braked and his companions turned around to face him. "I believe that when I come to the Gate of the City, the Lord will recognize me because . . . because the Narrow Gate leads to the cross and there I became a new person, a child of the King. He gave me a new relationship with him and a new name. I'm even wearing his clothes." Christian motioned down at his crested khakis. "Because you didn't come in at the gate, you don't have these things. Without them . . . I don't know what you'll find at that final gate."

The two interlopers gave him no answer. Looking at each other and sharing a laugh, they turned around and began jogging again. Wealth made some comment to the effect that he was glad they were outfitting their people with such first-class gear.

The three continued down the path through the rocky hill country. Christian stepped up his pace and gradually moved quite a bit ahead. Over the chest-high wall, bluebonnets, Indian paintbrushes, and verbena waved in blue-scarlet-purple cheering sections. Serious rock faces beckoned in the distance. The view from each crest confirmed he was definitely headed for the rocks.

The prospect of a good rock climb energized him. He had accepted the firm's offer of senior account manager in part because their accounts included several resorts in the mountains nearby. Skiing, snowmobiling, hiking, mountain biking, rock climbing—his "Lord of the Manor" privileges afforded him coveted access to all his favorite pursuits. Even during the harsh winters he was a regular at the local rock-climbing gym. Perhaps it was because his everyday job and routine presented practically no risk. Perhaps he possessed some kind of Lewis and Clark gene. He loved the thrill of testing his limits on a sheer rock wall—and the rush at the top.

Hiking up the steeper slopes, he began to realize that something inside him had changed. His heart still quickened as he sized up the cliffs above. But his anticipation overflowed from a full heart rather than from a hole in his soul that needed some high-risk endeavor in order to feel alive.

By midafternoon the Way tapered down to nothing at the foot of a huge hillside of boulders. Yet there was no doubt about which way to continue. To the left of a bubbling spring, defined by stone faces and boulders that glowed luminously, the Way ascended straight up the rock. A Parks Department-type sign identified this as the "Rock of Difficulty." Christian drank deeply from the spring and discovered roast-beef sandwiches and fruit in his pack. After a brief rest he attacked the boulder pile.

Immediately, he noticed something extraordinary about his new shoes. While on the flat surface of the Way, the soles had seemed as sturdy as hiking boots (but as lightweight as running shoes); here on the rocks they proved to be very flexible—especially the toes. Just like his climbing shoes back home, they allowed him to curl his toes around the rocks for a better grip.

The ascent sloped up at a comfortable yet challenging angle. Anyone watching him scampering up the rocks would have thought he was part mountain goat, part wide-winged albatross—his reach and musculature well suited to the challenge. Pausing atop a nice flat boulder, he scanned the hillside below for his former companions, but they were nowhere in sight. Christian looked at the sun and determined that he had about three hours of daylight left. He set off again, attacking the rock wall with quick, sure movements.

His fingers and toes probed for sturdy holds. Although sometimes there was a more convenient hold beyond the edges of the "path" of softly glowing rocks, staying on the Way had become a discipline he intended to follow.

Overhead an eagle screeched a welcome to the neighborhood. An advance party of hyperactive chipmunks scouted the terrain, always about five yards ahead. The sun shone, the breeze blew—*you couldn't script a more perfect day!* A wisp of rock-climbing camaraderie tugged at the back of his mind, an echo of shared summit-conquering laughter. Ever since he had resumed rock climbing a year ago, little shadows of a long-ago family vacation climb had edged in on him. But today there was too much to enjoy. He shook off the shadows and vaulted over the boulders to the next vertical stretch.

Although Christian was a veteran, the climb became increasingly strenuous. The stretches of craggy cliffs became longer and closer to absolute vertical, requiring him to lift his entire weight with torqued-out, tightly drawn knees or climb with handholds alone. Sweat beaded his brow. He began to wish there were some other way to get his backpack up the hill than strapped to his back. On the top of every ledge extended yet another stretch of rock.

He paused on a small ledge to catch his breath. Time for a squirt from his water bottle. Noticing the Scroll in his pack, he pulled it out. Well, he could use a little comfort and encouragement right now.

Holding the Scroll in his left palm, he pushed the power button with his right forefinger. On the small keyboard he found the menu key and selected "Encouragement." A video clip from Evangelist's movie played on the three-inch screen—Jesus sitting with his disciples by the fire, laughing, talking, always encouraging. Over the clip scrolled his promises: "Trusting me, you will be unshakable and assured, deeply at peace. In this godless world you will continue to experience difficulties. But take heart! I've conquered the world."

"Ask the Father for whatever is in keeping with the things I've revealed to you. Ask in my name, according to my will, and he'll most certainly give it to you. Your joy will be a river overflowing its banks!"

Christian smiled and closed his eyes. *Well, Father, what I need right now is the strength and endurance to make it up this Rock!* As he soaked in the water and the words, the exhaustion ebbed from his body just enough for him to stand up and tackle one more sheer stretch. And another. And another.

Twilight was falling. The eagle and the chipmunks had long ago abandoned him. He was sure his muscles were way out of oxygen, but he hoisted himself up one more cliff on heart alone and heard the sound that all spent climbers love to hear—the sound of water falling into water. Approaching the last ledge, the welcome sound grew louder with every push and pull until a final effort landed him on the outer rim of a small basin.

Christian took in the scene before him. From a height that disappeared into purple mists, a slender waterfall careened down another huge cliff about a hundred and fifty yards in front of him. The rock face served as a back wall to a basin about three hundred yards wide. After a day suspended between a bright blue sky and silver-pink rocks, this turn of the color wheel salved his senses. The cascade plunged the last fifty feet into a lake of midnight blue surrounded by dark green pines and firs tossing their heads and leaning in chorus-line sync, blown by the wind that whistled through their needles and wrapped their fresh, pungent scent around him. Another Parks Department-type sign read, "Welcome to Pleasant Arbor. Built and Maintained by the Lord of the Rock for the Refreshment of Weary Travelers."

Good enough. So Christian sat and rested, and turned his attention to study two giant pyramids of reflective glass that towered thirty feet over the treetops on opposite ends of the basin. Their upper panes reflected the beautiful shades of the late evening, but from each base, softly glowing lights twinkled through the foliage. He wondered where the paths to the pyramids might be. His curiosity dragged him up off his feet and forward to the pool.

Rock-walled cabins surrounded the water on both sides, equipped with rustic but comfortable beds and furnishings. He entered one, slung his backpack on the table, and plopped down on the freshly made bed. The firewood in the fireplace awaited his match, and within minutes a cheerful blaze warmed the room and his aching body. In no time the embers would do a nice job of roasting one of the foil dinners in his pack. As relaxed and tired as he was, the puzzle of the pyramids drew him back out into the fading light.

Tomorrow's path lay up the rock face to the left of the waterfall. The rocks glowed in the approaching darkness. Back toward the edge from which he'd come, the luminescent Way divided around the pool, encompassing the shelters on each side. At the base of the waterfall the divided stone paths converged again. He looked for any sign of a branch off the path that connected over to the pyramids, but found none.

Well, it is getting so dark I either need to make a move or wait until morning. Surely this whole basin is part of the Arbor. Obviously, the path is not going to be ramrod straight all the way to Celestial City. Maybe once it reaches a certain site, the point is just to follow it out the far side. What's the point of laying a glowing rock-path floor over the entire ground area here?

After he tucked his dinner into the coals, he set off toward the left end of the basin. In less than five minutes he reached the clearing and gazed at the pointed tower of black glass. It seemed much larger up close—like a midsize hotel. He began to approach but noticed a sign: "Ladies Only." *Good grief. What are these? Exotic bathrooms?* He couldn't see a thing through the dark glass entry doors.

He wandered back to his shelter. But it was going to be another fifteen minutes before his dinner was ready, just enough time to check out the possibility of a "Gentlemen Only" designation on the right end. A short walk and he found the sign he was looking for posted in front of the other pyramid. *Just a few minutes to check it out.* There was clearly no pathway up to the door. He strode across the grassy carpet, took the few steps, and shoved open the door.

Behind the cherrywood counter, two unusually attractive young women—one blond, one brunette, each with her hair falling softly around her face—smiled at him. "Good evening." The cool, smooth voices washed over him. "Did you just make it in?"

"Yes, I set up camp at the shelters, but then I found my way over here. Great facility. At least a four- or five-star." Would they appreciate his insider's ability to appraise the caliber of their resort? "So, is this part of Pleasant Arbor?"

"You mean you haven't heard of us?"

"Well, I'm not from around here." He felt a great need to cover. "And," he added, flashing his trademark-winning smile, "you're a little off the beaten track."

The smile did its magic. Their laughter embraced him as they handed him a glossy, four-color brochure.

"The Pyramids at Pleasant Arbor." He read the headline aloud and opened the trifold to scan the copy. "So, why would anyone want to stay in the shelters if he could stay here?"

"*Was* anyone else staying there?" they asked.

"Actually, no. But I mean, why even offer both kinds of lodging? Who's going to camp when . . . "

"Exactly," one of them cut him off. "And you'll feel that way even more after you've strolled through the pyramid. The doors of the available rooms are open so you may choose your favorite interior. The elevators are around the corner to the right and there's a sports café on the left. When you make your room selection, just phone the desk and we'll register you for as long as you'd like to stay."

"Oh, I'll be taking off tomorrow." He remembered his pack and his dinner. "Actually, I've got dinner waiting back at the shelter, and I guess I need to retrieve my backpack."

"That's no problem, really. You can order dinner down here or catch the catering cart when it comes by your room. We'll send someone to get your pack for you. Let us know when you find your room." Around the corner on his left a green neon sign caught his eye: "sports.com." The giant television screen at the far end was tuned to a basketball game. A quick pass to the perimeter and a graceful rainbow shot arched right through the net.

"Is this the finals?"

"Yeah, first game. You just get in?" Another attractive hostess type moved toward him.

Christian nodded. "I'm surprised you don't have a full house." He scanned the dozen or so guys snacking on peanuts and buffalo wings and sipping their drinks.

"Well, most guys just like to watch it in their rooms. Been upstairs?"

"Not yet."

She smiled. "You'll see why."

On his right the elevator doors opened and two more men headed toward them. He hesitated for a moment, then slipped into the elevator before the doors closed. Of the seven possible floors, he punched number five.

Chapter 4

A warm, affectionate voice announced, "Fifth floor." The doors opened onto a well-kept lobby with custom-bordered carpet and brass fixtures. Across from the elevators the glass wall of the pyramid promised a beautiful view tomorrow. He decided to follow the hall off to the right. To his shock the hallway extended around the *outside* wall of the pyramid and absorbed every square foot of the fifth-story view. All down the right side of the hall the doors would have to open into interior rooms with no view. *This is crazy! What moron designed this?*

Then he reached an opened door.

In every detail except the view, the "moron" who had designed the room had done a breathtaking job. An involuntary "Wow!" escaped Christian's lips.

Actually there *was* a view: big men elbowed, screened, and fought for rebound position on a huge eight-by-ten-foot plasma theater screen. A fleet-footed guard ducked, wove, and drove to the basket. Even though Christian was standing at the door, the explosion of the crowd through the surround-sound speakers enveloped him in that front-row feeling. Swagged back on either side of the screen, heavy velvet curtains repeated the bright blue of the carpet patterned with "spilled" reels of film ribboning around a confetti of "Admit One" tickets and golden popcorn. The smell of the real thing wafted out of a large popper in the corner. Across from a bubbling Jacuzzi, ornately framed photos of movie stars beamed down on an overstuffed bright yellow sofa and lounge chairs.

Next opened door—same view. But instead of the movie decor, a safari beckoned. Canvas curtains, couch and lounge chairs, leopard-patterned throw rugs and pillows matched the drop cloth on the circular lamp table. On both sides of the Jacuzzi, gigantic elephant tusks arched up toward the mounted heads of a gazelle, a Cape water buffalo, and other ferocious trophies. A table and torchère lamps fashioned from horns and antlers accented the Great Hunter decor.

As tired as he was, Christian could have toured the rooms for hours, taking in the concept and extravagant detail of each room—most with the same view. And that view was pulling him. He longed to settle down in a Jacuzzi and watch the big game.

He paused at the door to a rain forest room, savoring the rock waterfall pouring into the Jacuzzi and the fresh, fragile orchids cascading out of urns atop marble pillars in each corner of the room. But then the travel room looked even better. Plush Oriental rug, realistic-looking logs glowing in the fireplace. From the plasma screen, 3D images of exotic, island gardens summoned him to collapse on the rich brown leather sofa and put his feet up on the large round ottoman. The accent tables looked like large stacks of beautifully bound travel books and the walls were painted with floor-to-ceiling murals of mysterious temples. Styled like a Roman spa, the faux marble of the Jacuzzi was decked with replicas of ancient statuary.

Finally, as he was completing his circuit and nearing the elevator lobby again, he found it. It might as well have had his name on it. Actually, he was thinking he would head back to the movie room when the framed photos of familiar faces over the Jacuzzi stopped him in his tracks. Ooo—this was like the movie room, only better. In individual and group portraits, mythic galactic warriors stood guard over the science-fiction sanctuary.

Christian surveyed the familiar figures and wondered how it could be possible that only his favorites hung there. It was almost spooky—like they knew he was coming. He checked the number on the door and found a speakerphone by the lounge chair. But it had no buttons and he couldn't discover how it worked. On the glass end table a leather-bound book caught his attention. "Starcruiser Log," it read. "Speak and it will be."

So he tried it. "Telephone, dial the front desk."

Through the speakerphone three beeps, two rings, and the cool, smooth voice. "Front desk, may I help you?"

"Yes, this is Christian. I've chosen room 512." He was grinning from ear to ear and shaking his head at the beauty of it.

"Yes, sir. We'll have your bag retrieved and sent to room 512. Congratulations on figuring the communications system out. Many of our guests who decide on that room have to come down to the front desk for help with the voice commands. The Starcruiser Log on the table explains how it all works, in keeping with the theme. Have a nice stay."

"Telephone, hang up." Christian smiled again and leaned back in the navy leather, modular lounge chair. He shucked off his shoes and socks and scrunched his toes in the deep pile of a navy rug spangled with gold stars. The soft, buttery leather enfolded him. His eyes wandered up to the black-domed ceiling where, projected from a miniature planetarium projector in the corner, a star-scape of red-glowing gas nebulas and hot blue quasars slid silently by. He was cruising toward a giant fiery-pink star cluster when he heard a knock at the door. Another smooth-voiced hostess stood beside a catering cart. "Are you finding everything okay? This room has a catch to it."

"Yes, I've already discovered the voice commands."

"Congratulations. I'll bet you're hungry. Our new guests always are. You can order dinner downstairs at sports.com, or you can choose something off the catering cart. Did you find the wet bar?"

"Yes, I believe it's right here by the door."

"You'll find a full assortment of beverages and fruit in the refrigerator and slide-out baskets of chips, nuts, and cookies beside it. If you want something you don't see, just let us know. We'll get it for you. This cart comes around every two to three hours with a different variety of hot and cold snacks. Would you like some?"

Christian could hardly believe his senses. As he selected a Chicago-style sausage-and-pepperoni pizza and an entire box of his favorite creamy doughnuts, he chuckled at the thought of his now-charcoaled foil dinner. The thought about the campsite surfaced one final nagging doubt.

"Miss, may I ask you just one question?"

"Of course."

"Are you . . . are the pyramids really an official part of the King's Pleasant Arbor?"

"You mean, you never heard of us?" Her face clouded with disappointment.

He found himself doing his front-desk backtrack and smile-flash. "Well, actually, I'm not from around . . . "

"Surely you ought to *know* the answer to that question by now." She looked earnestly into his eyes and brightened. "You may heat up your pizza using the wet bar's microwave. If you want more, I'll be back in a couple of hours. Now enjoy your stay. You picked a great room." She grinned and lowered her voice, "You can even tell the door to put out a Do Not Disturb sign, and it will hang one out of this little slot right here."

Christian returned her smile and stood there for a moment watching her push her cart down the hall. He gazed down at the pizza and doughnuts and then into the room. *Oh puh-lease, I'm just staying one night.* He kicked the door closed and strode over to the navy and gold faux marble spa. "Jacuzzi, power on." From overhead a column of red light beamed down into the water and the Jacuzzi bubbled to life. *This is so awesome.* "Screen on. Volume louder." The squeak of rubber soles on the wooden court floor filled the room.

Inside of four minutes he was sliding down into the bubbles, his ice-cold Dr Pepper and stash of warm pizza and doughnuts spread out on the ledge beside him. *Eight minutes to go in the first half. Score is tied. This is great.* He grinned and drowned the last niggling little doubt in the depths of the bubbling water.

Christian opened his eyes and stared into pitch blackness. "*What in the . . .* " He sat bolt upright and tried to collect his thoughts. *Oh yeah.*

Christian's team got the rebound, fired an outlet pass two-thirds the length of the court where it was . . . caught! And then it was one-on-one to the basket as the clock ticked down 5 . . . 4 . . . and the shot . . . 2 . . . went . . . in! The surround sound exploded with screams and cheers as the buzzer sounded.

Christian scooped in the rest of the chips and wondered why the post-game celebration on the court didn't lift his spirits more. Like *Alice in Wonderland,* with every bite he seemed to shrink, while the radiant faces dripping with perspiration and the fans jumping up and down and hugging each other grew larger and larger. *I should have gone downstairs. Why does it feel like it takes so much effort?* He surfed the sports web sites, checking statistics and reading post-game interviews until he fell asleep.

e next morning—or midday—Christian was channel surfing en he caught a commercial for the pyramids. From the "Ladies y" side, the women rhapsodized over the ultimate girl resort.

"My favorite part is downstairs," a dimpled blonde reported. re's a jewelry bar and a fashion boutique where you can go every and try on clothes and jewelry—sometimes for hours!—until ind the right outfit for dinner. And a Roman spa where these great ng hunks in togas massage your hands or feet or shoulders."

he camera switched to a perky brunette. "Every room has beautifully designed home theaters and I can tell you what m everyone likes to watch: *My Friend, Phillip.*"

oo yes!" The blonde nodded in agreement. "I'm in *love* with g head!"

t what a talking head!" Her friend's eyes flashed. "I don't ow they do it, but this great-looking, blond-haired, blue-eyed ed Phillip is individually interactive. He'll listen to us tell our r talk about our day and say, 'Oh, tell me more.' He loves to he details and never asks us to just give him the bottom line. he asks us how we *felt* about our day. And he looks deeply

"Lights on." Immediately a field of gold stars twinkled in the dark, domed sky. He looked longingly at the Jacuzzi, but decided against it. *This is no time to get mellow.* He did take a moment to pick up the Starcruiser Log on the table. Scanning its pages he was amazed at the room's electronic potential. He pulled out one of the Envirodiscs and inserted it into the DVD player. On command it scanned through scenes of everything from rain forests to snow falling on icy mountain lakes until he found a view of jagged cliffs with eagles soaring. *This ought to get me in the mood. Who needs windows anyway?*

He nuked the remaining doughnuts and pulled on his clothes. Rested and ready, he shouldered his backpack and opened the door. He looked back, taking in this ultimate guy resort room one last time.

"Screen off. DVD off. Lights off." He closed the door and started toward the elevator lobby but then stopped in his tracks. The view he had expected to see this morning out the pyramid's glass wall had not materialized. The glass was as dark as it had been last night. Maybe the hotel's designer wasn't a moron, but he certainly was strange after all.

In the main lobby he thanked the smooth voices for the great night's stay and was aware that their silence followed him to the main door. He opened the door and stood there in shock. Instead of the bright blue sky and silver-pink rocks, a blue-green twilight greeted him. He knew he'd stayed up late and was sure he'd over-slept. But maybe he hadn't. There were no clocks in the room and he'd run off without his watch. *It must be dawn. I can't believe I feel so rested.* He looked toward the front desk to find the attendants gazing after him, amusement curling their lips. "What time *is* it?"

"A quarter after seven."

"A.M. or P.M.?"

"P.M." Their amusement was no longer a hint.

Christian stared at the darkening cliffs above the treetops with mixed emotions. *The bad news is, it's much too late to tackle the rest of the rock. But the good news is . . . I can enjoy another night in room 512.* He didn't even look in the direction of the front desk as he headed back to the elevators and the fifth floor.

He was in such a rush, he almost collided with the catering cart. "Oh, excuse me."

"Hi! Are you enjoying your stay?"

"Yes, but . . . tell me something. How do you know what time it is around here? It's so dark or something . . . I slept through the whole day."

"Well, you looked really tired last night. Have you been traveling long?"

"Pretty hard for several days."

She smiled and laid a reassuring hand on his arm. "And have you been under a lot of stress lately?"

"Yeah . . . yeah I have been."

"Well, it's the weekend. Give yourself a break. And . . . here. We make great burgers."

He landed back on the couch with his bacon-cheeseburger, French-fried onion rings, and another pepperoni sausage pizza.

"Screen on." Monster trucks sprayed fantails of dirt and sailed over impossible hurdles of cars. With voice commands he surfed between the soaring trucks, the latest Bond movie, and a rerun of Super Bowl XVII.

Later, in the Jacuzzi, he pondered the simple logic of the hostess's words. *Didn't the sign say that Pleasant Arbor had been built for the rest and refreshment of weary travelers like me?* As the bubbles bombarded his back, it sank in how really tired he was. Tired of all the stress and strain at work—always another deadline. His ski vacation a couple of months ago had been a bust in blizzard conditions. And then there was the whole violence thing. He had almost died in the Dump. And he wasn't used to dealing with emotional issues like that session back at the cross. He was in pretty good shape, but after days of jogging and the challenge of the Rock . . . *What's the hurry? That Rock will still be there on Monday. I deserve some time off.*

He meant to get some sleep so he wouldn't have his days and nights so mixed up. But then he discovered the wireless keyboard and the directions for Web TV.

What do you do when you can do anything at all? That w
question of the day—every day. He wasn't sure how he had d
but after spending almost a week in his room, enough time t
four games of the pro basketball finals, he had given hims
he came to think of as a well-deserved vacation. He wo
after the basketball finals were over. And since the series
two games each, that would happily be at least a few day
to the question of the day. Get in the Jacuzzi? Take a wal
est? Hang out at the sports bar? Surf the hundreds of
millions of web sites?

"DVD on. Scan disc." The planet fast-forwarded
"Stop. Play." Palm trees, white sand, breakers on the
ting over the ocean. . . . He was going to get up, but
was so delicious. After watching for a while he tur
back, folded his hands on his stomach, and closed
just Meg and him alone on that beach—playing i
ning on the beach, sunning on the sand, kissing.

By the fifth game of the basketball finals he ha
He put his big plastic tankard of Dr Pepper and h
glass table. Then he opened a bag of sour-crea
chips and dumped a bunch on his chest. That
them in his mouth without even lifting his elb

During halftime it occurred to him that it
since he had stepped out of his room. The p
be part of the King's retreat—any time he
much time in front of a television screen, h
higher than a kite. If his feet were still on
sunk in the softness of the sofa, this must

He thought about going down to spo
This was such a great series—two evenly
ing a cliffhanger. He kept meaning to, b
another doughnut or douse himself wit
down to the last half of the fourth quart
If he took the elevator now, he might
team's guard went up to the right of
with him, but then he shifted the ball
and over, where it spun around the

into our eyes and tells us what he's been thinking and feeling. We all sit and talk to him for hours . . . "

Christian rolled his eyes and changed the channel. When the cart hostess showed up he surprised himself by choosing some huge, sticky cinnamon rolls instead of doughnuts. He actually wanted to visit with her, but she handed him a package and called back over her shoulder, "It's a special offer for those who decide to vacation with us."

"PyramidQuest," the box inside the package read. He inserted the disk into the DVD player and a preview of 3D accelerated visuals opened up before him. From craggy mountains to moldy dungeons, the detail staggered him. He could hardly wait to finish the tutorial and launch into this new world. Over fifty levels! Spells, skills, cool equipment. Energized by the prospect of adventure, he set off. *Maybe I've been spectating too much. This is just the ticket.*

Whacking and slashing the plagues of flies, grasshoppers, and locusts, his pulse skyrocketed. And it was hard! Just when you thought he had them licked, the creepy things would re-spawn and fall out of the sky. The more he succeeded, the more he was able to acquire better swords, better spells, and better clothes. He played as a commander of Pharaoh's army chasing the enemy through the desert wilderness. In this version, when the bad guys tried to escape through the divided waters of a big sea, his divisions chased them all the way to the other side . . . and annihilated them. He felt a little conflicted about that but moved on.

Other levels took him out of the world of the pyramids and into the world of Japanese shoguns or medieval knights and castles. Completely hooked by the ever-new challenge of graphic phantasms, ogres, and goblins—the world of the game enveloped him. *What a sense of power! It feels so real.*

His new world even afforded him companions. As he progressed to higher levels, the monsters banded together and there was no way to defeat them except by finding other players online and forming a team. His on-screen knight messaged other knights, wizards, and clerics.

They would play until Christian felt his eyes were going to fall out of their sockets, agree to a short nap, and resume the quest. After a brief pause for food and beverage, Christian messaged the Green

Knight, "I have just been re-provisioned by a real-world teammate (very cute) with pizza and barbecue. Now I'm ready to go."

The Green Knight messaged back, "If you are a true believer, you will not speak of the other realm."

"Sorry, Green Knight. The word of Draygon is my life."

Level 10, level 15.

While he waited for one of his teammates to take a break, he remembered the basketball finals. He clicked over and found the game underway. *Game number 7? How could that be?* Agonizing over his choice, he watched for a few minutes. But he knew his teammates would be waiting for him.

Level 20, level 25.

Their team did a great job of staying together. If someone was wounded, they would all wait until his health bar rose above the halfway mark. No one would abandon a battle until all the others were safely past the enemy. And it wasn't all slash and bash and buying stuff. Their camaraderie grew as they searched out abandoned orphans and found homes for them and serenaded the princess in the Great Hall on her wedding night.

In the darkness Christian awoke. Something was bumping his nose. He reached for it but his hands ran into something. He tried to raise his head and bumped his forehead. He tried to raise his knees, but it was like being in a box. And where was the light from the screen? He always left it on so his teammates' messages could wake him up.

"Screen on. Lights on." Nothing. He breathed more rapidly in the pitch blackness. *Is this another one of my "Help! I've been captured by the Cave Giant" dreams?* He reached up, exploring the obstacle above him, pushing against it. His arms straightened out, but when he quit pushing, he bumped back into it. He reached down below him. There was nothing. Only air.

CHAPTER 5

He hoped he was still in his room. There was no palming his way down the walls to find out—he floated with the buoyancy of a blimp. It made him thankful for the ceiling. But only for a moment before a wave of frantic desperation welled up from his gut and washed over him from head to toe.

"I'm floating again! Why now? I've been here for weeks. And why so high? Lord, I tried to find out if this place was on the Way . . . "

The lights blinked and then stayed on, the air conditioner kicked in, and an invisible force pulled him down off the ceiling, planting him back on the couch. The plasma screen flickered to life with a message summoning him, "Knight Errant, where *are* you?"

He stared at the screen, heart pounding. *Good question. Did what I think just happened . . . really happen?* He looked back at the ceiling. Was it a dream or was the "evil enchantment" broken for just a moment? His eyes fell on the game controller, but he fought off something very powerful, sat up, and forced himself to look, really look, around the room. Greasy pizza and doughnut boxes, assorted plastic cups and plates, empty Dr Pepper cans, stale popcorn, plastic bowls with spoons set in dried-milk-and-cereal plaster—he had created his own dump-scape topped with pizza crusts and French fry spikes. Except for a path cleared from the couch to the wet bar/door area and back to the bathroom, the floor behind the couch was a wasteland.

In the bathroom he took another good look. This time at himself—blue eyes bleary and bloodshot, hair that shouldn't go public without a baseball cap, the beginnings of a scraggly beard, dirty (no, filthy!) T-shirt and shorts that stretched across his at-least-ten-pound-heavier body. He leaned on the sink and stared at himself right in the eyes. *Who* are *you?*

"Certainly no gallant knight," he muttered out loud and dropped his gaze.

He wanted to pray, but felt too dirty. He took a shower, then poked through the garbage looking for his backpack and running shoes. Rescuing them from the rubble, he cleaned off the dried tomato sauce and cheese.

The powerful thing pleaded with him. *What if you go out and it's night? Maybe you should pack up, just go down to the lobby, and take a look. If it's nighttime you could message your buddies back and finish up one more level with them before you take off. You owe it to them, really.*

He swung his backpack up on his back and moved to the door. But the handle wouldn't turn; the door wouldn't open. Another wave of desperation rolled out of his gut. He wrestled with the knob. No results.

A smooth, sunny voice called to him: "Are you planning on ending your stay with us, sir?"

Christian whipped around, eyes scanning the room.

"Sir?" The voice came from the speakerphone.

"Yes, I was. Thanks, it's been great, but I need to go."

"We are disappointed, then, that you won't be staying with us any longer," the voice clouded noticeably. "Was there anything we could have done to make your stay more enjoyable?"

"No, thanks, now if you'll just . . . " he yanked on the handle again, "open this door, please."

"Was the food all right? And your Jacuzzi, did you find it relaxing?" The voice was getting cooler.

Christian turned suddenly, planted his left foot on the wall, and put his entire weight into another yank. It didn't even budge. There was clearly some locking mechanism beyond his control.

"Sir, our only purpose is to please all our guests . . . "

"LET ME OUT!" A thin film of sweat covered Christian's body. His jaw clenched. He kicked the door and then pounded it with his fists. He shouted to the catering hostess and the hallmates he never met, "HEY, SOMEBODY . . . "

"Please relax," the ominously pleasant voice said. "Everything is taken care of."

He ceased pounding the door, and leaned back against it, closing his eyes again. Consciously he tried to slow down his breathing. He turned and stared again at the screen. Of course!

In his best Starcruiser Captain voice Christian commanded, "Computer, open the doors . . . NOW!"

Nothing.

"Door, open!"

No response.

His mind frantically searched for some way to override the power that controlled his room. The keyboard!

He extracted the wireless device from the coffee-table clutter and pulled up a "picture in picture" view of the computer desktop. In the larger picture the Green Knight's message flashed with renewed urgency: "KNIGHT ERRANT! PLEASE! WE NEED YOU!" Chin tucked, eyes darting between the keyboard and the screen, he searched the software programs.

"If this room does not meet your needs," the smooth voice said, "we can easily move you to another more to your liking."

Pounding furiously on the keys, Christian searched one program and then another.

Suddenly the screen went black, as did everything else in the room. He felt his body float up and away from the couch. His stomach flip-flopped and he broke out in a full-fledged sweat. Gripping the keyboard with his left hand, Christian extended his right hand above his head to break his impact with the ceiling.

But he never touched it. He could hear something like a door above him slide open. He kept ascending through the darkness. *Oh, God, what have I gotten myself into?*

Something slid shut below him. The lights blinked on and Christian found himself standing in a room with medieval castle decor, like a smaller version of the Great Hall where he and his comrades had serenaded the princess on her wedding night. The Pyramid Quest battle blazed to life on his new room's plasma screen, but the perspective had shifted, completely unbidden, away from his character to his online comrades. Goblin axes hacked at their armor, beating them back, spilling computerized blood all over the 3D landscape. "KNIGHT ERRANT! WE ARE UNDER ATTACK! WE NEED YOU! WE ARE DYING! DON'T LEAVE US!"

"We know you'll like this room," the sunny voice said. "Enjoy your stay."

Christian stared at the game controller on the heavy oak table in front of him. The screen seemed to swim out toward him, and the powerful thing pulled him into the down cushions of the tapestry couch. He looked at the keyboard still clutched in his left hand. It probably wouldn't even work on this screen. He looked back at the electronic carnage. In another few moments his teammates would be dead. Their prerecorded cries of anguish filled the castle room. "KNIGHT ERRANT, FOR THE LOVE OF DRAYGON . . . "

Christian closed his eyes for a few moments. He opened them to see the goblin chief swing his hatchet and decapitate his friend, the Green Knight. "NOOO!" his character cried.

"NOOO!" Christian slammed the keyboard down on his lap and began hammering the keys. Responding to the keyboard from his old room, a picture in picture appeared on the new screen. "YES!" Ignoring the screams of digital pain, he began sorting through more files. Control commands. *This is it!*

Christian opened the program and scanned the lists of commands—keyboard commands, room settings. He opened the file and with a hint of a smile clicked the "keyboard override" option. His finger moved the cursor to "lights off." Left click. The room dimmed, lit only by the huge plasma screen. His throat tightened as he moved the cursor to "door open." As soon as he left clicked, he sprang off the couch, straightened his backpack, and . . . *Yes . . . it's opening!*

He sprinted down the hall and took the elevator to the lobby level. When the doors opened he bolted, but as he pushed the front doors open he froze. *Oh, whoah . . . In here there is obviously some kind of gravitational force that keeps us grounded. What if I step out, and float . . . and keep floating right over the edge of the basin?*

Behind him he could hear footsteps . . . commotion.

Dear God, please help me get back on the path!

And with that he burst out the door.

From a height of a couple hundred feet, clinging once again to the rock face, Christian looked down at the basin below. It always gave him the weirdest sensation to watch birds flying around below him.

He could no longer see the sign advising all but advanced climbers to take extra ropes and harness for safe passage up this more difficult slope. He had been so relieved to see the noontime sun, so glad to be out of the glistening glass trap below, he spurned the safety measures and banked on his years of experience to get him up the Rock.

Beneath his grasping fingers and toes the luminous path tested every ounce of his climbing skill. Even within its boundaries, there were places the rock became so smooth that the next handhold or toehold was completely out of reach. He would have to back down, move over, and start again. Ledges were fewer and smaller, and stretches in between longer.

Lungs gasping, muscles aching, he used more rest stops on this half of the Rock. Catching his breath atop a rounded little ledge, he reflected not just on the differences in the Rock above and below the basin, but also the differences in the climber. *I am so out of shape! I know what I need to do, but it's so much harder to get my body to do it.* He felt like he was lugging a great big, creamy doughnut around his midsection. His extra sweat and frame of mind reminded him of post-holiday fatigue at the gym—it hurt, but it was good penance for a season of grand indulgence.

As he drew in another rejuvenating lungful of the crisp, dry air, he heard voices and the familiar rhythm of feet rappelling off the rock face, accompanied by the whirring of nylon ropes through pitons. From above, two rappellers swung into view. Christian could hear the anxiety in their voices and see the grim looks on their faces.

"Hey, aren't you guys going the wrong way?"

Two grimy, sweat-streaked faces jerked toward him as the rappellers yanked to a stop. "We *were* going to Celestial City. Actually made it to the top of the Rock. But the further we got, the more dangerous the Way became."

"I'll risk mountain climbing with thousand-foot drops," his companion said, spitting into the air for emphasis, "but I draw the line at walking into a lion's den. Good luck to you. And watch out for all the loose rock at the top." Releasing their holds, both men dropped quickly out of range.

"But wait . . . " Christian watched them rappel through the expanse below. Their words pricked his balloon. For the first time since he had left the City of Destruction, he seriously thought about going back. *The sign said "Rock of Difficulty." I didn't expect a walk in the park. I've done a lot of tough climbs. But . . . lions. I've never done lions.*

On the other hand there's no guarantee of safety if I go back. His mind flitted between the bombed-out bank and the toxic dump. *Is there any real safety this side of Celestial City? Maybe just different kinds of danger.* He stared intensely at the radiant path ascending the rock face.

I'm going up. *I may never have done lions, but Daniel did, didn't he? I may just look him up.* He felt in his backpack for his Scroll, but didn't find it. He emptied the pack, unzipped every zipper.

No Scroll.

He forced his mind to slow down and retrace his steps. It shocked him to realize that he hadn't read it, hadn't even looked for it, during his entire stay at the pyramid. The first and last time he had used it was on the bottom stretch of the Rock. *So when I reached the shelter, it would have been on top in my pack.* He vaguely remembered taking it out to look for the foil dinner underneath. It was quite possible that whoever retrieved his pack had not seen it, *or didn't want to.* If not in the shelter, then it could have fallen out in his pyramid room, in which case . . .

He looked up the Rock and was pretty sure he could almost see the top. Hundreds of feet below him, the cascading stream on his left hurdled into the basin pool. Judging from the position of the sun, it was doubtful whether he had enough time to make the descent, find the Scroll, and finish the climb back to the top.

He let fly a few choice words, dropped his head, clasped his hands behind it, and rocked back and forth. Exhaling deeply he unloaded his rope from his pack and prepared to rappel down the Rock. What would he give for just an hour or two of all his wasted time at the pyramids? *There was no path; they never really answered my questions; my conscience kept pulling me back to the Way but I kept rationalizing, kept playing . . .*

Usually rappelling was such a thrill, but he was just going through the motions.

Stupid, STUPID! I thought I finally had it figured out . . . finally found God in my life. First temptation comes along . . . just a little more rest . . . another game . . . another movie . . . another night on the web . . . what an idiot!

Landing back in the basin, he dumped his gear and trudged back to the shelters. *How much further would I have been by this time? Now I have to do the same stretch three times, and it's getting later and later . . .*

As he crossed the threshold of the shelter, his eyes scanned the room. No Scroll. It wasn't around the fireplace. He spied it under the table. *Thank you, God! A little dusty but . . .* Flipping it open he touched the "on" button and smiled faintly when the menu appeared. He thought about catching his breath and looking up Daniel's story, but knew he didn't have the daylight to spare.

Once again he ignored the cautionary sign and charged up the Rock without the safety harness or extra ropes. He would rather try to climb in the dark than take all the additional time. As he revisited the same nooks and crannies, his mind replayed some of his earlier thoughts. The vigor of his health-club yeah-it-hurts-but-I'm-making-up-for-it mentality drained away.

Adding to his gloom, lengthening shadows smudged the silvery pink of the rocks to a taupe gray. In the azure sky, stars began to twinkle. Steeling himself to endure the consequences of his poor choices, he tried to pick up the pace a bit, but he was so tired. He paused on a ledge that marked the high point of his previous attempt and searched for the crest above. If he made good time he just might make it before he lost the light completely.

Handhold by handhold, he pushed and shoved himself up the Rock. The rappellers had been right about the loose rock. Wind and rain had eroded the last hundred feet into a shingle pile. Each handhold and toehold had to be tested for stability before he entrusted his weight to it. Even so, his hands and feet often slipped, and with every new hold he had to make sure he was always prepared to shift his weight back to the previous one.

In the gathering darkness it was increasingly difficult to find firm holds. As he was forced to rely more on touch than sight, his hands and feet probed the rocky surface. The only light remaining was the faint glow of the path itself. There were times when it took several minutes of groping to find the support for his next move.

With his left foot he felt out what seemed like a firm toehold and his left hand grabbed a hold directly above it. But as he hoisted himself up, the rock moved. The entire slab bearing the weight of his left hand and foot slid out into space. He let go just in time to watch it go crashing into the darkness below, leaving him badly extended. With a prayer (and a rush of adrenaline) he fought to draw his body back in against the rock face. As his bulging eyes watched the huge chunk disappear, the memory of two terrified eyes sinking into the abyss seemed to stare up at him. Above the clatter and smashing of rock on rock, an echo of a desperate voice screamed, "CHRIS . . . CHRIS, HELP ME . . . "

He finally succeeded in reeling himself in and hugged the Rock, shaking so hard he feared he might yet lose his grip. Smoke poured out of the cracks around the door holding back his memories, suffocating him.

No, NO! I can't think about that . . . think about surviving . . . think about just making it to the top. He stuck to the Rock, refusing to look back down, fighting for focus until his fingers and toes began to weaken and lose their grip. Only then did enough adrenaline kick in to get him moving upward.

Within fifteen minutes he lay gasping on his back at the edge of the summit. *Forget it. Move on. I can't go there.* Purposely, he tried to imagine big cat ears, alert, pricked forward, listening in the dark, big cat noses sniffing the night air. He lifted his head and strained to hear any sound, detect any movement in the shadows. Gradually, his strategy began to work—the ghosts in his inner darkness were crowded out by a very real fear of the four-footed kind. *What will I do if I suddenly find myself face to face with a lion out here in the dark?*

He sat up cross-legged and gazed at the starry night. God . . . *God I want to cry out to you. . . . I really thought after the cross things would be so different. But here I am still making stupid, selfish decisions . . . only now I feel even guiltier for making them.*

He drew his knees up to his chest and hugged them tightly. *I felt all this new love and excitement for you. Well, how long did that last? I want to think I love you more than basketball, more than big-screen TVs . . . but God, if you can hear me, I'm so sorry . . . really. All day I've been thinking, yeah, I blew it, but I'm paying for it and I'll make it up. But my screw-up's a lot bigger than I thought.* He rested his head on his knees. *Father, I'm exhausted, scared. I don't know why you would want to help me. This quest is a lot more adventure than I expected. I don't think I can do it. It's got to be you.*

He eased down the path in stealth mode, hearing only strange, sonar-like echoes of unidentified night creatures from every side. Five minutes down the path he rounded a bend in the terrain and saw a stately palace lit up like a fairytale castle, about two hundred yards ahead. And the Way led right to it.

Christian picked up his pace as much as he could, hoping this place was really *on* the Way. His approach took him into a very narrow passage about a hundred yards from the porter's lodge. Suddenly, in the reflected light of the palace, he saw two shadows close by—one lion on his right and one on his left. Crouching, eyes locked on Christian, their tails twitched in anticipation.

Now he knew why the rappellers had turned around. And he reconsidered joining them.

From his lodge the porter saw him pull up and cried out, "Come on, man, where's your courage? Don't be afraid of the lions. They've been put there to test your faith and to discover who has none. Keep to the middle of the Way and you'll be safe."

Christian heard the words but felt like he was back on the porch with their old gray-and-white tomcat. Before he died, Pussy Gato had turned mean and would crouch on the window ledge by the back door, amber eyes locked on any who dared approach. If you did, he jumped you. And Christian had the claw scars to prove it. How many times had he been held hostage on that porch, knowing that if he took one more step, Pussy Gato would get him? The porter's words directly disagreed with the amber eyes fixed on him.

From his left came a long guttural growl. Trembling, Christian looked down to make sure he was in the dead center of the Way and took one more step forward. He looked up to see both lions launch.

CHAPTER 6

Christian's heart cried, Run! But his faith kept him riveted to the middle of the path. Cringing, eyes shut, he heard chains yank taut and the big cats scream in frustration. When he opened his eyes, they were straining against their choke chains, biting and raking the metal links. They swiped at him, but their paws could not reach beyond the borders of the Way. Breathing heavily, Christian made a dash for the gate. "Sir," he called to the porter, "is this house on the Way?" He glanced back at the lions.

"It is. If you'll wait, I'll call someone," the porter said and rang a bell. Presently, a young woman approached, backlit by the castle's lights. A slight breeze rustled her long silk skirt and blew a few strands of dark, wavy hair across her face. As she drew near the gate, she scrutinized Christian's face and disheveled figure. "What is your name?" she asked.

"Christian."

"Where are you going?

"Celestial City."

"Still?" her dark eyes looked piercingly into his.

"Still," his voice was quiet, but firm.

She signaled the porter, who buzzed open the gate. As the grillwork slid past him, she reached for his arm and, smiling, looked him full in the face. "Come in, Chris. Welcome to Castle Beautiful. I'm

Lady Discretion. This house was built by the Lord of the Rock for the express purpose of entertaining questors like you. Come meet my family. We were just about to eat a late supper."

The words "family" and "supper" did it. He realized he craved the one about as much as the other. "Really, I should clean up first," he mumbled.

The heavy door to the castle swung open, and they stepped into the glow of the entry hall's giant crystal chandelier.

"Welcome, questor, welcome." He was surrounded by warmth and handshakes from two young men of athletic and dignified stature, and another young woman of gracious bearing who in turn introduced him to their parents—a knight of the Kingdom and his lady. Introductions complete, Christian escaped to a guest bath to freshen up.

Washing the grime from his face and hands, he marveled at the rich decor of even this small corner of the castle. Blue matte porcelain walls with baskets full of grapes and flowers in white relief reached floor to ceiling. *The detail is so fine. Like a whole room made of Wedgwood china.* One last look in the mirror at his matted hair and badly stained khakis, and he considered sneaking off to find a quiet corner to crash. But he was too hungry to care much about his image.

Escorted by Lady Charity and Lady Discretion down a long hall, he caught his breath at each room they passed. Truly palatial furniture, tapestries, rugs, and unique treasures—each room looked like a work of art. But what caught his eye most were the hanging chandeliers—some five and ten tiered, some with crystals the size of a fist, others in fantastic shapes like galleons in full sail and Saturn with its rings.

"Do you recognize it?" Lady Discretion nodded at a great fixture.

"I do, from Evangelist's pictures. It's a guardian cherub."

They took their seats in what his hostesses described as the family dining room. If the long mahogany table with sixteen chairs surrounded by huge, ornately carved buffets and sideboards was the *family* dining room, he would like to see the formal one. Overhead, a gold and crystal replica of Castle Beautiful bathed a table laden with gleaming silver settings and crystal wine goblets in a soft, rich glow. Silver platters groaned with cold, boiled shrimp, a stunning array of cold meats seasoned and sauced, and every fruit imaginable, including his favorite—chocolate-dipped strawberries. And the breads! Baskets bulged with piping hot croissants, dark rye with raisins and nuts, and huge crumble-topped muffins chock-full of fresh blueberries.

He heaped his silver plate high and disciplined himself to use his knife and fork despite his ravenous appetite and a month of eating with fingers and plastic. His eyes rested on the name card with "Christian" beautifully scrolled across it. If they had had to rustle up another place setting, it didn't show. Waiting until he had taken the edge off his hunger, they then directed their conversation toward him.

"Tell us, Chris . . . " the Great Knight laid his damask napkin beside his plate, "what moved you to leave your home and begin your quest?"

"I lived in the City of Destruction . . . does that ring a bell?"

They nodded. "The school shooting and bank bombing, all in one week."

"Awful play by the Enemy."

Christian nodded. "I was already so sick of the violence in my own heart . . . angry, empty. It was the last straw."

"So you started your quest. What has been the greatest highlight so far?" Lady Discretion asked.

"It would have to be Evangelist's Kingdom Story."

"Here, here." Smiles of agreement all around.

"I think the things I saw there will stick with me as long as I live."

"Especially that scene at the Judgment Seat of Christ," Lord Piety said, and stared right through Christian.

"Yes, that was probably the worst moment of my life. But . . . I'm glad I saw it. When you really see how the Story ends . . . "

Lady Charity folded her arms in front of her. "I like to think of the Kingdom Story as a kiss—the kiss that breaks the evil one's enchanted spell."

"Um," Christian replied in agreement, "you start watching as this ordinary frog, and as the Story sweeps you along, you realize . . . you are really called to be a Prince."

From the head of the table the Great Knight spoke. "Yes, and you realize the Enemy's power was broken and his dungeon doors flung open." He stroked his beard. The golden light of the chandelier illuminated the folds of his dark velvet cape and the burgundy satin of his brocaded tunic. He turned toward Christian. "But even princes still settle for life in the dungeons, fawning over their bars and chains."

Christian swallowed. His face hardened slightly and his gaze retreated. "Just one more game, just play to the next level. . . . How come I get sucked back in so easily?"

"Let me ask *you* a question," the Great Knight said. "Why are you so passionate about computer games and basketball? What is it about them that captures your heart?"

"Because so much of life is so boring and the games are so exciting. It's this great adventure—full of surprises, testing your mettle. When you're watching the championship game, the stakes are so high. Or, when you've finally made it to level fifty, there's this great sense of history and accomplishment. You've come so far. And the thrill of being so close to winning, to standing on top and being king of that little world." He paused, allowing his own words to sink in. "Why does it have such a grip on me?"

"Good question," the Knight said. "Remember the small stories on the dam across the Dump—the ones that made the big screen fade?"

"Oh yes."

"The sports story, even the 'game' of business, is one of the most powerful small stories out there—along with romantic love—because they echo so closely God's Kingdom Story. Some call the Kingdom Story a 'Sacred Romance' because of the way God loves us so passionately and woos us like a bride," the Great Knight said. "God's Kingdom Story is also a romance in the tradition of the great romances of King Arthur, El Cid—a tale of grand adventure with kings and castles, foul fiends, deep magic, and damsels in distress."

Christian's eyes swept the extravagantly furnished table illuminated by the crystal chandelier and the suits of polished armor on either side of the fireplace.

"When we're young," the Knight continued, "we want to set our course and pursue it, caught up in our illusion of control. And then life happens—all these unpleasant surprises. We retreat and settle for playing things fairly safe. We may take a few well-calculated risks, but mostly we just get used to living in some version of a smaller story.

"But Life was written as a romance." The Great Knight's lively eyes focused intently on Christian. "The Good King woos his beloved. He summons his royal family and sends us out to slay this dragon, take that fortress, be his agents of deliverance, champions of those nobody notices—the beaten down and forgotten. He calls us to play a part in his Kingdom Story so much larger than the ones we choose for ourselves."

Christian nodded. "In my head I believe every word you're saying, but in my heart . . . "

"You wonder why you long for excitement and adventure. Perhaps it's because you've been born for it and called to it. Not the virtual kind with an off button, but real adventure with real risks and real stakes."

The Great Knight's words stirred a longing in Christian's heart. The Knight embodied so much of what men of Christian's time, what he himself, so often lacked: *gravitas*—weight. If the Knight were the lead actor in an epic adventure movie, he would not need any scenes up front to establish his moral authority. He wore it as easily as his velvet cloak.

"I want to believe that Life is an epic adventure—to have my life count like that." Christian hesitated, trying to put into words the powerful, new desires at conflict within. "And when I listen to you talk about it, it seems grand and exciting, but when I'm just out there living my everyday life . . . well, it doesn't seem as real or exciting."

"And the basketball games and computer games seem more real and exciting?" inquired Lord Prudence.

"To be honest . . . yes, certainly more exciting. And the chat rooms and the late nights of web surfing . . . "

"And the romantic fantasies and books and movies," added Lady Discretion, "I know. But doesn't the fact that it's *not* real life discourage you?"

"Only when you think about it," Christian said, grinning and looking down quickly, as he twirled the stem of his crystal goblet. "You're right," Christian said, meeting her earnest gaze. "It's not real. But let me play devil's advocate: So what if it isn't real?"

A hint of concern clouded her eyes. "I think that's for you to answer."

The Great Knight bowed his head and dispelled the uneasy silence with a concluding benediction. He led the company into a deep and powerful gratitude for God's care and presence.

At his amen, Christian felt an urge to throw his arms around the old gentleman's neck and thank him for his humility and dignity and greatness of heart. But that would be awkward—and in marketing they didn't do awkward. He settled on a handshake and a deeply felt "thank you."

The Knight's lady came and took his arm. "Dear Chris, I'm sure you're exhausted." She escorted him up the stairs of one of the castle turrets to his guest chamber. His aching calves reminded him of his day of rock-climbing penance. She opened a door with a sign on the lintel, "Peace."

"This window opens toward the sunrise, and the morning view is glorious." When she was sure he was comfortable, she said good night.

A hot, foaming spa jet-washed the dirt off his bone-weary body. *It feels so good to have a stomach full of real food and real wine and to go to sleep in a real bed.* The lady had even turned down his covers and misted the sheets with evergreen scent.

He pulled the cover up, savoring the other real things around him—real marble, real books on the shelves, real glowing coals in the fireplace. He snuggled more deeply under the feather comforter, warmed as well by the rich fellowship of a real family committed to such service. And through the top of the great arched window, real gold stars twinkled in a true night sky.

From the delicious depths of his bed he peered out at distant snowy mountains glistening in the morning sun. *Finally—a place where you wake up and it's actually morning.* Outside eagles swooped and circled over a sloping land bridge that connected the castle promontory back to a landmass of low mountains. From the castle the Way appeared to follow the land bridge down into a shadowy valley.

So what if it isn't real? Last night's question returned, interrupting his reverie.

He was a man who liked his movies. And his music. And just about anything that booted up, plugged in, or turned on. When he was not skiing, climbing, or playing team sports, he liked to watch other people do it on a screen. He remembered one night when Meg pried the remote out of his fingers and shoved him off the couch with her feet. "Come on! Let's go do something *real!*" She dragged him through the moonlight to a neighborhood park where he pushed her higher and higher on the giant swing set. Running through the great pecan trees catching fireflies, sweet kisses under falling stars—it was magic. Real magic. And he had almost traded it for an evening of hip, funny sitcoms, where angst-filled urbanites, who never struggled or bled, lobbed snappy one-liner grenades at those who did.

Christian sat up on his bed and surveyed the uncivilized terrain below. *Oh well, from the looks of things, I don't know that there will be anything to plug into for some time.* He found his clean khakis hanging on the door and headed downstairs. The men were already off on the King's business. The ladies welcomed him to a richly furnished Belgian waffle bar. He had one with strawberries and a small mountain of whipped cream and a second with pecans.

As he was pushing his sausage around in his syrup, Charity asked him, "Tell me, Chris, do you have a family? Are you a married man?"

"No . . . I wanted to, but it didn't work out."

"Any brothers or sisters?"

Christian paused. This line of questioning was always a killer. "I have an older sister, but I lost contact with her about five years ago. We were never close. Rachel was born with heart problems. It always meant special diets, special treatment, special care by my parents. Trips to the emergency room. Bouts in the hospital.

"It was a struggle for her to keep up in school. She fought a lot with my parents . . . and me. She used her health as a crutch sometimes, I think. My parents were always so focused on her special needs that they didn't seem to have as much time for me or . . . " Christian caught himself, "me or my problems. She dropped out of high school. Started living with one guy and then another. Last I heard she was with some guy in a band."

"And your parents?"

Christian sighed deeply. "They still live back in the city."

"Chris"—the lady of the house had this way of moving things along—"I have here the guest book of Castle Beautiful. If you look through the names and dates you'll notice that all our guests stay awhile to enjoy the castle."

She was right. Most entries signed out after about a week. He sighed at the vacation that could have, *should have,* been.

She must have read his thoughts. "You're not the first one to arrive after a long vacation below. Even so, the King likes for all the guests to spend at least a day." The knight's lady had the most gracious smile and no-nonsense way about her.

Christian spent the day inhaling the scent of ink and leather among the beautifully bound first editions filling the shelves in the study. Sunk into an exquisitely comfortable, overstuffed leather wingback, he spent hours reading biographies of saints little known to the world, strategic builders and agents of grace in the Kingdom.

At dusk the men returned just in time for dinner. Lord Prudence apologized for their appearance. "Please forgive us, Chris, if we eat first and clean up afterward. We are *starved.*" They dragged into the dining room and collapsed at a table spread with lobster bisque and stuffed tenderloins.

Looking at Prudence's exhausted face, Christian said, "You must have been hard at work. You've even got a little . . . " he touched his left temple to indicate where Prudence needed to wipe the blood off his forehead.

"Sometimes we receive assignments," Prudence said, wiping the trickle of blood off his forehead. "We're not free to share the details. But whether we're here visiting with questors or out on assignment, yes, it's hard work. We help redeem failing relationships, broken governments, schools, businesses, adventures in the arts. We make disciples, teach—engage in conversations . . . "

"A *lot* of conversations." Piety's head nodded vehemently in agreement. "A lot of face-time with people."

Revived by the tenderloin, the Great Knight responded. "Chris, you might be surprised how much our daily lives are like yours. Full of routine. We serve our family. We keep up this great palace. But we're not just a 'rest stop.' We use hospitality to move into people's lives. That's where the real action is. A great deal of the Kingdom work Prudence talked about can be accomplished right here at this table." He patted the polished mahogany with his hand.

"What about you?" The Great Knight searched his face. "Have you gained any insight? Does it matter so much if you engage in the real world?"

"To be honest, I can't say that my desire has done a 180. But what you've said about Life rings true. I look at you and think, 'That's what I want—a passionate love for God. To spend myself for the Kingdom. Show up in the throne room with that depth of camaraderie. A track record of real Kingdom adventure and accomplishment. Not just a tally of thousands of hours of fun that go up in smoke.'"

"Now Chris, don't get the wrong idea." Charity's warm smile lit up. "Life around here is rarely 'boring.' We have fun, but, well, it's just not the ultimate value in the universe."

Christian tapped his head. "I know it in here. We'll see how I hold up the next time I'm starved for something electronic."

"Who knows," Discretion said, arching her brows playfully. "Maybe one day other questors may find *your* biography on the shelves of the castle library!"

Reflecting on his track record so far, he responded, "Gee, I hope not."

The Great Knight rose. "Ladies and gentlemen, a toast. L'chaim!"

Christian's mind hung, but then he remembered. "L'chaim—to Life!"

The next morning after breakfast he was loading his backpack when the men knocked on his door. "We brought you something for your quest. Do you mind if I do an upgrade on your Scroll?" Piety asked.

While Piety was working on Christian's Scroll, Prudence presented him with what looked like a handle. "Here, Christian, put this on your left hand. Now squeeze it tightly twice . . . very quickly."

A circle of light about three feet in diameter flashed out from the handle. "Wow!" exclaimed Christian. "What is this? Some kind of shield?"

"Yes," replied the Knight. "And you will find that the greater your faith, the wider its circumference and the stronger its protection."

"Squeeze it twice again and it will go off," Prudence directed.

Christian squeezed twice and the lightforce shield vanished.

"This is awesome!" Christian grinned and flashed it on again. "Throw something at me."

The Knight fished a coin out of his pocket and tossed it toward Christian. A small thrust of the circle of light and the deflected coin went sailing into the bathroom.

Piety stood up with the Scroll. "Okay. We've taken this Scroll and given it the capability of a lightforce ray. Be careful when you activate the ray; treat it like a gun and don't point it at anyone unintentionally. Let's take it outside to show you how it works."

"Oh, before we go," the Knight motioned Christian over to the big window. "See those purple mountains in the distance?"

"Yes."

"Those are the Delectable Mountains. Beautiful wooded slopes, vineyards. Absolutely gorgeous land. Like our castle, it's for the refreshment of questors on their journey. When you make it there, our good friends the Shepherds will take you to a lookout point where you can see all the way to the gate of Celestial City."

On the way outside Lord Piety instructed Christian how the lightforce ray worked. "It's tiny but extremely powerful, and sharper than a two-edged sword, or even a laser. Because it's so small, it's the perfect concealed weapon. Tap twice anywhere on the surface and the ray comes out the front with a range of up to twenty feet. It will melt away deception and expose the true nature of anything."

"Thank you so much." Wielding the Scroll like a sword, Christian swished the ray in figure eights and a great big Z.

The Great Knight put a calming hand on Christian's shoulder. "It is a *real* weapon to use when you're in *real* danger. And you will need it in the valley below."

CHAPTER 7

Buoyed by the blue sky, his backpack stuffed with castle goodies, Christian charged after Lord Prudence down the gravelly land bridge. They whooped down the gravel slide in a barely controlled, crashing descent. As the incline played out, they slowed and caught their breath enough to talk.

"Thanks again for . . . everything." Christian grasped his new friend's hand. With their free hands they clapped each other's backs.

Prudence's eyes looked concerned. "Take care in the Valley of Humiliation ahead. It's a hard place . . . " His eyes swept the valley. "And remember what we showed you about your shield and the Scroll."

"Will do." Christian smiled and saluted his comrade and watched him head back up the bridge. Out of his pack he pulled the elusive Scroll and adjusted his headphones to listen to a little encouragement for the journey.

I love you, GOD—you make me strong.
GOD is bedrock under my feet, the castle in which I live,
my rescuing knight.

You've always given me breathing room,
a place to get away from it all,

A lifetime pass to your safe-house,
an open invitation as your guest.
You've always taken me seriously, God,
made me welcome among those who know and love you.

Christian marveled at the uncanny sampling of Psalms. *How does this thing work?*

He hadn't gone far before a glint of something caught his eye. About fifty yards ahead, a large satellite truck spanned the entire path. Beneath the call letters KDVL emblazoned on the side of the truck, a guy with a microphone was engaging an animated audience.

"So *you're* going to make me an offer *I* can't refuse to try to get on the show?" Laughter from the crowd. "Sorry, that's not the way it works. Hold on everybody, we're about to go live . . . this is it."

Bass-thumping, backbeat-pounding theme music swelled. The hard-bodied deejay, blue eyes flashing, circled his forearms and swiveled his hips in sync with the music. Roars of approval as the audience joined in. Christian flipped the headset off his ears and down around his neck, checking things out from the back of the crowd.

"This is the Prince of Power coming to you live from the Valley on KDVL where we rule the airwaves. Got a great show today, some hot new releases ready to sizzle up the charts. And right ahead, a new edition of the game that's got everybody talking: 'Who Wants to Get an Offer You Can't Refuse?' Here's today's qualifying question: Back in the Garden of Eden, from what tree did Eve pull down that red, shiny apple?"

The scene from Evangelist's movie flashed through Christian's mind. "The tree of the knowledge of good and evil," he heard himself say.

"There in the back, you are correct! Make way, kids. Let him through!"

Stunned at the sudden development, Christian hung back, but those closest to him grabbed his shoulders and pushed him forward. The deejay welcomed Christian and draped his bulky gold watch over his shoulder. "Okay, so tell us your name."

"Christian."

"Hello, Chris. I'm the Prince of Power. Everybody calls me Prince. Now, where are you from?"

"I'm from City of Destruction."

"Well, I can see you've been away for a while. You know, all that violence has really brought the people together. (Cheers, whistles from the crowd.) Yeah, posse, that's right." The Prince gave them a thumbs-up. "They've had lots of meetings, candlelight vigils, the place has a whole new identity. They've even renamed it—the City of Light."

Only his years of training in front of a microphone helped Christian mask his incredulity. "Well, I'm really glad to hear it."

"And you are on your way to . . . "

"I'm on my way to Celestial Cit . . . "

"Well let's just see if we can make you 'an offer you can't refuse.'" The deejay slipped out of his cheesy announcer voice. "Hey kids, you can watch a live feed from the monitor on the back of the truck while we go inside."

Not wanting to make a scene, and being curious, Christian let himself be escorted into the truck. *There's no question this truck's parked in the middle of the path, and besides, I'm pretty good at game shows.*

Inside the truck, a large bank of video monitors lit up two chairs and a microphone. "See for yourself, my friend. Things really have changed." On a monitor Christian saw familiar faces and scenes from his hometown—the Northside funeral scene he had watched from his motel room, and a memorial service for the bombing victims killed on the day he left. Like news clips strung together, he watched the candlelight vigils, protests at City Hall, large town meetings, and concerts where people joined hands and sang together.

"It's a different place, Chris. And you've really been missed." His parents' faces filled a monitor—sad, dispirited. His mother walked to the piano and picked up the photograph of Rachel, Phillip, and him in front of the Christmas tree. Taking it to her chair, she held it in her lap, then pulled it closer, studying each face. She sighed heavily and her eyes welled up. Jackhammers of remorse broke up Christian's composure. He noticed as never before his mother's softly crinkled skin, his father's shrunken shoulders.

"And this will be news to you, but your ex-fiancée, Meg, left Jason." Next to his parents' monitor, a living color picture of Meg flashed on the middle screen. Moving her things into a new apartment, unpacking boxes, stopping to look through an old photo album. Christian held his breath as she fingered snapshots of their hill-country escapes and wiped the dust off crazy photo-booth muggings with her shirttail. She closed her eyes and lay back on the couch, the album in her lap, her shoulders shaking softly.

"She married Jason because he was safe, you know. No eggshells to walk on. But she's always loved you."

Christian reached a hand up to the video monitor as if to brush her wet cheek. "Oh, Meg . . . Meg . . . "

The third monitor lit up with the picture of his bank, his friend Brad busy with one of his customers. A few strokes on a keyboard and Prince pulled up his bank statement. It still showed the few thousand dollars he had left in the account. A few more strokes on Prince's keyboard and a new balance appeared . . . one million dollars.

"Chris," Prince's voice was gentle. "Maybe your decision to leave was a bit hasty. It was a bad time. You're not the only one who left. But it's not like that today; you can go back. You don't even have to make the trip back. Just say the word and the next instant you'll be on Meg's doorstep. You can have dinner with your parents. I told you I'm the Prince of Power. I rule the air; I own this town. I can make all this happen. That money in your bank account is real. You can have your old job back. You can have any job you want. Just say, 'Yes, Prince,' and in one moment you can have the life you've always dreamed of. Just say it, Chris."

He was there. He was on Meg's doorstep, burying his face in the scent of her long brown hair, feeling the warmth of her body wrapped within his embrace. They would build a new life, build the dream home they had sketched in front of the fire that snowy night. He could start his own marketing firm, make it the best in town. He knew how to do it. They could invest in the resorts, enjoy VIP access to every one of them.

He dragged his eyes off the monitor and looked down at the floor. "What did you say?" He focused on Prince in the reflected TV glare. "What did you just call me?"

"I said Chris . . . or Christian, whatever—it doesn't matter. I'm making *you* this offer . . . "

Unnoticed, Christian slid his hand into his pocket and tapped his Scroll.

"What in the . . . what are you . . . "

In an instant the monitors disappeared. The walls of the truck fell away; the watching crowd vanished. Christian stared into the deejay's eyes, which widened and morphed from blue to yellow while the pupils shrunk into reptilian slits. Only he wasn't a deejay anymore. His huge shoulders and long neck towered over Christian, iridescent scales glistening in the sun. Shaking his dragon head, he folded his wings close to his body. Twenty yards behind his large lion-like mouth and padded, clawed, bear-like feet, his tail thrashed the air. He snorted and blew over Christian's head, the fire from his mouth whiting out the valley.

Quaking, his stomach doing flip-flops, Christian still had the presence of mind to reach in the top of his pack and grab the handle of the shield. "It was a lie! Everything you've told me was a lie!"

"Not so." The dragon wagged his head. "A slight misrepresentation about the atmosphere of your hometown. There's still plenty of action underneath, but on the surface at least, there's a lull for now. All the rest is true." The creature arched his neck and extended his wings. "I am Apollyon!" He let it echo down the valley, "Prince of the Power of the Air. All your homeland is mine and you are my subject." He bent down to eye level. "Still I am willing to make you this offer."

"I am no longer Chris; I am Christian." His voice rose steadily. "I am not just on a road trip. I am a new person with a new mission. I've given my faith and allegiance to the King, not some lizard Prince." He enjoyed letting his famous temper fly. "And I like this King, his service, his wages, his servants, his government, his company, and his country better than yours. So get out of my way." *Yeah, yeah, this feels good, you jerk.*

"Reconsider, dear Chris," the dragon said, furling his wings. "His Way is full of pain and shattered dreams. For the most part his servants come to a bad end. It's not wise to go against me and my way." Rearing up, the dragon shouted, "Is there any doubt that this land, this new millennium is mine? The momentum of history has shifted. This is *my* golden moment!" Again he snaked his head close to Christian. "Turn on the TV," he hissed. "Look in the back halls of the courts and Congress. Peruse the university course catalogs. Is there any doubt that my word, my ideas, hold sway?"

The dragon Prince paced back and forth. "Nobody respects your King anymore! They used to think he was good, but too hard to serve. Now they see him as the narrow, intolerant, uncompassionate bigot he really is. A self-seeking, self-possessed whiner! If all things do not serve him, he throws an earthquake tantrum and cries a hurricane. He's never there to help. How many of his followers have been put to shameful deaths! You think his service is better than mine? Really! He never shows up to deliver those who serve him. But as for me, how many times, as the world very well knows, have I showed up? I keep my appointments! By power or fraud I deliver what's mine."

"You are twisted!" Christian fired back. "If he waits to deliver his own, it's to prove that all we really desire can be found in him. He shatters our lower dreams so we can seek higher ones! As for the bad end you say we come to, you forget: death isn't the end. If we endure his delay, we do it for glory. And *we will have it,* when our King and his *better* angels come in all their glory!"

"*Better angels!*" Apollyon's absolute rage filled the valley. "I am an *Enemy* to this King. I hate his person, his laws, his people, and his 'better angels.' I retract my offer. Now it's me against you."

Thoughts of the Great Knight and his sons emboldened Christian as he squeezed his shield handle twice and the protective lightforce flared out. "Careful, Apollyon. I am in the King's highway."

Legs wide, Apollyon straddled the entire width of the path, laughing. "I swear by hell itself you will go no further. I'll spill your soul right here!" And he blew a flaming dart straight at Christian. With a deft move of his shield, Christian deflected the arrow. Apollyon closed quickly toward him, blowing darts as thick as hail. Christian tried to maneuver the shield to get the fiery darts to ricochet right back into the dragon. But when he succeeded he was disappointed. The darts bounced off Apollyon's scales as cleanly as they bounced off his shield.

With the precision of an experienced handball player, Christian wielded his shield with increasing skill and less effort. But he also realized he would never win the battle on defense alone, so he reached in his pocket to grab his Scroll. As he did, he exposed his right hand for only a moment, but enough for a dart to smash into it. As the pain shot through his body, he lifted the shield a bit too far up and another flaming arrow caught him in the foot. As the searing pain registered, the protective arc of his shield receded.

Christian had to work harder to protect himself, but he was in good shape, and the battle dragged on. Again and again he tried to force his hand into his pocket, but his right hand was almost useless. His breath came in gasps. Out of the corner of his eye he could see a pool of his own blood collecting around his feet. The circumference of the shield shrank again. He tried to transfer the shield to his wounded right hand and reach in his pocket with his left. But he bobbled the shield and a flaming arrow smoked off his left temple, laying him out.

Apollyon seized the opportunity to close in on Christian. "Dear Chris," the monster mocked, "don't you see I'm only playing with you? I can take you out anytime." Christian managed to sit up and was moving his hand toward his pocket.

"But before you depart my realm, I'd like to send you off in the right frame of mind. We can't have you flying to glory feeling like you've fought the good fight. I've already told you what your King's really like. Now let me show you what *you're* really made of."

With his legs splayed, Christian's wounded hand could not push into his pocket far enough to tap the Scroll. In his vulnerable position he still managed to hold the shield, but it was only about a foot in diameter. The beast swaying over him lightly exhaled his smoky breath, which somehow bound Christian to the spot, bleeding profusely, unable to move a muscle. Suddenly a giant picture materialized in front of him.

"You know, ever since you joined your King's service you've been pitifully unfaithful. In fact, I don't think you're going to see much by way of glory."

Unable to speak, Christian silently pled his defense. *I've made mistakes, but the King knows my heart. He won't call me 'unfaithful.'*

"Oh, but he will."

So you can read my thoughts. Good. You'll know how much I despise you without having to dredge up my old vocabulary.

"How quaint." Apollyon mashed Christian's foot and made the blood run faster. Huge, stadium-theater-sized pictures of the early days of his quest flashed before Christian. "You barely started out before a little name-calling from Worldly Wiseman sent you scampering off into the Hills of Inner Light, a lovely part of the country, but not one your King particularly cares for. You almost choked in the Dump of Despond.

"And you wanted only to indulge yourself in the pyramids at Pleasant Arbor, where you forgot your Scroll, your quest, and nearly your existence. You were almost persuaded to go back at the very thought of the lions. And even when you talked about your journey in Castle Beautiful—all the things you had seen and heard—you took a little too much credit, didn't you?

It's true, all that and much more. But my King is merciful and ready to forgive.

"You think so, do you? You know, you're pretty impressed with yourself."

The scene changed to his ten-year class reunion. He arrived in his brand-new BMW, smoothing his new power suit and tie. He made sure to check the time often on his new, slim gold watch—scattering the names of 5A resorts and restaurants like pearls before swine. All the girls too cool to notice him ten years before lined up to dance with him, and he reveled in their long overdue attention.

"Ah pride . . . just about my favorite sin. Yours too, I'd say. So easy. Really just as bad as rage. You think he's ready to forget violent rage again and again?" Christian's soul cried out at giant images of him assaulting Meg—tossing her aside, throwing her into a wall as he exploded out the door; violently shaking her by the shoulders over some forgotten, petty disagreement. And the worst—his fingers around her throat as he screamed at her, veins bulging, right in her face.

The picture did not follow him out of the room. It lingered on Meg's tears and humiliation, showed her looking in the mirror the next day, touching the bruises as fresh tears fell. And there were pictures he had never seen—pictures of Amy, head down, walking the silent gauntlet of protestors into the clinic for a "procedure." Throw-away Amy—the woman after Meg. Amy with her knees up and her clinic gown on, head turned, staring at the wall. A picture-in-picture shot of him playing pool with the boys. Eyes scanning the room for the next Amy.

But the scene didn't end in the clinic. The view followed the baby's fragile hands and tiny toes into a medical waste container—from the "procedure" room to the waste disposal truck, and finally from the truck to a landfill, where the birds and the bulldozers had at it.

"You think he forgets that?"

The pictures took him down into a pit of inner darkness. Monstrous pain suffocated him, making it hard to breathe—pain ten times worse than his physical wounds. "Is that close enough to murder for you? Apollyon blew a perfect smoke ring. "If not, I've got another episode for you. Do you think he forgives and forgets murder?"

Noooooooo. Dear God, please don't let him, please don't . . .

"Oh, oh . . . okay . . . let's see if God stops the picture. Well . . . no, it's moving right along."

Christian strained again to close his eyes, to redirect his focus.

"No, I think you really need to watch this."

He stared in horror as his eighteen-year-old self talked his younger brother into climbing up the steep rock face. He had known it would be a huge challenge for him and even more so for Phillip. "Well, you can stay down here and watch," he had said, taunting Phillip. "You're right, I guess, it's totally out of your league." He flashed his brother a younger, nasty version of his killer smile.

Instead of a long shot of their ascent, a tight shot of Phillip's red hair and face filled the air. Eyes that fought back fear with determination, an angry set to his jaw and his cheeks scarlet with humiliation. The further they climbed the more the fear absorbed the determination. Fear that mushroomed to panic as Phillip slipped a few times and the climb became even tougher. "Hey, Chris, I can't do this. Let's go back. I'm not kidding . . . I'm scared."

"Go ahead. Wimp."

He had said it without even turning to look at his brother. But he looked now as the picture blazed with the pain and desperation in Phillip's eyes. His brother paused, then tried once more to catch up to him, only to slip again and then scramble about ten feet below him. His younger self glanced down just as his brother completely lost his grip and fell backward more than fifty feet, landing with a snapping thud on the boulder pile below. The image was so real, so intense. Just like that day twelve years ago. Thick smoke poured out from behind the closed door in his heart.

Then the funeral appeared and images of the empty bunk below his. Driving to school alone. The vacant place at the table. Pictures he had never seen of his mother's sickened, black looks as he excused himself from dinner.

The door blew off and a fire of guilt and recrimination consumed him. He looked down again at the growing pool of his own blood. It was good to see so much of it. Even if there was no glory, at least there would soon be an end. Apollyon roared with delight.

A faint noise scratched at his ears, pulling him back to the present. From the headset still circling his neck, his Scroll played loudly enough that he could hear:

"God is sheer mercy and grace; He forgives your sins—every one."

Even murder?

". . . every one."

"Stay alert. The Devil is poised to pounce. Resist him . . . "

Resist him . . . Resist him . . . Resist him . . . Christian focused his entire being on those two words. His hand moved ever so slightly deeper into his pocket. *He forgives every one. Resist him. He forgives every one. Resist him.* Over and over Christian silently repeated the life-giving words. His hand moved deeper into his pocket. Finally it reached the Scroll pointed in Apollyon's direction. He had no idea if he would blast his foot off or find his mark, but he pressed his forefinger twice.

As Apollyon inhaled to deliver the final fiery blow, he looked down. His armor was peeling; iridescent scales broke away, littering the valley floor. Then his exposed skin began to peel. Over the entire length of his body, his own blood began to ooze and drip. Spewing curses, the Prince of Power spread his dragon wings, mounted the air he ruled, and sped away.

Christian slumped back full-length on the bloody ground, his hand still in his pocket. Even without Apollyon's pictures, his own stirred memories continued to fuel the inferno. He remembered his frantic descent down the cliff, then hovering over Phillip's crumpled body and colorless, freckled face. He didn't really know how to do CPR, so he went careening back down the path to the campsite, screaming for help.

Then he was following his dad's terrified wake. Even before he reached the boulder pile, his dad rushed past him with Phillip in his arms.

The car tore out for the resort town and its medical help fifteen minutes away. In the backseat, his mother and sister cradled Phillip's blood-soaked yet ashen body. His father was driving so fast, Christian became afraid to look out the windshield as the car skidded around one hairpin turn after another. He thought, *At what point do you accept that it's hopeless and give up this rush for help that's going to kill us all?* Then in the next moment, *So what if we go over the edge?*

Later he could only stare at the Rorschach blood-stain patterns on the waiting room floor, waiting for his mother's wail that announced his brother's death and his own damnation.

In the background the muffled waiting room conversation buzzed on. One voice buzzed more distinctly than the rest: "God is sheer mercy and grace. He doesn't treat us as our sins deserve." The waiting room faded, but the voice continued: "And as far as sunrise is from sunset, he has separated us from our sins." The headset around his neck called him back to the smoke and ashes, and the solid ground beneath it. "As high as heaven is over the earth, so strong is his love to those who fear him."

Scenes from Evangelist's movie floated in and out of his broken-life memory stream. His power suit pride; Jesus taking the whip. Meg's bruises; the nails in his hands. Amy's shame; Jesus' public, naked exposure. Phillip's body, crumpled on the rocks; Jesus' body, spent and limp on the cross.

His own experience at the cross tugged at Christian, wrenching him out of the blackness, back to the barren hill. He could almost feel his hands touch the well-worn knots and grooves again; his arms wrapped around it, holding on for dear life. Tears spilled down his face, mingling with his blood on the stony ground. *Ah, Jesus . . . back there . . . I felt the burden . . . the consequences. But today . . . this is who I am.* A sharp crescendo of tears and pain gradually subsided. *Still . . . even with all this, you love me . . . and forgive me . . . everything.*

He lay there for a while, God's grace tending his self-inflicted wounds.

Then he saw absolutely the strangest sight he'd ever seen: a hand in thin air—just a hand—holding some leaves.

Chapter 8

Christian squinted at the vision before him: the strong, clean hand hung there motionless. His headset crackled, "The leaves of the Tree of Life are for healing the nations."

With supreme effort, he raised his wounded right hand and touched . . . real leaves. Immediately his hand was healed. Slowly, he withdrew it, rotating it, staring at it in wonder. He took the offered leaves and brushed them over his forehead. Head pain gone . . . instantly. With a loopy grin on his face, he sat up, pulled off his sock and shoe, and feathered the leaves over his burned and bloody foot. Same result. So much so that he stood up. *No pain. Incredible!*

The hand had vanished. Just like his wounds.

He stared at the tiny fragment of heaven in his hand. *Just three leaves, and my whole life changes in an instant. Just . . . one touch.* He probed his fresh new skin. No tenderness or trace of the smoldering lesions.

He tried walking and found everything in working order. *This is . . . this is . . . Lord, if this is three leaves' worth of Celestial City . . . what will the real thing be like?* He closed his eyes and inhaled their faint but distinct aroma—like a forest after a rain, with a touch of mint. Opening his eyes, he searched the gray horizon, then closed them again, breathing in the heavenly scent. The incense of his own prayer rose to the Father. He felt known, down to the bottom of his motives and deepest longings, and still loved. A quiet delight in God ascended with his prayer.

Late-afternoon hunger pangs sent him scrounging in his pack—a sure sign of his recovery. After a honey-glazed ham sandwich and some grapes, he could not wait to close the gap between this valley and Celestial City.

For the remainder of his trip down the valley, he held his Scroll in his hand. *Just in case Apollyon comes back.* But his journey was uneventful. The path sloped up at the end of the valley, then immediately back down into another. A rusty sign nailed to the trunk of a gnarled tree read: "Valley of the Shadow of Death." A splash of red graffiti at the sign's base added, "Abandon All Hope—You Know the Drill." Even as he wondered who the pranksters might be, two young men came panting up the Valley slope, red paint on their pants and shirttails.

"Where are you going?" Christian hailed them.

"Back! And unless you wanna go psycho, you better turn it around right here."

"Why, what's the matter?"

"Man, that place is black as pitch. You can't see a thing, but you can hear and feel stuff." Eyes wide, the two older teens were obviously shaken.

"You believe in hell?" the shorter one asked, lowering his voice.

Christian pointed at the telltale paint on his shirttail. "Probably more than you do."

"There are people down there . . . howling and yelling," the shorter one continued.

"And things that whoosh and fly at you," his buddy added. "Scared the devil out of me. No way I'm going back there."

"Better to walk *through* it than wind up *in* it. Doesn't that prospect scare you even more?"

"Nah," the taller one shook it off. "Hell is one big rave, man, one big party. Bad dudes. Bad music. Bad women. Not a bunch of losers freaking out and crying, like they are down there." He jabbed his thumb back over his shoulder. "Come on, Ace, we'll just be leaving the same way we came in." The two headed to the top of the valley path and turned off the Way into the gray hills. The shorter one looked back at Christian, dark eyes filled with honest fear.

A recent convert to believing in hell himself, Christian gazed after them in sympathy. *There are times it would really be convenient if we could make our private realities the real thing.*

Descending the path, he didn't know if the sun was setting or the Valley shadows were deepening. The light continued to fade until, only a short distance from the sign, he found himself swallowed in the darkness that so alarmed the two kids. The only way he could continue was by the soft glow of the stony path. He could barely see more than a step ahead. The further he went, the faster his breathing became. He desperately wanted to run, but if he did he would outrun the light.

He scuffed along, kicking a few pebbles off the path to his left, but he never heard them land on anything. Curious, he took a coin out of his pocket and flipped it off the trail to his left. He held his breath waiting for it to plunk into water or hit some sort of bottom. Nothing. He flipped another coin off to his right and heard it roll down and away, swallowed by some huge coin-gulping vortex off in the darkness.

He couldn't shake childhood images of the Bottomless Pit in the depths of Mammoth Caverns. The tour guide, who had tossed in pennies that never plunked, had explained how they had lowered miles of rope into the yawning blackness, but never found the bottom. He had kept a death grip on his father's hand as they passed by, fearful beyond reason that if he didn't, he would somehow get sucked off the path and fall forever into the Black Nothing. Now he walked in the dark along a narrow path just inches from the void. A light sweat misted his entire body.

Slowly, step by step, Christian made his way forward. He began to hear voices out of the pit, far off and unintelligible. The further he walked, the more he caught snatches of whispers and laments.

"You ruined my life! I should never have listened to you."

"Who, me?" Christian instinctively asked. "Who's there?"

Oblivious, the tight little voice shrilled, "If you hadn't made me move, taken me away from all my friends . . . uprooted the children . . . kept looking for that pot of gold . . . just one more sweet deal, one more new partner . . . how could I ever settle down and make friends, build a home, a life?"

The female voice grew louder. "Why couldn't you ever say 'no' to your mother? We never could enjoy our *own* family, our own friends. Oh no, we always had to be with *your* family, always sticking their noses in our business, loaded with holier-than-thou advice on how to raise our kids. . . .

"Why in the world did I ever marry you? Should have married Robert. At least he gave his wife and kids a steady home. . . . I could have had a happy life with Robert. Why didn't you . . . "

The eternal harangue faded in the distance. Christian shook his head, wondering how someone could wind up in this black hole of bitterness. How someone with a life—a husband, a home—someone who had stood joyfully at the wedding altar, held her newborn children in her arms, and smiled at her future, could degenerate into this small, furious voice. A victim for eternity. *Why would you choose this, instead of Life to the full with the Father? Why pride and anger instead of forgiveness and trust in God?* Yet even before that thought was fully formed, another formed behind it. *Why did you go for thirty years before* you *chose Life?*

Eventually he could make out another voice.

"Okay, there was that scene in *Whoah, Romeo!* where Juliet fell off the balcony and woke up her parents."

Christian almost smiled. "Yes, that *was* funny. Who are you?" he called out.

"And then, oh yeah, that great moment at the end of *Buddies* where Pooch walks up to Lester's grave and puts the balloons on it and says, 'There you go, buddy, that ought to keep your spirits up.'"

The movie highlights reel paused. "I'm *so bored!*" the voice wailed.

Christian's almost-smile faded. "Can you hear me?"

"I'm *so bored!* This is *no fun!* There's nothing to do. *Forever!*"

As loud as he could Christian yelled, "CAN'T YOU HEAR ME?"

"Okay, get a grip; then there was the little girl who goes to her mom and says, 'Mommy, there's a dead person sitting beside my bed. I can *see* her.'" The voice laughed. "'I can see her.' Oh yeah, kid." He began to laugh hysterically. "You can 'see' a dead person? Well, that's a crock because I CAN'T EVEN SEE MYSELF!" he screamed." OH

PLEASE! IT'S SO DARK . . . AND I'M SO ALONE . . . and there's nobody . . . nobody but me."

Christian felt like a rubbernecker slowing down to pass a human car wreck. Crashed into the wall of final reality. Entertained to death. How many funny movie moments had he reminisced about for hours on end with the boys? *But for hours with no end? Alone?* Like a guy who drives past the glass confetti and pretzeled metal of the car of the reckless driver who just passed him, Christian felt the narrowness of his escape. With great effort he picked up his pace.

Christian looked right to see a fiery light—blue-yellow and orangey flames licking out of a cavernous, molten crater. Overhead an unseen creature muttered and peeped as it whizzed by. Startled backward, he stumbled and barely recovered. From all around, invisible beings buzzed him so close he feared he would be slashed by the razor talons of some demon-thing whooshing by his head, driving him off the path.

Continually fighting back his impulses to sidestep or duck, he focused instead on keeping his balance and moving forward. He pulled his Scroll out of his pocket, tapping it as he swept the darkness on all sides. The Way approached the crater. Huge whirlwinds of flame roared out of the cauldron lake below, blasting him with heat, singeing his eyebrows. Seized by the same terror he had felt in his virtual visit to the throne, Christian could hardly keep moving. The same reeking, nauseous stench wafted up, mixed with screams of agony. This time it was real, too real. Real people burning and burning and never burning up. The smoke of their torment stung his nostrils and made his eyes water.

Entire gangs of shrieking fiends rushed him. He stopped and prayed aloud, terrified they would run him off the narrow Way and into the fiery crater. They pressed in close behind and beside him, whispering accusations and threats in his ears. "You're an arrogant liar and a murderer—a user. You use women, light them like so many candles on your altar of self-worship. You belong here." The more he ignored them, the louder they raged. "You're slipping! We're going to leave your corpse as carrion for hell's birds of prey. Your God isn't watching. Where is your big, powerful God?"

Eyes glued to the path, one foot in front of the other, Christian steeled his mind against the grossest obscenities and blasphemies he had ever heard. He longed to stick his fingers in his ears but needed his hands free for balance. In response he began to shout prayers, matching decibel for decibel. "Okay, God, death is staring me in the face but you rule even the armies in hell. Please, save my life, God. Deliver me!"

His unholy tormentors finally backed off. In the relative silence that followed, Christian's breathing slowed. The murmurs from the outer darkness on his left became intelligible. An almost childlike voice mourned plaintively. "Ahhhh . . . if I could just sleep. Just for an hour. Dream and not wake up. Do we toss and turn forever? Is there never any morning to all this darkness?"

"Hello! Can you hear me?" Christian really didn't expect a response, but he couldn't help trying.

"Maybe . . . maybe this is all a bad dream. If it is, it's time to wake up! Wake up! Please wake me up! Surely this isn't it forever. Or sleep, if I could only sleep, just drift away. . . . How can this be real? Surely it isn't real. I'll wake up and everything will be . . . "

"You, on the Way . . . "

Christian startled at the voice in the black distance. "Who, me?"

"Yes, you. You're on the Way, aren't you?"

"Yes, where are you?"

"I'm out here on the other side of the chasm."

"Who are you?"

"My name is Regret."

Stunned, Christian searched for an answer. "I'm . . . I'm so sorry . . . "

"No, I'm the one who's sorry." Her voice was thin and weary. "I was one of those who considered the King's Way, but I never could believe, never could commit."

"Why?"

A loud sigh. "I couldn't bring myself to give up the only thing that was really mine—my life. I felt like I had this one opportunity—this one life—to do what *I* wanted. I had so much talent, so much ability. I knew I could follow my dreams, accomplish my goals. And I wanted them."

"Did you . . . achieve your goals?"

"Yes, a distinguished medical career, my share of fame and fortune . . . enough. Rich relationships and experiences. Something of a hero in my own circles . . . but what is a few decades of that compared to an eternity of this?"

Christian had no answer. He tried to think of some comfort for the melancholy voice. "I've heard lots of other voices from my path. Have you found any company?"

"No."

"But I've heard people crying out for help."

"Yes, I suppose we can't help it. But we know there is never any help. We rarely look up, because there's nothing to see. Only endless time to think about the small stories of our lives."

Yes, stories finally so small—just a pinpoint in the dark. The cosmic irony rolled over Christian. If "it's all about me" then, in the end, it really is *that* and absolutely nothing more. No plot. No setting. No other characters. Just me. Just endless dramatic monologues with no audience. "I am . . . truly sorry."

"So am I. Everything, everyone I really love is somewhere else. And others will enjoy it forever." The tired voice began to weep. The weeping faded to nothing.

Gradually, the cave-bottom black began lightening—as if moonlit followed by a gray dawning—which allowed him to walk faster. Desperately tired and hungry, he made the most of it. When he could actually make out his surroundings, he shrank at the blood and bones, ashes and mangled bodies. Heaps of dismembered bodies surrounded the entrance to a cave from which Christian could hear a monotone chant. Above the cave entrance hung an ancient warning sign: "Pagan and Ritual." Inching forward, he peered inside at two giants.

Judging from the sign, he guessed the one sitting at the table absently swirling his wineglass was Pagan. Completely absorbed in the business section, the well-heeled ten-footer never looked up. Kneeling in front of a small altar, enveloped in flickering candlelight, Ritual's prayer book hung down at an unreadable angle. As Christian tiptoed even with the genuflecting giant and sneaked a look at his gently bobbing face, it seemed that his mouth was engaged, but his brain was in neutral. Neither took notice as Christian eased out of their line of vision.

The Way sloped gently up through the nether gloom, but Christian could not break out of a trudge. The reality of hell clung to him, the voices echoing in his thoughts. Unlike the weight of his own guilt that was lifted at the cross, or that Apollyon had falsely dredged up, he felt the burden of others' guilt, something he had never felt so keenly before.

He agonized over all his lost friends and family. *Oh, God! What about my brother, Phillip?* He stopped walking and turned around, staring back into the black depths. *Oh, Phillip!* More tears flowed from that freshly tender place in his heart. He combed his memory for any hint that his brother might have found the Way. He seemed to recall that he had attended some kind of church or Bible group with his friend Andy that last summer.

Another voice caught his attention. "Even when the Way goes through the Valley of the Shadow of Death, I'm not afraid when you walk at my side." It was coming from up ahead. Squinting, Christian thought he saw movement and took off to catch up.

Chapter 9

Out of the valley and into rocky hills, Christian pursued the living voice. A few evening stars rose on the horizon, waiting for the rest of their spangled companions. Although his aching legs slowed on the steep grade, he had no complaints. He had had quite enough of valleys for awhile.

"Hello up there! . . . Hello! . . . Wait up and I'll join you."

The sluggish shadow pulled up and turned around. Christian closed the gap and with straining eyes made out the familiar face of his neighbor and running buddy. "Fidel, is that you?" he cried. "It's me . . . Chris."

"Chris? Man alive, you made it through that hellhole too?" Somehow a handshake was not enough and they embraced, if awkwardly.

Christian zeroed in on the familiar crest on Fidel's khakis. "Hey, I like your outfit," he said, swinging his pack off his shoulders.

"Yeah, about time *you* put on a uniform. Before you get comfortable I thought I'd spend the night just up ahead where the path bends a little under that rock overhang."

Christian peered in the direction the ex-Marine pointed. "Looks good. You're the survival guy, not me. I think my rubber legs can make another fifty yards."

For five years, ever since he had moved into his brick and cul-desac neighborhood, they had jogged together most mornings. Although the guy had fifteen years and twenty pounds on Christian, his drill-sergeant discipline kept him jogging in the snow and sleet even when his pansy partner stayed in. On the next running day Christian would always find him at the end of his driveway, stretching and making salty remarks about his mental and physical constitution. Christian had shrugged off his dictator-style approach to fitness. "Yeah, yeah, Fidel." The nickname had stuck.

Once in a while they played racquetball together, or, more correctly, Fidel *played* with *him*. Toyed with him. The one time Christian had actually beaten him, he had gone to the office the next day and reprogrammed the electronic property advertising banner outside to read, "Chris 15, Fidel 11."

For the only time in their history, Fidel had dropped by his office. He demanded a rematch that very evening, and cleaned Christian's clock 15 to 3, after which Fidel looked at him and said, "Put *that* on your sign." Christian just returned fire: "When you have *your* own sign *you* can put it up yourself."

For all that, Fidel understood how much Christian admired him. He was a farm boy turned Marine, turned prison guard, who had worked his way up through the system to oversee all the prison's agricultural work projects. Even though they shared little of their lives outside sport, Christian whispered a quick *Thank you, Thank you!* to God.

Fidel shook his head. "Wasn't that awful? Those voices wailing, carrying on . . . "

"Yes, the voices . . . the people, real people. And thinking that the people I love are headed . . . "

"I know, I've got a lot of family back there too, two girls, both married, even . . . even my wife."

He could hear the pain in his friend's voice. "You left your wife?"

"I spent nearly two weeks *begging* her and the girls to come with me and finally she agreed. But every fifteen minutes she'd crane her neck around and stare at the City skyline behind us. The next morning. . . she was gone. Left me this note; said she decided she loved her life in the City more than she loved me. And she couldn't care less about some far-off City where she didn't know anybody."

"But you decided to keep going."

"Hardest thing I've ever done," he said quietly. "I got to the cross and just bawled. But . . . " he paused and looked at Christian, "that wasn't my first visit to the cross."

"What?"

"Twenty-five years ago I made the trip up that hill. But I got derailed working and raising a family in our fair City. You know, I've seen a lot of violence in my time. I've worked in the prison system ever since I got out of the Marines, but all those dead kids and then the car bomb . . . You know, when you took off, it was the talk of the town."

"Really?"

"Yep, made the evening news, all the papers. Once I heard, I couldn't stay any longer."

"Did many others leave?"

"Well, there was plenty of gossip and talk show action about the 'imminent destruction' and your 'desperate journey to escape.' Endless replays of the stretchers coming out of the school, the bomb crater, limbs poking out of the rubble. People wringing their hands and tearing up at all those powerful images. But after the funerals the pictures faded."

"And the passion." Christian exhaled, shaking his head. "There's no clear battle plan to pour it into. They don't really understand why it's happening."

"And if someone tells them, they don't believe." Fidel softly added, "But I do."

"What was it like going back to the cross?"

The ex-Marine stared off into the middle distance and exhaled audibly. "Not nearly the same burden. More tears than the first go 'round. That was such a relief. You know? I *found* it! This was . . . well, it was the prodigal going home. I *wasted* it. Empty hands, empty life. Years of smoke and ashes. But when I asked Christ's forgiveness and told him I was ready to pick up where I left off, he welcomed me with open arms. Even confirmed the new name he gave me all those years ago . . . Faithful. Ironic, isn't it?"

"So, your name was Faithful all along?"

"Yeah, this ole guy who started and then quit and then started his quest again, split from his wife. Still he calls me Faithful. He must see something in me that I don't." Faithful's tough-as-a-boot voice cracked.

"He specializes in that." Christian clapped his partner on the back. "Nice to meet you, Faithful. My name's Christian."

"Chris," Faithful looked straight into his eyes. "Well, looks like we're in this for the long haul." And then, with a slight twinkle, he asked, "You going to stick with it?

"Are you going to keep up?"

They came to the bend in the road and slung their backpacks and tired bodies down against the rocky hillside. A fire would have been nice, but they contented themselves with fresh peaches, hunks of bread, and well-seasoned smoked chicken from the Castle kitchen's stores. Munching on white chocolate and macadamia nut cookies, they compared notes on the lavish hospitality of the Castle. Conversations around the Great Knight's table had made an indelible impression on both of them.

"Yep, they pushed and probed and exposed a bunch of hard things about my marriage—how my lack of spiritual leadership over the years contributed to Julianne and the girls' decisions to stay. Opened up a big door of regret."

"And I'm guessing Apollyon waltzed right through it and had quite a field day."

"Ugh."

A quietness settled over them. It was too dark to see Faithful's face, but Christian suspected it looked a lot like his at that moment. "I thought I was so ready to take on the Devil. Pulled out my shield. Ready to use my lightforce ray. Kind of thinking . . . "

"Thinking, come on Big Boy, I'm ready. Let's go!"

"Exactly! Ha! I made some smug remark to Evangelist about Satan 'getting his' at the cross. He warned me then, 'Don't underestimate him!' That dragon knew how to get past all my defenses."

"And crack open your ribcage and rake your heart and guts out and stomp all over them."

A full house of starry hosts twinkled over the softly dark terrain. Off to the men's left the luminous path angled and bent around another hill. No breeze, no moon. But this was so unlike the darkness of the Valley of the Shadow—somehow friendly, comfortable. They stretched out alongside the rock wall head-to-head, pillowed by their packs.

"Did you . . . did the hand come to you?" Christian grinned in the dark.

"The hand and the leaves, yes. I wonder what's ahead between us and that Tree."

Christian watched sleepily as Faithful did some stretching exercises. "Faithful, did the voices in the pit make you think about going back?"

"How could we walk through all that and *not* think about it?" Faithful shook out his blanket and began to fold it up. "But we're not just leaving them there. We pray every day that God will move their hearts to believe the Truth."

Faithful gazed over Christian's head at the Way. "It's good to have a terrible longing for people to believe the Truth. Let's look for every opportunity to share with lost people on the Way ahead. But, trust me," he said, shaking his head emphatically, "going back, even for a visit, is dangerous."

Christian rose, dusted himself off, and began to stash his gear in his pack. "But I want mercy! Mercy for everyone!"

"Careful," warned Faithful. "You want mercy for those fellas that bombed the bank and shot up our schools?"

"No." Christian's face darkened. "I want justice for them."

Faithful gathered up his pack. "Thankfully, it's not up to two guys who need a bath to figure out who gets what." His eyebrows furrowed as he watched Christian turn around and take a long look at the shadowy valley behind them.

Christian's heart was yanking on his leash. *Why does God ask me to lean into the emotional punch time and again and push right into the pain?* His will finally overrode his aching heart and spurred his body to turn around. He stared straight into his buddy's worried eyes. "Let's do it."

They set off at a steady pace through the cheery sunshine. Christian kept digging his spurs in, moving forward, dragging his yip-yipping heart along behind.

After a sojourn in total darkness, even the slight variation in the gray rocks and gravelly draws seemed interesting. Along the Way, weedy little plants were making a spring comeback. The two men shared a comfortable silence through the cool morning hours.

As the day warmed up, so did their conversation. Because they would be traveling together, they decided to take turns sharing their stories. Christian growing up in the suburbs, Faithful on the family farm. By evening the terrain offered some scrub brush with which to build a bona fide campfire. Christian poured hot chocolate mix and steaming water into Faithful's cup.

"Visualize a heaping mound of fresh whipped cream, some chocolate shavings, and a sprinkle of cinnamon."

"Thanks. I'll just visualize it plain."

Christian chuckled. "I wonder how my life might have been different if I'd been more content with 'plain.'"

"How'd you get into 'whipped cream' and 'chocolate shavings'?"

"Like I told you, my dad was a jeweler. Over the years he developed a list of clients who wanted to buy and sell jewelry, rare items, collectibles. I remember flipping through the magazines he advertised in—the elegant dinner parties and exotic resorts of the rich and famous splashed across our worn oak-and-glass coffee table. He'd take us with him to resort areas where we'd camp in the parks and he would meet clients in the five-star hotels. We might go swimming at a hotel for an afternoon, but our place was always someplace else. I felt like Alice peeking through the keyhole, catching glimpses of Park Avenue "Wonderland"—very different from life on our little Park Lane.

"And I wanted some of that world. My dad made a good living, but I would lie on my bed at night trying to figure out how I could get through the keyhole. Get a piece of Wonderland for myself."

"Well, you finally made it through."

"Yeah, but I felt too small to enjoy it."

Chapter 9

The next morning Christian awoke to find Faithful absorbed in his Scroll.

"Read me something good," he mumbled.

"Actually, I was doing a word search."

"A 'word search.' What's that?"

"It's where you enter a word like 'compassion' and the Scroll searches and lists all the verses where that word is found."

"Why would you want to do that?"

"I'm studying theology."

"Theology? I always thought theology was just a lot of religious trivia."

Faithful looked over at his companion with a mixture of restraint and amusement. "There's more to the Word than just encouragement. This time around I want to know God—know his heart and mind. That's theology—the Truth about God. When you're short on Truth, all you're left with is experience. And experience runs hot and cold. You tell me about the peace you feel while you're getting a divorce and I'll tell you about the peace I feel asking Allah's blessing on my second wife. But where's the Truth?"

Christian thought for a moment. "Faithful, could you teach me to dig in like you do? To get closer?"

"Sure."

Every morning they would start out studying the attributes of God together. Fueled by Christian's questions, their discussions carried them through their mornings, rising and falling with the hilly terrain. Afternoons they spent sharing their stories. College, Faithful's tour of duty in the Marines, Christian's adventures as a rank amateur in the world of advertising and marketing.

Every few days they would re-provision at a Shepherd's stand attended by lean, weathered folk, welcoming and generous. There they would exchange their empties for full water bottles and various snack meals, including what Faithful dubbed "quail on manna" sandwiches.

When he looked back on that part of their journey from further down the road, Christian remembered miles and miles of compassion, rolling hills of holiness, and long, flat stretches of sovereignty. He remembered Colossians and lying by the path at night feeling antsy for the next adventure, yet knowing from his previous adventures that he needed to fill his mind with the Scriptures if he was going to finish his quest well.

Faithful was a marvelous storyteller, and Christian remembered nights of incredible God-stories around the campfire. Like the one in the hills of holiness, staring at the campfire while Faithful told about a valley with a fire pit deep and wide where deceived and rebellious Israelites sacrificed their children to Molech. Where the drums beat late into the night to drown out the screams of the infants being consumed by the flames. Where the fathers and mothers turned their backs on the massacre in hopes that the idol would bless them—give them good crops and herds, sacrificing their own children on the altar of prosperity. "When the foreign armies lined up, poised to destroy Jerusalem," Faithful concluded, "God's prophets pointed accusing fingers back to the fire pit in the valley, 'something I did not command, nor did it enter my mind.' Even God, who knows the hearts of men, was horrified at the thought."

For a plain-spoken guy, Faithful knew and used a lot of "-ology" words. And in the middle of Christology, a study of Christ's résumé, they at last encountered a sign of civilization. They crossed a border where a large sign read, "Welcome to HeartLand," in slightly peeling paint.

Faithful pointed to the big red heart on the sign: "Well, that's encouraging."

Ribbons of trees and creeks wound through the fallow fields of dried-out crops blanketing the rolling terrain.

Squirrels and rabbits ignored Faithful and Christian as they jogged by. "They act like they own the place," Faithful said, squinting into the setting sun. A summer evening breeze dimpled the surface of a river as they crossed a bridge and landed on a silent street. The two questors' reflections ambled along the dark, dirty store windows. A large red heart perched atop a water tower base marked the center of the vacant town.

Chapter 9

Making their way to the heart tower, they passed long, warehouse-like buildings running down each side of the street. Christian pulled out his flashlight and gingerly pushed back a creaking door. Inhaling the stale, moldy air, they traversed a small, littered lobby into the long hallway beyond.

"Must be fifty doors off this hall," Faithful murmured.

Christian pushed one open, his light illuminating a ten-by-ten cubicle. Between two molded plastic berths padded with flimsy mattresses, a molded plastic nightstand held a phone. Beside each bed, built-in electronic panels accommodated a disc and controls for individual televisions mounted on the far wall. Molded plastic desks under each television allowed the guests to sit on the end of the bed and work at the desk.

"Who would pay to stay here?" Faithful asked.

"It's like a kid's plastic motel," Christian said, "except the colors are too drab—gray or tan, who can tell?"

"What do you make of that?"

Christian's light rested on a small alcove recessed into the wall by the bed. Protruding from the alcove, a mostly burnt candle slumped on a shelf. Flashing his light to the other bed revealed a similar nook. "Hmm. Maybe a little aromatherapy?"

It was hard to tell how long the place had been abandoned. Long enough for the cockroaches and spiders to take over. Back outside, Faithful swept the cobwebs off his cap and shoulders. "I'd just as soon sleep outside."

"Yeah, I guess," Christian said. As they headed for the heart tower, he still held out hope for a little running water somewhere.

Another warehouse building yielded aisles of rusted-out washing machines and dryers. Another, some sort of production line. In one, endless rows of steely, dead arcade games stretched off into the gloaming. Another held a maze of empty racks and shelves, and looked like a discount superstore stripped of its inventory.

The street emptied into what used to be a park. The skinniest pigeons Christian had ever seen flutter-walked among the broken benches and abandoned kiosks. He stared at a crude, concrete fountain—a giant birdbath structure, cracked and dry except for one puddle in the deepest fissure, putrid with algae and bird droppings.

As they neared the bolted base of the heart tower in the center of the park, their eyes flew open. Faithful's jaw dropped.

"Wh-whoah!" Christian stammered.

Both men stopped in their tracks and gazed upward.

CHAPTER 10

The burnished face, ringed with soft, silver curls, gazed down at them, radiant in the late-summer sunlight. Christian could almost see glistening tears slip from the corners of tender eyes, trickling over the statue's monumental cheekbones. The luxuriant folds of a sleeveless gown enveloped the ten-foot torso. Giant silver feathered wings arched up and over the shoulders. Her golden arms extended slightly from the body, gentle hands open, palms up, beckoning.

Christian let out a low whistle as he slowly circled the statute on its pedestal. "She's beautiful!" He reached up and slid his hand down the silver folds of her gown.

"And popular." Faithful pointed to the rows of melted candles encircling her base.

Christian settled back on an old mattress—perhaps a prayer kneeler for the statue's one-time devotees. His beauty-parched eyes feasted on the angel shining in the candle fire Faithful and he had made. And yet, she didn't look a thing like any of the fiery angels in Evangelist's pictures. She was all mercy, no might, no power.

Late the next afternoon they wandered through another abandoned town. Where were the houses and neighborhoods? They did discover what appeared to be a large boarding school complex surrounded by knee-deep weedy playgrounds and soccer fields. Standing in a central meeting room, they stared out over scattered rows of upended orange plastic chairs.

"I never thought I'd miss hearing a roomful of noisy kids," Christian said.

Around noon on the fourth day of their journey through HeartLand, they began to notice a difference in the countryside. A field of green corn rolled up and over a gently sloping hill. A clutch of buildings and trees materialized on the horizon. Then a truck pulled to one side in front of them and stopped, and they ran to greet the driver.

"Hello, you live in the town up ahead?"

"Yeah," the friendly faced man said. He wore a gimme hat and jumpsuit. "You can hop in the back and I can drop you at SwankyInnda. Real nice place to stay."

"That would be great." Christian put his foot right on the "I ❤ HeartLand" bumper sticker and hoisted himself in, with Faithful right behind. The driver shifted, but instead of going into gear, the transmission ground ferociously before the truck jolted forward.

Soon the familiar warehouse buildings lined the street, and traffic picked up. To the left, jumpsuited children kicked balls around a dusty, littered playground. The bleached plastic playground equipment teemed with dozens of others, swinging and bouncing, making plenty of noise. There were also dozens of babies strapped into infant seats under the sprawling shade trees. "VillageCare," the sign over the entrance read. Some of the babies had dumped over and were crying. Others were just taking in the world horizontally. A few caregivers watched over things, but obviously not enough.

"Must be hundreds of kids there," Christian said. "Lots of teenagers too. Looks like that boarding school we saw back in the deserted town."

Faithful's face clouded. "Maybe it wasn't a boarding school."

Ten minutes into the city the truck rolled to a stop just off a familiar-looking central square with another heart tower—a town called SafeHaven. They shook the driver's hand and Christian surveyed the real estate. "Do all your towns have a similar, uh, master plan?"

"Yeah, I guess. 'If it ain't broke . . .'" the farmer said. He lifted his cap, slicked his hair, and screwed the cap back on his head.

He was still grinding as they pushed open the door to the inn. A dimpled grin greeted them from behind a counter. "Hello," the fifty-something redhead chortled.

Christian wished he could just walk into the lobby of new property and not see the trash under the Formica-and-metal furniture, the crooked lampshades, and the runs in the carpet. He deducted staff evaluation points for dandruff. *And what is it with all these jumpsuits?* The attendant even wore a jumpsuit under her blazer.

"How may I help you?"

You could put me in a room that's not plastic.

They walked down a hall to the "HearthstoneSuite." The perky redhead had promised a "very comfortable, understated decor with tremendous access, loads of entertainment options, and a full-service work station."

The door swung open into a cookie-cutter copy of the warehouse inn rooms they had already seen. Except this one had two worn chenille bedspreads.

Christian stood underneath the hot, pounding water feeling his plastic anger melt. *You can forgive a lot of things in a hot shower. Maybe the rest of the quest is through boring, unexciting towns and country. Maybe a hot shower is as good as it gets.* He thanked God for the really big water heater.

When Christian returned to the room, Faithful was snoring slightly in his plastic berth, the wall-mounted TV murmuring into his headphones. Christian walked back to the door, peering into the hallway. The occupant across the hall had left her door open enough that Christian caught a view of a doe-eyed young woman—barely twenty, he guessed—pulling items out of a suede drawstring pouch in her lap.

She stroked something she held in the palm of her other hand, then placed the object in the wall niche beside her. One by one, she arranged a collection of five little winged dolls, different sizes and different dress, in a semicircle in the niche. From her pouch she extracted a votive candle and some matches.

She flicked off her lamp and the candle blazed, reflecting off the gold and silver and polished stone of the angel dolls. Some strong and masculine, others Madonna-like and childlike. None was a replica of the angel statue, but all shared her mystery. The young woman, tucking a few stray strands of auburn hair behind her ears, looked up past the ceiling, her left hand resting lightly on the angel circle, and closed her eyes.

From her slightly open lips the breath of a soft chant fluttered the candle flame. Her hands rose and fell with her voice, slowly passing over and around the angels. She bowed her head, silent once more, her hand resting on the angels. Slowly she drew her knees up to her chin, her misty eyes locked on the angel faces. She talked to them and paused as if to listen. Then talked some more.

The next morning, Christian pushed his tray down the PoshtaGrille line, collecting sausage wafers (you couldn't really call them patties), pancakes, and coffee. He didn't trust the eggs. Faithful evidently did and piled them onto his plate. A big egg crumb fell off the serving spoon and bounced on the floor. Twice. He looked into Christian's eyes. Neither spoke.

At one of the few tables with both a salt and a pepper shaker, Christian glanced around the room, scanning the jumpsuits. As his thoughts focused, so did his gaze. He began to scrutinize every diner, even those behind him.

"Faithful," he asked, after a complete inventory, "have you seen any old people since we came here?"

Faithful scanned the tables and his memory, then shook his head. To their right two women a little older than Faithful munched on their toast and cereal. Everyone else was Faithful's age or younger.

"Maybe there's a retirement center somewhere," Faithful said.

They walked in silence through the town. On the open, luminous road again they turned for a last look at SafeHaven. After a while Christian broke the silence. "I discovered what the niches in the rooms are for."

"What's that?"

Christian recounted their neighbor's ceremony. "I've heard some of those warnings in the Scroll about making idols and worshiping them. And I've thought, 'That is so bizarre.' I just don't get why people would want to do that. I mean, what's the appeal? And then standing there, watching her . . . it was really beautiful. And simple. Very concrete.

Like, this is what you do—you sing and chant and wave your hands. You just go through these steps and you connect. None of this intangible walk-by-faith-in-a-relationship-with-an-invisible-God stuff."

Faithful rolled his eyes. "I saw something about angels on local TV."

"Really?"

"It was called an 'Angel Moment.' Had this big swelling music and a five-minute story of this gal and how she was so lonely and running up credit cards because her lover ignored her. He was always out hunting or fishing. Then one day, her 'angel-father' told her to 'offer up her credit cards.'

"She told him she couldn't because shopping was the only thing she had left. Her lover was always gone. She said her 'angel-father' promised her that if she would 'offer up' her cards, he would turn her lover's heart back to her. So she did. It showed this reenactment of her burning her credit cards in one of those niches with angel dolls. And right after that, her lover's gun broke and his fishing rods were mysteriously stolen. Since they didn't have any money to buy new ones and the credit cards were toast, they wound up spending all this time together and it saved their relationship.

"Then at the end it showed the couple arm in arm in front of one of the big angel statues and this kind of sappy angel theme song swelled and the screen said: 'Another Angel Moment.'"

They walked in silence for a while. Several vehicles passed them. Unsolicited, a big white van pulled over. A tan, cropped head leaned out. "We're going to the capital. Need a lift?"

Christian looked past the driver at the ocean of monotonous fields rolling into the distance. "How far a drive is it to the capital?"

"About four hours. Right down this road."

Christian turned to Faithful, his eyes silently pleading.

They bounced along as Faithful and Christian listened to four college students debate the merits of a twenty-five-hour workweek. When the conversation ebbed, Christian addressed the driver. "Hey, I have a question, NuDave. We've been through several towns and . . . where are the houses? The neighborhoods?"

"What do you mean?"

"You know, like where . . . how do families live together?"

"They don't." NuDave smiled an amused smile. "We all grew up in VillageCare."

The others nodded. In the second seat ShellyGirl turned around. "Did you grow up with your parents?"

"Yes, my mom and dad and brother and sister and I, we all lived together in our own place."

"So is that normal? Does every family have to keep up their own place and cook their own food? Care for their own kids?"

"Basically . . . yeah. Sometimes they get a little help with the kids."

"Wow, sounds very high maintenance to me," ShellyGirl said, wrinkling her nose.

"Oh my angel, can you see me taking care of kids all day every day?" HotJane rolled her eyes. "Even when I was little I looked around at the VillageMoms and wondered how they did it."

From the shotgun seat BlueJay spoke up, "Well my mom did it. I always wondered . . . I think she did it to be near me."

"Right, you were such a special child." HotJane reached forward and tousled his short, slick do. "I'm so glad I'm a HeartLander, where 'Compassion is the essence of morality and no one . . . '"

All the students recited in unison, "'no one should have to shoulder an obligation not freely chosen.'"

Christian pondered the shared ideal. "But don't you *have to* work?" he asked. "Don't you *have to* 'shoulder some obligation not freely chosen' to make the whole thing work?"

"Well, yes," NuDave said. "That is the Great Exception."

"But," BlueJay said, "even that is negotiable."

"Yes," HotJane said, "that's why we're going to the election."

"Election?"

"Yes," BlueJay said. "Every four years at the capital we elect a new king or queen."

"You *elect* royalty?" Faithful asked.

"Yeah, about ten years ago everybody decided that presidents were too boring," HotJane pulled her lipstick and compact from her hot-pink plastic handbag. She sighed, "I just love watching all those jewels and that velvet and ermine. When I'm an angel, I want a robe with a little ermine on it."

"Now tell us about the angels," Christian said. "Who are they? I mean, how does everyone get so connected with them?"

"It's pretty simple, really," ShellyGirl explained. "You die, you become an angel. And then you help out your friends and family still on this side."

Christian met her matter-of-fact gaze. Faithful covered his reaction with a little cough. "Well, how do you know that's true?"

"Haven't you seen the Angel Moments?" HotJane looked sideways at him and tucked her head. "They watch us and counsel us. Help us make big decisions. My angels have helped me deal with some very difficult issues."

"And do you do the little ceremony thing in the niche?"

"You mean, do I chant? Of course I chant. Everybody chants."

All heads nodded.

"If you don't honor them," ShellyGirl added, "they won't take care of you. But they're so compassionate. If you just do your little part, they'll really watch over you."

"I take it you don't chant." NuDave glanced at Christian in the rearview mirror.

"No, I don't." Christian hesitated and then ventured out. "I pray to God in the name of Jesus, his Son."

"Well, Jesus may be the Son of God for you, but he's not the Son of God for me," NuDave said.

"No way." Christian's pulse went up a notch. *This is it. We're out of the boring in-between and back in the game.* "NuDave, two opposite ideas can't both be true."

NuDave's words carried an edge. "Words mean whatever we want them to mean. To me, Jesus is part of Spirit."

ShellyGirl turned around and spoke in a soft, but deliberately instructional tone, "God is Spirit. Spirit is beyond us, but also surrounds us. Spirit is totally a part of everyday life."

"Yes," HotJane affirmed, "and all the angels are Spirit . . . "

"But, how do you know that?" Faithful asked.

In unison the foursome responded, "Haven't you seen the Angel Moments?"

Christian scrambled for mental footing. Trying to talk to these students was like trying to nail Jell-O to the wall. He shot Faithful a "Help me!" glance, but Faithful seemed content to let him go it alone. He tried a different tack. "Okay. Do you guys go to classes? You take exams?"

"Yes."

"Of course."

"If words mean what you want them to mean, how can you understand what the prof is asking on a test? If you just write an answer that means something to you, but not him, how can he grade your exam?"

For the first time since they joined the company, the van was quiet. Christian struggled upstream against the logic-challenged current, trying to get the conversation back to the main thing. *The "essence of morality is compassion." Well, Jesus was the soul of compassion. Focused like a laser on "the least of these."* "What about your word 'compassion'? What does *it* mean? Is it compassionate to nurture life, or harm life?"

NuDave's eyes steeled in the rearview mirror. "That depends on what the meaning of the word 'life' is."

Christian moved forward in his seat. "Unless I'm missing something, words mean what the author or speaker intends them to mean. If you're going to answer the prof's exam question, you have to know what *he* meant when he asked the question."

Christian looked at NuDave in the rearview mirror. "To understand what the meaning of the word 'life' is, I would check with the Author of life. I believe he means 'every human being,' because he says we all bear his image. What do you think he means by 'compassion'?"

BlueJay turned and stared at him, his face and voice dripping with moral superiority. "I don't need an 'author' to tell me some lives are not worth living, and the compassionate thing is not to burden others with their care."

Christian ratcheted it up. "How do you show compassion to people who are old and weak? Do you just kill them off? Where are they? I haven't seen *any*. And what about the young? All those crying, ignored little babies at VillageCare. Who nurtures them, gives them the love and attention they need?"

"So what would you have us do?" steamed HotJane. "Translate them *all?* Some of us have to deliver the goods or there's no future. There has to be a balance. Compassion is about protecting our rights and happiness from burdens too heavy to bear."

"Protect whose rights?" Christian demanded. "If you're young and strong and able, are you more worth protecting than the very old or the very young, the frail and the weak? What about their burdens? Where's the compassion for them?"

"They are better off as angels!"

"You mean they're better off *dead!*" Christian's voice rose several notches. "So that's the compassionate answer—to kill the very ones that need the most compassion? Kill the old! What about the helpless babies in your wombs? Do you kill them off too?"

HotJane's face was a picture of fire and ice. "For angels' sake, let's just all go back to slavery then. Go back to being slaves of our reproductive systems. That is tyranny. Tyranny and the complete opposite of compassion. NuDave, stop the van."

NuDave screeched to a halt on the shoulder.

HotJane threw back the door. "Get your uncompassionate hearts *out* of our van."

A minute later Christian and Faithful stood by the roadside, staring as the "I ❤ HeartLand" bumper sticker receding from sight.

"Well, that wasn't very compassionate," Faithful muttered.

It wasn't the mild, breezy day but his clumsy witnessing that sent a trickle of sweat inching down the small of Christian's back as they walked. He wiped his brow and stole a glance at Faithful. As usual, no clues.

Finally he tried to make contact. "Faithful?"

The ex-Marine didn't look over but grunted.

"Faithful, what did I do wrong? I so wanted to say the right thing. Shine the light." The tiniest hint of reproach leaked out. "Why didn't you help me out?"

Faithful looked down and back at the road ahead. "Buddy, I've been pouring my life into you." He reached over and cupped his hand on Christian's shoulder. "Been trying to teach you what I know. I just felt it was time for you to try your wings."

"Well, obviously I wasn't ready. I crashed big time."

"You *were* a light." Faithful patted him. "Maybe a little too bright . . . kinda scorched everybody."

Christian heaved a big sigh. "What do you do when people's basic ideas about life are so different?"

At that point a familiar pickup truck pulled off the road in front of them. The driver waved and they stepped it up.

"Where you headed now?" It was their friendly farmer again. "Want a lift to the capital?" He pulled out a piece of gum and flicked the wrapper out the window.

Christian watched it flit along the pavement and tangle with the soft drink cans and fast-food wrappers in the roadside weeds. *Nobody cares and nobody cares.*

"Thanks. By the way, my name's Faithful." He offered his hand. "This is Christian."

The farmer touched the greasy bill of his hat. "JoeBob. You going to the election tonight?"

"I'm sure it's only for HeartLanders."

"You can come. Heck, you can vote. Arena's big. Crowds aren't what they used to be."

Faithful and Christian thanked him again and slung their packs and their bodies over the rusty tailgate.

The two questors' gaze swept HeartLand Capitol Plaza as the farmer's grinding gears faded into the din of traffic. Like an official gold stamp on a legal document crammed with fine print, the domes and pillars and gleaming marble contrasted markedly with the rest of the anonymous buildings crowded together in the monotonous city. Christian smiled. *A link to real civilization, even on a modest scale.* Dominating the plaza rose the mother of all angel statues—same face and beckoning pose, only times ten and solid gold. From their angle she seemed to be crowned by the capitol dome rising behind her and flanked by flights of marble stairs and pillared porticos. To their right, HeartLand Centre's fountains danced in the afternoon sunshine, its marquee announcing the coming schedule of performing arts.

Immediately across the street from them, the HeartLand Convention Arena was decked out with banners and balloons. Campaign workers filled the sidewalks, laughing and waving their red MP and green DP signs at one another. Christian and Faithful fell in with the steady line of people entering the main doors and the huge O-shaped lobby encircling the arena. Inside the lobby a bazaar of political trinkets and literature lured election-goers to enlighten their minds and lighten their wallets.

Faithful eyed a guy with five green DP buttons sharing a laugh with a guy with MPs plastered all over his red tie. "Is this an election or a convention?"

Christian followed his gaze. "They certainly seem to all get along, don't they?" The heavy cheese-and-salt scent of nachos came from a concession stand against the inside wall. "Hey, let's grab a bite to eat."

Standing at the bistro tables, they watched the lobby slowly empty as thumping music signaled the main event. Christian wadded all the fast food up in a lump in his esophagus, and tried to shove it down a little further with a big, final gulp of his drink. "I'd like to take a quick look at the tables before we go in."

Still chewing, Faithful nodded and picked up his drink. The first booths on either side of the aisle were larger and more official looking than the rest. On the right, green T-shirts emblazoned with "The Official Seal of the Daddy Party" faced off against their red Momma Party counterparts across the aisle. In the Daddy Party booth, brochures touted "The 30-Hour Work Week—What It Can Mean for You." On the Momma Party side, large full-color postcards simply read, "Save Our 25-Hour Week."

The entire back wall of the Daddy Party's booth consisted of a huge fifteen-by-twenty-foot portrait of the Daddy candidate, a man in his forties with dark hair, sensitive eyes, and, under his moustache, a wide, winsome smile. His smartly tailored jumpsuit sported a few medals. From the back of his booth, his poster beamed a broad smile at the huge image of his opponent, facing him from the back of her party's booth directly across the aisle. She reminded Christian of an older beauty queen—her smile a little too electric for her years, with piercing blue eyes, angular features, and a bright red jumpsuit jacket and skirt. A little hot and strong for the Momma image, he thought.

Caught in the cross-gaze of both big sets of eyes, Christian stared at Big Brother and then Big Sister. *Well, maybe that was the wrong metaphor.* He was glad for the HeartLanders' sake they had a choice. They probably weren't tyrants, but what an interesting way to do politics—every election some kind of giant custody battle with the children as the judge.

Next to the official Party booths, more colorful vendors offered an array of bumper stickers and pins: "Red Hot Momma Rules!" and "I'm Daddy's little girl."

In front of another large booth towered the omnipresent angel statue, and overhead, a banner: "Translation . . . when it's time." In each corner, video monitors ran Angel Moments in a continuous loop. All around hung huge glossy pictures of a rich, beautifully appointed building full of glass, brass, and marble; a magnificent interior waterfall; gorgeous floral arrangements gracing plush seating areas; private "chambres," some intimate, with the "translation candidate" hooked up to an IV and surrounded by a handful of tender and supportive faces. In others, the soon-to-be-deceased, in the middle of a festive crowd, watched some kind of tribute on a small stage. Several pictures featured the candidates pushing a wheelchair past the waterfall or holding the hand of someone reclined on a couch or leading a toast in one of the small theaters.

As they headed to the arena, Christian's gut kinked. The whole angel/translation thing took him back to grainy documentaries of the Holocaust, to the lost souls in hell, to the prophet-kings of Israel who tore down the Asherah poles and ground them into tiny pieces. He had a vision of leading a Gideon-style midnight assault on every angel statue he could find.

Chapter 11

Inside the darkened arena they slid into two of the many empty seats and focused their attention on a slight, jumpsuited young woman alone in a single spotlight on the vast stage.

" . . . After seven hours of hard labor, I wanted to hold my baby girl." The small face and dark eyes glistened with tears on the huge arena screen. "But the VillageCare nurses, after they cleaned her up and wrapped her in a blanket, they brought her in for about . . . a minute. One minute!" She struggled to maintain control. "I traced her perfect little bow-shaped lips, the curve of her cheeks. I stroked her velvety little head, and then it was 'off to the nursery.' They tell you you can visit anytime, but never for very long. And it's not the same. Just holding your child briefly in a room full of other children. Or even taking a walk when she was older through the playgrounds crowded with other children.

"I want a life with my own daughter!" she sobbed. "Is that so radical? Am I a bad person? I'm not saying VillageCare isn't great. Or that it doesn't work for most people, because, obviously, it does. But caring for my own daughter would not be a burden. It would be . . . the greatest joy . . . " She broke down and couldn't finish.

The spotlight faded out. Behind her on a giant screen, black-and-white images of HeartLand's frontier ghost towns haunted the assembly. The plaintive notes of a pop ballad swirled through the darkness. "Remember when . . . remember when . . . " The towns that once celebrated love and life loomed large and empty. In the darkness, displaced HeartLanders snuffled, mourning their empty streets and plastic beds.

The music faded and a soft, blue light washed over the stage. Blue-lit figures slowly converged on five microphones. Stage right, downstage: a tall fellow leaned closer to the mike. "At first we thought it was just rumors. I mean, how do you shut a town down? Yeah, we knew the service was getting worse and worse. Some jobs going without filling. But then one day they called a meeting on the plaza."

Stage center, upstage, a fortyish woman with frizzy hair: "And the mayor got up and read this piece of paper. It talked about our 'population decline,' our 'depressed economy,' gave us all these even more depressing numbers. It was awful. Gave us a big pep talk about a 'voluntary consolidation.' But when he asked for a show of hands of who wanted to leave Splendora, no hands went up."

Stage left, downstage, two college-age kids chimed in: "So we protested."

"We fought for our little town. Told the mayor we'd work harder. We didn't care if lines got longer and choices got scarcer."

"It was the only home we knew."

Stage right, upstage, a woman with a long braid: "And then it was on the news and in the papers—'Lights out for Splendora.'" Her voice caught as the headlines appeared on the giant screen. "We had thirty days before they cut the utilities and forced us out."

Stage left, downstage, an older, wide-bodied man: "Looked like something out of a war zone. Folks loading up everything they could carry in wheelbarrows, suitcases. People weeping and hugging at the plaza every night. Long lines of bikes, scooters, a few cars and trucks headed out of town, lots of people just walking." The news footage filled the screen behind him.

Slowly the stage filled up as, one by one, the HeartLanders displaced from Splendora and Eden and other declining towns gave blow-by-blow accounts of the final days of their small civilizations. Then on the giant screen a giant close-up of the Daddy candidate's face, slightly biting his lower lip and gently brushing away the tears.

After the last story, the blue stage lights faded and a montage of excerpts from the Daddy candidate's speeches filled the giant screen. "I have vivid memories of being in Splendora and Eden when they were being evacuated. I remember walking out of town with our poor, distraught comrades, helping to carry their luggage . . . "

The lights came up on the candidate himself on stage, continuing his remarks live, but for several moments they were completely drowned out by the cheers of his supporters. He paused, hands extended, and gave a slight bow before continuing.

"My friends, my HeartLand family." More roars from the crowd. "You have heard me speak of our great success during this campaign. Ever since our beautiful, beloved Princess returned to us as the Great Angel of Mercy, ever since she encouraged us to lay down our fears and join her, when it is our time, on the other side, we have seen the solution to so many of our problems. No more health-care crisis, no more threat of Social Security bankruptcy, no more horror stories of technology prolonging a life that becomes insufferable."

Christian's gut kinked tighter. Faithful discreetly wagged his head.

"But we have become the victims of our own success. As the popularity of translation has soared, especially for the preborn, our population has dwindled dangerously. And so I have focused my campaign on two issues: first, a slightly longer workweek—just five hours—to increase worker productivity. If we all work just one hour more a day, we can make up for the decline in our labor force. In fact, with just one hour more per day, we can see an increase in our standard of living. I have heard your complaints about the quality of HeartLand goods and services. You long for nicer inns and rent-a-dens. A more beautiful environment. Better food. These goals are within our reach, if we will all assume a little more responsibility. The trade-off will be well worth it!

"The second issue of my campaign is a new incentive program to encourage our young women to have more children. I have listened in profound sorrow as many have confided to me that they didn't want to have a baby because they couldn't bear to part with it. Our VillageCare program has been so successful. But a new day is dawning. A day of choice. We all agree that no one should be compelled to carry a burden she has not freely chosen."

The audience erupted in sustained applause.

"But the time has come to do everything within our power to encourage new life."

Cheers, applause.

"To allow young mothers to choose to keep their babies."

Cheers and a few boos.

"Our children are the future!"

More cheers.

"They are precious! They are gold!"

Christian and Faithful had to stand up to see as most of the crowd around them rose to their feet.

"We need to do this for the children! Elect me your king! For the children's sake!"

As the crowd roared, the room exploded into lights and music. From all over the arena children poured onto the stage. The stage lights blazed and the banks of house spotlights swept the wildly cheering audience. Supporters sang along with the Daddy Party's official anthem: "I will leave the light on. Stand with me. Together we'll be strong . . . "

As the children reached the stage, the Daddy candidate was a blur of motion—scooping them up, swinging them around, kissing them, gathering them under his long, extended arms.

On the giant screen, huge prompts: "VOTE, VOTE!" And the red decibel bars crept up . . . 60 percent, 70 percent. "VOTE!" "Feel my arm around you . . . " Eighty percent.

The noise was deafening. Christian and Faithful covered their ears. "Let me be your Daddy!" "Ninety-two percent" flashed on and off in giant red letters on the screen. The music ended and the house lights came up.

"Ladies and gentlemen," a voice called for attention, "Ladies and gentlemen, the vote for the Daddy Party candidate stands at ninety-two percent. Please take your seats so the election may continue." Over half the audience was floating and it took about five minutes for everyone to settle back in their seats. The arena blacked out again, and a primordial drumbeat issued from the darkened depths. Thum-THUM, thum-THUM. The keyboard sounded out eerie high notes. Another keyboard echoed back the same notes, only an octave lower—like spirits wailing to one another. Little eddies of applause and cheers swirled around the arena. Thum-THUM, thum-THUM. Christian found himself holding his breath.

The keyboard warbled again and from the back of the arena the Great Angel of Mercy materialized in an indigo spotlight, hovering at about the height of the lower balcony. Christian gasped and elbowed Faithful. At the same moment, a close-up of her face appeared on the giant screen at the opposite end of the room, and Christian recognized the blue eyes and angular features of the Momma Candidate. From her hairstyle to her gently flowing gown to her fabulous arched wings, she looked every inch the Great Angel, and the HeartLanders loved it. As if on cue, the Momma Party faithful rose and clicked on their penlights. In smaller indigo spotlights, four other angels appeared with the "Momma Angel," two on each side. Christian tried to figure out whether they were floating or suspended on wires, but in the dark it was impossible to tell.

"You come and touch me, Momma. You find me where I wait . . . " The half-whispered lyrics swirled around her in the dark. Gliding over the sea of penlights, the "angel" and her attendants floated in formation over the whistling, adoring audience toward the stage. "You cry my tears for me, Momma, and kiss the pain away." The audience sang along on the refrain, "Come see me, free me, Momma. Help me fly tonight, yeah, fly tonight."

Christian almost had to yell at Faithful to be heard. "Now that's what I call an entrance!"

"Yeah, puts those long, backstage hallway marches to shame."

Instead of landing on the stage as Christian anticipated, the five angels turned to face the audience and hovered about fifteen feet over the stage. Gradually the music faded, the lights came up, and the attendant angels floated down to the microphones onstage and told their stories.

The first two shared vivid memories of how terribly stressed life had been back when they had a thirty-hour workweek. They spoke in agonizing detail about the loss of sleep and good eating habits. About the terrible lines at the food and laundry services. About fighting for time to visit their children in VillageCare or spend time with friends.

Christian sat back and tried to imagine what a twenty-five-hour workweek would be like and what his old ex-Marine buddy must be thinking. He was expecting to be nudged toward the exit. But Faithful seemed as curious as he was about the outcome of this "election" extravaganza.

The final attendant angel began speaking in passionate defense of VillageCare. "When they visited my grandfather's house, they found my father, five years old, still running around in a diaper. He didn't know how to talk. His hair was long and tangled and encrusted with dirt and feces. The social workers guessed he had never had a bath, because when they tried to give him one he went absolutely berserk. The tub in my grandfather's house was full of excrement from the dozens of dogs and cats that lived in the house. The carpet was so full of urine that it squished when you walked on it. My dad was covered with fleas and head lice.

"I don't think my grandfather had a clue how to care for him. He spent most days in an old single-family house in front of a television, sitting in a broken-down, ratty old chair. Behind his chair, there was a five- to six-foot pile of aluminum soft-drink cans where he would just toss them when he was done. The house was so full of garbage and the stench was so awful that the social workers brought masks on their return trip. That is why VillageCare was set up—so that no child would have to suffer like my daddy suffered.

"And if you elect someone who takes those babies out of VillageCare," her voice quivered and cracked, "it will be like you dragged my daddy back to my grandfather's house all over again."

Christian heaved a sigh and lowered his head onto his left hand, rubbing his forehead with his fingers. The call for compassion—always compassion for the hard cases. The wedge that gets hammered and hammered until laws and institutions built upon the wisdom of the ages finally crumble.

"Some individual mothers say they want to care for their children, but it's a 24/7 job and too many women aren't up to it. The caregiving of young children quickly becomes a burden that is too hard to bear. Let the women who want to be with their children serve as VillageMoms. If mothers decide to care privately for their own children, we won't have enough VillageMoms. VillageCare as we know it will collapse. We cannot let the sad stories of a few disappointed mothers undermine what is best for everybody."

Christian shook his head in amazement. But he was pulled back into the moment as the Momma candidate began her slow descent to the stage. In anticipation, the crowd came to its feet, chanting, "Angel Queen! Angel Queen!"

She held out her arms as if to embrace them all. She tried to quiet them but they cheered even louder. Gently shushing them, she tried to begin her speech. "Shhhh . . . my fellow HeartLanders . . . " They yelled and whistled in response. "My . . . shhhh . . . my fellow HeartLanders . . . "

Christian studied the face on the giant screen. Charisma radiating from her Mrs. Universe smile, eyes shining with tears. Resistance to her guardian angel/Momma-*loves*-you appeal seemed futile.

"Tonight we stand at the crossroads and you must choose. Do you follow this vision of increased responsibility and reward offered by the Daddy candidate? Do you take the risk and throw away the safety net, *or* . . . " she gave a long pause, "do you want to walk into the future knowing that someone cares for you, someone is watching over you, ready to catch you when you fall?" At this suggestion they cheered and stomped loudly. "To those of you who have been seduced by this vision of a *better* HeartLand, I want to remind you: we live in a world where there is no reality, only perception. If you live life thinking that our streets are dirty, our buildings are drab, and our food service is mediocre, well then, to you that will be your reality.

"But you fail to perceive the glory, the absolute beauty of a life unencumbered by heavy burdens, a life rich in time and opportunity to spend long afternoons and evenings relaxing, having fun with your friends. What could be *better* than that? And from that perspective our environment, our goods and services are enriching, because they require less of us. And *that* is a *better* HeartLand. Besides, who says plastic is not beautiful? I say plastic is very beautiful and *that*, my friends, is my reality. Will you make it yours?"

The crowd roared, "Yes!"

"As for the choice of VillageCare or private care for our children, you've heard these true stories of private care. You think our children are precious? You think they are gold? Then how could you send them back to the oppression of private care? How could we not provide the very best for all of them?"

Slowly, from all over the arena, children began to file on stage. But they were not running or skipping or laughing. They came on wheelchairs, crutches, leaning on others for support. The electorate took a collective breath at the sight of so many children—bandaged and broken, limping and weaving—who should already have been translated.

"As our time together draws to a close, I want you to hear the most eloquent voice in support of VillageCare. In support of a shorter workweek and more time to spend with the children, every child here tonight postponed translation so they could talk to you personally and share their hearts with you." The Momma candidate took the microphone to each child. While the camera projected their broken little bodies and hollow little eyes on the giant screen above, each testified to the strength of the system and the goodness of the status quo. And she held their hands and kissed their foreheads and cradled them in her arms.

And when they had all spoken, she stood at center stage, arms extended just like the statue, cheeks wet with tears, and in a pleading whisper begged her countrymen, "Save our twenty-five-hour workweek. Save our VillageCare. Elect me queen," she urged. "But not for me . . . do it . . . 'for the least of these.'"

Thum-THUM, thum-THUM. Once again the keyboards wailed softly as the Momma candidate strode over to a five-year-old girl slumped in her wheelchair and lifted her, one arm under her shoulders, the other under her knees. Thum-THUM, thum-THUM. Against the soft lyrics, the murmur of the drum machine, and the sad, minor chords, the candidate straightened, turned and faced the audience, the child hanging completely limp in her arms. Thum-THUM, thum-THUM. She slowly walked to the front edge of the stage and then stood there. With each stanza, the intensity of the music ratcheted up. "Oh, Momma, it's time; now please, show me how your *heart beats!*"

The angel spotlights flashed from indigo to blood red. The big drums kicked in and the electric guitar soared. The candidate flew up and over the audience, the child still in her arms. Thum-THUM, thum-THUM. "Can't you feel my heart break?" The banks of house spotlights crisscrossed and circled the audience. Twenty feet above the floor the candidate hovered in her crimson light, a grieving Madonna Angel, holding the almost lifeless child in her arms.

The keyboards climbed another octave, pulling in synthesized ranks of organ pipes, while the bass and drums kicked in even harder. The vocals nearly screamed, "Now see me, free me, Momma. Don't you fly away. Don't go!" And the frenzied, crying, dancing crowd shouted along, "Don't go!" Slowly the Momma candidate floated toward the rear of the arena, her constituency writhing below. When she got to the back, instead of exiting, she turned and paused, looking back over the crowd.

Christian noticed that at this point, something changed. Those who had been floating sank back to the ground. People all around him began weeping and crying in earnest, screaming, "DON'T GO! DON'T GO!" She didn't. She floated back toward the stage. And as she floated overhead her followers chest-butted and screamed in ecstasy. Many stood in an open-armed salute, their eyes glazed, their mouths quivering with gibberish. Others fell down on their knees, bawling, their hands clasped as if in prayer.

At that very moment the giant screen called for the vote.

The entire arena shook as HeartLanders screamed and jumped up and down and body-slammed one another. The decibel bars on the screen quickly hit 100 percent and hung there, unable to rise higher. Onstage the Mommy candidate returned the child to her wheelchair. While the arena thundered its approval, her attendants unfastened her wings and drew the red velvet robe lined with ermine around her. She kneeled and the crowd quieted as they placed the glittering crown upon her head and handed her the orbed scepter. But when she rose and extended the scepter, the crowd exploded again.

"We love you, Momma! Don't go!"

Christian and Faithful looked around the arena. Chances seemed good that the party was going to last awhile longer. Some of the Daddy partisans had had enough and were moving toward the exits.

Christian and Faithful walked up the stairs just ahead of two distraught Daddy supporters.

"It's the music, CoolJoe. We have *got* to find a better song, or we're *never* going to win this thing."

Christian smiled at Faithful. "You think it's the music?"

Faithful waited until they were out in the lobby again. "Well, that music . . . man, it *hit* you . . . *aroused* you. The heartbeat drums, the way it kept ratcheting up and up, her biblical imagery. It was scary is what it was. Sheer stoked-up emotion—sacred, sexual . . . Mercy! I'm glad all she asked them to do was vote."

"Yeah, I think if she had asked them to bring down all their jewelry, she could have fashioned a golden calf on the spot." They filed back out the arena doors onto the sidewalk across from the plaza. Christian looked up and down the street. "Let's go find some good plastic beds."

They headed in the direction of the performance arts center accompanied by a brisk tailwind and a colorful assortment of dumped-off campaign literature swirling along beside them. Watching the postcards cartwheeling down the sidewalk, Christian remarked, "Well, they saved their twenty-five-hour work . . . Oh, watch . . . Oh my gosh!"

The pedestrian in front of them had stepped off the curb to cross the street when a blue sedan, taking a quick left turn off the plaza, plowed into her. She was thrown into the air from one side of the street to another, where she landed in a mangled heap. The blue sedan jerked several times as the driver struggled with indecision, but then fled. When Christian and Faithful reached her, she was lying on her back, her hands covering her face. At the sound of Christian's voice she let her hands fall away and tried to focus.

"Miss?" Christian pushed back long strands of blond hair from her face. "Can you hear me?" Her breathing was labored, but regular. The car had hit her on her right hip. It looked like her right leg was broken and she could easily be suffering from internal bleeding.

"I'll try to find help." Faithful sprinted for the arena.

"Miss, can you hear me?" Christian took her hand and felt a weak but steady pulse.

"Oh," she groaned, "what a bloody mess."

He shot a glance at her sideways-bent knee and the blood-soaked, torn jumpsuit covering God-only-knew-what terrible wound to her hip and thigh. "I don't think you should move. Just be still."

She reached down to her hip and quickly recoiled, crying out at the pain and the horror of what she felt.

"Miss, can you tell me your name?" He leaned closer to her blanched face, trying to make it easier for her to focus on him and maintain consciousness.

"Who . . . who are you? What happened?" she mumbled.

"My name is Christian. My friend and I were walking behind you when you were hit by a car. Came out of nowhere and plowed into you. He didn't stop."

"What's wrong? I feel this terrible weight . . . my whole right side, the waist down . . . "

"Yes, I think you're in for a long stay in the hospital."

She turned her head away and stared at the curb, tears running across the bridge of her nose and onto the pavement. "So . . . this is it."

"Hey, don't go there." He mopped her brow with a handkerchief from his pack. "Just be quiet, Miss. What's your name?"

"BabyGrace. Could you . . . could you please call my boyfriend?"

"Sure, how can we contact him?"

"SpinDoc, 25-790."

By the time Christian had written it down, Faithful ran up and bent over them, grabbing his knees.

"How is she?" he panted.

Christian nodded toward her injuries and raised his eyebrows.

Faithful reached for her hand to take her pulse and then dropped it as a white van turned quickly off the plaza and braked to a stop five feet from them. No lights or siren, but immediately two men jumped out with a canvas stretcher. "You the one that called in the hit and run?"

Faithful straightened. "Yes, here she is." He eyed their crude stretcher. One grabbed her under her arms, the other under her left hip and knee and, on three, they jerked her onto the stretcher. BabieGrace's screams doubled as they slid her right leg over next to her left. "You guys going with her?"

Christian and Faithful silently exchanged the same fear. *What happens to burdens like this in the land of low-maintenance compassion?*

"Yes," they both responded in unison, and jumped in the van.

"Where are the paramedics?" Christian whispered to Faithful as the driver and his assistant slid into the front seat. "Here." He handed the driver his scrap of paper. "She gave me this name and number to contact." The driver eyed him in the rearview mirror as he radioed the information to the dispatcher.

Illumined by the occasional flash of streetlights, BabyGrace's face gradually drained of terror, but also of the fight and determination to live. Tears of mourning and resignation streamed into her hair. Her unseeing, unblinking gaze was fixed on the ceiling of the van. Christian touched her arm. "Hey, we'll have help in minutes. You're hurt, but you're going to get through this." She blinked and stared at the ceiling.

They sat in a clinic driveway waiting for several minutes before the driver returned with someone in a white coat. *Finally!* Christian and Faithful popped out of the van. But instead of unloading her, the doctor stepped into the van with a flashlight and, as BabyGrace tried to swallow her screams, began to examine her injuries. Within minutes he emerged, shaking his head and looping his stethoscope back around his neck.

"We can't handle her here," he informed the driver. "You'll have to take her on to LoveJoy."

Christian was fuming as they climbed back into the van. *You idiots! Where is the emergency room? How could you not see that she needs major surgery . . . now!*

With perceptibly less haste the driver and the attendant climbed back in the front seat. Christian could swear they were driving back exactly the way they'd come. When they turned onto the plaza, he *knew* they were backtracking. Underneath BabyGrace's leg the canvas stretcher was completely blood-soaked. He would have given anything for a hand with a few leaves.

"Now listen, BabyGrace," he said, trying to rally her. "This is a leg injury. Your heart, the big stuff, is fine. I've seen it when it's really bad. But you're not there. Come on, you can fight this." He squeezed her arm. Slowly, BabyGrace turned her head and strained, searching his face, trying to reconcile his words with her mangled leg.

Opposite the HeartLand Centre, a beautiful glass and marble structure fronted the plaza. They approached and slowed. Although Christian and Faithful had not explored this end of the plaza, the building seemed familiar. Inside the glowing lobby, plush upholstery, exquisite flower arrangements, and a large waterfall stirred Christian's memory. On the marble fascia above the glass doors, gleaming backlit brass letters confirmed his suspicions: LoveJoy Translation Centre.

Chapter 12

"You may see her now." The blonde with swept-up hair and a coral-and-cream jumpsuit escorted them to BabyGrace's "chambre." Weaving among the seating groups of mostly empty lounge chairs, Christian and Faithful padded behind her on the plush taupe carpet.

Across the lobby, a few clusters of guests awaited the final farewells, some gathered around flickering votives, immersed in angel vespers; others were sneaking on their party hats and getting into the confetti. The place was crawling with angels—angel lamps, angel upholstery, angel murals on the walls.

Of course BabyGrace had known from the beginning—when she touched her wound and knew she couldn't move. Her tearful withdrawal, no hospital, the slow return to the plaza—it all fit with the macabre scenario through which they were now being ushered by Ms. French Twist, with her angel hairpins.

"It's Auschwitz with a marble lobby," Christian whispered to Faithful.

"Which hallway leads to the ovens?"

Off the lobby and down a couple of halls, the usher slowed and gently nudged open a door with a handmade calligraphy sign: "TranquilityChambre." *Why can't these people find the space bar?* BabyGrace had chosen a room with claret-colored damask wallpaper and a rich, jewel-toned Oriental rug. Propped up on huge tapestry pillows, her long blond hair was brushed out in a radiant halo around her face. An aquamarine silk kimono softened the gray-white of her face and highlighted her blue eyes. *At least they don't have to die in jumpsuits.* Under the richly textured blanket they could tell her leg had been splinted and she was already hooked up to an IV.

With a relaxed smile she turned from the Angel Moment playing on the large screen facing her to welcome them. "Hi," she offered in a surprisingly strong voice.

"Hey, look at you—you look so much better!" Christian allowed his heart a small leap. Maybe they sometimes combined hospital care with their translation "service." He squeezed her arm softly and took a seat beside her bed.

"Looks like they patched you up a little," Faithful said.

"Yes." Raising herself up to look down at her unmangled leg, she explained, "They stitched up my thigh and hip a little, just on the outside, and splinted my leg. I still can't move it, but it's a relief not to have it in such a mess. Thank the Angels for morphine." She dropped back on her pillows. "Translation is the most awesome, most transcendent moment of our lives. They want us to enjoy it."

Christian sank further into his chair and stole a glance at the IV. "Have they . . . Is it already starting?"

"No, not yet. I asked them to wait until Doc gets here." BabyGrace covered Christian's hand, still resting on her arm, with her other hand. "Thank you," she said, and turned to smile at Faithful, "and *you* for helping me so quickly and then sticking with me. Everything that was happening was so overwhelming. . . . I didn't show it, but it's hard to express how much it meant not to go through this alone. And, I was wondering," she said, hesitating, "would you stay? I'd be so honored. I've only summoned Doc . . . my boyfriend."

"Well, uhm, *we're* honored that you would ask." Christian stumbled a bit and cast a help-we've-got-to-do-something glance at Faithful.

A tap at the door and the usher appeared. "I found your bag."

"Oh, great. Thanks." BabyGrace took her black plastic bag and began searching through it as the usher withdrew. Eventually, she extracted a turquoise suede pouch. Her eyes lit up as she lined the fragile angel dolls up on the table beside her bed.

"BabyGrace," Faithful asked, watching as she pulled her votive candle and her matches out of her pouch, "have you ever wondered who made the angels? Who made you?"

BabyGrace lit her candle and dropped the matches back in her pouch. "Would you please dim the lights?" Faithful obliged. She sank back into the pillows, candlelight flickering off her exhausted face. "Yes, sometimes. I've always had this image of life as a burning rose—beautiful and terrible at the same time. Far beyond the creative possibilities of time and chance." She punched the button on the morphine pump.

"So when our Princess appeared from the dead with her assurances of eternal angel life . . . I remember coming to the Convention Arena here in the capital with my other college buddies to hear the big announcement in person, watch her video. It didn't give all the answers. But I think we all breathed a huge collective sigh of relief. There was Hope instead of Nothing. A future instead of 'The End.'

"And the part about a safety net—you know, *this*," she weakly gestured at her surroundings, "this option to becoming a burden on those we love, it seemed like a nice footnote at the time. And now . . ." her glistening eyes turned from Faithful to her leg, "Pretty pathetic, huh?" She lifted her hand off Christian's to wipe her cheeks.

"BabyGrace, you do have a future. There *is* a God who made the angels." Faithful gently continued. "Made this incredibly complex and magnificent world. Didn't you sense it sometimes when you asked your questions?"

"Yeah," echoed Christian, "when you stood outside on a summer evening and looked at the stars? When you enjoyed so many blessings not of your own making?"

"Yes, angel blessings. I don't know about God, but haven't you seen the Angel Moments?"

"Yes, we've seen them." Christian and Faithful gritted their teeth at the always-present, never-ending fabrications flashing on the far wall.

The door slowly opened behind them, and a bittersweet smile lit up BabyGrace's face. "Doc!"

"Gracie!" In a moment he had squeezed between Faithful and Christian and scooped BabyGrace into his arms. For a full minute they held one another, weeping softly. SpinDoc drew back the blanket to look at her leg, then embraced her again and kissed her deeply. "I . . . I am so sorry . . . I can't believe . . . "

"Shhh." She quieted his lips with her finger and then, regaining control, turned to Christian and Faithful. "Well, speaking of the Angel Moments, this is my boyfriend, SpinDoc." With a hint of pride she lightly stroked his hair. "Doc is the producer of the Angel Moments. Doc, these are the gentlemen who called for help, called for you even, and then stayed with me—from the accident all the way here."

Christian shook the man's hand. "Nice to meet you." His veteran marketing radar picked up signals from the man's handshake. It was more than a tad shaky. "I'm Christian and this is my friend Faithful. We are just passing through HeartLand, visited the election tonight . . . "

"Nice to meet you. And . . . I can't tell you how thankful . . . I'm *so glad* you were there for Gracie," he responded with a two-handed handshake and earnest eye contact.

"We were walking down the plaza right behind BabyGrace when she was hit. But, you know, she's only injured below the waist—that one hip and leg."

"I know," SpinDoc said, his face darkening. "I called and talked to the doctors here and at the clinic."

He really loves her and he knows the endgame here. Christian drew a deep breath and plunged in. "We were just talking about the God who made the angels, when you came in. The God of power and majesty who created the world and holds it and us in his hands." Christian looked hard into SpinDoc's face. "The God who offers eternal life as a free gift to those willing to receive it. Unfortunately, many reject it."

Alarm flashed across BabyGrace's face. "What do you mean?"

SpinDoc eyed Christian with obvious interest.

"The God who created us loves us so deeply. He longs for a relationship with us. But if you're like me, you live your life just ignoring him. Living pretty selfishly. For a long time my soul was like BabyGrace's leg. Pretty messed up. So many failures, so many mistakes. But I'd keep patching it up trying to look good on the outside. On the inside I was hurting."

Faithful finally recovered and caught up. "I've struggled with God too. Found out God has an Enemy. And this Enemy's greatest weapon is spinning lies." Faithful made a point not to look at SpinDoc. "Lies about God's existence, lies about God's great love and compassion. And I'll tell you one that is widely believed here in HeartLand."

SpinDoc sat very still and quiet. But BabyGrace's consternation was stronger than the morphine. "What?" she challenged. "What lie do we believe?"

"Here in HeartLand, you believe the Enemy's lie that the essence of compassion is not imposing any burdens on people, not making them have to . . . what is the line?"

BabyGrace defended the HeartLand mantra: "No one should have to shoulder any responsibility they have not freely chosen."

"That's it. But the problem," Christian said, "is that, left to our selfish, greedy little selves, *nobody* wants to lay down his own needs, his own agenda to care for others. And so here we sit in the ultimate expression of that lie—the transla . . . the *LoveJoy* Translation Centre—looking at a beautiful young woman, with the potential for a rich and full life, preparing to die. BabyGrace," he said, pleading, "with the help of a surgeon and about two or three months of caregiving . . . "

"Doc, say something!" BabyGrace's wan face flushed with anger. SpinDoc's drained, except for the dark circles around his eyes.

Faithful's voice reached out with gentleness and respect: "BabyGrace, Doc, the true essence of God's compassion is just the opposite of the lie you've been sold. No one has greater love than this: that he lays down his life for another.

"And the amazing thing is that although we are lost and broken, seduced by the Enemy's lies, God, the Author of our lives and this Kingdom Story in which we live, God sent his Son, Jesus, to do exactly that—to lay down his life for ours . . . pay the penalty we deserve for all our moral failures in a gory, horrible death by crucifixion on a cross. Then to prove he could offer forgiveness of our sin against him, he raised Jesus up from the dead—a guarantee that everyone who believes this truth will have forgiveness and real eternal life. Not as angels, but as yourselves, living and reigning with God for eternity."

Christian couldn't tell if BabyGrace's frustration arose from Doc's silence or her own vested interest in HeartLand's beliefs. "But," she said, pulling herself almost upright, "how could you believe *this* is the truth? What about the Angel Moments? Doc?"

"Yes," Doc whispered, gazing over at his latest production on the screen, "how *can* you believe it's true?" The words slowly surfaced from deep inside. "How do you know that the people in Jesus' time and place didn't just make up the story . . . to serve *their own* purposes?"

Faithful prayed over every word he was about to speak. "Most of the key players who wrote about, who 'produced' Jesus' story actually *saw* him resurrected in the flesh. Saw him many times. And they were so convinced that God had raised him from the dead and that his message of forgiveness was true, they willingly laid down their lives for what they believed." Faithful's eyes were riveted on SpinDoc. "Do you think they would have died for a lie?"

"But honey," BabyGrace clung to SpinDoc for support, "you know our Angel stories are true, right? You've got the Angel of Mercy on camera, right? Taped her story as it came to you and the other Planners? Taped all these people and their angel stories . . . Doc?"

In the silence that followed, the usher tapped again on the door and entered. "Oh," she said, apologizing, schooled in the manners of intrusion in a business of delicate situations, "I'll just be a moment. And before any of them could grasp her intent or intercept her, she slipped over to the IV with her hypodermic needle and plunged a lethal solution into BabyGrace's slowly dripping IV. "Angel blessings, BabyGrace."

"Just call us over the intercom when you're ready to leave," she said, directing her parting comments to SpinDoc, and closed the door.

SpinDoc stared, eyes frozen on the plastic tube taped to BabyGrace's hand.

"Doc? Doc!" BabyGrace reached for his chin and pulled his face to meet hers. He threw her hand from his chin and began furiously pulling the tape off. "Oh, Gracie, I never could have dreamed that choices made so long ago would have led here—to this room tonight. You sit in a planning meeting, trying to solve a problem. You come up with a strategy. It seems so compassionate. Salves the economic woes. Takes care of the hard cases. No more wrestling over feeding tubes and respirators, stretching between your job, your personal life, and caring for those who can't care for themselves. You have no idea that what will solve so many problems . . . Who could have foreseen that the hospitals would dry up and blow away, that people would be forced into choices . . . "

"Forced . . . Doc, who would *want* to suffer—to be a burden and make others suffer, when they can become an angel sooner, rather than later. I'll still be with you." She tried to pull back, but he held her hand firmly as he wrestled with the tape. "Doc, what are you . . . "

"And besides, we rationalized. Who's to say what happens on the other side? Maybe we do become angels—a lot of people talk about seeing them." SpinDoc wadded the tape up, threw it on the floor, and then gently extracted BabyGrace's IV needle, applying pressure with his thumb over the prick wound.

"Doc!" BabyGrace moaned. "Stop, you're scaring me!"

Faithful quickly scouted the private bathroom and returned with a cotton ball and a Band-Aid. SpinDoc stared straight into the eyes of his lover. "Gracie!" he whisper-shouted. "I need you to be quiet. Don't make them come in here." Securing the cotton over her wound with the Band-Aid, he grabbed both of BabyGrace's hands and took a deep breath.

"Gracie, I don't just produce the Angel Moments. I write them. I make them up."

"Doc, what . . . what are you talking about? BabyGrace shrank back, her eyes wide, her hands wriggling, trying to pull back from this unthinkable new reality. "This is no time . . . "

"This is absolutely the time, because if it isn't true, then we need to get you help. We need to get you out of here." He glanced at Faithful and back at the woman he truly loved. "Gracie, I will not let you give up your life for a lie."

Christian reached the entryway to the lobby and paused, hoping the jackhammers in his heart would ease off just a bit. He made sure SpinDoc's car keys dangled from his right hand where the front-desk ushers could see them. *See me, ladies? I'm walking absently toward my car . . . lost in my own thoughts . . . nothing out of the ordinary here. Please, Lord . . .*

Outside his pace quickened, although he tried to hold back. He begged God to make the others invisible to the ushers monitoring the chambers. *Death chambers! How ironic.* He punched the unlock button and the black sedan parked along the curb three cars down flashed and softly whistled in response. He slid into the leather bucket seat.

Christian followed the deserted street down the lengthy side of the Centre until it came to a dead-end at the river. The street was barely wide enough to turn the car around. Wheeling the vehicle around, he glimpsed several large sluices connecting the rear of the Centre to the river-blackness below.

He cut the lights and waited by the LoveJoy rear exit.

A fine, gritty mist began to settle on the windshield. He rolled his window down and stuck his hand out, palm up. The "mist" wasn't wet or even moist. Christian rolled the powdery stuff between his thumb and forefinger and suddenly froze. With a violent shake he withdrew his hand into the car. *Unclean! Unclean!* He couldn't see the smokestacks, but death floated in the air and slushed down the large drainage conduits, defiling the silent, dark waters behind him.

Sitting in the midnight shadows of the narrow, dead-end street, the walls of HeartLand's "civilization" looming on either side, Christian watched the clock, glancing anxiously in his rearview mirror for any sign of Doc and Faithful. The ashes streamed silently down, thicker and thicker, making it hard to see the exit. He considered getting out and waiting by the exit, but feared attracting attention. The minutes crawled by.

Like dirty snow the ashes piled up on his windshield so thick he turned on his wipers. He stared through the ashes at the LoveJoy Centre. Still a fire pit, but no screams or drums. Just another silent night of slaughter on the plaza. "Something I did not command, nor did it enter my mind." The clinic scene from Apollyon's film played large in his head. *Father, forgive us, for we know not what we do. And so many times we don't even want to know.* He prayed for BabyGrace, and his own abandoned girlfriend, Amy, and their child.

Christian glanced at his watch. Fourteen minutes since he had left the room. What would he do if they didn't make it? He prayed for all of them. *Father, there is no Plan B . . . please . . .* Suddenly their whole scheme seemed bush league. How do two men carrying an invalid in a blanket "sneak" anywhere? And the city with the hospital was so far—beyond the HeartLand border. How could they not get caught in the only luxury sedan . . .

Oh me of little faith. Christian hit the unlock button and popped out to open the back door while Doc circled round to the other side. Faithful gently threaded a dozing BabyGrace though the door and Doc lifted her legs onto his lap. They closed the doors and dusted the ashes off their hair and clothing. Christian had to turn the windshield wipers on high to see through the organic grit.

"Where to?"

Doc directed Christian to the major outbound artery. A block from the plaza Christian could turn the wipers off and pick up some speed. With relief he noticed that the thoroughfare glowed perceptibly.

From the back seat Doc thrust a sizable bottle of pills over Faithful's shoulder. "Here, this ought to last her until you make the hospital—two every four hours."

"You would not believe this guy," Faithful grinned over his shoulder and took the bottle. "Not only did we kidnap a candidate, but we made a drug heist on the way out!"

In a few minutes Doc motioned them over and disappeared with his briefcase under a blinking "Lock'NKey Security" neon sign. Returning, he dropped the briefcase into Faithful's lap and slid in the back seat beside BabyGrace.

Faithful opened the briefcase. "Now what did you do? Rob a bank?"

"Okay, guys, listen up. That is my life savings. You should be able to buy admission into the hospital, pay for the surgery—anything she needs. In a couple of blocks we're going to reach my office . . . "

"Hey, why all this? I thought you were going with us?" Christian's grip tightened on the wheel.

"We're in the middle of a top-secret rescue op and you're bailing? We need you!" Faithful insisted, the rush draining away.

"Yes, you do. You need me to create a major disturbance here so you can make it out of the capital . . . "

"Oh sure, you create a disturbance and immediately an APB goes out on this car . . . "

"No, you don't understand the system here. Our cars don't even have license plates. And law enforcement . . . " Doc rolled his eyes, "let's just say that in the land of infinite compassion, law enforcement is *not* a big priority—they can't handle too much at a time. Which is why, if they are tied up with me, they won't care about you, especially if you make it out of the city. Besides, if I do this . . . " he paused and looked over at BabyGrace's face, "maybe I will save more like Gracie. . . . Pull over here."

Christian parked the car a block up from a building with KHRT arranged vertically over the entrance. "I think there *must* be a God." Doc leaned forward and put his hands on their shoulders. "He sent you into my life—our lives—at just the right moment. I wish we had more time—I don't even have time to write anything down for Gracie." He closed his eyes for a moment and made a supreme effort to control his voice. "Tell her," he said and turned to look at her, "tell her that I love her. Deeply, passionately, soul to soul, now and forever. And that I'm so thankful for the years she has been a part of my life. Tell her . . . " a tear spilled down his cheek, "that I lay down my life for her. For her and for the Truth."

He turned to his lover and gently folded her in his arms. "Gracie, Gracie!"

Her eyes fluttered open and her lips parted in a beautiful smile of recognition. "Hi, Doc . . . " She stretched her arms around his neck and snuggled into his shoulder and promptly drifted back to sleep.

"Gracie, I love you," he whispered. He gently leaned her back against the door and tucked the blanket in around her and got out.

Reaching through Faithful's open window, SpinDoc clasped the travelers' hands. "This road takes you all the way to the border." He turned, wiping his cheeks, and strode quickly toward the four bright letters

"God will watch over her," Faithful called after him, "and our prayers will be with you."

Doc didn't turn around. He crossed the side street and entered the building underneath the big KHRT.

At the security checkpoint he slid his passkey through the scanner, then entered a lengthy series of reprogramming numbers. He jammed the elevator doors open behind him with a tenth-floor lobby table. In deference to the red "on the air" light, he slipped softly into the studio and hand-signaled a greeting, then a summons, to the engineer on duty. Checking the clock, the engineer removed his earphones and walked with Doc to the studio door. The engineer was still looking inquiringly at his superior when the door slammed in his face and he heard the bolt slide into place.

It took a minute, after Doc had thrown the switch on the regularly scheduled Angel Moment, to exit the control room, line up the camera, and take his position in front of the microphone. At 11:30 on that Saturday night Doc prayed to the God of Christian and Faithful to take care of Gracie and give him courage and a big audience.

"Hello from KHRT, this is SpinDoc, HeartLand Planner and producer of the Angel Moments. I'm sorry to interrupt your program, but I have a very important message for each and every HeartLander. Those of you on KMUS radio, welcome to this special simulcast with KHRT TV.

"Let me start with a little HeartLand history: All of you know how we feel about imposing obligations on people that they do not choose freely. That's why our children are in VillageCare facilities. While we've been able to enlist the help we need to care for the children, over the years it became increasingly difficult to give care to the elderly, the sick, and the disabled. The cost of that kind of medical treatment and care skyrocketed, and we could *not* attract enough people to caregiving positions.

"For years we worked on the problem, but it was mushrooming beyond our control. Our tax burden for entitlements suppressed economic growth and brought us to the brink of national bankruptcy. We had laws on the books that allowed physician-assisted suicide, but initially the threshold to qualify for that kind of solution was very high.

"We were so desperate, we experimented with lowering the requirements—one doctor, no terminal illness, just an honest desire not to live. You may remember that for the first time, our economic free fall leveled off. But we could see that if we really wanted to turn things around, we would have to provide more motivation for people to choose to opt out.

"In highly confidential meetings we wrangled over how to do this, sifting through hundreds of proposals, trying to find a way out. Our market research told us that most of our people believed in God, angels, and the afterlife. So we started talking about ways to make the afterlife seem like a more desirable option. To get people to connect health-care decisions to what they already believed."

Over at Momma Party headquarters, a precinct chairman standing in front of a television screen whistled to quiet the celebrating campaign workers. The pollster next to him waved the crowd over to the big screen.

On the outskirts of the city, Christian topped off the black sedan's gas tank. Inside the gas station, on a television above the register, SpinDoc's confession carried the banner: "Simulcast on KMUS 89.3 FM." Back in the sedan, Faithful tuned in the broadcast as Christian steered back onto the deserted thoroughfare.

"And then something happened," SpinDoc said, "that seemed to give us the opportunity we'd been looking for. The great Sister of Mercy died. In one of our meetings, I tossed out an idea: What if we adopt this woman—so famous for her compassion for the sick and needy and dying—as our patron saint? Elevate her to the status of guardian angel or something? Broadcast the idea that just as the sister had gone on to be with God and the angels, so others could end their suffering and join her. We could even develop an ad campaign around this idea.

"I was totally unprepared for leadership's response. They bought in, only they took it much further. They decided that we would go ahead and promote our patron saint as an angel herself. A small step, but one I could live with. Who knows exactly what happens when we die? Then they proposed that we suggest that everyone becomes an angel when they die. Another small step. Again, who knows? Maybe it's true. There would be such great benefits from advocating these small adjustments to beliefs people already held, surely it would be worth it."

The phone lines at the Capital Police Station lit up. The dispatcher woke up the chief and patched the calls through. Within minutes the ranks of duty officers at the station began to swell.

SpinDoc continued: "There was universal agreement that no one had done more for the very kind of people that we wanted to encourage to join her than this simple, homely woman. However, some pointed out that her followers might not go along with our plan. This woman held an extreme view of the value of each human life. She often spoke out against abortion and assisted suicide—minority views that rankled almost everybody. But, we reasoned, maybe if she 'spoke' from the 'other side,' she herself could testify how delightful it was, encourage others to join her. One senator even suggested 'finding' new writings after her death that softened her undesirable opinions."

The new queen stormed into her office to make the call personally. She was told that the chief was expected momentarily and would return her call promptly.

"With each new 'suggestion' like that," SpinDoc said, "I felt a little uncomfortable. But then I would think, 'What if we don't solve this problem? It will be the end of our civilization as we know it.' So I undertook to write a sample script . . . the very first Angel Moment."

The engineer finally "unstuck" the table from the elevator door only to find that the elevator was still not working. Out of shape and out of breath after running down ten flights of stairs, he could not get his passkey to unlock the security checkpoint. He shouted that the control room had been taken over and someone must have reprogrammed the door, but the gathering angry crowd would not stop yelling and listen.

"The week I began writing," SpinDoc said, "something else landed in our laps. The king's daughter died suddenly in a boating accident. Famous as well for her compassion, minus the worrisome views on abortion and assisted suicide, we started shifting gears. A stunningly beautiful woman, the media had been in love with her. They had hyped the time and effort that she dedicated to her charity work, so that it seemed she was on par with the great Sister of Mercy."

Two police vans full of officers in full riot gear sped away from the police station. Moments later, the dispatcher answered a call from the LoveJoy Translation Centre regarding a missing candidate. He apologized to the head usher but informed her that all personnel were currently being redirected to an emergency situation at the HeartLand TV production studios. Besides, it wouldn't be the first time a candidate had gotten cold feet and left without checking out at the desk.

SpinDoc's black sedan slowed as it reached the city limits. It paused at the blinking red light next to a heart tower and then sped away as the scattered, gray building-blocks of the suburbs gave way to the open road.

SpinDoc's narrative continued: "For me it was a no-brainer. Back at the keyboard later that night, I wrote the first script for our Princess Angel. I heard her voice and the message flowed. She shared with our grieving citizens how heaven was a place of clear, endless sunny days. 'No more pain, tears. Why linger? Why suffer? Let all those who are hurting come to me.'

"And you did. By the tens, then the hundreds, then the thousands. And we had to build the translation centers to handle the load. And the economy took off. So, the twinges of conscience I felt when I saw people drop what they were doing and glue themselves to the TV, panting for another Angel Moment, were relieved by the assurance that I was doing my duty—doing the Lord's work, actually. The whole thing began to be something of a spiritual exercise for me."

The bomb expert lit the fuse and a controlled blast sent the security checkpoint door flying. The engineer peered out from under the desk where he had taken shelter to see a dozen rifles rush past.

"And then it wasn't just the Princess," SpinDoc said. "We had all these other 'angels,' encouraging people, doing little miracles. The genie was out of the bottle. People started writing books about angels, giving interviews about their own angel sightings. We were swamped with 'eyewitness reports' of angel encounters, mostly with dead family members and friends. Aside from the herd mentality, I have no explanation for this phenomenon."

The SWAT team struggled up the ten flights of stairs. The captain held up in the hallway waiting for his winded troops to regroup before they moved in on the control room where SpinDoc's professionally delivered, detailed account was riveting the country.

"Some entrepreneur came up with the little angel friends and family members—the little figures that we see everywhere today. And someone else came up with the little altars. Suddenly, we were all lighting candles and chanting. And we Planners figured if we were still going to try to steer this thing that we had better incorporate and assimilate a lot of what was going on. So the Angel Moments expanded, and we commissioned the big sculpture that is copied in every town plaza in HeartLand.

"My friends, you know me. You know I have enjoyed the honor and prestige of being a part of our Planning Commission for over twelve years. I swear to you that what I'm telling you is true. If there is a God who made the angels, then I will have to give an account of the lies I have spun and the deaths I have encouraged. And I humbly ask your forgiveness."

Bursting through the studio door the captain, his communications officer, and six other officers crammed into the control room, rifles aimed and ready to fire at SpinDoc. The rest of his men covered the only exit into the hall. Frantically, the communications officer plied the control board.

Doc maintained a steady voice as he stared at the troops through the glass. "I knew that if I confessed the truth to you I would pay dearly for it. But I have become convinced that the greatest expression of compassion is to care for one another—to lay down our lives for . . . "

The officer found the right switch. The red lights over the window and out in the hallway changed to green.

"Good evening, gentlemen," Doc's voice went flat. "Well, it appears there are *some* limits to our compassion."

The bullets shattered the control-room window glass and found their mark. Moments later the chief telephoned the new queen, reporting that the situation had been resolved and he was most apologetic for the delay. She responded that she would like a police escort at once to the KHRT studios to reassure the people that the rantings of a sadly deranged fellow-HeartLander should not shake their faith in the system.

Under a moonless sky, SpinDoc's sedan sped north to Vanity Fair.

Chapter 13

Through smarting eyes Christian registered his progress across HeartLand's "ForbiddenZone" border. Surely a nuclear strike zone could not look more barren or hostile than the terrain through which SpinDoc's car bumped and shuddered—alkaline flats pocked with rocks and occasional boulder piles. But the radiance of the Way rolled out in front of him—a road through the white sea, the only distinguishing feature through the seemingly endless miles of cracked ground ahead. From the back seat BabyGrace moaned an occasional descant to Faithful's snores.

After another twenty minutes on autopilot, a shimmering glare broke through the heat and haze. Straining to bring the distance into focus, he could make out shiny dark hills of something clustered along the base of something big and white. *A wall?* Yes, there was an edge at the top, but it kept going and going—the most massive structure he had ever seen. *A fortress? A walled city?* Gleaming white, it stretched out for miles along the horizon. Twenty to thirty stories high with gigantic towers shooting out of each of its four corners at least a hundred stories into the too-bright afternoon sky.

The distance quickly closing, Christian studied the towers. It was hard to think "corporate office space" here in the middle of the wilderness, but what else could the reflective glass cylinders sliced off at forty-five-degree angles be? And now he noticed, between the skyscraping towers, spanning most of the structure, a vast circle of glass—a clear bubble-dome. Between the corner towers and the big dome rose four smaller glass domes, each about the size of large sports stadium roofs.

In the foreground the dark heaps grew bigger. *Glass? What would reflect in the sun like that? And birds!* Diving, wheeling, circling, a small civilization of white gull-like scavengers were doing business on the mounds.

"Faithful! Check this out!"

Faithful awoke to discover they were wending their way through foothills of garbage. Watching the birds swoop and pick their way through the rubbish, it slowly dawned on him why his companion was so taken by the dump-scape.

"Have you ever seen so many big-screen TVs and dish satellites in one place?"

Faithful rubbed his eyes and sat up staring at the double-doored refrigerators, tower speakers, monitors, computers. "Pretty slim pickings for the birds." True for any bird trained in an average dump. But watching them claw and peck through the plastic, these gulls had obviously become masters at winnowing out bugs and bits of organic bonanzas from the techno-heap of last year's models.

"The glass may be busted on a lot of screens, but this stuff doesn't look that old."

"No, looks a lot better than most of the electronics at my house. Hey!" Faithful finally saw the gleaming wall and the bubble above. "What is that?"

"I think that's the city. Some kind of municipal/corporate Taj Mahal. Those must be office towers at each corner, and I'm guessing the entire city must be tucked inside."

"The Taj Mahal of monster malls."

Christian grinned at his buddy. "That's pretty good!"

"Yep, I could have made it in marketing. But too many wimps with espressos."

The sedan rattled by a hill of huge doughnut-shaped CAT-scan machines, junked X-ray tables, and ventilators. "I smell a hospital." Christian flashed a relieved smile at Faithful, who reached a consoling hand back to BabyGrace.

Suddenly, Christian braked.

Faithful followed Christian's gaze. "Well, look at that!"

They cocked their heads to line up with a brightly lit widescreen television on which Evangelist's unmistakable head talked through fractured glass. Christian powered down the window.

"Hello, my friends! Grace and peace."

Christian felt like jumping out of the car to go hug the television. "Evangelist! What are . . . this is great!"

"Man alive, you're a sight for these sore eyes." Faithful and Christian rolled out of the car, leaving the motor running.

"So," Evangelist said, beaming, "how have you fared since our last encounter?"

Christian and Faithful gave him a five-minute update, moving aside from the car windows and pointing in the backseat where BabyGrace lay dozing fitfully.

"I'm glad to hear it—not about all the trials, but that you've been victors and are staying with it. Keep running!" he said. "The crown is waiting for you. Run to win. Run hard for the finish line. Fix your eyes on the Kingdom. Can you see it?"

"Well, no there's this huge bubble . . . " Christian began.

The great old man shook his silvered head. "Can you see what's *invisible* with the eyes of faith? Don't let anything get hold of your hearts and distract you. Now go. Set your faces like flint." And he blessed them: "You have all the power in heaven and earth on your side."

"Wait, wait!" Christian hailed the fading picture. "Evangelist! We need your help, I mean," he said, pointing at BabyGrace in the back seat. "How do we get help for her? How do we get into or through this town and what's going to . . . "

"What's going to happen?" Evangelist leaned forward, his face filling the screen. Christian glanced over at Faithful's subdued face and hedged slightly. "Well, uh, we probably don't need all the details, but maybe a helpful tip or two. You know, how to deal with what's ahead, how to . . . " He paused. Did he really want to know?

Evangelist's face looked even more sober than Faithful's. "My friends, you've heard that the path to the Kingdom takes you through many hardships."

Christian sighed. Evangelist's tone reminded him of his accountant at the end of a bad quarter. Evangelist continued, "You shouldn't really expect to go far on your journey without encountering difficulties. More are immediately ahead. But stay on the Way as it descends under the edge of this city. There you will find help for your friend." The muscles in the back of Christian's neck relaxed just a little.

"In this city you will attract many enemies. They will direct their hatred for the King at you. One or both of you will seal your testimony with blood. But be faithful and the King will give you the Crown of Life.

"For the one who dies—although your death will be unnatural and your pain great—your lot will be better than your friend's. You will escape many miseries and arrive at Celestial City sooner. As the battle unfolds and you remember these words, acquit yourselves like men. And commit the keeping of your souls to God, your faithful Creator. Grace and peace." And with a flicker he was gone.

It was all Christian could do to climb back in the car and keep driving. He tried to focus on doing the next thing. As Evangelist had predicted, the Way slanted down as if toward an underground parking garage. At the security checkpoint underneath the wall, a greeter approached.

"Good afternoon, sir," he said, nodding appreciatively at SpinDoc's sedan.

"We've come to Vanity Fair from HeartLand. Our friend needs a hospital." All Christian's PR chat had vaporized in the blast of Evangelist's words.

The greeter glanced at BabyGrace and immediately radioed for assistance. "We should have an ambulance here within a few minutes. Welcome to Vanity Fair. I'm sure you'll find our health-care system the envy of the world. You came to the right place."

Christian rested his weary head on the top of the steering wheel. Faithful gathered their packs as the greeter directed Christian over to a loading zone. In moments the greeter approached, arms brimming with giveaways. "Here is your parking receipt. I just assumed you'd be needing valet parking."

"Um yes, thank you."

"That will be fifty dollars—valet deposit."

"Oh, okay. Faithful?"

"Got it."

"And here is our complimentary seasonal shopping bag and a T-shirt."

"Thanks."

"Inside the bag you'll find a coupon book worth hundreds of dollars of discounts for shopping, dining, and the Fair. Oh, and a map and a directory." The greeter smoothed his Vanity Fair–monogrammed jacket and opened Christian's door. "You'll find very comfortable accommodations and a world of fun while your friend recovers."

As soon as the small, white, electric ambulance stopped, the attendants expertly unloaded BabyGrace from the back seat onto a collapsible stretcher. Christian and Faithful barely had time to thank the greeter and throw their stuff in before the ambulance whisked them out of the entry bay.

The shock of Evangelist's words melded with wonder as Christian and Faithful stared at the interior of the bubble. Behind them, like a gigantic lobby of a downtown luxury hotel, the balconies of twenty-five stories of meticulously designed condominiums overlooked intimate lanes of shops and cafés that delivered a new surprise around every bend: a small plaza with fountains and flower carts. A huge bookstore with an autograph party—lines snaking between the outdoor coffee bar tables. More shops and arcades that suddenly opened onto a larger approach to a forty-screen theater complex.

Faithful nudged Christian, pointing to floaters with small jet-propulsion belts, who wove in and out of the regular floating traffic. The average Vanity Fair floaters had refined their skills to a level Christian could never have imagined. The ambulance swung onto a boulevard where, along both sides, artfully ornamented poles provided floaters with push-off points. A sleek monorail whooshed toward the other side of the mall-town. From big plasma screens at every corner, a woman infotainer with great legs snagged the interest of passersby with her endless newschat loop.

"Ambulance please. Ambulance please." On the ground level

their driver politely beeped his horn and dodged a few pedestrians—mostly adults with young children. Surprisingly swift and agile, their stretch golfcart-style emergency vehicle neared the southwest corner of the city-mall, where one of the huge, iridescent office towers disappeared above the condominium balconies.

At a smoked-glass edifice with a stunning gilded cupola above the portico, they slowed and Faithful read the gold letters to the right of the main entrance: "Nu Image Retreat." The ambulance swung around to the emergency entrance. Christian and Faithful lit up at the sight of a gurney with concerned-looking attendants awaiting their arrival.

With SpinDoc's briefcase savings lightened considerably, Faithful rose from the admitting desk and headed back to the nuclear medicine waiting room.

"Maybe not for us, but this is a great place for Gracie. They don't even fool around with X-rays. Go straight for the big machinery."

He sat down by Christian, who offered him a coffee and some snacks. "Take your pick. We've got 'Millionaires,' 'Golden Nuggets,' and 'Rich'NChips.' What's the word on Gracie?"

"She's going straight from here to emergency surgery. They know they will have to operate. They just have to find out how many screws and plates to use. It's going to be a long rehab. But they have that here too."

"That's what I wanted to hear." Christian clinched a fist in victory. He closed his eyes briefly, savoring the good news and his candy bar's gooey pecans and caramel. "Hey," he motioned to the huge plasma screen on the waiting room wall, which he had been watching while Faithful checked BabyGrace in. "Get a load of this."

"What?"

"Body sculpting. As far as I can tell, emergency cases are sort of a sideline here. They do mostly plastic surgery. They have an incredible menu of procedures to choose from. I'm already thinking about unwanted hair removal, laser skin rejuvenation, and the anti-aging program." He sucked his gut in and flexed his pecs for effect.

Faithful humphed and rolled his eyes, but within minutes was sucked into the promotional video. Footage shot downtown at the Fairgrounds took the viewer into the Body Pavilion where "graduates" of Nu Image programs floated in spotlit alcoves. Elaborately coifed, skimpily gowned, and bejeweled, the Nu Image women rotated slowly, holding long-stemmed red roses—sirens magnetizing every adolescent boy floating by. Hovering clusters of women and preteen girls swarmed their male counterparts, appreciating their silk-and-spandex tuxedos. The camera faded back and forth between slow, head-to-toe close-ups of the "after" versions on display in the pavilion to identically produced "before" shots. Christian picked up the remote but felt powerless to push the button as Mr. Lower Body Lift and Miss Ultrasonic Liposculpture hung and spun while the narrator described how the surgeons had siphoned off more than ten liters each of dimples and pooches.

Misty eyed, Mr. Nose Job, Miss Ankle Reduction, and Miss Brow Lift each testified how Nu Image had lifted them from the depth of despair over deficiencies, which Faithful swore he could not detect, to ecstasy over their new "look."

"What happens when they get to seventy or eighty?" he groused. "They're still going to be wrinkled and liver-spotted and eating dinner at 4:30."

"I don't know, but you could ask *her*." Christian nodded toward the approaching physician.

The surgeon introduced herself and spoke in a clipped, serious tone that made Christian's neck and shoulders tighten up.

"I'm afraid the pictures and blood tests reveal a great deal of damage—internal bleeding, the beginnings of infection in poorly treated wounds. There will be . . . " She paused, searching for words, "a lot of scarring. And, I'm afraid, a bit of a limp. But in rehab they will teach her to float so smoothly, you shouldn't notice it often."

Christian stared at the surgeon, trying to square the substance of her report with her I'm-sorry-you-have-cancer tone. "S-s-so you'll be able to save her leg?"

"What?" the doctor shrank back.

"And she'll be able to walk?"

"Yes, she'll walk, but," she put her hand on Christian's shoulder, "not normally. I'm sorry. We're prepping her now. The surgery will be lengthy—two to three hours. Again, I'm sorry we can't offer you a better outcome."

The weary questors followed the surgeon's directions to the surgery waiting room. Once inside they gave each other a tired clap on the back.

"You probably saved lots of lives in the Marines, buddy," Christian said, "but this is my first. This is great! We rescued the beauty from the belly of the beast!"

"Yep," Faithful rubbed his aching neck muscles. "We did it."

They collapsed into the chairs as the television voice proudly narrated the surgeon's success with thirteen-year-old Little Miss Lip Enhancement and fifteen-year-old Little Miss Breast Augmentation.

In recovery BabyGrace opened her eyes briefly, trying to surface. "Where's Doc?" she barely whispered.

"Hey," Christian said, ignoring her inquiry. "You came through great!" He patted her arm. "Doctor says you'll be up and walking in no time."

"Doc says I'll walk? Where is he?"

"Sh-h-h." Faithful shot a nervous look at Christian. "You're in the best care Doc could find. These people have fixed your leg and you just need to rest and get better."

"Just sleep it off, Gracie," Christian said. "We'll be here when you wake up." Christian watched as a curvaceous, tightly uniformed nurse checked the IV and injected a shot of something.

Noticing his apparent concern, she explained, "Vitamins—E for skin repair, C and D for bones, anti-aging therapy. Our goal is never just to repair. We turn back the clock here. We make you better than your genes ever intended." As she gave them a top-to-toe once-over, her smile faded. "You might want to check out our Adonis Reinvention Program. The brochures are in the main lobby."

Christian stared at his face in the mirror across from the bar. There were no fast-food places in Vanity Fair. Only trendy "grilles" and watering holes where hamburgers cost ten dollars. At least people actually sat down to eat them. The face staring back at him seemed different from the one he used to see every morning. The one that swiveled slowly from side angle to full front, preening in all his "manly man" glory. *Where did these little lines come from?* Today's education in "frown lines," "brow lines," "laugh lines," and "crow's feet" gave him a new and completely unwanted vocabulary for thinking about his "look."

His friend returned from the restroom. "Hey, Faithful." Christian pointed—discreetly—around him. "Have you ever seen so many mirrors? I think most of the building exteriors here are reflective glass, and half the interior walls are mirrors."

"Yeah, I can't remember the last time I saw so much of myself."

"Me too. But I was just thinking how long it's been since I thought much at all about the way I look."

Faithful nodded. "Been too busy fighting battles."

"True." Christian perked up at the sight of the club sirloin and steaming baked potato coming toward him. Faithful inhaled the sizzling scent of his rib eye.

"Ah, *m-m-meat!*" he growled.

Back out on the street Christian and Faithful walked in silence. "A Day of Profit, a Night of Pleasure"—the glittered letters on the back of a floater's purple organza shirt signaled the dress code change. Instead of suits, khakis, and sweaters, the women wore tiaras and flowing capes or dresses in holographic colors. Their faces literally glowed with cosmetically induced, pink and lavender radiance. The teen and preteen floating floozies preferred exposure, drawing attention to their curves and budding cleavages with eye-catching applications of the radiance-inducing makeup in designs of contrasting color. Lest anyone miss anything, arrows were a big favorite.

Many of the younger guys sported a similar look, except for makeup. Chests were in. Vests with no shirts for the younger guys; for the older ones, unbuttoned shirts sprouting gray hair and glitter. On young and old alike, little clumps of gelled and twisted hair were all the rage.

"Looks like they've been attacked by a baby goat." Faithful struggled to process the strange reality.

"Baby goat?"

"Yeah, those boys' hair looks like a nanny goat's tummy when her little kid keeps planting and sucking but can't find the teat."

Christian lost it, dissolving into laughter at Faithful's uniquely agrarian window on the world.

Not even the snobby twitterings of the floaters overhead staring and pointing at his un-glam look and clothes dampened his pleasure. Reaching for Faithful's shoulder, his heart welled up, savoring this God-given partnership. "Let's see how proud they are of their accommodations."

Very proud, as it turned out. "It's a good thing Doc had deep pockets." Christian sipped his breakfast latte.

Faithful looked around. The condominium food court offered a variety of fruit, bakery goods, a waffle bar, and a hot line featuring eggs Florentine and peppered bacon. "How do people afford to live here?"

The waitress delivering their check overheard. "Well, you work, you risk, you buy, and if you come up short, you serve six months in the DC—Debtor's Corps. Like me." She laughed. "Hey, the worker bees have to come from somewhere. Then after six months you get a little investment egg and start over again—start climbing that golden ladder."

Christian caught her eye. "Why?"

"Why? Why climb?" her eyes widened.

Christian nodded. She searched her mental files and came up with an invitation.

"Tomorrow at 11:00 A.M. Come to the CWC—our Corporate Worship Center. You'll catch the vision."

The Nu Image Recovery Center had promoted Gracie from ICU to a private room. She was tilted up in bed looking for them when they arrived.

"Hey, Gracie." Again Christian was struck with the brightness of her eyes, even on a morphine pump.

"Hi! I've been hoping you'd show up."

"How did you sleep?"

"In and out. The vampires here come out early—6 A.M.!—and suck your blood. They wear lab coat disguises, but I know . . . "

Delighted with her good humor, Faithful and Christian enjoyed delaying the inevitable. But after several minutes of banter, the unspoken question crowded everything else out.

"Gracie," Faithful ventured, "you haven't asked about Doc."

"It's so much safer to joke about my 'lovely' hose." Completely sobered, she stared down at the opaque white stockings that covered her incisions and protected her from blood clots. "I've got such a hard road ahead that, I've thought if, for some reason, he can't come . . . maybe it would be better not to know."

Faithful took her hand in his and sat on the edge of the bed. "Gracie," he said, glancing at Christian, who moved closer for support, "we have followed Doc's instructions to the letter. He wanted to rescue you from all the angel lies and death at the Translation Centre. He wanted you to live—to come here and have this surgery and walk again and live to remember his love for you . . . "

"No!" she wailed and closed her eyes. But she didn't pull her hand out of his grasp.

Faithful waited a moment and continued, "Gracie, this God who laid down his life for you, do you remember what we talked about? Well, Doc, I think, was inspired by that love. Because . . . he laid his life down for you."

From Gracie's closed eyes tears began to stream and her shoulders shook.

Christian picked up the narrative. "We drove him to the TV station. It wasn't till then that he told us he wouldn't be coming with us. I think . . . when he saw you so ready to join the angel ranks, I think he felt the weight of the consequences of his lies. I think he felt an obligation to put the truth out there. Save others like you from . . . "

"Well, maybe I didn't *want* to be saved!" Gracie cried, jerking her hand back. With tight jaw and short, shallow breaths she continued, "Maybe I wanted to die—angels or not! Did anybody ask me?" She shot an accusing glance at Christian and then at Faithful. "Let me guess. So he went to the station and spilled his guts on live TV until . . . until . . . " Her words dissolved into sobs that shook the bed.

Faithful's eyes mirrored the pain in Christian's.

"Why did you mess with his head?" she sobbed, hands over her eyes and cheeks. "Who are you to think you have the gift of Truth! If you hadn't been there, none of this would have happened!"

"Oh, Gracie," Christian said. "I understand why you might say that, but think about it. Doc had phoned the doctors. He knew your injuries were serious but not life threatening. I think he walked into that death camp thinking, 'Rescue.' We happened to be able to help. Doc knew it was a lie, remember? He couldn't let you give your life for a lie."

"No, it's not," she said, shrugging his hand off. "Reality is what you make it."

Faithful stood up. "Maybe we'd better go," he offered, his tone very gentle. "We don't have to sort this whole thing out right now."

After a long silence, Gracie pressed again for an answer. "Isn't it? Isn't reality what we make it?"

"Well, if reality is what you make it, then how do things like this happen?" Faithful asked. "Your reality crashed into God's laws of physics and here you are.

"Gracie, reality is what *God* makes it. You can believe all you want that you're going to die and become an angel. But if you had died without crossing the line of faith to God, right this moment you would be alone in outer darkness or even worse. You would be in pain and misery that makes this look like a walk in a HeartLand plaza."

"My world used to make sense." Gracie opened her eyes and took the tissue Christian offered. "It used to be angels and translation and the love of my life. Now Doc is gone, and you tell me everything I believe is wrong and God is asking me to 'have faith in his Son.' How am I supposed to know what's true?"

"Because," Faithful answered, "it is the Truth that agrees with reality. And here's the universal reality that we all experience: All of us, if a video were made of our lives, someone could edit together all the times we said, 'This is right,' 'That's not fair,' 'You did something wrong to me.' All of us. We all draw lines as to what is right and wrong. I've run into some folks that swore it was all personal opinion, but they always back down when they got asked the right questions: 'So you think torturing an infant is wrong, or is that just an opinion?' 'You believe bribing a judge for selfish gain is always wrong, or is that just an opinion?'

"We all draw lines. Don't you?"

"Yes," she whispered.

"That in itself proves there's a God. If it were just survival of the fittest we'd all rip each other to shreds and not give a whit. But all of us have his law written on our hearts. People who have never heard of God's law show that it's real by instinct. God's Word says his law 'is woven into the fabric of our creation. There's something deep within us that echoes God's yes and no, right and wrong.'"

Faithful looked for signs that Gracie was nodding off, seduced by the morphine. But her eyes, though tired, were glued to him.

"Now here's the kicker—if we were to sit down and watch that edited video of all our right and wrong judgments, would our actions support our own words? Could that same editor go back through the tape and find scenes from our lives where we didn't measure up to our own standards? You bet. He could probably make a feature-length film out of all the times I've wound up doing things I absolutely despise. Several, in fact.

"What about you, Gracie? Ever wind up doing something that missed your own mark?"

She dropped her gaze and didn't answer.

"The Scroll says, 'I realize I don't have what it takes. I can will it, but I can't do it. I decide to do good, but I don't really do it. . . . I obviously need help! So God did it for us. Out of sheer generosity he made it right himself. And he did it by means of his Son, Jesus Christ.' *That* is reality, Gracie. *That* is the Truth. We screw up. God's Son pays the penalty. We ask forgiveness. He forgives."

"Gracie," Christian said, "he loves you so much. He has been wooing and pursuing you for a long . . . such a long time."

BabyGrace closed her eyes. They waited, but she lay there silent, motionless. Finally she opened her eyes and spoke very deliberately, "I want you to leave now. And I really don't care if you come back."

Chapter 14

Eye candy. Everywhere they looked. Outside the monorail, trees leafed out in flaming reds, purples, and neon greens. Little shops and cafés twinkled with lights, even in broad daylight. Corporate-sponsored fun beckoned from every corner; crowds browsed rows of easels under the "Chocolate Monster-O's Ghouls and Fiends Art Show" banner; rows of spectators cheered the "Farizon Jet Belt Drag Races." The retail area whooshed into theme-park-like fairgrounds as they neared the center of the bubble. Thrill seekers tilted and whirled in a giant roulette-styled Ferris wheel ablaze with a computerized light show. Weaving in and out among holographic swans, flamingos, and waterfalls, hovercraft-style gondolas navigated a "river ride" without ever touching water.

In the seats across from Christian and Faithful, older couples with enough important look-at-me jewelry and "timepieces" to buy Christian's old neighborhood sipped exotic brews from fancy cups and read the paper. What the younger set lacked in baubles they made up for in bosoms and biceps, displayed in spiky latex fringe dresses, credit-card/chain-mail vests, silver lamé, shredded pantsuits. Mugging and flirting, their mood contrasted sharply with Christian's.

His heart wasn't in this at all. If they were going to try to see Gracie again, then he would have preferred to lay low in the condo. Why hasten the opportunity for Evangelist's prediction to come true? But Faithful held out hope that at the Corporate Worship Service they might find a hymn or a creed, some vestige of a real church gathering.

The monorail glided to a stop and deposited most of the passengers into the embrace of a semicircular colonnade of shiny steel pillars. Extending from both ends of the colonnade, giant silver hands with outstretched fingers gathered the faithful in toward the basilica in the middle. Inside the vaulted lobby, a fifty-something boardroom type with gold-rimmed glasses and chiseled features paused, then extended a cordial but not hearty welcome. He steered them over to the visitor table, where nametags were dispensed, and promptly disappeared.

"Hi." With a smile fastened on her lips and a diamond-studded ancient coin necklace fastened around her neck, a volunteer filled out their visitor tags. "Name?"

"Christian."

"Title?" She adjusted for Christian's obvious embarrassment. "Profession?"

"Uh . . . questor," Christian smiled.

"Ohh. That's nice." She wrote it on his tag and handed it to him. "Name?"

"Faithful . . . also a questor." Her lips never unfastened but her eyes did—scanning, scanning, and brightening at the approach of a woman in a hot-pink silk duster unbuttoned over matching slacks and shell. "Name?"

Christian and Faithful put on their tags and looked around. As they made their way to the sanctuary entrance, a guy in cashmere denim greeted Christian with a solid PR handshake and a look that swept to his nametag and then on out over his shoulder in search of something or someone else.

Another greeter in an impeccably tailored, merino worsted suit handed Christian a program and observed his scrutiny of the elaborately carved entryway. A note of pleasant surprise warmed his whisper. "Beautiful detail, isn't it?"

"Oh yes." Christian soaked in the beauty. "You don't see craftsmanship like this too often."

The greeter caressed the doorjamb. "Gothic trefoil arches. And the foliate friezes were all hand-carved and gilded."

Inside, gold encrusted everything—light fixtures, pipe ranks, the walls on either side of the stained glass behind the gold-and-crystal altar. Even the pews sparkled with decorative bands layered with gold. Christian caressed the hand-carved cloverleaves. *Nice "foliate friezes."* As they turned into a row about midway down, their eyes caught sight of the second balcony. Solid skyboxes aglitter with golden corporate logos. Shadows of corporate titans moving and shaking behind the tinted glass.

Christian searched Faithful's face for any hint of imminent departure. Disappointed, he sank onto the luxurious cushions and looked at the program. With his forefinger he traced the laser-cut image of the basilica on the outer cover bound with gold-tasseled, elastic ribbon. The fine detail piqued his marketing instincts. He turned the contrasting inside cover over and ran his finger down the back of the information page. *Engraved.*

Two worshipers slipped in beside Christian. "There are about ten other places I'd rather be right now," the man remarked to his partner.

"Me too," she whispered. "Shall we turn and wave up at the Box?"

"No, but you know they're up there giving points."

A baroque flourish of pipes called the stragglers to be seated. Slowly, a massive organ rose old theater-style into the chancel and parked in front of the floor-to-ceiling stained-glass window. On cue the choir processed from the rear of the nave, the right half singing, the left half speaking in syncopated unison to the music. *Whoah, the Solid Gold Singers!* What else could you call these people floating down the aisles in metallic gold body suits under their sheer, billowing gold robes, their faces shining with gold cosmetic radiance? Each held high a staff or vertical banner decorated with gold corporate emblems matching the ones on the balcony—a stylized check mark, a piece of fruit with a bite out of it, a castle, triple shields.

Reaching the front, the two lines turned to approach each other. At the meeting point in front of the altar, they floated upward, one line to the left, the other to the right. Below, on platforms rising out of both sides of the chancel, pounding drums kicked in with the organ. The choir filled the front of the basilica with such intricate maneuvering and hoisting and waving of staffs and banners that it was hard to take it all in. Worshipers sprang to their feet or floated well above their seats. Christian was momentarily mesmerized by the throbbing and spinning of it all. Faithful, too, was smiling.

As the audience cheered wildly and the drums launched a thrashing techno beat, a fifteen-piece band rose on another platform, playing a strangely juxtaposed expansive movie soundtrack-style piece over the pulsing rhythm. In rapid-fire succession, holographic images seemed to play right on top of the altar: people hitting the jackpot at a gaming table, bringing in a gushing oil well, throwing confetti on the trading room floor, sneaking up on and ambushing the enemy. Two of the singers vocalized endless pop diva riffs, never landing on the words to the next verse. Feeling weird and wired, Christian found himself cheering with the others at the victories exploding over the altar. Fog machines, lasers, fireworks—taking them higher and higher until everything crashed to a stop except for one organ note piercing the darkness.

High up in the golden walls on either side of the stained-glass window, two figures stood in flowing silk robes, arms outstretched in the spotlights. They leaned out and swan dove into the chancel. Even the Vanity Fair audience gasped before they swooped up again in full float. Under softly dancing lights the band segued into a lush ballad. A soloist sang what had to be a love song, but in a strange and unfamiliar language. Trailing long, opalescent silk scarves, the dancers soared, spun, and entwined in long, clutching spirals through the five-story expanse—an exquisite aerial *pas de deux.*

The ballad faded and the spellbound audience quieted as the dancers took one more dive and the fluttering scarves disappeared into the chancel fog. The pastor suddenly stepped out of the fog and took his position behind the altar.

"My friends," the mellow voice reached out to the hearts opened wide by the images, movement, and music. His suntanned face dripped with charisma, radiating almost as brightly as his 22-karat gold pinstripes sparkling in the stage lights. "My friends, what are you prepared to do?" He let the question hang.

"I see ripples of restlessness out there. A crisis of contentment.

Too many settling for too little. Are you prepared to do what it takes, to take control of your own destiny? My friends, in accumulation we find *salvation*. We buy, therefore we belong. We consume, therefore we control.

"Shopping is the great adventure! Show your passion; show your creativity! Seek, spend, and you shall find: sacks full of significance, portfolios full of pleasure. Every purchase is an exercise of control, a promise of redemption. That's *you* at the counter, *finding* your religion. With your getting, you give meaning to your life. When you risk great debt, you show your commitment.

"We are consumers. So let us consume with excellence. What are you prepared to do?" The words echoed through the great assembly.

"We are also adventurers, scaling the heights of that golden ladder. How long have you been maintaining instead of pushing ahead? Are you prepared to take the leap, even if you can't see the net? Even if there *is* no net? Can you roll the dice, plan the attack, keep on holding when everyone else is folding?

"I lay down this challenge: *Are you ready to double down?*

"Too many of you are standing at the table, savoring your little pile of winnings, thinking, 'Well, I'm pretty comfortable here. I live the good life. Why put it on the line for more?' These are the voices of those who want to settle. They whine about the pace. They complain that they're going as *fast* as they can go and there is *no more* to give. With one eye on the clock and the other on their social calendars, they nitpick about their quality of life. These are the many, the wimps, the whipped. The ones who clutch in the clench. Stuck on the thirtieth floor, never making it to the top.

"After all you've put into it, do you really want to hug the rail while someone else passes you by? While someone else gets the cash, the investments, the titles, the access that could be yours? Where are the brave hearts, the ones who draw to an inside straight flush? Who gather all their chips, risk *everything*, regardless of the outcome or cost, and bet it on the winning move? Today, in this place, among those gathered here are hearts too big for mediocrity, souls too strong to compromise. And so I ask you—come to the altar and double down! What the mind can believe, the will can achieve! Make the commitment. Take the risk. Claim your reward!"

As the pastor spoke, the choir "ahhhed" and "ohhhed" along. Worshipers of all ages streamed out of the pews and made their way down front.

"You in the boxes up there. You didn't get there by holding anything back. Set the pace. Again, today. Show the others what it takes to risk even the biggest stack of chips, not just for personal control, but for mastery of your universe. Come on down!"

When the altar was full, they still came, stacked up in the aisles. Brushing away tears, the couple beside Christian moved out of the pew, joined hands, and walked the aisle. Like the others, their eyes and their hearts were lifted up. They could see that doubled pile of winnings.

"Thank you, band. Now will you all repeat the Creed with me:

We believe in a Higher Power, higher than Truth and Justice—
We believe in WINNING!
Blessed are those who run after the newest, fastest, and best;
Their treadmills keep our machinery humming.
We believe in the triumph of the Strong.
The weak can be warmed and filled somewhere else.
Blessed are the beautiful;
They are gods in the flesh among us.
We believe in moral freedom and radical individual choice;
We control our destinies with the things we buy.
Blessed are the hip and the cool;
Their compass guides us.
Above all, we believe in Opportunity
And risking our soul to gain the WHOLE WORLD!

In the name of Progress, Education, and Technology,
Amen.

"And now, my friends," the pastor concluded, "your reward awaits. Double down!"

"Double down indeed!" they cried.

The music swelled as the crowds surged toward the exits. Christian and Faithful stood, waiting to file out of their row. The couple that had been sitting next to them approached. The adrenaline had peaked and Christian could see the fear in their eyes.

"Well, it could have been worse." Faithful pulled up at the giant hand.

"Oh?"

"They could have had angels."

Christian laughed and fished his map out of his pocket. "There are no words. No words . . . " a flash of recognition caught him in mid-sentence. "Faithful! You know who the pastor was?"

"No."

"Oh yeah, you weren't with me then. That was Guy Wealth. He came tumbling in over the wall of the Way instead of coming in at the gate. Pastor Wealth. Well, the man found his true calling. Had a buddy . . . Health . . . Jimbo Health. Probably in management over at Nu Image."

He unfolded the map. "So," he said, surveying the central Fairgrounds sprawled in front of them, "what's your pleasure? The Foods Pavilion? Pets?" He looked over at the Body Pavilion. "I think I've seen enough skin buffed and puffed to last a lifetime."

"What's that in the middle up there?" Faithful asked.

"It says it's the Acropolis—Top of the City, whatever that means."

"Well, it must be important if it's sitting smack-dab in the center of everything. Wonder why they'd leave a big old rocky hill in the middle of their man-made bubble."

"Let's check it out."

Remarkably, the entire Fairgrounds radiated the unmistakable glow of the Way. Following the crowds toward the Acropolis, they paused at a small historical marker most Fair-goers floated right over without a glance. Brushing away the dirt and cobwebs, they read the inscription:

> Vanity Fair is the oldest fair ever known. Thousands of years ago it was observed that pilgrims passed this way en route to Celestial City; so the Chief Lord of this place set up the first recorded year-long fair named 'Vanity' because of the lightness of the town and its people. And because all that has ever been sold here is vanity: houses, lands, trades, honors, titles, countries, kingdoms, lusts and pleasures of all sorts, including whores, lives, blood, bodies, souls, silver, gold, precious stones, and what not.
>
> The Prince of Princes himself, when here, went through this place on the way to his own country. And the Chief Lord of this fair showed the Prince from lane to lane and invited him to cheapen and buy some of the vanities offered here, even kingdoms from all over the world. He offered to make him Lord of the Fair if the Prince would have given him the slightest reverence. But appraising the merchandise, he found it worthless and left without spending a penny.

The glammed-up Fair-goers hustled by, hungry for the eye-feasts offered in every direction. Christian reached out to touch the dusty bronze marker. He slid his fingers around the edge, gripping it firmly and looked up at the bubbled sky. This marker and his Scroll in his backpack—two touchstones of Reality in the midst of all the craziness around them. *"God made men and women true and upright; but we have gone in search of many schemes."* A flock of angel wings and tiaras floated by. *So many crazy schemes.*

On approach to the rocky rise they could make out a collection of buildings on top. Up a wide and well-worn staircase, dozens of Fair-goers ascended the heights, pushing off every fifth or sixth step as they floated up the hill. They started their climb behind two tufted-haired young men. Christian tried not to think about the goats.

"Yeah, I went. Same old same old," one of the young men said. "My old man makes a run to the altar just about every week. If he keeps 'doubling down,' he may as well move out of the house into his office. Even when we do see him, he's totally wasted."

"Yeah, my dad too. And mom," the other replied. "All that

'money gives you meaning,'. . . what is *that?* If I have a 'religious experience' it's *not* buying something. It's sitting in a dark movie theater wrapped up in some really awesome story."

"Amen, brother!" They both laughed and bounced up a few more steps.

"And it's not just the stories, it's like . . . when we're all sitting there in the dark together, there's this . . . thing . . . this feeling like, wow, we are all *in* this *together*."

"Yeah. Just give me enough money for my movie tickets."

"And my home theater."

"And surround sound."

"And video games."

"And CDs."

"And concert tickets . . . "

They bounced out of earshot. Another ten minutes of brisk climbing brought the questors through an enormous stone arch into an ancient-looking center of worship laid out with temples. Not just a few, but scores of them in every direction. An absolute glut of Corinthian columns, cupolas, pediments, and porticos. The air was drenched with incense.

"If they don't worship God, they'll worship something." Faithful surveyed the crowds moving in and out of the temples. Visiting a dozen or so they found that inside each temple stood a statue of a different celebrity. Constant movie, music, or sports clips playing on giant plasma wall screens fed the fantasies of adoring worshipers. In front of each statue stood a marble altar whose prominent feature was a gold star surrounded by tiers of flickering votive candles. Many who lit candles and placed them in the holders also took small charms and hung them on little pegs in gold display cases mounted on the backs of the altars. The questors watched as a tall, graceful brunette hung what looked like a miniature condo balcony from one of the pegs, then kneeled in silence.

"What is she doing?" Christian asked Faithful.

Faithful stared at the miniature mirrors, tiaras, pets, clothes hangers, computers—you name it—hanging from the pegs. "I have no idea."

They moved on to a particularly delicate circular temple with a sort of teardrop roof. One minute they were standing, watching a red-haired diva belt out her signature tune on the plasma screen. The next minute their noses were almost pushed into the screen by manic worshipers enveloping the Star who had unexpectedly showed up *in the flesh*. Immediately overrun with flowers, notes, and charms, she personally greeted as many worshipers as she could, before handing the offerings to an aide.

"One at a time, please, one at a time." She tossed her long red curls spritzed with gold glitter and flashed her big-screen smile. "Now, how may I help you?"

"Please, Crystal, I just got out of Debtor's Corps and I need a whole new wardrobe." The petitioner pressed a handful of silver coat-hanger charms into the palm of the security woman, who in turn handed it up to the Star.

"Okay, I want you to close your eyes and create this new truth. Make it your new reality. Are you ready?"

"Yes!"

"Here is your new truth: I have more money than I could ever spend. Say it!"

"I have more money than I could ever spend!"

"Believe it and the money will find you! Now, say it again!"

"I have more money than I could ever spend!"

"Do you believe?"

"Yes, I believe!"

Outside the teardrop temple Christian and Faithful noticed a little kiosk selling charms.

"Excuse us, we're not from around here." Christian rotated the display of gold and silver miniatures sitting on the counter. "What are these for?"

"These are happythoughts." The vendor sized up their khaki outfits and paused, but then launched into his pitch. "You want a hard body? Thicker hair? You buy this little mirror and put it up in the temple and sometimes, like today, the Star herself comes and puts her hands on the happythoughts and sends her energy and helps you find a new reality. You want a new condo or some hot, pricey item? You put the computer or new condo or full-wall plasma TV up there; she helps you get anything you want."

"You know," he winced at their khaki, "for starters, you look like you could use some new clothes. If you hurry you can hang some of these coat hangers on pegs in the case before she . . . " He stopped, waved off by Faithful's hand and their obvious lack of interest.

"Hey, it works."

"I don't think so," Faithful replied.

With the arrival of the Star, worshipers were descending on the kiosk, lining up behind Faithful and Christian. Incensed by Faithful's very public rebuff, the vendor fired back, "What do you mean? What's your problem?"

"I think it's a great sales gimmick, but that's not the way life works."

"Who are you, telling me my religion is wrong?"

"Now," Faithful asked, "do you *really* believe the Stars have that kind of power?"

"What? You have something against the Stars?"

Faithful glanced over at a nearby temple. "Actually, I'm very close to a great celebrity. See that temple behind you?" He motioned to a classically domed temple with a pillared porch.

Still put off but also intrigued, the vendor backed off a little. "Yeah."

"Across the entablature is an inscription."

"Yeah, that's the temple dedicated 'To the Star We Overlooked.' In case we missed anybody."

"Well, let me introduce you to this celebrity. He is the God who made the world and everything in it. He doesn't visit your custom-made shrines or give you new truth to make a new reality. He *is* the Truth. He made reality. Starting from scratch he made the entire human race and made the Earth, with plenty of time and space for living so we could seek him."

The vendor's eyes squinted slightly. "Why should I seek him when I've got my own truth, my own reality?"

"And what reality is that?" Faithful twirled the happythought display. "That if you earn enough money and buy enough things you'll be happy?"

The man grabbed his twirling happythoughts and drew the display back toward him. "Hey, cut it out! Who are you to attack my truth?"

"You know, as I look around," Christian joined in, "I see people who are working harder and spending faster and expecting more and more. But even when they satisfy their desires, their desires don't stay satisfied. They just morph into bigger desires. There was even an article in your paper this morning . . . "

"Yeah, I saw that," Faithful said. "Income went up by about 20 percent at the same time happiness went down by 20 percent."

"Right. It said the economists were 'totally mystified,' looking for a 'big idea.' A 'breakthrough.' Something to explain the facts—the reality—that money doesn't seem to buy happiness." Christian turned to the vendor. "What do you think?"

"I think you guys need to buy something or shove off."

Faithful leaned in with a twinkle in his eye, "We buy the Truth with a capital T. Got any of that?"

"Look, buddy," the vendor practically shouted, "I sell happythoughts. These people buy them. They get what they need. That's the truth that works for me."

Faithful deliberately calmed his voice and slowed his pace. "I look around here and I see that you Fair-goers are pretty religious. What do you have to offer when people lose heart? What are you selling that's real, that's eternal—a Rock that will take you through all the heartaches and failures life throws at you?"

"What's real here is that *you* are full of . . . "

"Hey, Profit, these guys giving you trouble?" A surly looking man with longish black hair parted down the middle stepped out of the line and into Faithful's space.

"Man, these guys are crazy bigots. They think they've got the only truth about some celebrity god who 'made the world.'"

"What if he did make the world," Faithful said, addressing the growing crowd, "and he's calling for you to seek him and experience a radical life change? What if he has set a day when every person will be judged and everything set right?"

"Oh, here we go." A Nu Image makeover broke out of the line and stepped toward Faithful. "It's God's chosen with the ultimate superiority complex. You've got the truth and everybody else is going to hell. You're never happy until you've convinced people of different faiths how inferior they are."

A large audience, both standing and floating, had gathered. Christian glanced around, shaking his head. "I can't believe what I'm hearing. We never said anything like . . . "

"Hey, we saw these guys this morning at the CWC." The couple that had sat by them at the Corporate Worship Center pointed at the questors. "Sitting there in their freaky clothes. Sitting! They don't float! They even made fun of Pastor Wealth!"

"You what?" The vendor's friend grabbed Faithful's vest under his chin and gave him a sharp yank. "We don't put up with mockers and bigots around here. You didn't come here to buy. Where are your shopping bags? You just came here to make trouble."

"Sir, let go of my vest." Christian heard an unfamiliar tone in Faithful's voice. "I am a peaceable man. I'm not looking for a fight."

"No, you're just a *bigot* looking for a *beating!*" The man hauled off to slug Faithful, but with a smooth combat-trained maneuver, Faithful deflected the blow and flipped his assailant. The guy flew back up at him and several of his buddies joined in. Christian moved in to help, but somebody tackled him from behind. They went crashing into the kiosk, which exploded, sending happythoughts flying in every direction.

Free happythoughts! The spectators dove into the dust. Enraged, the vendor piled onto Christian, pelting him with blows to his ribs and head. The other guy was twisting his legs, trying to turn him over and deliver some damage where it would really count.

Jetpacking in, sirens wailing, the police drowned out the vendor screaming at Christian. The crowd scooped up happythoughts and scurried away, leaving Faithful and Christian bleeding beside the wrecked kiosk.

"These . . . these intolerant BIGOTS!" the vendor could hardly speak through his rage.

"All right, Mr. Profit, calm down." One of the policemen tried to get a statement while the other pulled up Faithful and Christian and cuffed them.

"This was a hate crime! Everybody here's a witness. They attacked our religion, made fun of the Stars and Pastor Wealth. Then they attacked me and smashed my kiosk. I've lost all my happythoughts!"

You and me both, buddy. Christian longed to wipe away the trickle of blood that crept down his cheek.

"Welcome to The Cage, gentlemen." The steel door clanged behind them and the officers disappeared into the crowd of spectators gathered outside. It was just Christian and Faithful and about fifty extremely aggressive looking men and women in a large, barred, free-standing enclosure—a single open-air cell, where only a locked cubicle and a privy in the middle allowed any privacy. The Cage was elevated about four feet up and ten feet out of reach of the live audience behind the concrete barrier. "No Feeding" signs were posted on the barriers.

"The first thing you'll learn is that we play for ratings." The six-foot 250-pounder hiked his thumb at the cameras suspended from the ceiling every few feet. "Cage TV. Cameras run 24/7." He draped his hairy arms the shoulders of both of them. "A couple of the Stars even got their start here. But if you're up for hate crime," he said, laughing a sick, hyper laugh, "you won't be around long enough to gain much of a following."

"Hey, boys and girls!" He yelled at his mates and pushed Christian and Faithful toward them. "Look! Fresh red meat!"

Chapter 15

In twos and threes the veteran prisoners filed past the rookies, leaning in their faces, laughing, sharing inside jokes. The backs of their black T-shirts read: "The Cage: Where There Are *No* Survivors." A little shaken by the receiving line, Christian felt relieved when they huddled on the far side and Faithful and he could wash up their cuts and bruises.

"Remember, buddy," Faithful whispered, away from the cameras, "this is the battle. We are the King's men." He nodded to the cameras. "This could be our finest hour."

Christian found an unmade bunk and carefully lowered his newly beaten body down. Gradually, the throbbing in his head subsided, but his ribs registered no relief. He tried taking shallow breaths rather than breathing deeply, and settled on breathing deeply. It hurt more, but not as often. *Adventure! Battle! It sounded exciting. But it was* so hard. *God,* why *does it have to be so hard?* A yawning vise of fear clamped down on his gut. *And Gracie? What happens to Gracie?*

Occasionally peering in Christian and Faithful's direction, the inmates were writing a script they could hardly wait to act out. They argued; they laughed; finally, they broke into smaller groups lounging against the walls and sprawled around the floor, pulling out cards and dice. Christian wondered if he had an overactive imagination. But they kept looking up at the clock.

Soon after 7 P.M. they gathered briefly, did a nice high-five for the camera, and closed ranks on the bunks where Christian and Faithful were resting. Expecting a fight, eight guys so buff the letters on their black T-shirts stretched way out of shape grabbed them both by the hands and feet and dragged them out of their bunks to the center front of The Cage. Christian could see Faithful hanging limply in their grasp and was glad he too had decided not to fight back. *Tonight, Lord, let them see two men of the King!*

To offer the live audience and outdoor cameras a first-rate view, they lined Faithful up against the bars facing them, unzipped his vest, and ripped off his shirt—an opening maneuver greeted with whistles, catcalls, and applause. One strongman stood to Faithful's right with his hand on the back of his head, mashing his face into the bars.

"Reach wide, you hate-monger! Grab the bars!" Strongmen on each side secured Faithful's fully extended hands. "Put your legs together!" Two more sitting on the floor pinned his feet.

Whatever was happening was happening to Faithful first. Three bouncer-types positioned Christian at a forty-five-degree angle about ten feet back so he could see Faithful and the crowd could see him. Overhead a camera zoomed in on his face. "If you don't watch," the biggest whispered in his ear, "it'll go harder on him." Christian gasped as they pinned his arms behind him. Every breath turned the knife in his left side.

Ringing the action and facing Faithful's back, the remaining forty or so prisoners looked to their hairy-armed leader.

"Drum roll, please!" he said.

On cue, the "percussion section" rolled their air drums, accompanying themselves with loud "d-d-ds." The leader dropped his "baton" and everybody crashed a "cymbal." From behind the drum corps, a woman in a Cage T-shirt and black jeans slinked forward, obviously experienced on a fashion model's catwalk.

"Catwoman! Catwoman!" The live audience joined the prisoners.

A feline stretch. A pouting purr. Catwoman mugged for the camera and crouched right behind Faithful. Then stretching up as tall as she could, she posed, cat claws open over Faithful's bare back.

"Catwoman! Catwoman!"

Slowly, she dragged her long fingernails across his shoulders and down to his belt, leaving light red scratch marks as Faithful winced. Whoops, hollers. She did it again. And again. After five times she drew blood, which she wiped onto her finger and held aloft. The audience screamed with pleasure.

Ten times. Twenty times. Fifty. Her hands and fingernails dripped with blood. Faithful's body stiffened at every pass, but he never opened his mouth. Christian blurred his eyes so he couldn't see the detail. Finally, when Faithful's back was marked with deep red, brimming furrows, she turned in triumph to the other prisoners. They ran forward, enveloping her in hugs. She reached out, smearing their faces and arms with blood.

The strongmen released Faithful, who slumped to the red-spattered concrete floor. Painted for war, the inmates danced and chest-butted for the camera, then descended once more on Faithful, kicking and beating him. Faithful managed to curl up in a ball on his side, his hands over his face, trying to protect himself.

The memory of Apollyon's paralyzing breath swirled around Christian. The urge to fight back drained away and he begged God over and over, *Please let it stop. Please let it stop.* He tried to remember the words from the Scroll that had saved him. *He forgives . . . yes . . . he forgives our sins, every one.* The kicking continued. Christian's captors finally released him and he sank to the ground, unable to see his friend through the forest of kicking legs. The sharp pain in his ribs made him feel sick. Crawling, then lurching up, he stumbled to the nearest commode and threw up.

A few mates at the edge of the fray turned and burst out laughing at Christian's pain-induced nausea. Eventually, the rest left off their kicking and joined in. Satisfied with this fitting conclusion for tonight's primetime episode, they celebrated with a big round of high-fives, then lined up behind Faithful's curled body. A few ran over and lined up beside the open door to the toilet. To wild applause they took a bow. Lifting a hairy arm to the center cam, the leader flashed the producer a thumbs-up.

He turned around and signaled the same to the troupe. "Oh yeah! Ratings'll be through the roof tonight!"

Miraculously, Faithful could still walk with Christian's help. He collapsed, face toward the wall, on his bunk. "Thanks, buddy."

"Faithful, what can I do?

"Just . . . pray for me."

Christian found his friend's ripped shirt and did his best to clean the gashes on his back. Then he slid gingerly into his bunk, aware of the gloating eyes savoring his pain.

He forgives our sins. He forgives your sins. He forgives you. The vise on his gut loosened slightly. *He forgives you. I forgive you. At least I want to. You are so deceived. God, I can't fathom how you could allow this. But, Lord, I'm trying to hang on. I look back at that line of faith on that barren hill and I'm sticking on this side. Just, please, Lord, strength. For Faithful, for me.*

"Get up!" The policeman dragged Faithful out of his bunk and shoved his camo vest into his hands. "And you! Up!" Christian had finally drifted off, but the officer was unlocking the cubicle in the middle of The Cage and ordering them inside. Christian carefully stood up beside a tall, suited black fellow backlit by the morning sunlight. Faithful limped by, struggling to pull his vest over the scabby mess on his back.

"This is your OP." The policeman shook the black hand adorned by French cuff links and a gold-and-diamond watch and said, "Call me if there's any trouble." He locked the door and stationed himself beside the only window, shooing away the other prisoners.

The OP drew a sheaf of papers from his briefcase and spread them on the table. "Mr. Christian and Mr. Faithful, which one is which?"

"I'm Christian. We need some medical attention for my friend, Faithful."

The OP's expressionless face softened slightly. "I'm sorry. As long as you can walk they don't call the medics. Especially with the gravity of these charges. The policy is not to waste money on prisoners who may not be around long anyway. Sorry, that's the reality we're dealing with here."

Christian tried to be patient. Of course they would have to submit to due process before these trumped-up charges could be thrown out.

"It's okay, buddy. I'm fine," Faithful said with a lisp.

Christian did a double take. Under his friend's blue, swollen upper lip, his two front teeth had been kicked out and two more were broken off on a severe diagonal. Christian looked away, glad there were no mirrors around.

"In a few days," the OP began, "you will appear before the Power Table."

"Power Table, what's that? Why are we here? What law have we broken?" Faithful asked.

"One question at a time, please. In Vanity Fair we have no laws. Oh, we have them somewhere in the Power School archives, but we outgrew them long ago."

No laws, no due process? The vise clamped back on Christian's gut. "So how do we know what we've done wrong, if there are no laws?"

Unflappable, the OP straightened his black-and-silver tie. "Why don't you let me explain our system and then I'll take your questions. At your hearing, the Victims' Plea Voice, or VP, will help those whom you allegedly oppressed put their grievances before the Table. I'm your OP, your Oppressor's Plea Voice. My job is to cross-examine the victims. Both sides will present closing arguments.

"The citizens of Vanity Fair have elected representatives from each perspective and power group to share the power pie. We've found that laws are too rigid and circumstances change so much that the best way to address grievances is to give every group a place at the Power Table—let these nine Power Voices review the victim's grievances from their group's values and point of view. They will hear your defense, examine your beliefs and your motives, and then decide what is most useful for the community—how to compensate the victims and what punishment, if any, is deserved."

"So these Voices, who are they?" Christian asked. "How do they decide what's right and wrong?"

"The Voices' great strength is that they know their groups. As members of the groups, they identify with what they value, what motivates them, what their deepest needs are. And in their positions they develop an acute ability to listen and to identify."

Christian squinted and scratched the stubble under his chin, pondering a system with no laws and a jury elected to make up today's right from yesterday's wrong. He turned back to the OP. "I've been a part of community groups that were great for deciding policy—do we sell school bonds and raise taxes—that kind of thing, but morals and basic beliefs? What if the people in five of your groups get together and decide to offer a sixth Voice at the Table a bribe to vote with their Voices and give them a majority? How do you decide if bribing a Voice is wrong?"

The OP shifted uncomfortably in his seat and looked at him. "I would not get into this with the Power Table. You are not going to change the system."

"Just out of curiosity," Faithful asked, "who are the Power Voices representing your citizens at the Table?"

"As I said, there are nine: two Corporate Titans, three Middle Managers, Ms. Debtor's Corps Minority, Mr. Lifestyle Minority, Mr. Ethnic Minority, and Ms. Handicapped Minority."

Christian sat back in his chair and looked at Faithful across the table, absorbing the true weight of their situation. Finally he said, "Well, all we can do is speak the truth about what happened and what we believe and leave the rest in God's hands."

"I wouldn't mention 'god' either. You saw what happened at the Acropolis when you did." There was not a hint of malice in the OP's words. Just strategy.

"You seem very good at this. Why did you take our case?" Faithful asked.

The OP pulled out his laptop. "I'm intrigued by your case, Mr. Faithful—your truth claims, and, to be honest," he said, meeting Faithful's gaze, "the ratings. Now, I need you to give me your perspective of what happened. Start at your entrance through the gate of the Acropolis."

"And then we have some important things to tell you," Christian added.

Chapter 15

An hour and a half later the OP tapped on the window. Christian and Faithful walked out with him and watched the officer usher him through the crowd.

"Ratings or not, I like him," Christian said.

"Me too," his buddy replied. "He's smart as a whip and, once we got him going, he did a great job of thinking outside the box."

"Hey, Snaggletooth!" the leader yelled, "Nice smile!"

"Whoah, I didn't know vampires came out during the day!" From inmates and audience the jeering comments and jabs continued.

They had missed breakfast and Christian was starving. Taking their lunch trays from the mess cart, they stood, wondering where to sit. Faithful looked at the hairy-armed leader and Catwoman sitting cross-legged on the darkly spattered concrete floor, right where he had been beaten the night before. He looked at Christian, then limped over to his tormentors and sat down beside them. All the catcalls and laughter stopped. Christian followed and sat down with them. The silence was deafening.

"Hi, I didn't catch your names last night. I'm Faithful."

They stopped in mid-conversation and stared at him.

"I just want you to know that I don't hold any grudge. I know that in prison food is a scarce, kind of sacred commodity. So here's a peace offering." Faithful offered his tray to them.

Christian looked down at his tray for a few *lóng* seconds. "Yeah, peace." He extended his tray as well. "And good will toward men," he boomed. Grinning at Faithful he added, "I may just break out into a Christmas carol any minute."

The camera above zoomed in on the stunned faces. Slowly, the leader reached out and took Faithful's piece of cake and Catwoman took Christian's apple. Then the questors stood up and passed their trays in offering to the other prisoners until all the food was gone. They returned to the lead couple and sat down. Hungry, but excited.

"So, why are you in here?" Faithful asked.

"Stealing—embezzlement," the leader said. "Why are *you* in here?"

"Would you like to hear my story?"

Still chewing on Faithful's cake and Christian's apple, they nodded.

The questors' account of the school shooting and bomb blast back in the City of Destruction caught the inmates' attention and more of the prisoners drifted over. For the next two hours Faithful and Christian told their stories: from Evangelist and the Hills of Inner Light to the cross, then up the Rock of Difficulty to the Pyramids at Pleasant Arbor (several laughed and asked how they could make reservations). The inmates and thousands more watching television were swept up by the beauty of Castle Beautiful and the horrors of Apollyon and the Valley of the Shadow. Then HeartLand and finally Vanity Fair. They didn't mention BabyGrace's name or the money, in hopes of protecting her.

"I've heard rumors about desperate HeartLanders sneaking into our hospitals," the man who had shoved Faithful's face into the bars said. "It always got me going because I knew it made our insurance go up. But man, no wonder. I broke my leg once. I'd be ashes in the river if I had a HeartLand address."

"Hey, Mr. Bleeding Heart," one of the inmates standing on the fringe said, "you going soft on Snaggletooth here?"

"I think a lot of what he said makes sense."

"For crying out loud, you're as bad as they are. Maybe you're the one that needs a date with Catwoman tonight instead of Mr. Christian here."

A few laughs and whistles, but nothing like the energy or unanimity of the previous night. Catwoman herself retorted, "When was the last time one of you beefcakes offered me your food? I'm thinking there are a lot of jerks out there more deserving to be in The Cage than these two. You can count me out for tonight." She got up and headed toward her bunk. "This kitty's taking a nap."

One of the biggest and buffest stood in her way. "Now Ms. Kitty, you need to think that one over." He raised his voice and clamped his hands on her shoulders. "I don't give a rat's you-know-what about their story *or* their food. I want ratings, you hear?"

The leader jumped up and got in the man's face. "Let go, you idiot, before we smash *your* face against the bars!" He looked around at the inmates circling up. It was hard to tell who sided with whom, until Mr. Buffest sent Catwoman sprawling and let fly a left hook into the leader's jaw. Yelling and cursing, the leader's defenders charged his assailant, tackling him and provoking *his* buddies until the fight seemed evenly divided. Outside The Cage, the live audience got into it as well, some defending Christian and Faithful, others attacking. Faithful limped over to help Catwoman sit up. Christian retrieved the napkin from her tray to tend her busted lip, expecting any moment to be pounced on and dragged into the fray.

Instead, the officers arrived with the OP. Ignoring the brawl, they cuffed Christian and Faithful and escorted them out of The Cage. The camera panned the prisoners pounding one another and dissolved into a close-up on Catwoman's face gazing after Faithful, her eyes misting.

"Oyez, Oyez. All victims draw near to the Power Table and lay your grievances before the Honorable Voices and you will be heard."

The nine Power Voices strode into the ornate hearing room, black robes flowing, and assumed their positions behind their nameplates. Ms. Handicapped Minority walked with the same easy gait as her colleagues, no wheelchair, no cane, but her squinty, close-set eyes and sloping shoulders must have posed a severe disadvantage in the Fair.

The Power Table looked powerful indeed—a great mahogany semicircle elevated three feet off the floor. Christian marveled at the gorgeous decorative band on the panel. *Hand-carved "foliate frieze," no doubt.* Behind the Table rose a sweeping mural of a classic, white-robed Lady Justice, black-robed, sober litigants clustered at her feet. But it was Lady Justice with a twist: still wearing the traditional blindfold, but in the pans of her Scales of Justice, two ballot boxes. One marked "yes." The other marked "no."

The Honorable Mr. Titan #1 banged his gavel and gave just a slight glance up at the Voice TV camera over the OP's table. "This hearing is called to order. First victim."

Chapter 16

Mr. Profit stood up. "I run a kiosk up on the Acropolis, your Honor. Yesterday morning, as the Corporate Worship Service emptied out and all the worshipers came up, these men stopped by and wanted to know what people were doing with the happythoughts.

"I took the time to explain about our religion and our worship, and these men," he said, stabbing a finger at Christian and Faithful, "began attacking me. They attacked my truth, my reality, my livelihood—everything we believe about the Stars sending their energy, helping people find new realities, new truth, about wealth bringing happiness—in front of everybody they said it's all lies and they claim *they* have the only truth. And when my buddies came to defend me, they started a fight and wound up smashing my kiosk. And the crowds made off with most of my inventory."

Mr. Lifestyle Minority peered over her glasses at the documents in front of her. "So you are accusing them of hatespeech and hatecrime?"

"Yes, your honor. The only reason they attacked me was because of my beliefs—beliefs shared by all our citizens."

Grumblings from the gallery matched the looks on the Voices' faces.

With an easy, relaxed stride, the OP circled around to the VP's table. "Mr. Profit," he said, leaning in slightly toward the victim, "is it true that this morning you received compensation from your oppressors for the full value of your kiosk and your happythoughts, plus one thousand dollars extra for the pain and inconvenience you suffered?"

The vendor looked down for a moment. "Yes, but that doesn't take away the pain I suffered. And I know some of the worshipers who heard their hatespeech. They were wounded too; their beliefs were shaken to the core. I saw it in their eyes. And I saw the same look in the eyes of some of the inmates in The Cage today. You need to stop them, your Honors, before their hate spreads out of control."

"Mr. Vendor," Mr. Debtor's Corp Minority said, giving him a reassuring smile, "we are well aware of what was happening in The Cage today. That is why this case was expedited and you all received special summons. The Voices apologize for the inconvenience, but we are taking this case *most* seriously. Next victim."

A woman in a white nurse's uniform arose. "Your Honor, I am a nurse at the Nu Image Recovery Center. I overheard these oppressors attacking one of my patients, deeply wounding her with their hatespeech. She had to ask them to leave and not visit her again." With an icy glare, she pointed at Christian and Faithful. "These men told her that reality is *not* what you make it. There is only *one* reality. *One* perspective. *Theirs*. Ever since that conversation two days ago, my patient has been inconsolable. Bless her heart, she was watching The Cage today when these two went at it again and she just burst into tears." The nurse herself teared up. Her VP handed her a tissue.

The OP rose and waited quietly for the nurse to regain her composure. "Nurse Superior, didn't you and your Victim's Plea Voice offer to take a statement from your patient to present at this hearing today?"

"Yes," she sniffed.

"And what did your patient tell you. How did she respond?"

"She wouldn't make the statement."

"Did she say why?"

Nurse Superior's tender tone hardened. "She wouldn't make a statement because . . . because she was so confused. It's just like the vendor said; their intolerant, bigoted ideas have poisoned her brain. She's so confused she doesn't know what is true or real anymore."

Under the table, Faithful lightly bumped Christian's arm with his fist.

The OP continued in his gentle manner. "But your patient had absolutely no wish to make a statement or make a victim's claim?"

"She just had surgery and she's on drugs! What do you expect? Your Honors . . . "

"Nurse Superior, I hear your voice. I share your concern." Middle Manager #2 nodded in empathy. "Thank you for coming in." She addressed the VP, "Are you representing any other victims?"

"Yes, your Honors, I represent . . . Pastor Wealth."

The hearing room hummed at the dramatic turn. Pastor Wealth entered and swept down the aisle and up to the Power Table, barely floating before the Voices. In the Voice TV control room the producer clapped his hands and thanked his lucky Stars.

"Your Honors," Pastor Wealth thundered, "I come today to testify to the long-standing hate and bigotry of these men." He thrust his right hand toward Christian, flashing a whopping diamond ring directly into the Voice TV camera. "*This* one I have known for quite some time, and he is just as extreme and hate-filled as the day we first met.

"I had no sooner turned into the Way to Celestial City than this fellow hailed me and lost no time telling me I had turned into the Way in the *wrong* way. That there was only *one* way to turn in, and I had better go back and do it the *right* way, the way *he* did it. He puffed up like a peacock and told me that if I didn't have *clothes* like *his* . . . " he smiled while the hearing room tittered, "that I would not be allowed into Celestial City. Well, my friends, here I AM. What city could be more Celestial than this one? Not only have you welcomed me, you have honored me and shown this man to be a fool.

"Furthermore, I join the others." He motioned to the nurse and the vendor. "We are united in our resolve. These men must not be allowed to spew their filthy hatespeech in our immaculate city. They are not even worthy of life in The Cage. Their abuse of Mr. Profit may not seem so great; they may have paid for the damages, but their lies and hate are doing incalculable damage to the men and women of the Fair, deluding them, and seducing them into bigotry. Even now there are citizens of our city who are being sucked into their cesspool of deceit. For the common good, for the protection of our lifestyles and everything we hold sacred, we must put an end to their crimes by silencing their actions, their speech, and . . . " he paused for maximum effect, "their very thoughts."

"Here, here!" The gallery erupted in applause and a hail of attaboys. Pastor Wealth turned and waved briefly, acknowledging their admiration, and flashed his most charismatic smile at the Voice TV camera.

Refusing to look up at his witness, the OP floated up even with the pastor. "Pastor Wealth, are you a tolerant person?"

"Absolutely! That's why I find their self-righteous, moral judgment so offensive."

"Why do you not tolerate Chris and Faithful?"

Pastor Wealth's eyes widened and his suntan deepened. "Because . . . well, just listen . . . I mean, you've heard . . . " he cleared his throat. "I do not tolerate their extreme, bigoted lies, because . . . you have to draw the line somewhere."

"Precisely," the OP said and bounced his fingertips together. "And I suppose you draw the line at torturing infants?"

"Of course."

"What about the perverted abuse of little children?"

"Unquestionably."

"What about homosexuality?"

Pastor Wealth floated up another foot in indignation, and shot an I'm-sorry-you-must-suffer-this glance at the Honorable Mr. Lifestyle Minority. "Absolutely not. Everybody knows they are born with a predisposition toward their orientation and have every right to enjoy a full sexual life."

"Ah, exactly the same defense offered by many child molesters I have dealt with in this system. And yet you heartily *condemn* them." The OP paused, letting him wriggle in the net. "Isn't that exactly what Mr. Christian and Mr. Faithful have done? They have drawn the line on what is true and good. They have just drawn it differently than you. Who are you to say their line is unacceptable? That's being awfully . . . judgmental."

Pastor Wealth rose another foot. "I draw the line at spiritual racism!" He flashed an anguished look at the ethnic minorities at the Table.

The OP floated up to eye level. "Pastor Wealth, do you consider yourself something of an expert on spiritual matters?"

"Yes!" The pastor crossed his arms, a picture of nonverbal defiance.

"Don't all religions draw lines? Don't they all make truth claims that say this is right and that is wrong?"

Silence.

"Don't Muslims believe that Mohammed is the greatest prophet and deny Jesus is the Son of God? Wasn't Buddhism born when Buddha rejected basic truth claims of Hinduism? Aren't Hindus uncompromising when it comes to their basic beliefs of karma and reincarnation? Even atheists, when they claim, 'There is no God,' aren't they drawing a line that excludes everyone who does?"

The pastor seethed, unresponsive.

"Mr. Christian and Mr. Faithful are being accused of hatespeech and bigotry and now spiritual racism, when in fact, they are making exactly the kind of truth claims that every major religion makes, indeed, that we all make."

Pastor Wealth shot up another three feet, fumbling in his pocket, finally extracting a photo from his wallet. "See this?" He raged down at the OP. "This is my nephew! Dead at sixteen! Suicidal because of spiritual racist bigots like these!" he pointed down at Christian and Faithful. "Murderers!" he screamed, floating around the room holding out the picture, another Momma Angel with a lifeless child in his arms. "The blood of our gay and lesbian children is on your hands!" Like an untied balloon he blew around the room in a descending spiral, letting everyone observe his nephew and his grief, until he finally collapsed on his chair at the VP's table, all blown out.

The OP floated down and offered Pastor Wealth his handkerchief. "We are deeply sorry for the death of your nephew. But the fate of these men should rest on reason and facts and evidence, not on inflammatory posturing, character assassination, and name calling."

The VP laid a restraining hand on his victim as the OP took his seat.

The Power Voices summoned Faithful and Christian to stand before them. "You are accused of hatecrime, so we must question you directly about your motives. Please, tell the Voices, why have you spoken and acted in such an oppressive way to all these victims testifying today?"

Christian began, "Your Honors, you think your bubble here is the ultimate reality—all there is or will be. Your Corporate Titans sit in their control rooms at the tops of their towers, masters of this little universe; manipulating with fear and greed. We told the vendor, 'We buy the Truth!' But it is not for sale in this city. Vanity Fair is a bubble of deceit and lies and the Titan *behind* the Titans, the Chief Lord of this Fair, sits up in *his* control room, directing the shots.

"Well, we poked a hole in your bubble, sir, because we care about your people. And if they can see this bubble for what it really is, if they look through the hole and see God's Kingdom reality—his promise of unconditional love no matter how well people perform—once that happens," Christian said, turning to face the audience, "they will never be content to stay, even if the Titans make every one of them Stars with their own temples on the Acropolis."

The galley boiled over in anger, ready to take up where The Cage left off.

"Bigots! Hate-mongers! Shut these guys up!"

Mr. Titan #1 banged his gavel. "Order, order! The oppressors may sit down."

The OP waited for silence and then approached the Power Table. "Your Honors, where will you draw the line? At their actions? They have already more than paid for damages accidentally resulting from a fight that police cannot conclude was started by these men. At their speech? Whatever happened to freedom of speech? Will you draw the line at their thoughts? Are we now willing to debate thought-crime in these chambers? What ever happened to freedom of conscience? You are champions of moral freedom. But at what price? I implore you, do not condemn these men. For if you do, our freedoms established in our founding charter are condemned with them."

The OP sat down. Christian caught his eye with a look that said more than thanks. *You were my champion today. Nobody could have said it better.* And there was something in the OP's eyes that hinted he was not just for hire. *Please, Lord, let his own words sink in.* He looked back at the Voices and took a deep breath. From somewhere, peace. A surprise. A gift.

The VP stood up, buttoned his jacket, and laid a comforting hand on Pastor Wealth's shoulder. "Honorable Voices, there has been much talk of drawing lines in this hearing room. But as we have seen, we cannot agree on where to draw the line between good and evil. Every statement we make about what is right or wrong is ultimately just a matter of our own personal opinion. That is why we have elected you. We trust each of you to draw your own lines and let the majority prevail. We commit the plea of these victims into your all-powerful hands." The VP sat down and the eyes of the hushed hearing room turned to the Table.

The Honorable Mr. Titan #1 looked down both sides. "Are you ready to vote?"

All heads nodded.

To the left all the Voices extended their right hands. Every thumb turned down. Mr. Titan #1 looked to his right. All thumbs down. He looked straight at Faithful and Christian, and no longer hiding his scorn, extended his robed right arm and slowly rotated his thumb down. "The oppressors will rise."

Christian and Faithful slowly stood beside the OP, quiet, but with their heads held high.

"Mr. Christian and Mr. Faithful, you have duly compensated your victims for your hateful actions. We commend you. But free speech and reason are merely tools of the oppressor. Our charter is a living, *evolving* document; we must adapt and modify these immutable ideals that have guided us from the beginning, the greatest being the right of our citizens to pursue happiness. You have left a trail of tears and broken beliefs through our fair city. You are enemies to and disrupters of our trade; you have disturbed our peace and robbed our happiness; you have won some of our fellows to your dangerous beliefs. Therefore it is our perspective that you should be remanded to The Cage, and the inmates there be furnished with whatever supplies they request to dispatch you to whatever god you pray to and go to when you die."

Applause burst from the gallery. Others surged forward to console Pastor Wealth.

But Faithful was on his feet shouting to be heard. "Please . . . your Honors . . . please . . . may I say something?"

Mr. Titan #1 gaveled the room back to order. "To demonstrate our deep compassion and great tolerance, we will allow it."

Pastor Wealth bristled and started to object, but again the VP laid a calming hand on his arm. "You've already won," he whispered. "Besides, look at him. He looks terrible. Even lisps."

"Your Honors, we did not steal your happiness. The cupboard was already bare when we got here. Even Pastor Wealth, at the Corporate Worship Service, addressed the great restlessness of your citizens, their 'crisis of contentment.'

"There is only one Person in the Universe who sees things exactly the way they really are. It is the Creator God who made the Universe, who made us. He doesn't sit at anybody's Power Table. He is the One who sits on the Throne. Only he sees clearly where to draw the line. 'Let God be true, and every man a liar.'

"Yes, he draws the line at *any* moral failure, because his character is perfect. But our God is also our Voice. He made us and knows our weaknesses. And his Son, Jesus, didn't regard his position of Power as something to be grasped, but humbled himself and walked among us, experiencing our perspective, feeling our pain. The God of the Universe became a victim, betrayed and unjustly oppressed. At the hands of a powerful elite he suffered dearly and gave up his life. He paid our sinprice and offers Life to all who respond with faith enough to take him at his word.

"And when we do, God teaches us where to draw the line, and softens our hearts, and molds our wills through his Word, his Holy Spirit, and Jesus, the King of kings. And whether you pray to him or not, sir, you *will* meet him when you die. May he have mercy on your soul."

Christian sat on Faithful's bunk. Out front The Cage TV crews were setting up extra cameras and sound equipment. The officers were in and out unlocking the doors and ushering in deliveries: cans of gasoline, several large crates. Some of the inmates were huddled together putting the finishing touches on the script for what was anticipated to be the highest-rated episode of all time. Others opened the crates and pulled out an assortment of whips and knives and clubs. The Cage cracked and popped and rang with clashing steel blades. The questors spoke quietly, watching their opponents warm up for the deathgame.

"If I'm first, I don't want you to watch," Faithful said. "I want you to find a quiet place behind the cubicle and pray for me."

"I feel the same way."

"You know," Faithful said, "I was thinking while we were sitting in that hearing. Even Jesus lived and died by public opinion. But whether the thumbs down come from Pilate or the Voices, God's hand is the one in control."

Christian knew it was true, but he could not shove his heart back down his throat. He wanted to die well, like the martyrs in Evangelist's pictures. He also wanted to take something strong and pass out. Just wake up in time for dinner in Celestial City.

"I keep thinking about Evangelist's words," Christian said, "that maybe only one of us will be taken today. So I want to go first. If somebody comes galloping to our rescue . . . " he put his head down between his hands, "Faithful, I don't want to go on without you. Besides, you're the stronger warrior. You do better in battle. I mean, today was brilliant." He made himself look straight at Faithful. "I was so proud of you."

Faithful smiled and shook his head, "Not any prouder than I was of you." He clapped Christian on the back. "You've come a long way from that afternoon in the van in HeartLand."

The theme music swelled. Christian's heart raced even faster. They stood up.

"Listen," Faithful's tone turned serious "If God provides a way for either of us to escape, it will be a flat-out miracle. So we escape, agreed?"

Christian looked around at the bars, the crowds, the knives. "Agreed." *Safe bet*. "Faithful, what about Gracie?"

It was the worst part. Neither had any idea what to say.

The leader approached, hesitant. "No matter what you see tonight, I'm not really game for this." His voice faltered and he did not look them in the eye. "Sometimes you just don't have a choice."

"Camera, action!"

The announcer finished the introduction and the red light on the camera over Faithful's bunk came on.

"Mr. Christian, Mr. Faithful." The leader held up his hand with two toothpicks sticking out. "Short one goes first."

The drums rolled as Christian reached out and drew. *The long one!* He turned for a last look at his friend. Faithful embraced him in a big bear hug. No words. Too many words. Finally he whispered into Faithful's ear, "How will I find you?"

Faithful paused and whispered back, "Remember Apollyon? The hand with the leaves? Meet me at the Tree of Life." He drew back and smiled at his buddy. Then he turned and followed the leader to the front of The Cage.

Everybody had a whip. It should have been Catwoman's finest hour, but she and about eight others sat on the left side of The Cage with their backs to Faithful. Evidently, they did have a choice after all.

The whip whistled, then whistled again and cracked. The audience roared. Crack! Crack! Crack! With all the popping and cracking, the live violence, the mob soundtrack, nobody noticed when Christian slipped around to the back side of the cubicle. He stuck his fingers in his ears and tried to pray. *Dear God, take him. Take him quickly, please.* The whipping continued until the first commercial break. After break the thud, thud, thud of clubs. If Faithful ever screamed, Christian didn't hear him. *Lord, use it. If Gracie is watching, let it break her heart and bring her to you. And for all the others who are watching . . .* "

There was a hand on his shoulder. He looked up to see the OP, his finger over his lips, pointing him to the back door of The Cage, slightly ajar. He wanted to keep praying. He wanted the City. But here was the miracle, standing smack in front of him. *Ah Lord, I can't do it. Not alone. And what about Gracie? Lord, what will happen to her?*

It was as if someone whispered, "Go, you will not be alone. Neither will Gracie."

The OP closed the door and locked it behind them, slipping the key in his pocket. They ran three doors down an empty lane to a deserted coffee shop. Casting a parting glance over his shoulder, Christian saw above The Cage a dazzling shaft of light piercing the bubble, and in the light, the outlines of a blazing chariot and two white horses. His eyes welled up as he ran after the OP. *Only one chariot. Goodbye, my friend.*

Opening the door behind the counter that said, "Employees Only," the OP motioned him through. "Down those stairs!"

At the bottom they pulled up at an intersection of cramped lanes that ran between dark, dirty buildings. The air smelled of mold and garbage.

"I'm so sorry." The OP shook his head, "We just couldn't think of a way to save you both. Here." He handed Christian his backpack and then held up Faithful's. "We didn't know which one of you it would be. What should we do with this?"

Christian stared at the pack, trying to tear his thoughts away from the clubs and the chariot and his friend's face. "We . . . uh . . . oh." He unzipped it, and fumbled around inside. Finally, pulling out Faithful's Scroll, he held it up to the OP. "Can we get this to someone in the Nu Image Recovery Center?"

"You mean Gracie?"

Christian almost smiled, remembering the man's astounding investigative abilities. "Yes, Gracie."

"I don't think *we* can. But maybe *I* can."

"It could mean the difference for her."

The OP nodded his head and thought a minute. "We're in the Debtor's Corps basement. Take this lane straight. Don't make any turns. It will finally come to a door that opens into the exit bay on the far side of Vanity Fair. There's usually nobody there. Very few leave this place." He raised his eyebrows. "Things may change soon, though, you think?"

A smile flitted across Christian's face.

"Follow the Way through the dump and across the flats. Before midnight you should reach a ravine marked by some bushes at its edge. I'm told you can't miss it. I'll meet you there before morning." The OP disappeared down the intersecting lane.

Christian took off running through the dark, graffitied concrete buildings. He had only gone a few blocks when the pain in his ribs became unbearable. The best he could manage was something between a power walk and a slight jog. Thankfully, the lane was deserted. The Debtors were working and playing in the beautiful bubble upstairs. The basement was a giant flophouse served by a few cheap convenience stores. Through the only window he passed, he glimpsed a warehouse-style interior lined with rows of bedrolls. Against the far wall a dozen Debtors whistled and clapped at something burning on the screen of a small black-and-white television.

He slipped out of the exit bay and past the glistening black plastic mounds. He tried to think of Faithful, standing strong in the presence of the King. Beautiful smile. And the King's welcome embrace.

As the miles stretched out and his ribs throbbed with every step, the image faded and the darkness flooded in. The evils returned in force, dancing, raving in the dark. "You think you've won the battle? Where's your victory? Where are all those fellows bailing out of the hole in the bubble? And Gracie. You're abandoning her. So much for your great HeartLand escape. You're pathetic. You're alone. Your God is cruel."

Chapter 17

Way up near the surface, voices hummed and hovered. But Christian sank back into the fog, ignoring them. The delicious comfort washed over him as he drifted back down.

He neared the surface again, drawn toward it, yet sensing somehow that if he did break the surface, something heavy and terrible would crush him. He turned and nestled back into the fog, but it swirled, thinned, and drained away completely. Opening his eyes to darkness, he tried to get his bearings. He squinted, searching for contours, outlines, any hint of where he was and what was going on. The squinting pulled at something tight and painful on his forehead. He reached up and discovered a knot on his right temple covered with new, tender skin.

I was . . . I was walking and my ribs were killing me . . . Tentatively, he inhaled. A little and then more and more filling his rib cage. *No soreness. Ribs feel okay, but my head hurts. What in the . . .* He uncurled from his fetal position and struggled to sit up. But the room whirled and tilted and he collapsed on his back. When he opened his eyes again he could make out a door on the left and what must be a curtained window on the right.

He was on a bed inside something, somewhere. He was not outside. He was not running from . . . from what? Released from above, the giant, heavy thing smashed down onto him, taking his breath away. *Faithful!* The nightmarish soundtrack rolled—pops, cracks, thuds, the mob's gleeful voices. He curled back up on his side, begging the fog to roll back in, to cradle his head in its comforting arms and help him forget. The pain in his head was swallowed whole by the pain of this crushing weight. *Faithful and Gracie and escaping the Fair and . . . the OP! Where is the OP?*

He looked down at his hospital gown. *I was running. I didn't think I was going to make it. Did I stumble, hit my head on a rock or something?* He stared at the dark wall seeing nothing—hearing everything, again. They could have been beating Faithful behind him, over by the window. Christian absorbed each lick of the batons and cudgels, but the invisible weight crushed even his groans. He couldn't wince, couldn't grieve; he could only lie there and listen until it faded away.

I'm in a hospital. Where? He stared at the doorknob. He could get up and go to the nurse's station, figure this out. *What if they found me, and I'm back in Vanity Fair?* He closed his eyes and tried to slip back beneath the surface, sink far, far below this lead weight that crushed his spirit.

He dozed, but fitfully. His muscles demanded a stretch. *Maybe slower this time.* He sat up carefully, feet over the side, giving his head time to settle on his body before he opened his eyes. Finally, he slid off the bed, untucked the catheter bag, grabbed his IV pole, and wove across the room to the window, poking his head through the curtains. A familiar downtown—from his memory or in truth? No condos or corporate towers, no monorails or Acropolis. Through the bars he saw a city sloping up into foothills with mountains beyond. Across the street, short afternoon lines cued up outside a movie theater box office. The Angelique Film Centre looked just like the one back home. He leaned his forehead on the fifth-story glass, eyes sweeping right and left, his breath fogging a small patch of window. To the right the familiar downtown park, to the left . . . *how could this be?* The sidewalk tables at Common Grounds and beyond, his old office building, and parking garage. The bank next door was framed with scaffolding, still under repair from the car bombing.

He scanned the mountains again, *his* beloved mountains—the only thing he missed about the City of Destruction. He recognized the shape of each peak. Every landmark he could think to look for, he could locate. He knew the sign on the street level down in front before he spotted it: "Doubting Castle Glen: When there's no hope, and you can't cope."

He pulled back from the curtains and shuffled over to the door. *Locked, of course.* He fell into the dark-green vinyl recliner by the side of his bed and leaned back, staring at the ceiling.

It was impossible. He laughed aloud at the sickness of this nightmare, the worst of everything: Gracie's hospital room plus the locked door at Pleasant Arbor, plus the cursed city he so desperately wanted to leave. He congratulated the Enemy on the totality of his defeat. He struggled over to the window again. The people in the movie lines were gesturing, traffic was flowing—if it was some sort of holographic fraud, it had been commissioned on a grand scale.

He retreated back into bed. *Yeah, that's it; this whole thing has been crazy from the start. What a crock! I'm the crock, just full of it!*

Again he dozed in and out of an exhausted but shallow sleep. He kept scratching at a door, trying to escape. Or was the scratching at his door? He opened his eyes and thought he saw the doorknob wiggling in the murky light. A giant figure in a white coat barely cleared the door jamb and flipped on a naked overhead bulb.

"Well, I see the traveler has finally woken up. Welcome back, Chris." There was nothing welcoming in the man's tone or face. Big nose, big bushy eyebrows, big teeth, everything about the man was huge. "Do you know where you are?"

"My name is Christian and no," he responded, not bothering to sit up.

"No, our records indicate that you are Chris Adams. You were admitted to Doubting Castle Glen here in City of Destruction subsequent to a brief stay at the county hospital where you were treated for head injuries sustained in the car bombing at First City Bank two weeks ago." He leaned in for a close-up at the knot on Christian's forehead, but made no comment. "You've been drifting in and out for a while now, giving us a travelogue about 'faraway places with strange sounding names.'" His lips parted in what was supposed to be a smile, but instead came off as a patronizing leer.

Christian looked back at the dark-green wall. For all he knew, he could have been picked up by another one of Apollyon's trick vans. He sympathized with Gracie and the worshipers on Vanity Fair's Acropolis. Maybe reality wasn't as simple as he thought.

"I'm your doctor, Dr. Despair," he said, turning the recliner so Christian faced him. "Do you remember the bomb blast?

"Yes."

"And what do you remember after that?"

"I remember seeing something and running to my office and then to my car."

"Interesting." The doctor opened his chart, took his pen out of his pocket, and began writing. "And then . . . ?"

"I got so sick of all the violence in this God-forsaken town and the violence creeping into my own heart, I left. Threw stuff in my backpack and just ran."

"Uh huh." Without looking up from his writing the doctor asked, "So, tell me, where did you go?"

Christian gave him the five-minute version, ending with his escape from Vanity Fair.

"Would you like to get your old job, your old life back?"

Christian hesitated, thinking briefly of Meg. "No."

"No, why? Too much violence? Did you lose family or friends?" he asked without a hint of sympathy.

"No. But the life I was living here and the person I was becoming . . . it scared me. I hated it."

"What about that journey of yours? Would you like to be back out on the road, heading to Celestial City?"

Christian turned over on his back and stared at the wintergreen ceiling. "No, not really."

"Why is that?"

"It's too hard. A little more adventure than I bargained for."

"Finding out that this god of yours will not really come through for you?"

Christian squirmed.

"Well, if you don't want back your old life here in the City, and you have no hope of going on with your faith in your god, then what's the use? Why choose life if it's so bitter?" Christian stared at the ceiling. He had no answer.

"Think about it." The doctor rose. "I'll be back tomorrow." He flicked off the light and closed the door, leaving Christian in the dark.

He's right, you know. Hope, longing, expectations, they're all just a setup for another fall. Christian couldn't tell if the whispers came from the evils lurking somewhere in the darkness or from the depths of his own heart. *You ran away from here crying, "Life! Life!" Is that what you call this? Having your heart whipped and bludgeoned and reduced to smoke and ashes just like your buddy Faithful?*

Who's the enemy here? It's God, isn't it? Isn't he supposed to come through for you? You gave your heart to him and he promised to give you Life in return. Wasn't that the deal? YOU CALL THIS LIFE?

The seed of doubt left behind by the giant doctor quickly mushroomed into a horror movie plant, leaves shooting out, tendrils climbing into every corner of the room, making it hard to breathe. Christian curled back up in his bed.

Maybe I didn't run off in search of life. Maybe my head got cracked and all this has been a dream, some kind of fantasy turned nightmare. Maybe the only way is just to embrace the doubt and the cynicism; live without hope. If I'm strong enough, clever enough, maybe I can find a good woman, settle down on my little half-acre, and ward off the violence. But isn't that holding onto hope? Hoping to find another Meg? Hoping my kids aren't the ones lined up in coffins in the stadium?

He couldn't imagine life without hope. At least not a life *he* wanted to live. And yet he couldn't imagine picking up where he left off back in this City. His heart longed for so much more than his old tap-dancing-to-get-approval-big-bucks-and-the-girl small story.

A nurse appeared with his dinner tray. While he nibbled, she deftly unhooked his IV and catheter, then left. He got up, turned off the light, and wobbled back over to the window. Twinkling with lights, the foothills stretched up to embrace the soaring mountains. He stood there for a long time until the last of the twilight disappeared before he crawled back into bed.

"I think we can talk this through. Don't let that old donkey of a doctor get the best of you."

Christian opened his eyes, but the door was closed. He rolled over, searching the room, and saw a five-foot face on the wall opposite his bed. He craned his neck, searching for a projection beam, but couldn't find any.

The face continued, "You know, Chris, you are reasonable, intelligent, a fairly good-looking guy." The face winked at him.

"Who are you?"

"I'm Nellie. I know you've been through a lot and I think you're being pretty hard on yourself."

Nellie had the look of a thirties movie star of alien descent—all finger waves, eyelashes, dark Kewpiedoll lips and greenish-black hair. A studio starlet shot in old-style dramatic contrast through a green-tinted lens. He had no idea how her greenish-white skin showed up on the dark wall.

"You are definitely not the oppressor," she consoled him. "You are the victim. Just think about your family—your parents' attention always consumed by your selfish, needy sister. And then Phillip was the baby who got what was left. There was never any for you. Phillip's accident was a *terrible* tragedy. But it was just an *accident*. It wasn't your fault. Your parents just made it worse by turning away from you. Where were they when you needed them? They were the adults. You were only eighteen. They should have known all brothers carry on a rivalry and not blamed you. You've been bearing this big load of guilt because of their weaknesses and failures. If they had been better parents, they would have walked with you through that dark time." With no encouragement, Nellie went on and on about his childhood and the raw deal he'd gotten. "If you can see how you were the victim, it gives you strength. Strength to go on and fight back against *all* the oppression in your life."

Her voice was sweet and tender. Very expressive, just like her face. Fluttering her big eyes and flashing her dimple, she rambled on about his dad's lack of involvement in their home, until Christian fell asleep.

Chapter 17

Christian awoke, but regretted it. Every time he did, the giant weight crashed down on him again. Regardless of *which* reality was real, he was angry. If *God* was real, well, then he was mad at him. Nellie had never mentioned God, but the more he thought about it, the more he felt like the wounded victim of his Maker. *I thought you loved me and were inviting me to be part of this grand adventure.* The highlights of his quest played in his mind, especially his time on the road with Faithful—memories that sharpened his loneliness and stirred his grief. *I wish the hand had never brought the leaves from the Tree of Life! Why didn't you let me die in Apollyon's valley?* By mid-morning his anger had overflowed into a full-fledged eruption.

"I thought you brought me someone to share the journey! Someone to learn from, to fight side by side together!" he railed. "I thought we were going to clasp arms and walk through the Celestial City gates together! *Or,* if you were going to take one of us, why did you have to leave *me?* Faithful gets the party in Celestial City! I get a dungeon with Dr. Despair and Neptune Nellie—the bad cop telling me I should just end it and the good cop stroking me and telling me I'm just a victim. What do you think you are doing?"

His rage was still fully engaged when Dr. Despair made his morning round.

"Good morning, Chris."

"What's good about it?"

"You tell me."

"Nothing. It stinks! I don't know if I'm crazy or being held captive. I don't know if I'm back where I started or on the far side of Vanity Fair, and if God is real I don't know how he could do this to me if he cares for me!"

The doctor nodded in agreement. "Yes, if he's really all-powerful, it seems he would have prevented this from happening. Maybe he is in control but he's a little more dicey than you thought."

Christian ranted on, "I thought life was supposed to be this great adventure with people you love. Winning! Victory for the

Kingdom! But there's a trail of dead bodies behind me—Doc and now Faithful. I didn't see any victory. That's not life; that's death and too much of it. Just like back here in the City of Destruction. What's the difference?"

Dr. Despair sighed, "You're right, you should probably just give in to the fact that *this is life*. And, if it's too overwhelming . . . " he reached into his pocket and took out an unlabeled prescription bottle. "If it's too overwhelming, take four of these." He plunked the pills down on the nightstand beside Christian's bed and, inhaling deeply, rose to his full height. "To live without hope is not for the weak of heart."

Christian glared after the doctor as he let himself out. Then he glared at the pills, angry at the damage this man enjoyed inflicting. So opposite from Faithful. He thought again about his friend's sacrificial efforts to reach out to Gracie, Catwoman, and the rest.

From deep inside, a long sigh escaped. *Dear God, there are so few really good men, so few who are courageous and bold and willing to lay down their lives for other people. Why did you have to take one of the best?*

Every night Neptune Nellie returned, rearranging the old furniture of his life in new places. She spent countless hours exploring his victimhood, dredging up every grievance he'd ever suffered and showing how he was not to blame. She exposed how it was really the fault of his family, his teachers, his schoolmates, his friends in high school and college, his girlfriends, and especially, Meg. She explained away his shame over Phillip's death and his horrible abusive outbursts toward Meg. She even revealed that Amy had stopped taking birth control pills because they made her gain weight, so it was her own fault she got pregnant. Nellie talked incessantly of ways he could fix things to find enough happiness to live on, assuring him that he *could* find a new life back in his old life, that it could be arranged.

Every day the doctor returned, scarcely hiding his frustration that Christian could not find it within himself to either pop the pills or get over it, give up his loss of hope and sign on with the cynics. Christian himself wondered how long he could live in such miserable doubt. Over and over he approached the precipice of faith and stared out at the future. If God was down there, he was distant, sitting with his hands in his lap. *Something has to die here. Will it be me or my heart?* The grave looked easier than his dungeon. Easier even than life with no hope.

One day the doctor came in with a wheelchair and strapped him in.

"Where are we going?"

"We're going to review your options."

He wheeled Christian down a long hall. Through the rectangular windows in the doors he could see other patients like himself, curled up in bed or sitting slumped and glassy-eyed in the recliners by their beds, some secured with a strap. At the end of the hall the doctor pushed Christian up to a large window overlooking the Castle Glen yard. Tombstones stretched as far as the eye could see.

"These once were questors as you are. They chose the peaceful nothing of this yard rather than the grief and agony you are so loath to give up."

"What happens to the ones who embrace the doubt, who live with no hope?" Christian asked.

"When they've stabilized they go back out into the City. They tend to be either criminals or professionals. Many of them teach in universities."

"And what of the rest?"

Without a word the doctor wheeled him into the elevator. On the next floor, two giant day rooms stretched the entire length of the hall on both sides. Televisions hung from the ceiling every twenty-five feet or so. Thousands of patients slouched in gray metal folding chairs in the cavernous windowless rooms, clustered around the hypnotic boxes.

"They find their little addictions. Some get strong enough to go out into the city and find harmless addictions there. Sports, work, collecting . . . the possibilities are endless."

"Small stories," Christian murmured.

"Very small. Some fall into destructive habits and have to be brought back."

Back in his room Christian lay on his bed and stared at the bottle of pills. *Something has to die.* He thought of the graveyard and the TV dungeon, and the pointless tap dance of his own chosen addictions. The dead-end, empty games of Pleasant Arbor. Adventure with an off button. Seemingly under control, but never large enough for his heart. On the other hand, there was the Kingdom adventure. Technicolor, alive, more joy and Life than he had ever known. But completely beyond his control. A role in a story that seemed far *too* large. *And the pain! Dear God! I can't live with this pain. The more you hope, the harder you fall. I had such great hope in you, God!*

He got up occasionally and paced around the room, holding the bottle of pills in his left hand. They took his untouched supper tray away as he again watched twilight fall over the mountains. With one hand he clutched the little bottle. With the other he traced the peaks with his finger on the glass. What is real? This room with a view? The bars outside his window? How could his quest be a dream? He had learned too much. Grown too much. The change in his heart and soul was more real than these towering peaks. Unbidden, snatches of the Psalms scrolled through his mind. *"I look up to the mountains; my strength comes from God who made the mountains."*

"Before the mountains were born, from everlasting to everlasting you are God."

For the first time since he woke up, he cried out, not *at* God but *to* him: "Where is the Life you promised? Please show me!"

"You are such a creative guy, Chris. You just need to take that creativity and actualize yourself." He had learned that you couldn't turn off Neptune Nellie. A continuous fountain of self-promoting happy talk, she gushed for hours each night. "Focus on your needs and desires, and you will create a plan, the door to all the happiness you could ever want. And you need to go to your father and tell him, 'Father, you have sinned against me, and you don't deserve to be called my father ever again. . . . '"

The best he could do was stuff his head under his pillow and try to fall asleep. His dreams were mostly nightmares of The Cage. But this night he dreamed he was in the mountains, climbing up through quaking aspen groves and twilight meadows where moose waded and drank deeply from gurgling, icy streams. Swinging up their racks they watched him pass, water dripping from their muzzles. Unlike the Rock of Difficulty, it was an easy, joyous climb. In the rocky meadows above the tree line the columbine and lady's slippers danced in the breeze. Twilight deepened and one by one the stars showed up, rehearsing their nightly praise songs.

In his dream, Christian finally neared the crest, a ragged edge of gray against the inky sky. At the top of the ridge directly ahead he spied the dark silhouette of a soldier with his back to him, pants tucked into his combat boots. About twenty feet from where the soldier stood, the ridge leveled out. Christian stood up, dusting his hands loudly in hopes that the sentry would turn around. But he didn't. He lifted his right arm and pointed to the spangled expanse. Christian looked out at the heavens of eternity, filling the Earth with their silent voices. Their cry shot clean through him, piercing his cracked, stony heart. The sentry spoke in a familiar voice tinged with quiet urgency, "Hey, buddy, there is *so much more*. You are needed." Christian desperately wanted his friend to turn around, but Faithful stood there, his face to the heavens. Christian stood, gazing after him until his vision blurred and he wiped his eyes with his hands. When he looked again, the silhouette was gone.

He woke up. But for the first time, the crushing weight of Faithful's death did not smash down on him. He lay there in the dark, listening to his rapid breathing and pounding heart. *Faithful, what are you telling me?* It shocked him to think of his buddy in combat gear. Wasn't he peacefully at rest? He smiled. His uniform seemed much more fitting than walking around with a harp.

Somehow Christian had lost perspective on the battle—the armor of God, the forces of darkness he was up against. Another thought occurred to him: *If we live like we are in the greatest of all battles, then it won't surprise or defeat us when we come under vicious attack. We won't feel betrayed by God.* Prodded by this new thought he sat up, his mind racing. Eventually he moved to the window, staring past the streetlights at the blackness beyond.

Ah, but Lord, the battle is so hard. I never counted on bleeding so much. I can't take another hit like this. This one's already over the line. And I'm not a very good warrior.

Why not, came the thought, *if you've trained under the best?*

He didn't have an answer for that one.

Christian spent the rest of the night talking it out with God. His vision had become so narrow. As he talked with the King, the walls blew out and he could again see and think about the journey.

"Why is the quest so painful and the country so dangerous?"

"Because everything is at stake," came the reply.

So why should I be surprised when the enemy uses live ammo? He faced the precipice of faith again, conscious that his fear of the past had consumed his hope for the future. He caught a glimpse of the arms open wide to catch him, carry him if need be, but his pain was so real and hurt so deeply, he still couldn't step out. He wasn't afraid of dying. It was the prospect of more and more pain that paralyzed him.

An orderly brought in his breakfast tray and, with one eye on the little window in the door, moved Christian's plate slightly, revealing something sticking out underneath. Then the orderly exited without saying a word.

Leaning forward in his recliner, Christian stared at the little piece of brown poking out from under his plate. He checked the window, tipped the plate up, and pulled it out, immediately sliding it under his hospital table. After watching the window for a few more seconds, he looked under the table to discover a twig with three leaves on it. A scrap of brown paper was wrapped around the bottom of the twig.

"I found this in the bottom of your backpack. Remember!" It was signed, "hOPeful."

Prickles radiated over his body and down his limbs. Faded but still amazingly green, the leaves from the Tree of Life rested in his palm. Cupping them in his hands he pressed them to his face. The leaves for healing. The meeting place to find Faithful. Tissue paper thin, but still neither shriveled nor brown, they held the promise of Celestial City.

He remembered nights around the campfire with Faithful gazing at the heavens, twirling these leaves and talking about what it would be like to finally stand before the throne of the One they loved so much. Christian remembered holding his leaves aloft against the starry night sky, picturing the trees in Celestial City planted on each side of the River of Life—right down the middle of the Great Boulevard.

He paused for a moment, his eyes opening wide. *River of Life, Tree of Life, Crown of Life. Life! I ran off to find it. Gave my heart to God in exchange for the promise . . . but . . . I'll never really find it here. It's there!* He'd been so desperate to find Life in his small story, and he had finally tasted Life in the Kingdom Story—real joy, intimacy, Truth, so much of what his heart desired. But this chapter of the Kingdom Story was more about battle and hard pain and unfulfilled longing. The ancient words scrolled through his mind: "Hope deferred makes the heart sick, but a longing fulfilled is a Tree of Life." *All my heart's deepest longings will be fulfilled, but there's a lot of overcoming to do first. Then comes the Tree of Life.*

He pulled a pen out of the nightstand and scrawled his own message on the back of the little brown paper. He prayed the OP had found his Scroll, or had been given one of his own. A little shaky, he rolled the paper around the stem of the leaves and tried to eat his breakfast. *If it works, I'm going to need this.* What if the same orderly didn't come back? What if he wouldn't deliver the message?

The door finally opened and the orderly entered, not making eye contact. Christian pointed to the little brown stem poking out from under his plate and softly asked, "Would you please return this?"

The orderly flashed a look out at the hall but said nothing. He took the tray and locked the door behind him.

"Please, Lord, let him deliver the message. Please, deliver *me!*"

He paced the room as the minutes ticked by. Out of the corner of his eye he noticed the little bottle of pills lying down by the baseboard where he had thrown them. A smile broke out. The thing that needed to die. It wasn't him; it wasn't his heart; it was his *will*, his will to find the full measure of the Life he'd always longed for on this side of Celestial City. He talked to the Father and laid it down. It didn't take away the pain, but it opened a way to get past it. He prayed for Gracie and for the OP—Hopeful. Another friend to share the journey. He couldn't wait to see him. The prospect soothed a little of his pain over the loss of Faithful. Already God was using it. A living victory from the ashes. He still couldn't understand why God allowed so much hurt and sorrow, why he didn't hedge and protect a little more, and he told him so. But then he left it there.

An hour passed and then another. As the day wore on, he tried to relax, praying often. He hoped he would not have to face the doctor again. The nurse brought lunch. About an hour later the key scratched in the lock and Dr. Despair's giant frame filled the doorway. At the same time, the room began to shake and the walls began to crumble. Christian stood at the edge of the precipice of faith, clutching the leaves of promise. He caught a clear glimpse of the passionate love in the eyes waiting below, and finally jumped.

CHAPTER 18

A deep, low-pitched rumble shook the room. All around him the building rocked and quaked, but Christian stood stock still, the ground under his feet rock-solid. The wintergreen walls froze and degraded like a computer screen crashing and dissolved into rough-hewn stone. White-coated Dr. Despair sprouted locks of snarled, matted hair that plunged to his shoulders and a long, tangled beard. Big eyes bulging at Christian, the giant pulled back his huge fist. But the enormous muscled arms and legs and blood-stained tunic began to vibrate and fade as well. What had become dungeon walls opened up, and finally Christian stood alone in his khakis, free and clear of the giant and his castle. Behind him he heard a familiar voice.

"The . . . thing really works!" He turned around to see Hopeful about fifty feet behind him, right hand still extended, gripping a Scroll. A slow Cheshire grin parted over his perfectly white teeth.

"You!" Christian greeted his new friend with a back-clapping hug. "You have no *idea* what it meant to see those leaves! What it means to see you! Great move!"

"I *knew* you were in there!" Hopeful's eyes mirrored Christian's delight, although he barely hugged back.

"Well, if anyone could investigate and track me down, it would be you."

"Tracking you here was not hard. Getting to you . . . " Hopeful shook his head. "I tried to bribe the servant to take you your pack, your Scroll, my army knife, anything. But he was afraid someone would catch on. The others talked about . . . "

"There are others?"

"Oh yes. We tried everything we could think of, but nothing worked. The castle was too secure. Finally, it had been over a month . . . "

"A month?"

"Yes, you've been in there a long time. We camped at a Shepherd's stand, not too far from here. Yesterday we prayed again, long and hard, asking God what to do. I went through your backpack one more time and somehow those leaves popped out at me, *fresh, green leaves* in the bottom of a backpack. I told the others to go on and I came back and finally persuaded the servant to take them. I knew they meant something to you and they seemed safe to him."

Christian admired Hopeful's fresh khakis with the King's crest. "You look . . . great! Faithful would be so proud, so delighted." Christian smiled, remembering his dream. *Maybe he* is *proud.* "How did you find me?"

They both shouldered their packs and began walking. "When I reached the ravine and you weren't there, I had to wait until morning to pick up your trail. It looked like you had stumbled off the Way and crashed on a big boulder. There was blood on it."

"I wondered about that possibility," said Christian, pointing to his forehead.

"From the boulder there were huge prints all the way to the castle. The giant must have found you and carried you home."

"Did it really look like a castle from the outside?"

"Turrets, moat, the works. Why, what did it look like from the inside?"

Christian tried to explain his sojourn through the hopelessness of the giant's castle. He was still not in the best of shape. As he told his story they traveled slowly and decided to camp for the night instead of pushing on to the Shepherd's stand. Christian's old bedroll never looked so good. He scrolled for a while by the campfire and then shut it down and gazed into a real night sky.

"I finally came full circle," he said. "I realized I could fight to understand, or I could have God. I was drowning in the whys."

"Maybe I'm a 'why.'" Hopeful's tone was so different from the courtroom slick Christian remembered. "And all the others. I've heard even more will take their time and follow us. I've struggled . . . " His silky voice trailed off. "I'm torn between being so thankful for what God showed us through your lives and especially Faithful's death, and feeling . . . guilty. Maybe if I had believed without the witness of such a tremendous sacrifice, he wouldn't have had to die."

"Listen," Christian said, inhaling deeply. "I had a dream last night. I saw Faithful." He paused. His heart felt as tender and fragile as the new skin on his forehead. "He pointed to the heavens and said, 'There is *so much more*.'

"I've been thinking of Celestial City as the Grand Prize. The thing to be bagged. The joy of being face to face with Jesus. But it's 'so much more.' For one thing it's Command and Control for the battle going on right now." He looked down at his khakis. "I think I lost sight of that. Or maybe I never fully bought into it to begin with. This chapter of the Kingdom Story is so much about battle and overcoming. Then Celestial City is reigning with the King. I have no idea what that's about. Can't imagine. Anyway, the unseen is so huge. There's so much going on out there. When Faithful dies and you bust me out from the dungeon, it's not just for your benefit or mine. It's part of the Kingdom Story, the Kingdom strategy; we're pushing back against everything the Enemy is throwing against us *and* we're getting ready. Because we're getting *closer*."

Christian stared at the glowing embers, his heart yearning for Faithful's presence. But, along with the ache, thanks and praise welled up inside. Hopeful was the King's man! He left all the glitz, glamour, and ratings for the quest.

"Thank you, Hopeful. That's twice you've pulled me out of the pit."

"I'm so honored to serve with you."

By midmorning they reached the stand where the Shepherds reported that over a thousand questors had recently passed that way, spurred out of Vanity Fair by the Truth they had seen on Voice TV. They celebrated with a round of high-fives and clinks of their icy mugs. Christian gazed up at the Way winding through twin peaks, an oasis of cool and comfort rising out of the wilderness floor. *All this and mountains too!*

After lunch they began their ascent of spacious paths that at times became actual staircases with rivulets of icy water cascading down the "handrails." The King of landscape design had included "snack bars" at frequent intervals—grapevines dripping with frosted claret-red grapes, boughs loaded with Bing cherries and apples. Alongside the Way mountain streams tumbled and pooled around rocks so flat they could walk out on them, splashing their faces and taking long, deep drinks.

They set up evening camp beside a small sapphire-blue pool surrounded by the wide, flat rocks where they perched, dangling their legs in the water and washing their clothes. From fifty feet above, the water plumed into the pool, providing a perfect background that lulled them to sleep. Christian couldn't remember the last time he had felt so clean and so refreshed.

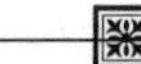

The aroma of fresh coffee broke gently into Christian's slumber. In the rosy morning light two burly Shepherds were frying bacon and cracking eggs. "Welcome, questors! Welcome to the Delectable Mountains." Christian and Hopeful dug into a mound of bacon and great conversation.

After using his bacon to mop up his third perfectly over-easy egg, Christian licked his fingers. "Are you traveling with us today?"

"Just to the top of Clear Ridge," one Shepherd replied, patting a long leather pouch hanging from his belt. "We'll show you something we think you'll enjoy seeing."

If he'd had just a little more energy, Christian would have jogged up to the Ridge. In spite of the altitude he felt so much stronger today. They finally reached the top, where they had a great view of the mountain slopes below, another desert wilderness beyond that, and far in the distance, another blue ridge of mountains. The Shepherd opened his pouch and pulled out a shiny brass telescope. "Here," he said. "Look straight across at that ridge of mountains on the horizon, up at the very top of the tallest one. What do you see?"

Through the glass, Christian swept the line of peaks and paused at a bright reflection. "I see something shining."

"That's it. Can you make out any shapes in the shining?"

"A wall, maybe? And a gate?"

The Shepherd smiled. "That, Chris, is the gate to Celestial City."

A thrill shot through Christian's body. He strained at the glass, longing for more than this little glimpse. Finally, he lowered the scope. "It's so close," he whispered. Knowing where to look for it, he could still see the brightness, even with the naked eye. He passed the telescope on to Hopeful.

Hopeful gazed at the City. He lowered the scope and caressed the time-worn brass. "Any chance this thing takes digital pictures?" he asked.

The Shepherd chuckled. "Just remember."

Christian took the scope back, straining to see any hint of green trees beyond the walls. *Remember. Remembrance is such a big part of this journey. Every morning I wake up and forget so much.* He sympathized with Hopeful. He wished he had a picture of this on his watch face where he could check it every fifteen minutes. A constant contrast between time and eternity. A continual reminder that time is running out. The Marketing Guy in his brain began to spin out an entire line of "Teach Us to Number Our Days" timepieces with Celestial City gates that glowed in the dark. *Oh, stop it.* But the grin stayed on his face for the next five minutes as they said good-bye to the Shepherds and began the fun part.

Not really anxious to leave the aspen-lined meadows behind, they camped early at the foot of the mountain. Rising while it was still dark, they struck out into the wilderness. Through winding arroyos along dried-up stream beds, around flat-topped eroded mesas, the engineers of the Way had a hard time making a straight go of it. They took shelter at midday in the shadows of huge boulder piles and, when the sun sank closer to the horizon, pressed on through the brush and occasional cedar.

After two more days of rocks, gravel, and ravines, they topped a small rise and stared at the last thing they expected to find: the geometric grid of a city sprawled before them. Scratched into the flat desert floor—the playa—concentric half-circles were subdivided by spoke-like arteries radiating from the hub. In the empty center, inhabitants were busy erecting a large tower. The Way encompassed the entire city and headed out across the dusty desert on the far side. Christian and Hopeful exchanged a look of okay-let's-go and descended to the playa.

A shark car zigzagged through the shimmering heat waves and silently passed them by. From the large paper maché mouth, wetsuited legs and flippered feet poked out in black-humor fun. The driver of the shark grinned and waved. They would have waved in return, but just then a go-cart with a jet engine screamed past. By the time they recovered, the shark-car was well past and a glossy yellow banana three-wheeler zipped by. From a large hole in the banana, a girl with a tropical fruit-laden hat grinned at them. She returned their wave. A normal-looking truck passed, hauling a mattress, whipping up near-lethal billows of dust. Three mattress passengers in gas masks gave them the royals-in-their-carriage wave. Not wishing to choke in their wake, Christian and Faithful waited a minute or so before they traversed the last fifty yards to the city entrance. The fat guy in front of them straightened up on his furry rabbit motor scooter and punched the throttle.

The sign over the entrance read, "Nomads of the Heart:

Welcome." A girl in a Hawaiian shirt and ballerina tutu smiled as she stamped their hands. "Which tribal lodge do you prefer?" Christian and Hopeful surveyed the landscape of every conceivable kind of tent, pavilion, RV, car, truck, plane, and other assorted conveyances and lodgings, including one built out of old doors.

"We don't know," Hopeful said.

"Would you like to see a list?"

Hopeful scanned an extensive list of affinity groups: Windsurfers' Lodge, Rave Lodge, Geodesic Lodge, eLodge, Pyromaniac's Lodge. He pointed at an entry and showed it to Christian: "Questor's Lodge." Welcome Woman gave them a map and directed them to a lodge tucked deep within the desert sprawl.

The Nomad Camp was truly a rainbow gathering, ethnic diversity enhanced by colorful layers of body paint, mud wraps, and liquid latex. Sporting unpierced, untattooed skin or naturally colored hair was definitely passé. Four guys with giant Easter Island–style foam heads walked by. On the left a sign read: "Attention Lodge: Drop in to Attention Lodge and we will all pay attention to you." On the right in the Retro Sci-Fi Lodge, someone in a gray bodysuit, oversized white head, and big black eyes darted into a large gray tent marked by a sign: Hangar 54. The scent wafting from the Hemp, Hemp Hooray! Lodge almost bowled the questors over.

Winding their way among the lodges was like putting the car radio on scan, except the Latina, pop, metal, and polka strains overlapped. Christian held up a moment, perplexed by the raging of a thrash vocalist: "I wanna be an organist! I wanna be an organist!" When they moved on to where Hopeful could hear him, Christian threw up his hands. "For crying out loud, let the guy play the organ!"

Hopeful's brows knit and he burst into laughter. "He wants to be an *anarchist!*"

Christian had never seen such eclectic bizarreness in his whole life, but he tried to walk down the street without "Golly, Margaret, would you look at that!" written all over his face. This place went way beyond glitzy Vanity Fair. More a manic pursuit of life, liberty, and happiness translated, "How can I push the envelope with something—my outrageous clothes-vehicles-art-behavior—something that somebody isn't already selling on a T-shirt?" The style was "ironic juxtaposition": to come up with new cards to play, these Nomads took the old cards and shuffled them together in shocking and unprecedented ways—a barbershop quartet singing the Beach Boys, a fire breather with a Teddy Roosevelt monocle, safari hat, khaki shirt, and zebra leggings.

Floating revelers celebrated life in their own small stories. Some preferred to walk on stilts. A couple of small platoons marched by, chanting and drumming. One was festooned with ribbons and buttons that read: "Fun Is a Spiritual Path," "Born Again Pagan," and "I Read Banned Books!" The other marched to the beat of other drums: "Recovering Baptist," "Heretic," "I wasn't created in your image of God," and "My Karma ran over your Dogma."

The presence of the Enemy was more palpable here than in any other place Christian could remember outside of Apollyon's valley or the Pit in the Valley of the Shadow. They could not go more than a block without passing a tarot-card reader, sly eyes searching the crowds for weary faces. And such expressions were legion. Everyone here had hungry eyes and hearts, constantly cruising, scavenging for any morsel of fun they might be missing.

As shadows lengthened and the sun softened, the tarot readers lit votive candles that flickered seductively. Outside the Church Chateclysm, robed monks ignited oversized torches interspersed among giant totem poles and invited worshipers into their tent revival. Alone in the center of a full-size replica of Stonehenge, a lovely young "Eve," clad only in leaves, twirled slowly, eyes closed. Gradually she began to float.

Looking past Eve at the crowded stage in front of the Trust in Me Hypnotherapy Lodge, Hopeful mused, "It's the endgame opposite to the Fair's."

"Yeah, I was just getting that too," Christian replied.

"All these radical individuals dedicated to the search," Hopeful said, "but more for experiences and relationships than for money and all the goodies."

Right next to a twenty-foot-tall lamp mobile, they spied a small, ribbed, Quonset-like tent with a sign, "Welcome, Questors." They stopped and stared at the sign.

"I'm thinking 'questors' means something totally different to this crowd than it does to us," Christian said.

"Well, no totems or tarot readers; that's encouraging," Hopeful said. He moved toward the tent and pushed back the flap. Smiling, he turned to Christian and waved him on in.

Stepping through the flap, Christian surveyed about fifteen astonished faces. Men and women of all ages, all in the King's khaki, some seated, some on their knees. A fifty-something gentleman with distinguished graying temples rose to welcome Christian.

"This is an Acts 12 moment! We were just praying for your release . . . and here you are!"

"Unless it's my angel," Christian smiled.

"Believe me," Hopeful said, "he is no angel."

The questors surged around the new arrivals until a friendly guy somewhere in his forties and with intense brown eyes quieted them. "I think introductions are in order. I'm Colonel Vision, a former money junkie from the Fair."

"Ditto," said a salt-and-pepper Corporate Titan-type, extending a broad smile and firm handshake to Christian. "Warbucks."

The gentleman who had first greeted them introduced himself as Aquila and in turn presented his wife, Priscilla.

"Fine teachers, both of them," Colonel Vision said.

A stocky woman with beautiful brown eyes and a radiant face gave each of them a hug. "I'm Community Mom," she said, beaming.

"She was our Corporate Mom back at the Fair," Warbucks said.

"Yes," she said, "and I didn't think I could ever make the break and strike out, but I did. Thanks for the courage." She hugged Christian again.

"I hate to be ignorant," Christian said, "but what's a Corporate Mom?"

"Oh, I took care of everybody. Picked up cleaning from the corporate cleaners, checked on car maintenance at the corporate auto service. Pushed a refreshment cart around the offices. Even learned how to give a pretty good massage. But now it's so different. Every glass of water is a Kingdom touch, it's . . . sorry, I'm so excited I'm just babbling." She dropped her face in her hands and then quickly raised her head again, shaking her head and laughing.

"Hi, I'm Goodnews Man," offered a thirty-something with star-quality good looks.

"You look familiar," Christian said.

"He used to anchor the news at the Fair," Hopeful said.

"Yes," Goodnews Man said. "Yours was the big story that changed my life. Thank you."

Christian received the same message from Sonshine, Mercy Heart, and Prayer Walker. "Thank you, thank you." The change in their eyes swept over Christian. A whole garden planted and watered with Faithful's blood and his tears; now strong and healthy and ready to plant their own seeds. Other questors had moved on to Celestial City, but these had remained, praying about how to impact the Nomad Camp for the Kingdom.

Together they strolled to a nearby diner, three stories of scaffolding draped with a silver silk parachute that smelled of deep fat and a charcoal grill. Celtic bagpipes accompanied by violin and accordion provided overly loud background music.

"We think the key to reaching these folks is through the arts—music, performance, storytelling," Colonel Vision said. "We've been praying about reaching out from a café with live entertainment. Goodnews Man has written some songs. Camp will break next Monday after their yearly Ceremony. We have three days to run our café."

Goodnews Man smiled and clapped Warbucks on the back. "This guy is amazing! He went to Bartertown Lodge and came back with a guitar, some PA equipment, lots of chairs, tables, coffee machines—good stuff too!"

Christian eyed the Nomad at the next table. His sparse orangey-red hair was braided into a few beaded dreadlocks, one falling across his tattooed forehead. In addition to six nose rings, his face was completely rimmed with pierced rings across his brow, down each cheek, and under his neck. His eyebrows and the bridge of his nose were pierced with double-ended studs. He was engaged in animated conversations, his eyes happy, dead.

"It's a pretty tough crowd," Christian said.

"Yes, it is," said brown-haired, petite Prayer Walker. "But as I've walked these streets I've found this massive need for hope and Life.

They're incredibly cynical. They cruise around complaining there's not enough new stuff—just the same old stuff as last year. Can you believe it? I've had some great conversations about my future and my hope."

Colonel Vision turned to Hopeful. "We were thinking of calling it Café Hope."

Hopeful grinned, "Need a mascot?"

After dinner the group headed back to their tent. Christian excused himself and circled back the other way alone. His fellow questors were planning, strategizing, asking for a battle, while Faithful and he had stumbled into theirs. He scanned the neighborhood as he walked. *Do they have any idea what they're in for?* At Viva Lost Vegas, an Elvis impersonator lip-synced one of the king's rowdiest numbers, swiveling and sweating in the stage lights. Sleek young men in spike heels, sequined gowns, and lipstick backed him up, their dance steps tightly choreographed. Inside Hades Gates, on a giant red stage bordered with black gargoyles, a black-robed priest raised a ceremonial knife over the throat of a white-robed young woman. A priestess passed a chalice of red liquid among the crowd, while their cohorts blow-torched animal heads over fifty-five-gallon drums.

Not that long ago he would have gawked at all the flesh and snickered at the occult excesses. Tonight he wearily collapsed on a wrought-iron bench across from the sacrifice, next to the questors' tent, beaten down by a palpable sense of the Enemy's power. He watched the spectacle, absently fingering the intricate design on the bench seat. From behind him, tender hands began massaging his shoulders—gently at first, then with more pressure on the painfully tense muscles. After a few minutes the hands slipped around his neck and a smooth voice whispered in his ear, "Hey, you look lonely."

He looked around into long lashes, long honey hair, and a low neckline. "Hi, I'm Buyme. What's your name?"

Before he could stop himself, "Christian" came out of his mouth.

She looked over at the mock-sacrament making the rounds. "Pretty disgusting, isn't it?"

Christian looked at the crowd getting tanked on whatever was in the red stuff and dancing around the roasting animal heads, then gazed again at her luminous face and eyes just inches away from his. He took a deep breath. Delicious vanilla scent radiated from her body.

She straightened and continued rubbing his neck, working further down his shoulders and arms. After a few minutes she said, "I think we're neighbors."

Christian turned for a quick glance behind them at her red tent bordered with gold bullion fringe. Through the drawn flap he saw a garden of glowing candles reflecting off the turned-down, petal-strewn sheets on her canopied bed. A warning thought popped into his head, but as she began massaging his temples and his scalp, it melted away. Her hands circled over his body, radiating goose bumps, stirring delight.

She leaned down again and whispered, "Would you like to join me for dinner? I've just grilled some steaks and I've been saving a special bottle of burgundy." She kissed his ear lightly. Then his neck. And continued sprinkling warm, gentle kisses around the back of his neck to his other ear. "And for dessert," she whispered, "I put fresh satin sheets on my bed."

It would be so easy. He longed for more of her touch, more kisses. In that moment he realized that he was only one invitation away from the dead, happy eyes all around him. He closed his eyes for a moment as she continued kissing his neck and her hands began working down his chest. Finally, he opened them. As he stood and turned to face her, he saw Hopeful leaning against the outside corner of their tent. Christian paused, dropping his eyes to the bench. In the flickering torchlight his eyes gradually made out the design—circles within circles, like a giant web. He walked around the bench and clasped her shoulders with one arm, giving her a squeeze. "Thanks, but I just ate. Let me offer you an invitation instead. Maybe you can join us for coffee tomorrow night."

She flounced her long hair and pouted at him as he waved from the front of their tent.

"I was wondering if you were going to need another save," Hopeful said.

Christian raised his eyebrows. "You might pray that my hungry heart will not go rampaging through my private video catalog tonight. Here we have hooked up with this awesome group and . . . I feel so lonely." He gazed back up the street at Hades Gates.

Hopeful put his arm around Christian's shoulders and prayed for both of them. When he finished he looked at Christian. "Only three days here. Three days worth of grace and we'll make it."

After breakfast and a brief organizational meeting, the questors fanned out to accomplish their Opening Night assignments. Being wordsmiths, Hopeful and Christian discussed a publicity flyer as Prayer Walker led them to the eLodge. Twenty minutes later, they handed the flyer to her. "You're invited to Café Hope. Cynics welcome," she read.

"That ought to cover most of these restless natives," Hopeful said.

Starting at the outermost perimeter, they spent the whole day walking the Nomad Camp, passing out flyers and tacking them on message boards. They enjoyed occasional islands of whimsy in the sea of decadence, like the walk-in camera big enough to view the desert upside down, and a bubble fountain complete with do-it-yourself bubble wands. But what really flourished here were the body-painting pageants that attended the occult dramas about the "wound that never heals" (until a satanic priest has his way with you).

Late in the day they reached the central playa, which was still roped off so builders could put the finishing touches on their tower, which wasn't a tower as it turned out, but a three-story stick-figure man constructed of wood and lined with neon lights. Behind the neon man, a semicircle of bone trees lent the playa a sacred-burial-ground feeling. Big bleached bones hot-glued to gnarly "trunks" supported spreading "branches" of horns and antlers. Atop twin towers on either side of the man, the builders were installing pyrotechnic and laser launch pads.

"So, what do they do at this ancient techno-pagan super-ceremony?" Christian asked.

"They pour gas on the neon man's feet and hands, and strike a match," Prayer Walker answered.

"What's that supposed to mean?" Christian responded.

"Nothing. It only means what it means to you."

"Why do they do it?"

"You want the official answer?"

"Sure."

"Because 'if they didn't burn it this year, they couldn't burn it again next year.'"

"Okay." Christian preferred the homecoming bonfires of his college days when the meaning was clear: "Beat the snot out of State U."

Out of flyers, they headed back to their café and were astonished at the transformation. Colonel Vision had welded together a giant rebar cross and erected it out front next to the street. Mercy Heart had picked through the trash pile down at the central playa and come up with enough neon bulbs to fashion a Man on the Cross, neon-loop head slightly bent, neon arms outstretched.

"Look at this," Colonel Vision said. He taped his Scroll to the bottom of the neon Man's feet and switched on the lightforce ray. The Man on the Cross blazed against the desert twilight.

Warbucks had again scavenged the Bartertown Lodge and come back with a couple of spotlights, icicle-style Christmas lights that Community Mom and Sonshine had hung around the room, and candles for every table, a couple of which were angel candles. Christian shut his mouth. *Deal with it.* Goodnews Man was just finishing his sound check with Aquila and Priscilla, who had learned to run the mixing board. Christian leaned against the wall, absorbing Goodnews Man's thoughtful lyrics and well-crafted tunes. The whole set had a funky excellence.

Everyone except Goodnews Man, Priscilla, and Aquila divided into two teams: the people people—Sonshine, Community Mom, Mercy Heart, and Christian—discussed with Colonel Vision how best to greet the guests, work the room, and build conversational bridges to the Kingdom Story. Then Colonel Vision and Hopeful withdrew to tend the coffee pots. Prayer Walker fairly bubbled at the prospect of walking the room all night, waitressing and praying.

"Well," Colonel Vision said when they were ready to open the doors, "we built it. Now let's see if they will come."

They swung the doors open and the entire tribe from Hades Gates dimmed the room with their black presence. Priests, priestesses, the stage crew, filling almost all the chairs.

"It's our 'dark night'—no shows," explained Diabolique, in her long, black velvet robe lined with scarlet.

"Well, we are so glad you decided to drop by," Community Mom said, squeezing her hand with real affection.

With a hint of surprise in her eyes, Diabolique peered down at the big-boned, fleshy arm resting on hers. She jerked her arm back with a snarl. "What's that supposed to be? The 'Jesus love-touch'?"

"Why do you hate Someone who loves you so much?" Community Mom asked.

"Because I want control. The power of the satanic is real." Her eyes narrowed and her lips curled.

"I know," Christian said, "but the one who gives it doesn't love you. You can't trust him."

Diabolique turned to see Goodnews Man setting up on the stage. "When is this bozo going to start?"

That night gave new meaning to the expression "rough crowd." Not about to be taken in by Goodnews Man's media presence or intimate songs, the Hades crowd generated their own gothic shock atmosphere, rife with crude humor and overly boisterous laughter. When Priscilla shared her story of how God used Faithful's death to heal her Vanity Fair depression, the crowd wept dramatically and blew their noses.

Christian lay in bed that night exhausted, wondering if Buyme or any of the other guests had heard anything over their disruptions. *You can try and love these people but you pay for it. Dearly.*

Back home at Hades Gates, the priestly band gathered around one of their fifty-five-gallon drums for a private ceremony. Chanting darkly, they sprinkled mystic powders that flashed green and blue in the roaring blaze. When they passed the chalice, the red liquid dripping from their mouths was heavier and darker than the vintage they used for prime time.

After a good, hard night, they all straggled off to the black tent behind the gargoyle stage. In the gray dawn Diabolique fetched a jug of water to extinguish the fire in the metal drum. The embers hissed and smoked in the cold shower. And kept hissing. The black head of a giant pit viper rose from the smoke and stared at her with icy blue eyes—eyes like a shark, unblinking, no slits. She breathed faster and backed up slowly, a smile playing on her lips. When she had reached a reverent distance, she knelt down and began chanting, arms outstretched. The serpent hung, suspended like a vision, until suddenly it exploded out of the drum and raced toward the priestess. Jet black, over six feet long, it bumped her lightly on the wrist and streaked out.

"I've been kissed," she murmured, still smiling.

She pulled her wrist to her face and saw two bleeding holes. Her smile opened into a shrieking cry and the muscles in her arms and legs began quivering uncontrollably.

CHAPTER 19

Back at the Lodge the next morning, Christian and Hopeful cranked out another flyer. "Come meet the only Man who can cure the 'wound that never heals.'"

They rendezvoused with the others at the Hall of Records, a walkway between ten-foot-tall monoliths covered with old vinyl singles and LPs. From there they spread out, covering the Camp in pairs. Christian and Mercy Heart had been posting and passing out flyers for about an hour when they approached a small gathering outside the Big Medicine Lodge. Agonizing screams of grown men and women and a deathly stench came from the Lodge. Mercy Heart hit the brakes.

"What's the matter?" she asked a redhead swathed in bandana scarves.

"Five people brought in with snake bite, screaming they're on fire. Not responding to anti-venom or the shamans. And they're delusional, talking about this snake that charges out from hiding, bites them, and races off."

"It's nonsense," said her partner, hiking up his flannel pajama bottoms. "I'm a science teacher. Everybody knows snakes don't like to waste their precious venom on anything but food victims. Even when they're threatened. They don't *jump* out of the bushes and attack people."

"Well," said Mercy Heart, "their screams seem real enough." Before Christian could stop her, she slipped through the group and into the Lodge. Annoyed, Christian watched her go. A rescue operation, like Gracie's, was one thing. He did hospitals as little as possible, clueless on how to sit with the suffering. His idea of mercy was to watch television together and provide what he hoped would be distracting and entertaining commentary. Of course, that was BC and this was now. *Still, this is so awkward.*

The stench reminded Christian of the reeking Pit in the Valley of the Shadow. He walked halfway up the street to quiet his stomach. Torn between leaving Mercy Heart and finishing the distribution of invitations in their section, he finally moved on, keeping an eye on the camp clutter and vehicles that lined the streets.

He was helping the team prep for the main event back at Café Hope when Buyme burst in the door, trembling. "Oh my gosh, oh my gosh . . . *oh my gosh!*" Community Mom rushed over and put her arms around her. "What's wrong, hon?"

"I just . . . I was in my tent cleaning . . . there was all this candle wax," her words tumbled out. "Suddenly," she said, pulling up her sheer leopard skirt and pointing to two red dots on her calf, "suddenly, this snake *shot* in out of nowhere and *bit* me. I felt this burning fire run up my leg and then out over my whole body. The muscles in my arms and legs started twitching and tingling, and I got so nauseated. My heart started racing—and it felt like this lead weight was crushing it. I thought, 'I'm going to die. Right here in this tent; right now.'"

She held out an open hand to Priscilla. "And all I could think about was your story. And how God saved you from yourself. So I started . . . I tried to make it over here." Priscilla took her hand and put another arm around her. "I was screaming, but that freaking heavy metal from Hades Gates . . . nobody could hear me. I fell down about halfway over. I couldn't walk any further . . . my arms, everything was starting to freeze up. And this fire just kept burning. I looked up at the Man on the Cross and I . . . I don't know what I said . . . something like, 'I know I'm so screwed up, but I know you can forgive me and you died for me' . . . something like that. And all of a sudden, the fire died out. And I could breathe, and my heart slowed down. I'm not . . . " she looked around at the incredulous faces, "I know! Isn't it incredible?"

"Welcome to the family!" Community Mom and Priscilla both hugged her. Everyone else did too. Christian was last.

"Thank you," she whispered, "for not using me. For inviting me here."

"You're welcome," he whispered back—a guy who had screeched to a stop with one wheel spinning over the ditch. He could feel Hopeful's eyes on him.

"Buyme," Warbucks said, "what happened . . . where did the snake go after he bit you?"

"He just zipped out of my tent. It was so bizarre! This long, black snake with weird blue eyes. Oh my gosh, I don't even want to take one step back outside."

The men grabbed their Scrolls and headed out. Christian reported to his fellows what he and Mercy Heart had heard at the Big Medicine Lodge earlier. Colonel Vision and Goodnews Man began a cautious search of the perimeter of Café Hope, while Christian and Hopeful hustled back to find Mercy Heart. About halfway there they came upon her, down on her knees in the street, retching her guts out. She was shaking uncontrollably. Christian scooped her up, and Hopeful pointed to the two red dots above her left ankle.

"Mercy Heart, I'm so sorry I left you," Christian murmured in her ear. She tried to focus on his face and shake her head. Christian could feel her becoming rigid. "As soon as we get back, you look at the Man on the Cross. Somehow God used it to heal Buyme's snakebite. Do you understand?"

She tried to respond, but couldn't speak.

"You look at the Man on the Cross. Look at him, asking, believing. Blink if you understand."

Mercy Heart blinked.

They rounded the corner onto their street. When they got to the Man on the Cross, Christian pulled up at an angle so Mercy Heart could see him. Slowly she began to relax in his arms. Her breathing slowed. Goodnews Man and Colonel Vision rushed over.

"I feel terrible," Christian said. "I left her at the Medicine Lodge and, on the way home, that snake must have bitten her."

Mercy Heart reached up and took his face in her hands. "I shouldn't have run off like that without talking to you." Her voice was amazingly clear. Christian slowly lowered her down and Colonel Vision moved to pick her up. She waved him off. "Wow! I feel almost okay."

Christian and Hopeful looked at each other and at the Man on the Cross. But Mercy Heart gave them no time to meditate on the miracle. "You guys need to go tell the others back at the Medicine Lodge. They brought in three more after you left."

They ran all the way back to the Lodge, Scrolls in hand, eyes combing the roadside. Bypassing the little crowd, they told their story to a security guy in camo and cowboy hat standing by the door. Quickly, he showed them to the doctor and head shaman, to whom they told the story again. The doctor and shaman began a heated discussion. *Okay, Lord, here we go. The battle is shaping up again and here we are in the thick of it.*

The doctor walked back and told Christian to tell their story to the eight victims and their family and friends, so they could decide for themselves how they wanted to respond. The shaman hung back, glaring at them.

"My name is Christian." He looked at the convulsing victims and their stunned friends and families. "And, in a very real sense, I was snake bit—dying in the clutches of the Enemy. But the Creator God and King loves me, and his only Son, Jesus, gave up his life on a cross to ransom me. Paid the sin price for all my selfish desires for control."

At the mention of "Jesus," the shaman's hostility spilled over. The priests and priestesses attending Diabolique erupted, "Shut your freaking Jesus talk up."

"With just a look of faith at the cross and what Jesus did there," Christian continued, "enough faith to ask for it, I was given the King's gift of Life. And somehow, God has used the Man on the Cross we erected at our lodge to give healing from this deadly snake's bite to two women that looked to it for Life and healing. If you would like to bring your friends and loved ones, if they wish to seek Life and healing in Jesus Christ, then we welcome you to our lodge. We will do all we can to help you."

The head priest's eyes were about to pop out of their sockets. Christian and Hopeful were escorted outside while the victims and their families and friends decided how they wanted to respond.

"Please, Father," Hopeful said, "draw these lost, hurting people to yourself."

Christian shook his head, breathing rapidly, "Please . . . "

Three wanted to come. Not surprisingly, Diabolique was not one of them. The Hades Gates priests followed those electing to go outside, hammering them with ridicule and huge lies about the questors. Spying the opportunity, Christian slipped back in and neared the priestess's bedside. "Diabolique," he whispered, "can you hear me? Blink if you can hear me."

Gazing at nothing, eyes dilated, the priestess blinked.

"Blink if you agree. What's the reality here? Do you see you are not in control?"

She blinked.

"Do you see that you don't control this power? That it controls you?"

Again Diabolique blinked.

"Buyme and Mercy Heart, they were both dying like you. Now they're back at the lodge helping fix dinner. Your master's power is real. It can hurt us. It can kill us. But it can't condemn or destroy us. Because God's power is stronger. He took the guilt of our sin and nailed it to the cross. But your master is about to sting you *again* with death, and if you hang on to your unforgiven sin and go down with it, this will only be the beginning of a horrific misery that will never end. Do you still want to hold on to him?"

She blinked.

"Even if it destroys you?"

She blinked once more and stared into the nothing. Her hair and clothes were sopping wet, her labored breathing becoming shallower and shallower. Christian's eyes swept the circle of clenched faces around him—the same as the thumbs-down expressions of the Power Table, as possessive of their hatred as the angry voices crying out from the Pit in the Valley of Shadow.

It was going to be a sellout, blowout crowd. All day a steady stream of curious Nomads drifted by the Man on the Cross. Many tried to light candles and lay flowers, but Priscilla and Aquila politely turned them away, explaining that there was no special power in the symbol, only God who was at work through it. In anticipation of a larger crowd, the questors worked through the evening rolling up the walls to their lodge and scrubbing the additional chairs that Warbucks had miraculously scrounged up. Two Hades Gates priests showed up out front with signs that read, "The show's a fake, it's really their snake." and "Stop kneeling: fake healing."

As eight o'clock approached, Christian surveyed the scene: The chairs under the tent roof were almost filled, but the extra chairs and standing room outside their rolled-up walls remained empty. The crowd glanced occasionally at Colonel Vision, Hopeful, and Warbucks as they patrolled the perimeter with their Scrolls, but for the most part chatted away, making snake jokes around the flickering candles. When Goodnews Man began weaving his story around his poignant songs and haunting melodies, the room quieted. Then Buyme's story really seemed to connect. A hint of awe played across the crowd's faces. With the notes of Goodnews Man's last song hanging in the air, the crowd hushed as Christian prepared to take the mike.

But before he could fully rise from his table, a delicate young woman with long blond hair preempted him, closing in on the stage, obviously intent on saying something. Colonel Vision's eyes were on him, full of questions. Christian finally sat back down, unsure of what to do. From the back he could tell she was dressed in the King's khaki and she limped noticeably as she took the stairs to the stage.

"I too have been healed by the King's power," she began, opening a small notebook and finding her place. "I was stranded in a lonely place, broken, all my dreams in pieces. All I had was the Story of Jesus of Nazareth. But it was all I needed." She began reading a poem.

imagine a compassion
beyond any calculation.

imagine a purity
beyond any corruption.

imagine a cup
that never runs dry.

imagine how whole
it could be
if we stopped trying
to gain or grab or garb
these selves that only shiver
in dark slivers.

we say, "no, really, who
turned out the light?
a night without end
chills a heart to stone
& stumbling."

we thought these lives
were our own.

it seems we were mistaken.

bring what is broken
to the hands that first formed it.

In the silence that followed, the speaker closed her notebook and lifted her gaze to Christian. First a spark, then a glimmer, then her face broke into a dazzling, glorious smile as she wiped a tear with her finger. In the back, Hopeful brushed his cheeks. Christian slowly mounted the stage and folded her into his arms. "Gracie," he whispered, "oh, Gracie, you made it."

Christian sat up on his bedroll. He never did well with four hours of sleep. But the snake was "wasting a lot of its venom," randomly attacking people, and the questors had taken turns during the night tending to four more victims. Every victim that had been bitten yesterday who had not come to the Man on the Cross had died within twenty-four hours, including Diabolique. The drums down at Hades Gates beat all night.

A handful were packing and getting out of Dodge, but for most Nomads of the Heart, tonight's bonfire Ceremony was the most transcendent thing in their lives. Christian had talked to one fellow at length last night, a guy with a button that read, "Thank God I'm an Atheist." He claimed he had been to the mountains beyond, searched for twenty years. Like Dorothy in Oz he had pulled back every curtain he could find, but there was no one there. "All that is left is a few moments like these," he said. "I work and save eleven months a year so I can come here. For eleven months I rot in front of a screen—computer screen, TV screen. An embarrassing blob in a big, gold recliner to the screwed-up progeny I sired to succeed me. These people, this Ceremony, this is what gets me through. It's the only life I know. I will leave *after* the Ceremony. Period."

"But Celestial City is real. I have seen it," Christian said.

Atheist just laughed. "You dreamed it. There's no such place in all this world."

"But there is in the world to come," he said. And even as he said it, he realized again how the tectonic plates of his life had shifted. The best part of Life was out there, waiting for him, not here.

Community Mom walked over with a hug, a muffin, and a mug of coffee. It was a gift to be under the watch of such a champion caregiver. She was the glue that held the whole enterprise together. Christian smiled and blew her a noisy kiss as she headed back to the coffee bar. Over the rim of his steaming mug, Christian watched Gracie, Buyme, and about ten other rookies lounging around down in front. Seated on the stage, Priscilla, team teaching with Aquila, launched them into Theology 101, although, with the easy flow of discussion and questions, their "students" were not wise to it. Minus all the "-ology" words Faithful enjoyed so much, Priscilla was beginning at the same place—the glory of God. How we were made to "see it, savor it, and show it." *You go, Priscilla.*

He rose and walked to the door and stood there, sipping his

coffee, beaming at God. If anyone could have sneaked him a picture of this when he was lying in Doubting Castle Glen, he would have written it off as another monstrous attempt by the Enemy to mock him and grind him into the dust.

Hopeful walked over and clapped him on the back. "Enough grace for two days?"

Christian executed a nice save that kept his coffee from spilling. He wanted to ask his friend if he had been surprised at the turnout last night, but decided against it. "More than enough. Let's go for one more."

They prayed and by the time they had finished, Colonel Vision and Warbucks had joined them.

"I have an idea," Warbucks said, holding out a button that read, "Skydancing Tantra: Discover who is draining your energy." "I was over at the Wear It Lodge yesterday. They can make buttons or ribbons that say *anything*.

"Obviously," said Hopeful, taking the button.

"I wondered if, today, we should scratch the flyers. Everybody knows us now. Why don't we just send everybody out with some big buttons like this?"

"Like *this?*" Christian took the Skydancing button.

Warbucks was learning to ignore his offbeat humor. "You guys come up with something that fits us and I'll go get the buttons made."

After lunch everybody met at the Hall of Records and pinned on their new buttons: "Café Hope: Got some? 7-8 tonight!" The plan was to finish early, before the Ceremony started. Each veteran partnered with a rookie. Christian tapped Gracie and they headed to their section.

"Hey, last night I was so busy catching up on what happened to you I forgot to tell you how *much* I enjoyed your poem. You must have been writing a long time."

"Thank you." She blushed slightly. "It's been a long time since I shared my work. I filled dozens of notebooks when I was younger—then lost my momentum in college."

"Why?"

"I wanted to write words of Truth. But I gave up thinking it even existed. If everybody was going to read my work and say, 'I don't care what you meant when you wrote it, *this* is what it means to me,' why write? Just conversing with myself wasn't appealing.

"Then after watching the spectacle they made of you in Vanity Fair," she shook her head, "I swore off TV. Writing was my therapy. I think I sort of wrote my way into the Kingdom."

"Share something else you've written. Something you know by heart."

She thought a moment as they walked, then began:

the kingdom of God
can reign within, but in most
it is buried devastatingly deep
like a forgotten poem,
like a forgotten soul
in the night soil
begging to be unearthed . . .

She stopped. "Are you going to keep walking two steps in front of me? I mean, should I get a veil and a palm frond to wave over your head?"

"Gracie, I'm so sorry! There's some automatic walking meter deep in my head that says, 'Okay, if I just walk faster, she'll catch up.' I'm sorry."

"I'm getting used to it," she said. "But it's a double loss. I used to be pretty sweet eye candy. Now . . . " she said, keeping her eyes down on the dusty playa, "when I catch sight of myself in a mirror, walking . . . I see this crippled thing limping by, so unfeminine, so undesirable. And on top of that, it takes so long to do anything, get anywhere . . . oh, and did I tell you my new name? 'Graceful.' That's what the Shining Ones said when they gave me my Scroll. I didn't know whether to laugh or . . . "

"Stop!" Christian lifted her head with his hand and looked into her eyes. "When I look at you, I don't even see the limp."

"No, you just walk off and leave me," she said, turning her face away.

He gently turned her head back. "When I look at you I see a gorgeous, desirable young woman that I'm going to have to watch myself with. Someone whose inner beauty now outshines anything she was before."

They walked on in silence for a while.

"You didn't look like you were 'begging to be unearthed,'" he said.

"What?"

"The last time I saw you in the hospital. You didn't look the way you described yourself in your poem—like you were 'begging to be unearthed.'"

"But I was," she said. "Thank you for digging me out."

They reached their sector and tried to connect with the creative chaos that lined both sides of every street. All of the Reincarnational Vedic Astrologists at the La La Lodge wanted to hear about the healings at length. But this was not a generation "looking for a sign." Most of these Nomads of the Heart had heard about the snake, heard about the healings. It didn't matter. It was one more thing among the many unusual things they had come to see and experience. Like "Thank God I'm an Atheist," they had staked out their own "temporary autonomous zones," and nothing, not snakes or Jesus, would distract them from the soul-soothing tonic of their final few liberated moments.

"You seem pretty disappointed," Gracie said as they headed back to the café.

"I'm just blown away by the height of cynicism and depth of self-absorption. I mean, this is high drama, a demon snake on the loose, people dying in fiery agony, miracles happening before people's eyes—I expected revival. But all the buzz is about the Ceremony. We're not even a blip on the radar."

When they stopped talking for a moment to take stock of where they were, they saw billows of black smoke roiling up from what looked like their neighborhood. The closer they got, the more Christian fought to remain at Gracie's side and not rush ahead. Every time they turned a corner, they hoped they would see that the smoke was off target, wide of their destination. But as the flames grew bigger and closer, it was obvious the fire was on their street. With no fire trucks here in the desert, a crowd had gathered to watch whatever it was burn to the ground. Was it Buyme's red tent? The priests at Hades Gates smirked at them and made unsacred hand-signals as they passed.

Café Hope was burning. Like an oversized covered wagon after an Indian raid, the tent fabric had been incinerated and the exposed arched metal ribs were sagging and melting in the intense heat. What had been a stage, a coffee bar, furniture, PA equipment, all their bedrolls and backpacks, was now a mass of glowing embers and ash amid the flames. The Man on the Cross had been torn apart and stuffed back into the ground head first, all the neon tubes smashed and broken.

One of the questors was down, surrounded by Colonel Vision, Warbucks, Mercy Heart, and the doctor from the Big Medicine Lodge. Another knot of khaki hovered nearby, sobbing, praying, holding one another. Gracie joined them. Christian walked to where the victim, Community Mom, lay. Colonel Vision and Warbucks looked up with faces baptized by the grief and shock of the battle.

"You know she stayed behind to get things ready for tonight and help any victims that came by," Hopeful said softly. "Evidently, it was our neighbors from Hades Gates. They beat her up pretty good."

The doctor rose as Christian approached. "I'm concerned that her forearm may be fractured where she held it up to shield herself from the blows. There's no way to tell without an X-ray machine, which we don't have here."

He left in the company of Hopeful and Warbucks, who went along to retrieve some painkillers and other meds.

"Hey, lady," Christian knelt down beside Community Mom, "welcome to the martyr's club." He looked down into her bruised face and swollen right eye.

She smiled and then winced. "That was a whopping initiation fee."

"Yeah," he stroked her hair, "but the monthly dues haven't been as bad. So far."

Christian turned around to the crowd of two hundred or more who had gathered in the lane. It would not be long before the

Ceremony would start. Head down, he combed his hair with his fingers and walked slowly over to stand beside the Cross.

"We invited you to Café Hope tonight," he said to the crowd. "I'm sorry it's gone. If ever there was a place that needed hope, surely this is it. I have never seen so many people so burned out, so bored, ignoring and fearing the void beyond their last breath.

"You see us struggling. You see us engaged in a battle. We're not looking for violins here." He carefully grabbed the Cross, avoiding the shards. "Sometimes it's miracles. Sometimes it's blood and ashes. But it's Life to the full, every moment charged with meaning and purpose. And this isn't even the best part.

"The best part about Life in God's grand Kingdom Story is the end. 'What will you do in the end?' Truth wins in the end.

"In the end, God tells us we will live with him. We'll be face to face with the King of the Universe, who knows our names and invites each of us to dinner. His presence will dazzle more than any king of sports or music or nations. Yet he'll be more cherished company than our most inspiring author or dearest friend. In the neighborhood he has developed, the custom home he has designed for each of us will put the most luxurious designer showcase houses to shame.

"The government will be great. The Creator God and King will be on the throne. No more partisan positioning for advantage. No more political spin in the courts of the King. Every wrong will be righted. Every injustice corrected and compensated. And we will reign with him."

Christian glanced at the questors and caught their rallying smiles. Colonel Vision gave him a thumbs-up. Gracie and Prayer Walker pumped their fists.

"And if there is news, it will be the Truth. Things that are really important will be headlines. Things that are trivial will not be hyped for ratings. We will learn what went on in the Kingdom today that really matters for eternity and displays the majesty and Technicolor grace of God.

"And if there are schools, they will teach the Truth and the lessons will be fascinating and the laboratories may be in far-off galaxies. We may peer through some huge window on history and discover the Truth about God's work in the defeat of tyrants and the victories of his people.

"In everyday life we will live in accordance with our true natures—in complete love and justice with one another. Those old strongholds that we have fought to overcome all our lives will be torn down. Those of us who have diseases will be healed." He looked over at Gracie. "What is broken will be fixed. No more tears. No more pain. And those friends and loved ones who have gone on before us will fold us in their arms once again. And 'there is so much more!'"

He paused, still looking at the questors, unaware of the Hades Gates priests pressing forward through the crowd.

"So many of your lives are like worn, scratched CDs. You are so weary of playing the same old tunes over and over and over again. Your hearts are so achingly empty and bloated at the same time, staggering under the oppression of excess. But God has plans for you—'plans to give you a future and a . . . '"

Baring the curved blades of their sacrificial knives, two Hades priests jumped Christian, holding their knives to his throat. "Shut up and march," they screamed. Five more of their knife-wielding brethren lined up, separating Christian from the rest of the questors. In less than a minute they had Christian around the corner and out of the questors' line of sight. After another minute, the remaining priests backed off their positions and ran in the other direction.

From somewhere out on the perimeter the drums grew louder and louder. The day's carnival pulse slowed to a solemn cadence. Advancing torchlight reflected off the RVs, tents, and rows of skeleton buildings. A final turn, and the drums and torches swung into view. An expectant hush fell over the bright young pagans gathered in the center of the Camp. The sacerdotal corps of shamans, Chateclysm monks, Vedic astrologers, Hades Gates priests with their Wound that Never Heals cousins, and all their Tantric and guru brethren circled the bonfire three times and pulled up, drums still pounding. Three dark-robed Hades Gates priests dragged a noncompliant Christian down the roped-off corridor to the base of the neon man and up the steps. Standing him between the three-story man's legs, they poured gasoline over his head, drenching his body. The torch-bearing shamans climbed the steps and set fire to the neon man's lowered hands and feet.

A chorus of screams interrupted the rite. The shamans and priests looked down the corridor to see the black viper racing toward them. The crowd froze except for the torch bearers and Christian's handlers, who fled, leaving him to face the snake that whipped up the steps and coiled around, crushing him in its python grip. The serpent reared its head back, eye-level with Christian, who stared into the serpent's blue gaping eyes.

The snake struck Christian on the neck. Almost too quickly to see and very lightly. It felt more like a nudge, a lick. He did not even feel the fangs sink into his skin. Just as he was wondering if he had really been bitten, a fire blazed through his veins. It was as if someone had poured the gasoline *inside* his body and struck a match. The snake reared its head back once more, gazing at him briefly, then uncoiled and slithered over to the neon man, where it wound up his leg, unscathed by the flames.

Within seconds Christian's muscles began to quiver and he had trouble focusing his eyes and his thoughts. *Dear Jesus, is this it? I escaped Vanity Fair to make it . . . here? Please deliver Gracie and Hopeful and the others by your power. I know you can deliver them . . . and me . . . and if not . . .*

The thousands of silent faces reflecting the neon and fire began to dim and he swayed and staggered slightly. He tried to stay away from the flaming foot of the neon man fifteen feet away. But then, what difference would it make if he burned from the inside out or the outside in? He tried to keep standing.

As he looked up he saw a light piercing the darkness. Not high in the heavens, but low on the horizon, just over the heads of the crowd. One moment there was blackness, the next there was a cross, caught in a circle of light—a circle made up, he guessed instantly, of dozens of Scroll rays. *Oh, God, please, help me hang on.*

Immediately the fire in his veins died down. His heart began to slow and the vise that had been gripping it loosed. His limbs began to tingle as the control returned and his breathing became normal.

He extended his arms, raising his hands, and when he thought his voice would be strong enough, addressed the rapt crowd: "Nomads, please listen! In ancient times, God delivered his people from fiery serpents. He loved them and had mercy on their cry for forgiveness. So their leader, Moses, lifted up the snake in the desert, and anyone who looked on it was saved. In the same way God loves you and lifted up his Son on a cross like the one on the horizon." He pointed at the questors' shattered cross that their company had reestablished on the ridge overlooking the Camp. "He gave his one and only Son. And this is why: whoever believes in him shall not perish but have eternal life—a life of hope! Just for a look, just for the asking . . . "

The crowd erupted into a giant cheer. Christian stopped, stunned, his heart rising. Out of the corner of his eye he could see something moving. He turned around to see the hands of the neon man being slowly raised into the night sky. Festive Nomads began to float, whooping and chanting, as the fire consumed the neon man behind him. The drum corps recovered and resumed its familiar frenzy.

Christian lowered his arms and surveyed the weightless worship. A few maintained their silence, floating prostrate or mournfully on their knees. But most of the celebrants reacted as if to a touchdown at the Super Bowl. And Christian felt like he might as well have been wearing a rainbow wig and be waving a John 3:16 sign between the goalposts.

Descending the steps, Christian made his way back up the corridor toward the cross. Its beauty hurt. Behind him the flames consumed the neon man with the large, dark serpent looped around its neon shoulders, hollow eyes reflecting the thousands of adoring faces.

Chapter 20

Halfway between the ridge and the giant bonfire, the questors met up with Christian and mobbed him. Now everybody smelled like gasoline, but nobody cared. After they greeted him, they put their arms around the handful of Nomads that had followed him out of the Ceremony.

Christian slung an arm around Hopeful's shoulders. "They tell me erecting the cross there was your idea. That's *three* times now."

"You must have black-and-white circles painted on the top of your head." Hopeful's Cheshire grin shone in the darkness of the empty Camp street. "Actually it was Colonel Vision's idea to pick through the embers for the Scrolls: 'If they're supposed to last forever, what's a little fire . . . ' And he was right, thank God, because we didn't have time to build a fire or find another way to light that cross so you could see it. When we were hauling it up the rise and looked back and saw the snake, things got a little frantic."

"Again, thanks." Christian squeezed his shoulders.

Since the Nomads were fairly well distracted, the questors circled the perimeter of the Camp without incident and headed out along the Way. Worried that the Hades Gates clan might look for them, they kept up their pace until, a couple of hours later, they arrived at a hot springs surrounded by warm, flat rocks. They decided to rest for the remainder of the night.

Christian lay back in the hot-springs pool, letting the gasoline soak out. Perched on a rock beside the pool, Gracie's moonlit hair spilled around her shoulders. The exhaustion of his ordeal and their two-hour forced march ebbed away. But a night of sleeping on the rocks with no bedroll loomed.

"I feel like we steamed past a shipwreck in the middle of the ocean and threw down the lifeboats, but no one was saved."

"But people *were* saved. Buyme, a couple dozen others. Chris, *you* were saved. Did you have visions of being Moses and leading thousands of people across the desert to the Promised Land?"

"No, I could never be Moses."

"Why not?"

"I'm too good in front of a microphone."

She splashed him with her foot. "Seriously, is it about the numbers?"

He laid back again in the warm water, closing his eyes. *Is it?* He felt broken over Diabolique's present torment, her decision to side with her eternal murderer. He saw again the thousands of empty faces lit by the bonfire. But what else was going on? Disappointed expectations of revival? Had he treasured the secret hope of leaving Pharoah's army drowning in its indulgence and sweeping out with a great mass of people to meet God at the mountain?

"If it's about the numbers," she said, "that is *so* Vanity Fair. More, bigger, better. 'We must have results! Seeable, countable, bankable results!' Look at me. I'm a result. You *almost* didn't see me. What more could you ask from the body of Christ? Every moment I was there was beautiful. Hearts united, each gift shining."

"I always liked Gideon's story. Three hundred men and Gideon defeated what appeared to be an indestructible opponent."

"Maybe you don't have any more battles to fight."

Her words rippled through the dark. He pushed off the shallow bottom and turned around, following her gaze upward to the brightness glimmering from the highest peak.

Thank heavens for the Shepherd's stands. These oases provided the questors with comfort and nourishment as they traveled—smoked turkey legs, sausage on a stick, trail mix, bowls brimming with berries, served with life-giving smiles and words of encouragement ("Can you see the City?" "Keep looking up!"). Not to mention tent space and bedrolls. Each day Christian felt stronger, the mountains got closer, and the shining grew brighter. Everyone took turns helping Gracie and Community Mom keep up.

Gradually the dust and rocks gave way to rolling hills, and then bigger hills that merged into mountains. The nip of fall was in the air. At the end of an uphill day, they crested a ridge to find a gorgeous mountain chalet resort. Beulah Landing featured a stone fireplace where they spent the evening drinking hot chocolate. Through the plate-glass windows they could see the gleaming City at the far end of a gentle valley.

Their nearness to the City was confirmed the next day when they saw Shining Ones in transit up and down the valley. The Way passed through gardened landscapes on every side—fleur-de-lis sculpted hedges and towering fountains; romantic country rose gardens with gurgling bird baths, orchards, and vineyards—all manicured to perfection by the King's gardeners. The questors snacked on the orchards' vine-ripened peaches and grapes. At midday they had to don the sunglasses, which the Landing had provided, because the reflection of the sun upon the City up ahead was so dazzling.

Christian and Gracie, trailing the others, were closing in on a lunchtime Shepherd's stand when Sonshine and Mercy Heart came bursting back toward them. "You're not going to believe this! This is almost the end of the road!" Sonshine said.

"You're kidding!" Gracie said as she took her arm from around Christian's shoulder.

"No! It's twenty-six miles from here to the top!" Mercy Heart said, her enthusiasm bubbling over.

"Twenty-six miles!" Christian said, "I used to run that in four, four and a half hours!"

"Me too!" Mercy Heart said. "Even this out of shape, I'm sure I could do it in less than six—well, maybe more, since the valley slopes uphill so much."

They all looked at Gracie's face and stopped.

"Oh, Gracie," Mercy Heart said, "that was strictly hypothetical."

Head down, Gracie limped past them toward the stand.

Mercy Heart immediately caught up with her. "Gracie, we wouldn't think of running off and leaving you. It's just that twenty-six miles, well, that's a marathon. And to those of us who run marathons, we automatically think . . . "

"Don't worry about it," Gracie said, her voice sounding small and tired.

"How about a protein smoothie?" asked the stand's Shepherd attendant. "Gives you an extra boost for the final run. We have Miracle Mocha and Celestial Slush."

Gracie took her smoothie and followed Community Mom to a bench overlooking a rushing stream. Christian was finishing his when they walked back over to the group.

"Community Mom and I have been talking things over," she said, loudly enough to get everyone's attention, "and we have something we want to tell you." The two disabled questors smiled at the circle of hushed faces. "We've been thinking. We don't want to hold you back. We want you to go on and not wait on us."

Community Mom put her good arm around Gracie. "This is it! The race to the finish! We all want to get there as fast as we can. So no more carrying—or dragging!—us along. It's time to 'strip down, start running, and never quit'!"

"I think that's exactly the way it should be," echoed Gracie. "I think we should line up here at the Shepherd's stand, somebody say, 'Go!' And everybody just go for it!"

Gracie surveyed the quiet circle. They weren't buying.

"Look, I've traveled alone before," she said, "and I was never alone. Sometimes I even saw him out of the corner of my eye. This tall, strong figure walking right beside me. It's really okay." Her voice caught. "Only a few more hours in this tattered tent. Then I won't limp anymore. My injuries were the gift that brought me to the cross, made me who I am. But in just a few hours," her voice trailed to a whisper, "I get to give it back. So just go on now—all of you."

The rookies were the first to break the silence, responding with misty good-byes and hugs of encouragement. It was harder for the veterans. After several teary farewells, Community Mom broke it off. "Good grief, we'll be together for eternity. And I want you all to come over to my house tomorrow, so it's okay if we miss dinner together tonight!"

Everybody laughed and the cloud of indecision lifted.

"Hey." The Shepherd pulled out a starting pistol. "We do this for groups all the time. Just tell me when you're ready."

The sight of the pistol changed everything. The questors lined up even with the "Celestial City—26 miles" sign. Some jogged in place with their eyes closed; some squatted, stretching their hamstrings; others stared straight ahead, shaking out the muscles in their arms and legs. Their faces set with determination, Gracie and Community Mom joined them.

"Ready," the Shepherd said, pointing the starting pistol in the air. "Set." They all stared straight up the valley, eyes on the finish. "Go!" The Shepherd fired the pistol. All the rookies and a few of the veterans took off at a good clip.

Christian smiled, watching them go. *In ten miles they'll be dying at that rate.* He remembered his first few marathons. He was so excited and pumped at the beginning of the race that he ran much faster than his training runs. *Big mistake.* Community Mom held her bad arm with her good arm and managed a slow jog. Only slightly in front of her, Warbucks and Colonel Vision jogged just as slowly, falling rapidly behind the others. Gracie set off at a brisk limp.

Suddenly, black hands encircled her waist, lifting her cheerleader style, swinging her around and settling her piggyback on Christian's back.

"What are you doing!" she protested.

"Love never gives up," Hopeful rapped.

"Keeps going to the END." Christian sort of rapped back, tacking on a few vocal punctuation marks. "Gracie, if you think I'd rather get there faster than get there with you and Hopeful . . . you don't really get me. I love running the race with my eyes on the prize. And I love it even more in the present company."

Gracie let him jog along in silence. Unable to see her face, he wasn't sure how this was playing. After about a minute she squeezed his neck.

Every half-mile or so, Christian and Hopeful switched off carrying Gracie. Occasionally she took a break from the piggyback jolting, trying her best to keep up a limping jog with her arm around Hopeful's or Christian's neck.

Parks, fountains, orchards, gardens—the scenery continued to be a constant distraction from their discomforting efforts. They jogged past a huge fountain in the shape of a pipe organ, water cascading from "keyboard" to "keyboard," as majestic organ music floated through the air. Even with so much pleasant distraction, Christian's pains became harder to ignore. He found himself changing his rhythm to alleviate the pain in his hip, only to have his knee start complaining. Even during the stretches when he was not carrying Gracie, the run was no longer comfortable. The sweat was dripping off Hopeful's face too.

Every mile a sign marked how many miles remained to Celestial City and a sort of mini-Shepherd's stand provided water bottles, energy bars, and an opportunity to slow down and walk as they drank. But after they slowed down, it was harder to start jogging again. At the thirteen-mile stand, they paused a moment to "clink" their water bottles and bend over in a little huddle, hands on their knees.

"Halfway there. Should we stop?" panted Christian. "The City will still be there tomorrow. We don't have to make it tonight." He and Hopeful both looked at Gracie.

"You are the ones beating your bodies, not me," she said.

"Yes, but you're in pain too. I can see it in your face." Christian opened up his mouth for another long squirt from his water bottle.

Gracie dropped her head for a few moments and looked back up. "Why hold back? I'm game to go until one of us just can't make it any farther. We're not going to wake up sore tomorrow," she said with a tired grin. "Not going to wind up back in the orthopedics office."

"When I think of everything waiting for us just thirteen miles away," Hopeful said. "I can't stop now."

"Okay," said Christian, "ready, break on three. One, two . . . "

"Three!" They clapped together and Christian hiked Gracie back up on his back.

But it was torture. Their walking spans after each mini-stand lengthened, especially on the uphill stretches. The glorious sights and sounds of their surroundings hardly registered. With one exception: as they topped a hill at about mile six, they caught sight of Community Mom leaning on Colonel Vision, with Warbucks beside. They were about to crest the next hill. Christian pointed to them and squeezed Gracie's arm.

He almost hated to see the three-mile sign come up. In his experience it was synonymous with "the wall," the boundary of stamina and strength almost as solid as bricks and mortar. He stood at the mini-stand, feeling shaky, too tired even to grab a bottle of water. He honestly didn't think he could finish. Bending over, he stared at his legs, which looked far more solid than they felt. He knew finishing would require every bit of his determination.

He stared at a lush patch of blue-green grass next to a tree by the Shepherd's stand. He could easily go to sleep right there. Just lay his body down and finish after a rest. The glory of the City brightened the twilight, but his body knew it was quitting time. He finally recovered enough to stand up and grab a bottle of water. *If I tell them I'm finished, they'll stop. Then again, maybe they're ready to stop, but they'll keep on going if I don't bring it up.*

He took the earphones and his Scroll out of his pocket, searched the menu, and put his headset on.

"Ready?" he looked at Hopeful and Gracie.

Without exchanging a word, they nodded.

As they launched up the slope, Christian turned the volume way up. "Strip down, start running—and never quit! Keep your eyes on Jesus, who both began and finished this race we're in. Study how he did it. Because he never lost sight of where he was headed—that exhilarating finish in and with God—he could put up with anything along the way. And now he's there, in the place of honor, right alongside God. When you find yourself flagging, go over his Story again. That will shoot adrenaline into your souls!

"You've all been to the stadium and seen the athletes race. Run to win. All good athletes train hard. They do it for a gold medal that tarnishes and fades. You're after one that's gold eternally. I don't know about you, but I'm running hard for the finish line. I'm giving everything I've got!"

Okay, Lord, it feels like I have nothing left to give. So you've got to do it. You've got to lift this leg, and then that leg, and then this one, and then that one. You've got to keep my freshly cracked ribs from knifing into my side too much so I can keep breathing. You've got to take over my mind and keep me focused on the finish line.

At the top of each hill the City's jasper walls came into sharper focus, shining like diamonds into the starry sky, softening its darkness so that the night seemed to retain twilight's memory.

"Only three more hills!" Hopeful said, shooting a thumbs-up.

"Yeah, three more!" Christian managed a half-grin. He looked up at Gracie over Hopeful's shoulder. "Are you miserable?"

"Yes! But I'm counting it down, hill by hill!"

Three hills to go. And then two. Christian promised himself that if he made it up this hill carrying Gracie, he wouldn't have to do it again. He would help her walk up the last hill, if she could. Even after a downhill rest, he knew his ribs couldn't take it anymore. Feeling as if he were about to collapse, he prepared to lower her down just short of the top of the hill. Then Hopeful, already at the crest, let out a tired but distinct whoop. Christian carried Gracie the few remaining steps, after all, powered by the little shot of adrenaline he got from Hopeful's cry.

Towering above the far side of the valley on magnificent multi-jeweled foundations, Celestial City rose into the light-suffused sky. Directly across from them a giant, pearl gate marked the entrance. The diamond-like walls and the gate glowed with the reflected *shekinah* glory of God, as translucent as the amethysts, sapphires, emeralds, and other precious gems in the jeweled foundations.

But Hopeful's whoop was no doubt inspired by the valley below as much as the City above. For nestled there was a huge stadium filled to capacity with a great cloud of witnesses. A short downhill run would take them into a tunnel and out to the finish line.

Buoyed by the adrenaline rush, Christian beamed at Gracie, "Do you want to climb back on and finish the race?"

"Why don't you and Hopeful both put your arms around me and help me finish in a style more becoming . . . "

"More becoming of children of the great King whom we are going to see in person in less than *ten minutes!*" Christian grabbed Gracie and kissed her joyfully on the mouth. Then he embraced Hopeful, who gave him a hard hug back. It was truly the immense joy set before him that got him down that hill. Even though Gracie leaned on his "good side," his ribs were screaming; but he could hardly feel them with the cheers of the crowd floating out of the stadium.

As they entered the long dark tunnel, the deja vu sensation of his tunnel experience in Evangelist's pictures swept over him. But the memories only made it sweeter: memories of the yawning fears that had swallowed him when he walked the tunnel were consumed by the fiery joy that shot through his exhausted body. He knew who was waiting for him; knew him, loved him, and couldn't wait to see him.

As they emerged from the tunnel and turned into the homestretch, he *could* see him. Although the stands on their right grew wild with celebration, the sound seemed somehow distant. Christian could only see *that face* as it came closer and closer, his smile that warmed it mirrored in his own. He had this sudden urge to just run. Run as hard as he still could and throw himself at the feet of this magnificent Person who watched them jog-walk the last few yards. He looked over at Gracie and Hopeful once more and saw streams of tears flowing down Gracie's cheeks.

Leaning forward as one, the three questors broke through the silver cord across the finish and came to a stop before the King of kings and Lord of lords. Smiling at Christian and Hopeful, he went to Gracie first, hugged her, and with his scarred hand, wiped the tears from her cheeks. He whispered something in her ear that made her face light up like a fireworks finale, then greeted Hopeful.

Even as he watched the King greet his friends, they changed in front of his eyes. Gracie straightened up and put her weight firmly on both feet. The pain in her eyes melted away. Her beauty dazzled, her movement became free and easy. As he caught snatches of Hopeful talking with the King, Christian recognized the familiar voice, of course, yet the counselor sounded even better—his voice richer and smoother than before. His friends shone with as much splendor as the angels, but with an even greater sense of weight and moral authority, their mercy and strength clearly visible in their faces.

Christian took a deep breath and exhaled. No more pain in his ribs or anywhere else. He felt like he could run another marathon; but right then the King turned and walked over to him.

Christian still felt like throwing himself down before him, but knew somehow that wasn't what the King wanted. What he wanted was to put his arm around his shoulder, give him a squeeze, and turn him toward the infield. The King lifted his free hand, sweeping the entire stadium of waving, cheering veterans, and spoke softly in Christian's ear, "Welcome to Life! And . . . there is *so* much more!" Like a father standing beside his son who has won Olympic gold, the King's face radiated with approval and pride. "Are you ready for a victory lap?"

Christian shrank back, "Oh, no, not . . . "

"Not for you," he said, and his laughter was like a wave crashing on the shore. "For me!"

Immediately, the track behind them filled with white-robed victors. Musicians toting every kind of instrument joined the procession as well. A few participants were still in khaki. Christian broke out in joyous laughter as the khaki-ed ones came closer. Community Mom, Colonel Vision, Mercy Heart, Buyme, and the rest were there, possessed of the transforming stature and authority he had already seen in his closest companions.

"Have you been waiting long?" Christian asked Prayer Walker.

She paused. "I don't know how to answer that because time is so different here and there is so much to experience and . . . no . . . " She gave up trying to explain.

Behind them hundreds of veterans lined up with tambourines. A rear guard of cherubs and mighty flaming angels followed. The trumpeters blasted a fanfare, and Christian turned around to see four Living Creatures with four wings and four faces descending in front of the King, their bottom wings roaring like a cataract as they flew. Their top wings didn't flap, but touched, wingtip to wingtip. Beside each Creature, sparkling wheels covered with eyes flew in sync with their movements.

"This is so *other,*" Christian said to Hopeful, who nodded.

The Living Creatures hovered above and in front of the King, who had mounted a breathtaking white stallion with golden mane and tail. With a slight tap on the reins, the King wheeled him around to face the questors.

"Today," he thundered, "you are no longer questors, because you have completed your quest. You have found everything your hearts have ever longed for. Today you are conquerors!"

The stadium resounded with wild applause.

"You will march with me today in my victory parade and I will clothe you in white linen. Your names are written in the Book of Life and I will never blot them out. I will lead you up and present you by name to my Father and his angels."

The thrill touched the very core of Christian's being; he had a greater capacity for excitement than he had ever felt before.

Up ahead the Living Creatures cried out with a voice of rushing waters,

Applause for God!
Sing songs to the tune of his glory,
set glory to the rhythms of his praise.
Say of God, "We've never seen anything like him!"

The parade moved off around the huge stadium, the Living Creatures and their all-seeing wheels up in front, the Faithful and True King right behind. As he passed, the veterans threw rose petals, showering the track on which his stallion pranced. Behind him the questors, now conquerors, walked arm in arm, faces brimming with delight, eyes on the King. The trumpeters saluted Christian and his fellows with ten thousand welcomes, then launched into a brilliant and familiar melody. The Deliverer's theme! Another wave of goose bumps washed over Christian. The singers behind them sang the words to the first verse:

Bless our God, oh peoples!
Give him a thunderous welcome!
Didn't he set us on the road to life?

Didn't he keep us out of the ditch?
He trained us first,
passed us like silver through refining fires,
Took us to hell and back;
Pushed us to our very limit.
Finally he delivered us
To his City of light and Life
And we will reign with him forever!

Through the rose-scented confetti Christian looked at the faces in the stands, sensing a multitude of kindred spirits he couldn't wait to serve beside. On the front row one face in particular was waving furiously, shouting his name. He didn't recognize the face . . . and yet he did! He broke ranks and ran to the red-haired, strapping fellow who stretched out his arms to him.

"Phillip! Thank God! Phillip!"

His brother leaned out over the track wall and hugged him tightly.

"Oh, Phillip, what a . . . I'm so sorry!"

"I know. It's okay. I know where you'll be. I'll catch up with you later!" His brother waved him on and Christian caught up with the conquerors. The King turned around on his horse and smiled at him. Christian smiled back, shaking his head. *He doesn't miss anything.* Christian didn't know how his heart could hold any more joy, but it did.

When they were about halfway around the track, the Deliverer's theme ended and the Living Creatures cried out:

Let the heavens rejoice!
Let the Earth join in!
And let the Sea give a resounding round of applause!

Somehow the glory of the stadium dimmed and lightning filled the sky; the thunder melded with the roar of stadium applause. Rising around the rim of the stadium in live circle-vision, huge thunderheads cracked and blazed. The King raised his right hand. His messenger winds dispensed the thunderheads, and snow-capped mountains shot up covered with trees that danced as the wind whipped their boughs and blew through the stadium, swirling the rose-petal rain.

The King pointed at the mountains. The snow melted away; the mountains and the whole stadium began to rock and shake. Craters opened and fountains of molten lava shot into the sky. Christian could feel the heat on his face and marveled at the raging power choreographed like a laser light show at the word or gesture of the King.

"I've always wanted to watch one of these up close without getting scorched," Hopeful yelled above the roar, his eyes wide.

Again the King summoned the winds, which returned, filling the stadium with salty spray. Gigantic ocean waves billowed and broke all around the stadium. Dozens of dolphins leaped in salute. The band broke into an up-tempo praise song.

"I will worship," the singers belted out.

"I will worship," the stands echoed.

"All of my days . . . "

The dolphins jumped to the rhythm. Everyone in the stadium sang their hearts out and began to dance. The heavens echoed their song. In front of Christian, Gracie twirled with abandon. *Graceful.* Christian laughed. *He knows our names!* Through the tunnel on the far side of the stadium and up the final hill they walk-danced, the music lifting their hearts and bodies up to the gates ahead. Overhead a shower of meteors took Christian's breath away.

"You alone I long to worship, you alone are worthy of my praise," the company sang.

Over the City aurora borealis–like waves of rainbow radiance danced and pulsed to the song's rhythm. They approached the inscription over the great pearl gate:

Blessed are those who wash their robes,
that they may have the right to the tree of life
and may go through the gates into the city.

The King dismounted before the gate and walked to the pearl entrance. As Christian held his breath, his King opened heaven for him. A slight push and the pearl split along an invisible seam, the two halves swinging wide open. As Christian passed through, his fellow conquerors and he were transfigured, their khaki becoming white robes that shone like sunlight.

Inside the diamond walls, the City's golden buildings shone with the same translucence as the pearl gate. How could a heavy metal be so clear? Even the atomic composition of things must be so "other." From every corner of the City, bells began ringing. All along their route, white-robed conquerors in golden crowns saluted the King and then saluted the new arrivals. They traveled a broad boulevard. Down the middle of the street flowed a river clear as crystal shot with fire.

Drinking in the beauty, Christian's own reaction was different than he always thought it would be. Yes, it was achingly beautiful, way beyond anything he could have imagined as he looked at those rich-and-famous magazines on his old coffee table. Yet the beauty surrounding him was only the setting for the real action—the royal splendor of the King and his people and what they would do together for eternity. It was so real, but when he looked at it, what he really saw was God's glory behind it.

They must be nearing the Throne. Up ahead the sky was filled with angels. *Real angels*. Myriads, rank upon rank, disappearing into the sparkling firmament. A massive sapphire throne rose over the buildings ahead. High up, Christian recognized the four very "other" creatures he had seen in Evangelist's pictures, *completely* covered with eyes. They hovered before the One on the Throne, crying out to all who gathered:

Holy, holy, holy
is the Lord God Almighty,
who was, and is, and is to come.

At the presentation, the glorious King of the Universe proudly presented him by name to his Father and the angelic hosts. The closest thing like it on Earth had been commencement. Everybody won. Everybody got the prize. Some with more honor than others, but everyone knew the honors were deserved and everyone cheered for everyone else. And while it was a finish of sorts, it was much more of a beginning.

Afterward the crowd dispersed down the long, golden boulevard. Christian hugged Hopeful and Gracie as the other conquerors descended the sapphire steps. He looked down the boulevard. Beside him the River of Life gushed from the base of the throne and flowed down between the golden lanes of the great street. On both sides of the river, the Trees of Life spread their fruit-laden branches. Exquisite, incredibly huge, broad-leafed trees. Their minty scent filled the air.

Tripping down the last few steps, Christian ran to the radiant, powerful figure waiting under the first Tree. Faithful threw his arms around him in a big bear hug. They laughed and clapped each other on the back. Even though Faithful now looked about the same age as he did, Christian knew he would always see him as the older brother.

"Hey, buddy, I like the crown!" Faithful studied the gold circlet on Christian's head.

"Oh, I almost forgot." Christian said. "It already feels like a part of me, like the robe. Like I wasn't ever fully dressed before."

"That's the way everything here feels. I walk around constantly thinking, 'Oh, *this* is the way it was supposed to be,' or '*This* is what I always felt was missing.'"

"Well, that's kind of the way I feel about you!" Christian loved hearing the sound of Faithful's voice again, although it was less gravelly, and deeper.

"We'll never be parted again, buddy." Faithful put his hand on his shoulder as they walked alongside the river. "Hey, I was going back to the stadium. Want to come?"

"Sure. What's up?"

Faithful looked at him with his familiar twinkle. "There's another questor about to start the adventure."

Chapter Notes

I have greatly enjoyed freewheeling down the path of John Bunyan's heroic work, quoting him, paraphrasing him, and generally staying on his course, although, from time to time, I have throttled off on my own creative departures, sometimes for entire chapters (9–12, 18, 19) before rejoining his sturdy path. The copy I worked from, my grandmother's 1933 version published by the John C. Winston Company, used footnotes in the text of the story. While I don't want to distract with little numbers peeking out of the paragraphs, I do want to give attribution to the wonderful resources that inspired me and enriched my story. All Scripture is taken from *The Message* (MSG) by Eugene Peterson, except for references designated ESV (English Standard Version) and NIV (New International Version). Although some Scripture quotations are quoted exactly, others are paraphrased by me.

Chapter 1

Wiseman's counsel ("Jesus isn't *the Way;* he's one *option* . . . ") is adapted from Corey Hink's wonderful illustrations in *InterVarsity* magazine (Summer 1994). Billboard wisdom: Confucius and Gandhi quoted in *All Men Seek God* (Hallmark editions, 1968), and Woody Allen from the cover of *Time* (August 31, 1992). "The evil enchantment of worldliness," one of my all-time favorite images, is borrowed from C. S. Lewis's essay, "The Weight of Glory."

CHAPTER 2

Evangelist got his poetic words about love and tolerance from Josh McDowell (*Moody,* March 1997, p. 36). And the verse on his billboard is from John 8:32 (ESV).

CHAPTER 3

It is a sober assignment to write dialogue for Jesus on the throne of Judgment. Almost all of Christ's words are straight or adapted from Scripture: Matthew 3:12 (ESV), Psalm 50 (paraphrased), John 18:37 (NIV). Evangelist's fading whisper to "make a run for God" is Psalm 2:12. The variation on "You shall know the truth . . . " inscribed across the dam was inspired by Michael Weed's postmodern interpretation of John's words (8:32) inscribed on the Main Building at the University of Texas at Austin *(Veritas Forum,* April 1997). Peterson's version of Romans 6 helped me write the description of Christian as he emerges from the spring below the cross, a scene that hints of baptism. I didn't originally intend to go there, but being so terribly dirty from the Dump, Christian *needed* to wash up, and there it was, which, for me, brought to life the cleansing symbolism of baptism in a fresh way. John 16:33,23-24 provide the words of encouragement on Christian's Scroll.

CHAPTER 6

Discussing the *Sacred Romance* around the table at Castle Beautiful neatly fit not only with the setting, but also with Christian's need to probe his motivation for his adventure-seeking stay in the Pyramids at Pleasant Arbor below. John Eldredge has graciously given permission to incorporate ideas and wording from the book he coauthored with the late Brent Curtis (Thomas Nelson, 1997), which has been very influential in my own romance with the Lover of my soul.

CHAPTER 7

Descending into the Valley of Humiliation, Christian finds encouragement on his Scroll from Psalm 18:1; 61:2-5. In his verbal battle with Apollyon, Christian's comments on *shattered dreams* echo Larry Crabb's message in his book of the same name (WaterBrook Press, 2001). The idea behind the Scroll's message of forgiveness comes from Psalm 103. The power of 1 Peter 5:8-9 (paraphrased) enables Christian to resist Apollyon's attack.

CHAPTER 8

From Eden to Revelation, the Tree of Life serves as Bible bookends and fingers pointing to the glory God has in store for us (Revelation 22:2, paraphrased). "All hope abandon, ye who enter here," is the inscription above the gates of Hell in Dante's *Inferno*. The voice at the end is praying Psalm 23:4 (paraphrased).

CHAPTER 9

Sacrificing children for prosperity in the fire pits of Ben Hinnom—a wickedness God finds unthinkable (Jeremiah 7:31).

CHAPTER 12

Grace's beautiful image of life as a "burning rose" is from the poetry of Brooke Axtell (www.brookeaxtell.com).

CHAPTER 13

Apologists tell us that the two most successful ways to share the gospel with a person who thinks "reality and truth are what I make them" is to begin from Creation, or that innate sense of right and wrong, fairness and justice, with which we were hard-wired from the factory. BabyGrace's bedside witness is taken from Romans 2, 3, and 7. The idea of recording our own judgments and measuring us against our own standard was indelibly impressed upon me by the first Francis Schaeffer book I ever read, *Death in the City* (InterVarsity, 1969, p. 112).

CHAPTER 14

The inscription on the historical marker is Bunyan's original description of Vanity Fair. As Christian reads it and observes the "many schemes" around him, he thinks of Ecclesiastes 7:29 (paraphrased). Atop the temple-strewn Acropolis, Faithful's witness of

"The Star We Overlooked" echoes Paul's defense in Athens of "the God Nobody Knows" (Acts 17). The week I wrote this chapter, there really was an article in the *Houston Chronicle,* "Can't buy me love: Contentment does not come with wealth" (June 7, 2001).

CHAPTER 16

Cross-examining Pastor Wealth, the OP draws from Lee Strobel's interview of Ravi Zacharias in *The Case for Faith* (HarperCollins/Zondervan, 2000, p. 149). In his parting words Faithful proclaims, "Let God be true, and every man a liar" (Romans 3:4, NIV) and gives a cross-centered gospel that answers postmodern and multiculturalist concerns for the oppressed who are victimized by the powerful. Thanks to Andy Crouch for his thoughts on the subject in *Christianity Today* (November 13, 2000, p. 80).

CHAPTER 17

Much of the material in this chapter was taken directly from conversations with Christian counselors John Eldredge and Leighton Ogg. In his book, *Psychology as Religion*, Dr. Paul Vitz renders the Prodigal's lament in this biting reversal: "Father, *you* have sinned . . . " (as quoted on *BreakPoint* with Charles Colson, commentary 010601, June 1, 2001). The text on the Scroll is from Psalms 90 and 121.

CHAPTER 18

The reference to hope and the Tree of Life is adapted from Proverbs 13:12 (NIV). "Every morning I forget . . . " is an echo from *Journey of Desire* by John Eldredge (Nelson, 2000, p. 199). The greatest celebration of our "Age of Irony" is perhaps the Burning Man festival held each year in Nevada. With a strong occult presence and much more profanity and sexuality than I have depicted here, "techno-pagans" push the envelope of postmodern possibilities. For the Nomad Camp I drew from media descriptions of the festival, adding my own vision of the ultimate expression of the "whatever" lifestyle. The Attention Lodge posting is actual, as is the reference to "the wound that heals." Christian's encounter with Buyme was adapted from Solomon's description of the temptress in Proverbs 7.

CHAPTER 19

The poignant images of Gracie's poetry, "Jesus of Nazareth" and "from chaos may cosmos come" were created by Brooke Axtell (www.brookeaxtell.com) and used by permission. In their Theology 101 discussion, I picture Priscilla and Aquila interacting with the new believers over the clear, deeply inspiring vision of the Savior that John Piper has cast in *Seeking and Savoring Jesus Christ* (Crossway Books, 2001). The question for our times, "What will you do in the end?" is Jehovah God's challenge to unfaithful Israel in Jeremiah 5:31 (NIV). Plans "to give you a future and a hope" is from Jeremiah 29:11 (ESV). "But if not": code from Shadrach, Meshach, and Abednego that Christian is *confident* that God is *able* to deliver, but whether he does or not, Christian will not serve or worship anyone else (Daniel 3:17-18, ESV).

In Numbers 21 the bronze serpent was lifted up as a type of Christ. Here the serpent coiled around the blazing man is a stark anti-type of Christ. The Nomads have a clear choice: to celebrate the image of a man deliberately void of meaning, which is destroyed in the flames, or worship at the cross, the most meaningful image in the world, which gives eternal life (John 3:14-16).

CHAPTER 20

"Strip down, start running . . . " From his headset the Hebrews 12 imagery of a cloud of witnesses watching a race and the 1 Corinthians 9 athlete that trains hard for the gold prepare Christian for the final approach to Celestial City. At the finish, Christ greets them with a salute taken from Revelation 3:4-5. The Living Creatures summon applause for God from the crowd (Psalm 66:1-3) and heaven, earth, and sea (Psalm 96:11, paraphrased), as the words to the Deliverer's theme fill the stands (Psalm 66:8-12, paraphrased). If there is one praise song that, to me, fits this occasion, it's David Ruis's "You're Worthy of My Praise" (Maranatha Praise Inc., 1986; used by permission.) Over the gate to Celestial City is inscribed Revelation 22:14 (NIV), and the Living Creatures before the throne cry out, "Holy, holy, holy" (Revelation 4:8, NIV).

AUTHOR

In a world that beckons us to live small, live for today. Lael Arrington challenges her audiences to live large and finish well. A student of Bible and culture for more than twenty-five years, Lael shares how knowing God and his truth answers the "big questions" of life and satisfies our deepest longing for meaning and hope.

Lael's first book, *Worldproofing Your Kids,* has been featured in *Focus on the Family* and World magazines and has also been used as part of the worldview curriculum for Summit ministries and Focus on the Family Institute.

In her books and her radio and television interviews, Lael speaks as a fellow traveler in a culture that squeezes us into its mold. She offers practical push-back strategies with an Erma Bombeck twist. Her messages have inspired audiences across the country—at women's ministry events as well as for educational and leadership groups. With a master's degree in the history of ideas from the University of Texas at Dallas, she has taught about culture and apologetics at secular and Christian schools and colleges. Her writings have been included in *Beyond Today* and *Bright tomorrow.*

Lael and her husband, Jack, a pastor, make their home among the azaleas and dogwoods of the northwest Houston area and are delighted when their son, Zach, pops in from college. She enjoys working with the church's creative team and has recruited other

Women Who Read for biweekly discussions at the local college library.

Lael invites you to visit www.laelarrington.com to learn more about her ministry and access study guides for using excerpts from this book to teach Christian worldview.

For information on scheduling Lael to speak, or to share with her your response to this book, contact Info@laelarrington.com.

"Be honest. Do you skip over the 'classics' because you think they'll be hard to read or simply don't apply to today? If so, get ready to read a book that takes a timeless classic and dresses it in today's street clothes. What Lael Arrington does in retelling *Pilgrim's Progress* makes Christian's story read like headline news. And like a fast-moving fiction novel, you'll find Christian's quest for faith and love speaks to your own need to find God amidst all the distractions and trials of our day."

—John Trent, author; speaker; president, strongfamilies.com

"Does John Bunyan's *Pilgrim's Progress* still resonate in the 21st century? Certainly it does, but Lael Arrington helps make the necessary connections to our modern world in her fresh, insightful version of this classic tale. Join Christian and Faithful in their journey to such places as Celestial City and Vanity Fair. It's a disturbing but insightful trip."

—Kerby Anderson, president, Probe Ministries